Pride Pub

T

THE THOMAS ELKIN SERIES

Elements of Retrofit

Clarity of Lines

Sense of Place

N.R. WALKER

The Thomas Elkin Series
ISBN # 978-1-78430-775-2
©Copyright N.R. Walker 2015
Cover Art by Posh Gosh ©Copyright August 2015
Interior text design by Claire Siemaszkiewicz
Pride Publishing

Published in 2015 by Pride Publishing, Newland House, The Point, Weaver Road, Lincoln, LN6 3QN, United Kingdom.

ELEMENTS OF RETROFIT

Dedication

Dedicated to my husband.
For not always understanding my need to do what I
do, but putting up with it anyway.

Chapter One

Definition: Retrofit — To substitute new or modernised parts or systems for older equipment: fit in or on an existing structure, such as an older house; substitute new or modernised parts or equipment for older ones.

Source: Oxforddictionaries.com

Looking out of my office window over the darkening New York City skyline, I could see my reflection in the wall of glass before me. Beyond the expensive suit and shoes, there was gray hair at my temples, my once-black hair was now salt and pepper, and there were creases at the corners of my eyes.

Forty-four years old. *Forty-four. How did that happen?*

It seemed like I'd missed half of my life. In many ways I had.

The light on the intercom flashed. "Mr. Elkin?"

My receptionist was fifteen years older than me and had been my receptionist for ten years, since the day I'd started at the firm, and yet she never faltered in her professional etiquette.

"Yes, Jennifer?"

"Ryan is on line two. Would you prefer I take a message?"

"No, it's fine," I told her. "I'll take it." I pressed the speaker button. "Ryan?"

"Hey, Dad, yeah, it's me."

"Anything wrong?" I asked. It was unusual for him to call the office. "Still coming for dinner?"

"Yeah, yeah, it's all good. Just about dinner," he hedged, "I was just wondering if you'd mind if I brought someone?"

This surprised me. Since his mother and I had separated, it'd taken a while for things to get back to normal between us.

"Yes, of course, that's fine," I told him. "Someone special?"

"Oh no, nothing like that," he said with a laugh.

I could hear muffled voices in the background.

Then he added, "Just ran into an old buddy from school. He just got into town, he's by himself and I told him he could have dinner with us."

"Okay, that's fine," I said. Ryan was very social, and growing up, he had forever had a crew of friends who'd lived at our place as much as their own. I'd quite often got home late to a den of high-school kids pretending to be asleep. I looked at my watch. "See you soon."

I disconnected the call and pressed Jennifer's line. "Can you please order dinner for three to be delivered to my home address?"

"Certainly," she replied. "Thai? Italian? Japanese?"

"You choose."

"Very well."

There was a soft click in my ear and I went back to staring at the evening skyline for another half an hour, before packing my laptop into my satchel and walking out of the door. Jennifer gave me a polite smile. "Japanese, delivered to your door at seven-thirty."

I smiled warmly at her. "Thank you, Jennifer."

"Have a good weekend, Mr. Elkin," she said, knowing I'd be working all weekend. I worked most weekends. "I've taken the liberty to have lunch ordered for you tomorrow. Security will bring it up."

"Don't know what I'd do without you."

She smiled proudly. "Have a good evening, Mr. Elkin. Give Ryan my best."

"I will."

I took the elevator from the top floor of executive offices down to the executive marble lobby, walked a block to the executive marble lobby of my apartment building, took the elevator to the executive suite on the top floor.

Expensive. Polished. Predictable.

Those three words just about summed me up.

I'd been preoccupied lately, unsettled and lacking *something*. I'd quite often caught myself staring out of the window for some lengths of time, not able to recall a single thought. Maybe I needed a vacation. Maybe I'd take one after this next big contract was done.

I loved my job as an architect. Loved it. I loved the lines in structure, the quiet confidence in well-built, historical buildings, and I loved the superiority and functionality of modern design.

I loved my apartment, had some good friends and I even had an amicable relationship with my ex-wife, all things considered. My relationship with my son was better, good even. We'd had a rough patch when his mother and I had first separated five years ago, but now at twenty-two years of age, he could see all sides of the situation and had made peace with it. With me.

No sooner had I put my briefcase down, changed into jeans and a button-down shirt and poured my first glass of wine, there was a knock at the door. I checked my watch, and knowing the doorman would have sent Ryan straight up, I called out, "It's unlocked."

"Hey, Dad," Ryan yelled from the door.

I could hear a quiet conversation and I remembered he was bringing company. My top-floor apartment was a large, open floor bachelor pad and the kitchen ran along the inside wall, out of line of sight from the front door.

"In the kitchen," I replied. "You boys want a drink?"

Ryan walked in, followed by a face I didn't recognize at first. "Dad, do you remember Cooper Jones?" Ryan asked, by way of introduction. "We went to high school together."

The name yes, but he didn't look a thing like I remembered. Gone was the gangly, awkward teenager, replaced by a fit-looking young man. He had messy short brown hair, a wide smile and mischief in his hazel eyes.

"Yes, I remember," I said, extending my hand for him to shake. "You just grew up."

Ryan rolled his eyes. "That's what happens, Dad, when you don't see someone for five years."

Cooper shook my hand firmly. "Nice to meet you, sir."

"Can I get you boys a drink?" I asked again. "Dinner will be here in about half an hour."

I had my wine, they opted for a beer, and Ryan told me how Cooper's family had moved to Chicago and how he'd lost touch with him through college, but Cooper had come to New York City for the summer. He'd literally checked into his room and gone in search for something to eat when he'd run into Ryan on the street who had then pulled out his phone and called me to see if he could tag along for dinner.

"Hope you don't mind," Cooper said with a smile. "I was only going to grab something passable as food from a 7-Eleven or something."

My nose scrunched up at the thought and Cooper laughed, telling me, "That's the same reaction Ryan had."

Dinner arrived and as we ate, the two boys talked about people they knew. Although the conversation almost excluded me, I didn't mind. It was good to see Ryan laugh, and their college stories were rather funny. Very different from me when I was twenty-two, that was certain.

Ryan looked at me. "You're quiet tonight, Dad." He pulled at the label on his beer. "How's things?"

I think he wanted to know how things were with Peter, but didn't want to ask outright in front of company. "Good," I said, not about to say I was single again, after I'd told Peter I wasn't interested. "Work's been busy."

He got the message, because he gave a nod and went back to picking at his beer label.

Changing the subject, I looked to Cooper. "So, what brings you back to New York?"

"I have a summer internship," he said. He was just about to speak again, but was interrupted by Ryan's ringing phone.

"Hey," Ryan said loudly into his phone. "Hell yes, I'll be there. I'm bringing an old friend of mine who just got into town... Okay, see ya soon." Ryan clicked off the call and looked at Cooper. "Man, you *have* to come out with me tonight. We got tickets to the hottest new club."

Cooper shrugged and grinned. "Um, sure."

Ryan looked at me, somewhat apologetically. "Sorry, we'll need to cut it short tonight. Hope you don't mind."

"No, I don't mind at all," I told him. And I didn't. Hell, at twenty-two I'd been married, with a baby on the way and a house in the 'burbs. It wasn't until I'd almost hit forty that I'd realized what I'd missed out on, what I'd spent twenty-five years hiding...

"Go out, have a great time," I told them. "Be careful. And if you need a place to crash in the City, there's always here."

"Thanks," Ryan said with a genuine, appreciative smile. But then his brow creased. "You sure you don't mind?"

"Mind?" I scoffed. "I'm jealous!"

He laughed, though I doubted he knew the underlying truth to my words. I *was* jealous. I was jealous he had a social life, I was jealous he still had his youth, without the weight of mistakes and life wearing him down.

They left to spend their Friday night out doing God knew what while I tidied up after dinner, sat down with a glass of wine and opened my laptop, spending my Friday night working.

* * * *

I was in the office on Monday early, like always, and had forgotten about the intake of interns, until Jennifer buzzed me on the intercom. I looked up from the job specifications. "Yes, Jennifer."

"Sorry to interrupt, Mr. Elkin," she said. "If I could trouble you at my desk for a moment."

The only time Jennifer ever asked me to come to her desk was when she wanted me to have a visual of a client, or opposition, before I met them. "Sure," I told her.

Jennifer's desk ran along the left-hand side of my double doors, which ensured no one got to see me without checking in with her first. I opened the door and she handed me a file, which I opened. "Interns," she said quietly. "There are three to choose from, that's them over there." She looked pointedly toward the waiting room without moving her head.

I looked over to see two young men and one woman, all keen to impress and impeccably dressed. Usually the four executive senior partners got to choose from the top four candidates, so I knew any of the three remaining candidates were good. I read through the very brief credential lists first, not even looking at names or gender. I just wanted talent.

Academically, they were all relatively evenly matched, but then a name stood out. I risked a glance at the suited man who I hadn't even recognized as the kid who'd had dinner in my apartment just three nights ago.

He looked different. Gone was the backpacker look, gone was the kid who drank beer and talked about drunken antics with my son.

In his place was a professional, serious man, dressed in a well-tailored suit.

Without another thought, without *any* thought, I looked at Jennifer, handed her the file and said two words that would change my life.

"Cooper Jones."

Chapter Two

A short while later, Jennifer knocked on my door and upon walking in, introduced the man behind her.

"Mr. Jones, this is Mr. Elkin. He's a senior partner here at Brackett and Golding. You will do everything he asks, when he asks you to do it. You'll be here when he gets here, you'll be here until he leaves. Keeping up?"

"Yes, ma'am," he answered.

Jennifer sniffed. "You may call me Jennifer," she told him, then looked pointedly at me, signaling to the young man that he should address me.

In that split second, I wondered if he'd acknowledge that he knew me, or knew Ryan at least, and I wondered if I'd done the wrong thing by taking him on.

But he gave a curt nod and said, "Mr. Elkin, it's an honor."

I smiled at his professionalism, while Jennifer turned on her heel. "Right, come with me. I'll show you to your desk."

Cooper didn't smile, but his eyes flickered with humor before he followed her out of the door.

And for the next two weeks, I worked with him every day. He mostly worked with my team, but sometimes with me — sometimes for minutes, sometimes for hours. He was efficient, dedicated and very talented. For his age, he was one of the best I'd seen.

For his age. I had to keep reminding myself he was only twenty-two.

But even with the mundane jobs he was doing as an intern, it was easy to see he had a love for architecture, much like I had when I'd been his age. Much like I still did.

He would use his hands animatedly to describe something and his eyes would light up as he spoke. He was passionate, that was for certain.

And as an intern, I should have had him doing what the other interns were doing — the mundane tasks, still ensuring they learnt, but interns basically did the little jobs no one else wanted to do.

The other senior partners rarely saw their interns, and granted, before Cooper I'd rarely seen any of mine. But he was different. He had an energy, a presence. I didn't know what it was, but I was intrigued by him. He was fascinated by the work that went on around him, and that was refreshing.

Maybe because he was an old friend of Ryan's, or maybe it was because of his love for architecture, but instead of having him learning from other people on my team, I picked him to work closer to me.

It was his second week there, late in the afternoon, and we'd had a staff meeting in the conference room, which turned into a bit of a concept meeting then became a design think-tank. I liked those meetings. More casual, open and everyone was encouraged to discuss problems, allowing group discussions on possible solutions.

Cooper was merely an observer, he never said anything unless spoken to. His answers were well-thought-out and calculated. It showed a professional maturity that surprised me, considering his age.

The other staff came in and out, all busy with their own schedules, and by the end of the day, I found myself sitting alone with him at the large oval table.

"So, how are you finding your time here?" I asked him, just as the last person was walking out.

"Oh, I love it," he said quickly. "Everyone's great, very helpful. I tend to ask a lot of questions…"

I smiled at him. "An inquisitive mind."

"When I'm learning something, yes," he said. "And there's an awful lot to learn. I think I've annoyed a few of your draughts people."

He made me laugh. "Good. Pick their brains, ask them anything."

"I have already," he said. He shook his head, as though he couldn't believe something. "It's surreal, you know, that some of the most recognized buildings in New York have their blueprints framed on these walls. That I'm walking past them like they're just pictures…but they're not. They're real."

I was still smiling at him. "Some of them are incredible."

"Oh, they are, he said. He was so excited. "The Woolworth building is amazing. The original blueprints are on the wall," he said, shaking his head again. "I can't believe it."

"Well, that's a little before my time," I told him.

"Have you designed any?" he asked. "That are framed on the walls?"

"Sure," I told him. "Come on, I'll show you." I stood up and by the time I got to the door, he was right beside me. "All of the blueprints framed on walls were at some point either designed from original concept or had some work done on them by Brackett and Golding," I told him as we walked down the hall. "The company's one of the longest continuously trading architectural firms in New York. We've put our stamp on quite a few."

"Very traditional, very prestigious," Cooper said. "In design and in reputation."

I stopped walking and stood in front of one particular set of framed blueprints. Cooper stopped with me, but looked at me as though he might have said the wrong thing. I pointed to the gilded frame.

His eyes popped. "The Radiator building?"

The fact he knew the name of the building as soon as he saw it made me smile. "It's now called the Bryant Park Hotel, but yes, the Radiator."

"You worked on it?" he asked in a whisper. His eyes were still wide and staring straight at me.

"Not when it was originally built in the nineteen-twenties. I'm not *that* old," I told him, and he smiled. "But I worked on it in the late nineties, when it became the hotel it is today."

Cooper's mouth fell open. "It's stunning." He looked from me to the blueprints, as though he was mesmerized. He lifted his hand to trace his fingers over the drawn lines. "The black brickwork is brilliant. How it minimises the contrast between walls and windows, and in the nineteen-twenties. It was such forward thinking. And the gold on the tower..." His words trailed off, he shook his head again and pulled back his hand. "Sorry. I get carried away."

I was staring at him. The way he spoke of architecture, of buildings, of the art in them, was something I did. It was a passion in me, something that no one else really understood.

"Don't ever apologize," I told him. My voice was barely a whisper.

Cooper's eyes stayed on mine and it wasn't until someone walked past us that the connection between us was broken.

Something had just passed between us. A familiarity. An understanding. A moment.

I exhaled loudly and took a step back from him. I needed to put some distance between us. "Here, look at this one," I said, pointing to another frame down the hall. "It's more modern."

"The Citigroup Center?" he asked with an amazed laugh. "You worked on it too?"

"Not me personally," I told him. "Hard to believe, but even the seventies were before my time. But it's one of my favourites."

Cooper laughed out loud. "I didn't mean anything about your age," he said, still smiling. "I just can't believe all these buildings came from designs out of this office."

"It's incredible, isn't it?" I asked. Then I nodded to the blueprints in front of us. "See the angled roof line? They wanted to setback penthouses in the angled roof, but couldn't due to zoning restrictions. Now it houses a computer-controlled tuned mass damper, a four-hundred-ton block of concrete that slides on a thin layer of oil. The inertia of the damper reduces the swaying of the building by up to forty percent."

I stopped talking when I realized now it was me who was babbling on about the wonders of architecture. "Sorry, I get carried away," I said, repeating his words back to him.

Cooper smiled at me, but his eyes bore straight into mine. "Don't apologize," he said quietly. He stared at me. His gaze never faltered, and I was unable to look away. After a long moment, he broke the connection by turning back to the blueprints. "That is some incredible engineering."

I cleared my throat. "Yes, it is."

Then I looked around to find nearly almost everyone else in the office had gone. I checked my watch. "I hadn't realized it had gotten late."

"Is there anything you need me to do?" he asked.

"No," I answered. I had work to take home, but didn't mention it to him. "I think we might call it a day."

Cooper looked around, as though checking we were alone. "Can I ask you something?"

I had a feeling this was not a work-related question. "Yes," I answered, hiding the caution in my tone.

"Did you take me on because of Ryan?"

I blinked at his blatant question. "No," I half-lied. "I took you on as an intern because of your credentials. You were top of your class."

He nodded and smiled. "I didn't want to be here on some favor, that's all. I mean, it's a dream to work here. I'd just hoped that I earned my place."

Cooper was honest, almost to a fault. He spoke transparently. If he thought it, he said it. I liked that trait in people. I liked it in him.

"I'm sure you have," I told him. "I've been watching you. You have a very good eye for detail."

His face brightened and he tried not to smile. "Really?"

If he was asking if he really had an eye for detail, or if I'd really been watching him, I wasn't sure. I couldn't believe I'd just admitted to it. Instead of answering him, I gave him a smile and turned to walk back to my office. "Have a good weekend, Cooper."

"Same to you, Mr. Elkin," he called out behind me.

I packed up my satchel and walked out of the office with Jennifer. "Any plans for the weekend?" she asked.

"No, just the usual," I told her. Which meant work. My usual was work.

"If you need anything," she said, "you have my number."

I smiled. Dear Jennifer was the sweetest woman. She organized my entire professional life, and sometimes my personal life too. She knew what food I liked from which restaurants, she knew what cologne I wore, she knew birthdays, anniversaries and did it all without looking up from her computer.

"I'm sure I'll be fine," I told her. "But thank you. You're really worth more money."

She smiled, and just before we went separate ways on the sidewalk, she said, "Don't work too hard."

Every weekend, and most nights, was about work for me. I'd had a slew of one-night stands, I'd tried dating. And in the beginning, after the separation from my wife, it had been exciting. It had been new and exhilerating and everything I'd dreamed it would be.

I tried *everything*, once, sometimes twice, I did it all — safely, of course — but four years on and I was looking for something else. I just didn't know what. I'd met a guy, Peter, and theoretically, he should have been perfect for me. Similar age, similar interests, similar everything. But he was too passive, too agreeable to everything. I had ended things with him a few weeks before and had happily dove headfirst into work.

I had every intention of spending a quiet weekend at home, finalising two case files. I went to the gym once, treated myself to some online porn and ordered in food. It was perfect.

Except on Sunday night, I dreamt of Cooper.

It was vivid and hot. I dreamed I was fucking him. His head was thrown back and his mouth was open and I was inside him. He groaned with every thrust.

It was so real, I woke up so fucking hard, I could almost taste his cologne on my tongue.

I got to work a few hours later on Monday morning and almost tripped over my own feet when I saw him.

It was absurd. Ridiculous. Wrong, even. He was the same age as my son!

And yet there he stood, wearing gray suit pants and a matching vest over a crisp white shirt. His vest pulled in at the waist and showed the shape of his ass. He was talking to someone else, but he smiled at me and my heart thumped in my chest.

Fuck.

"Good morning, Mr. Elkin," Jennifer said with a bright, wide smile.

I cleared my throat and still croaked when I spoke. "Morning."

"Busy schedule," she said matter-of-factly. "First meeting at nine."

"Good." I needed the distraction. I needed work and meetings and appointments, difficult clients and over-budget builders. Anything to distract me from a certain twenty-two-year-old man, whose eyes I could feel on me, burning into my skin, from across the room.

Chapter Three

I managed to avoid Cooper all day. Mondays were always busy, and I told myself I was imagining the attraction. The thought of me being attracted to him was preposterous. He was twenty-two, and I was forty-four. He was just a kid!

But every day I saw him, and every day I looked for him. I had his schedule jam-packed and he seemed to thrive.

I'd managed to quash any notion that I could have been interested in him. The fact he spoke about my work with a passion like mine was nothing more than a professional admiration. Even in my line of work, it wasn't every day I met someone who loved architecture like I did, and it had just thrown me, that was all.

At least that was what I told myself.

It was late on the Friday evening of Cooper's third week when he dropped some files on my desk for me and looked at the board in the corner of the room. It was the first time he'd been in my office without anyone else with him. He eyed the draughting board in my office like it was the space shuttle to a young, wannabe astronaut.

The draughting board itself was rarely used these days. Nearly all draughting was done in CAD programs, which took precision to an art form, but I still liked to use the old-school draughting board and blueprints in paper.

"I've seen you eye it a few times. You can go look at it," I told him, looking up from my paperwork.

He grinned, walked over to it and ran his finger along the wooden frame. "It's like touching an artist's easel," he said quietly.

I smiled at that analogy. "I guess it is."

Cooper looked at me, then back to the draughting board. "This is the Mosconi job," he murmured.

I stood up and walked over to him. He'd seen enough job sheets and specifications to recognize it. "Yes, it is."

"It's a beautiful building," he said, almost shyly. He traced his fingers across the elevations of the plan, along the façade of the building. "The lines are definitive, it's streamlined and geometric. It speaks of elegance that comes with history, yet it's sustainable and retrofitted for modern living." He spoke as though he was thinking out loud, then his eyes darted to mine and he blushed. "Sorry, I get carried away."

I'd never seen him shy or even remotely unsure of his own words. It was an emotional reaction, and I liked it. Something else I shouldn't have noticed.

I shouldn't have noticed the blush across his cheeks, or the way his chest rose and fell with each breath. I shouldn't have noticed how his eyes darkened and I certainly shouldn't have noticed the lines of his neck, or his jaw, or those of his lips.

I had to swallow so I could speak. "Don't apologize. Architecture is a beautiful thing."

Cooper's eyes darted to mine and he held my gaze. "Yes, it is."

The air between us was suddenly static and it made my heart thump out of time. Cooper opened his mouth to say something, something I was pretty sure I didn't want to hear, so I walked quickly back to my desk, putting some distance between us. *Jesus Christ.* I couldn't think, I could hardly breathe. He was just a kid, for fuck's sake. He was the same age as my son.

I shouldn't be checking him out. I shouldn't find him attractive. Or smart. Or clever. Or funny.

I shouldn't like the way his eyes sparkled when he learnt something new. I shouldn't like the way his lips curled when he smiled. I shouldn't wonder what they felt like, how soft they'd feel against mine.

Oh, fuck.

I shook my head and cleared my throat. "I uh, I think..." I tried again. "I'll be working from home this weekend."

"Oh," Cooper said. I didn't know what his facial expression was. I didn't dare look at him. He sounded like he didn't care. "Okay."

"I have a few things to catch up on here, but you can finish early if you like," I said, dismissing him. I didn't watch him leave, but when the door clicked softly I looked up to my office and seeing it empty, I finally breathed.

I needed some space, some breathing room, to get my head cleared of this nonsense. And, like the weekend before, two days working from home where I could lose myself in my work without any distractions was just what I needed.

Only that was not what happened.

Saturday morning I got up, threw on some jeans and a T-shirt and set about making coffee. Which became looking for coffee, which became ransacking the kitchen, pulling the pantry apart looking for fucking coffee.

Then the intercom buzzed. I cursed at the interruption and pressed the button. "What?"

"Sorry to bother you, Mr. Elkin," Lionel the doorman said. "I have a Cooper Jones here. Says he's working with you today."

I stared at the intercom. "Pardon?"

I heard a muffled voice, then Lionel spoke again, "Cooper Jones, sir. He says he brought the Lewington files…"

Shit. Shit. Shit. I cleared my throat. "Um…"

Lionel's voice came through the intercom. "He said to say he brought the Lewington files *and* coffee." Lionel didn't exactly sound impressed. "Apparently the coffee is important."

I smiled. "Let him up."

I opened the door and went back to the kitchen, tidying up the mess, and wrote coffee on the shopping list.

There was a brief knock at the door. "Hello? Mr. Elkin?" Cooper called out.

"Yes, come in, Cooper," I replied.

He walked in, holding a briefcase in one hand, a satchel over his shoulder and a tray of take-out coffee in his other hand. He was wearing suit pants, but no tie or jacket and his shirtsleeves were rolled to his elbows. He was looking every part the relaxed professional, while I stood there in jeans and bare feet.

He slid the tray of coffee onto the kitchen counter and I looked at him questioningly.

"I called into the office and picked the files up," he said, putting the briefcase down and sliding the satchel from his shoulder. "And coffee from the café you like."

Cooper looked around my apartment, from the open living and dining room to the gourmet kitchen. The furniture was expensive, probably pretentiously so, but it was a direct representation of me. It was classic and traditional, with Chesterfield leather lounges and an antique dining table. The only modern furnishing was the kitchen. Cooper took it all in as though it impressed him. Finally, his eyes landed on me. "So, where are we doing this?"

I ran my hand through my hair. "I, um…well, when I said I was working from home," I said quietly, "I didn't expect you to work as well."

"Oh," he said, realizing he'd just turned up at my apartment without an invitation. "Oh, shit," he said, looking mortified. "But Jennifer said specifically I was to work when you worked. No exceptions. It was one of the first things she ever said. She was rather specific."

I smiled at him. "It's fine, Cooper."

"Jennifer scares me," he admitted, still not sure where to look. "I mean, I'm sure she's nice and all, but she has a ferocious glare. She makes me nervous. Anna, one of the other interns, is scared shitless of her."

He was clearly embarrassed, and rambling. I smiled and handed him one of the coffees he'd bought. "Cooper, it's fine. We'll set up at the dining table. Pull all your files out and we'll have a look."

"I'm really sorry," he said again. "I feel like an idiot."

I laughed at him and sipped my coffee. "It's fine, Cooper. It shows great work acumen that you'd be at work at" —I checked my watch— "eight o'clock on a Saturday morning."

His eyes widened. "Am I too early?"

I couldn't help but smile at him. "No, you brought coffee, so it's all good."

I picked up the briefcase and set it down on the dining table. I collected my satchel, pulled out my laptop and we settled into a comfortable working silence. He'd ask a question every now and then, while he worked on getting the energy compliance ratings for the Lewington job, and I spent the next few hours trying to ignore the fact that the man I'd dreamt about, whom I'd fantasized about while I'd jerked off in the shower last night, was sitting across from me.

I also ignored how he slipped the end of his pen between his lips and how he'd lean his head on his hand with his fingers in his hair. Making myself focus on my work, I somehow managed to get the specification sheet half done for the same job Cooper was working on. It was helpful to have us both on the same plans, running through the same file sheets, and I didn't realize the time until Cooper stood up and stretched. "Hungry?" he asked, checking his watch. "It's lunchtime."

I looked at my watch to see it was almost one. "Jeez, I didn't realize the time."

Cooper walked into the kitchen. "Can I make myself a sandwich?" he asked. "Want one?"

"Um, sure," I answered, not sure what I had in the kitchen in the way of sandwich ingredients.

I watched him as he rifled through the fridge and the pantry like he owned them, obviously looking for something in particular. "Have you got peanut butter?" he asked. "I can't find it."

"Peanut butter?" I asked disbelievingly. "No, I don't think so."

Cooper shook his head. "How can you not have peanut butter?"

"Um, not since Ryan was little," I said, then immediately regretted my choice of words. I didn't want him to think of me as a dad to one of his friends. I didn't want him to think I was implying he was a kid. I didn't want him to think of me as someone twice his age, or his boss, or... I didn't know what the fuck I wanted him to think.

Needing the distraction, I grabbed my keys. "Come on, we'll go out and grab some lunch," I told him. "I need to grab some coffee anyway."

"Uh, Mr. Elkin?" Cooper's voice stopped me as I neared the door. I turned to face him, and he looked down to my feet. "Shoes?"

Fuck.

"Does Alzheimer's kick in at your age?" he asked with a laugh.

My mouth fell open. "I'm not *that* old, thank you very much!"

He laughed again, then tried to hold it in. "I'm sorry, was that out of line?"

"What for?" I asked. "Making fun of Ryan's father, or your boss?"

"Neither," he said. His eyes shone and he grinned. "For making fun of the elderly."

I rolled my eyes and pulled on my shoes. "So, the attitude? Is that a hunger thing?"

"Yep," he replied cheerfully. "That's an 'I'm on my lunch break and can say what I want' thing."

I walked to the door and held it open for him. "Oh, is that the same as 'you work for me, you'll watch your mouth or you'll spend the rest of your internship sorting mail' kind of thing?"

He laughed as he walked to the elevator. "You win." He pressed the button and as the doors opened, he stepped inside. "So, the lack of humor? Is that a hunger thing?"

"No," I said with a smile, stepping in beside him. "It's an old age thing."

Cooper laughed. "Such a vicious circle."

Chapter Four

I shook my head but couldn't hide my smile. I liked his banter. He had a certain arrogance and boldness that came with age. Or lack of it.

When the elevator doors opened, Cooper stepped out into the foyer and gave a smug smile and cute little wave to Lionel the doorman.

I rolled my eyes. "Cut it out. He didn't let you up to my apartment because he was doing his job."

Ignoring the jibe, Cooper smiled as we walked from the foyer out onto the sidewalk. "So, what are you buying me for lunch?"

"An attitude adjustment," I replied quickly.

Cooper laughed. "I heard the little Vietnamese place up here is one of the best."

"It's one of my favourites."

"Where else do you go out?"

"I don't, really."

"Not at all?"

"I work a lot. The people I've dated don't understand the long hours."

We walked in silence for a bit, while Cooper obviously thought about what those long hours meant in the career he'd chosen.

"Does that scare you off?" I asked with a smile.

"What?" he asked quickly, looking at me. Then he shook his head. "No, no. Not at all. I don't mind the long hours."

We walked into the little café, I ordered some steamed vegetable rolls and a noodle salad to go, and I bought some ground coffee from the café Cooper had bought coffee from this morning.

The walk back to my apartment was quieter, his banter was gone. I grabbed some plates and dished up lunch for us both. The dining table had our work all over it, so we ate at the kitchen counter.

I was about to ask him where the impressive Generation Y mockery had gone, when he said, "Ryan told me."

"Told you what?"

He stabbed his noodle salad with a fork. "About your divorce from Mrs. Elkin."

I put my fork down and frowned. "And what else exactly did Ryan tell you?"

He took a mouthful, seemingly oblivious to my discomfort. "That it was hard on him, that it was hard on all of you."

"It was," I said quietly, still unsure of his point.

"He said you've dated a few...*people*, but nothing serious."

I cleared my throat. "Really. Is that what he said?"

Cooper nodded, took a drink from his water bottle and pushed his empty plate away. "You know, it's not easy for anyone," he said. "Jesus, I remember when I came out to my parents, I thought they'd flip their shit."

I blinked. Twice.

I remember when I came out...

"What?"

"When I came out," he repeated, as simply as discussing the weather. "When I told my parents I was gay. I knew I had to do it before college. I knew I had to be out *before* I went to college, or I'd spend the next four years in the closet."

He was gay. He was telling me he was gay after discussing my divorce, which meant he knew *why* I got divorced.

I shook my head, really not sure what to say. "Yeah." I snorted in disbelief. "God forbid you end up living a lie until your fortieth birthday."

I didn't mean for it to sound so biting, but I didn't apologize.

He looked straight at me. I was half expecting him to say sorry for bringing it up, for even discussing my personal life with me, but of course he didn't. "Is that what happened for you?" he asked me outright. "Did you get to forty and think—"

"I can't live a lie anymore," I finished for him.

He nodded. Then he did the darnedest thing. He put his hand on mine. "You're not living a lie anymore."

"No," I whispered. "I guess not."

He pulled back his hand then he brightened considerably. "So? Seeing anyone?"

I shook my head and laughed at the incredulity of the conversation. "No."

Then he stood up off the stool, leaning in close to me as he did. "That's a shame," he said. He was close enough for me to feel the warmth of his skin, to smell his aftershave.

Fuck.

Still leaning in close to me, he slowly took my plate then turned to walk around the counter and put the plates in the sink.

Apparently he spoke, but my head was still spinning at what had just happened, I didn't hear him ask me anything. He waved his hand in front of my face to get my attention. "You okay?"

"Yeah," I replied, though the smug bastard smiled at me.

"I asked you how your coffee machine worked," he said.

I stood up, walked around the counter and took the coffee from him, giving him a glare as I did. It didn't help that he smiled.

If it were Ryan speaking to me like that, I'd chip him for disrespecting me. Yet, I found it sassy in Cooper. The way his eyes danced, the way his lips twisted in that playful smirk.

The strong smell of coffee seemed to clear my senses a little, sobering me, as I filled the machine, but when I turned to face Cooper again, he wasn't next to me. He was back at the dining table. And he was back to being all business.

I put his coffee in front of him, answering his questions and discussing the insulation properties of different types of glazing and New York's planning requirements for retrofits. He was inquisitive and had a thirst for learning everything he could, and the way he just switched from flirting to professional left me wondering if I'd imagined the flirting side of it.

I mean, why *would* he flirt with me? Not only was I twice his age, and the father of a friend of his, but it could be career-ending.

Well, not for me. I might get a slap on the wrist, but his career would be over before it had even begun.

Why *would* he flirt with me? Who the hell was I kidding? What the hell was I thinking? I could have kicked myself for even considering the idea. First the dream, then the fantasizing about it. Now this?

I needed to go out and hook up. Find some one-night stand and fuck him senseless. Or be fucked senseless. I needed to lose myself, for just one night.

The fact that I'd fantasized about Cooper, about having him underneath me, should have been enough warning. It had been too long since I'd had sex. I was only interested in him, I told myself convincingly, because I'd gone too long without fulfilling sex.

I needed to go out. I needed to get laid. Then there'd be no more of this irresponsible infatuation with a twenty-two-year-old.

"Plans for tonight?" Cooper's voice startled me.

"Um, yeah," I told him. "I have plans." *Only very new, not-thought-through plans,* I thought to myself. *But plans nonetheless.*

"Where are you off to?"

"Just catching up with an old friend," I told him, when the truth was I had no clue.

"I'm supposed to be going out with Ryan and some other guys tonight. But I might cancel," he said, looking straight at me, as though he was trying to suggest something.

"You should go," I told him. "You don't need to be working here with me. Go hang out with the guys, have some fun."

Cooper stretched his arms above his head and yawned. He looked to the table in front of us and changed the subject. "We got a lot done today."

"We did," I agreed. "I have a bit more to catch up on tomorrow," I said, and he nodded. I quickly added,

"You don't have to come in tomorrow. I won't tell Jennifer."

He smiled at that. "We'll see," he said. "But yeah, I should let you go. If you have plans."

I nodded. "I do."

Cooper started to pack his papers up, he closed down his laptop and slid it into his satchel. "Thanks for lunch," he said. "Though, seriously? A peanut butter sandwich would have been fine."

He collected his things and he'd no sooner walked out of the door than I was in the shower. *Fuck.* I had a hard-on from just being around him, his smile and his smell. It was the second time in as many days I needed to jerk off in the shower because the thought of him was too much.

It was the second time in as many days I imagined it was Cooper underneath me, over me, or his lips around me.

I didn't even wait for nightfall. I got dressed and went downtown to a local bar I'd been to plenty of times. It was only early, so there weren't many people, but everyone I looked at wasn't right for me.

I just wanted some faceless, nameless guy, who I could take to a hotel. I only lived a block away, but I never took casual hook-ups home. I wanted the anonymity, the security. But as I scoured the faces of men for hours, and as other men approached me, none of them were what I was looking for.

None of them had that shine in their eyes, or that mischievous smile. None of them were young and vibrant, not like Cooper.

Fucking hell.

I ended up back at my apartment, pissed off and frustrated. I couldn't even have a one-night stand without thinking about him. I stripped down and climbed into bed naked and this time, with images of him behind my eyelids when I jerked off, I imagined him inside me. I imagined what it would be like to be pinned underneath him, while he buried himself in me.

I came so hard my head spun.

But I slept like a baby.

* * * *

The next morning I was up early, as always. Even being a Sunday didn't mean I couldn't get work done. Amazingly enough, for the first few hours I was up, I didn't think of Cooper at all.

Until it was about nine o'clock when my buzzer rang. Lionel's apologetic voice crackled through. "Sorry to interrupt you on a Sunday, sir."

"It's fine, Lionel."

"Cooper Jones is here again."

"Is he just?"

"Yes, sir," Lionel said. "He said to tell you he has coffee…" There was a muffle of voices again and Lionel groaned. "And peanut butter, sir. He said to tell you he bought you peanut butter."

I grinned into the intercom, grateful they couldn't see me smile. "Send him up."

Chapter Five

I unlocked the door and waited, and true to his word, he walked in with two large coffees and a jar of peanut butter.

I was smiling at him. "What are you doing?"

"If you work, then I work," he said, handing me a coffee. "Jennifer's rules."

"I work every day."

"I don't mind," he said simply. "If I want to be the best, I need to do what the best does."

"Is that flattery?"

He lifted up the jar of peanut butter. "No, this is flattery," he said with a heart-stopping grin. "I can't believe you don't have any."

I smiled at him, and he stared at me. Neither of us spoke, and the air was electric. *Fuck.* "So, how was last night?" I asked, changing the subject and putting some distance between us.

"Oh, I never went," he said, sipping his coffee. "Wasn't up for it."

I was oddly relieved he hadn't gone out, hadn't picked up anyone, or that he hadn't taken anyone home. Fuck, this was getting ridiculous.

Then he asked, "How was your night?"

"Uh, okay," I lied. "I was home pretty early."

"No hot date?" he asked lightly, but there was a seriousness in his eyes.

I shook my head. "No."

Cooper exhaled through puffed cheeks, seemingly relieved. "So, what's on the agenda for today?"

He was wearing jeans today, not suit pants. He had a button-down shirt, with his sleeves rolled up to his elbows, so I wasn't sure if he was here to work or not. It was definitely more relaxed.

"I, um, I'd like to get started on the Cariati file," I told him. I didn't exactly have anything for him to do, but didn't want him to leave either.

This kid was doing my head in.

"Okay," he said, excited "You're doing the façades for that job, aren't you?"

"Yes."

"Can I watch?" he asked.

I stared at him disbelievingly. "You want to watch me draw?"

He nodded, but his cheeks tinted with embarrassment. "It's like watching a masterpiece from the beginning," he admitted quietly.

I couldn't help but smile. "Flattery will get you everywhere."

His eyebrows flickered. "Really?"

He stared at me until I had to look away. I put my coffee down on the counter, pretending to be distracted. Jesus. I wasn't imagining things. This kid was seriously flirting with me. *Fuck.*

I should have stopped it. I should have said no. I should have told him from the very beginning that this was a bad, bad idea.

But I couldn't. While the logical, sensible side of my brain was telling me to put an end right now to this nonsense, the selfish, infatuated, stupid part of my brain wanted it.

My body wanted it.

I glanced back at him, at his smug little smile, then snatched the jar of peanut butter from his hand. I looked at the jar and turned it over in my hands. "Flattery in a jar, huh?"

He smiled as he sipped his coffee then assessed to the dining table. "So, are we working today?"

Work. Right. "Yes, we are," I said, getting my brain back on track. "You can keep going with the specs on the Lewington job while I get started. It takes a while to grid it all out."

"I can't believe you really start each job by drawing it out," he said, walking over to the table. "You know it's the twenty-first century, right? We have computers now."

"I like to see it develop in front of me," I tried to explain. "If I draw it out, it seems to give me a better feel for the overall tone. I've spoken to the Cariatis many times. I know what they want. I can see it in my head, and it comes out better by my hand than with a computer."

I looked up then, to find Cooper staring at me. He was smiling, as if some errant thought made him happy. "That's amazing," he said. Then he added quietly, "You're amazing."

I was taken aback by his blatant compliment, pleased, but a little embarrassed. I looked at the table instead of him. "Oh. I'm not sure about that."

"I am," he said confidently. "And there wasn't even any peanut butter involved."

It made me laugh and as I sat down, I opened my grid pad and pulled my draughting leads from my satchel. Cooper looked at the specialized pencils. "Do they still make those?"

I rolled my eyes. "It's not a quill and inkwell, you know."

He laughed. "No, in the museum they have the quills and draughting leads in separate displays."

I chuckled, despite his constant jibes at my age. "Comments like that counteract the peanut butter."

He grinned, and instead of looking even slightly remorseful, he looked at me like I'd just proposed a challenge.

I tapped the table with my index finger. "Enough with the smartass comments. Work."

Like I hadn't spoken at all, he said, "How about we have a little bet?"

"Pardon?" I asked. "As in a wager?"

"More of a professional, social experiment," he mused. "How about, for the next four hours, you do your drawing of the façade, and I enter in the exterior details into the CAD program. At the end of the four hours we'll see, one, who was more productive, and two, who was more accurate." He opened his laptop and looked at me expectantly.

"And what exactly is the wager?"

"The loser buys lunch."

I smiled at him, at the gleam in his eyes and at the daring of his smile. "Deal."

I slid the spec sheet across the table to Cooper. "You'll need that," I told him, and started with my grid paper and went by memory alone. It was a remodelling job on an old building, strictly confined by city building codes.

I knew those codes like the back of my hand, I knew what the owners wanted and I knew how to make it happen. So, picking up one of my draughting leads, I got started and not even the annoying *tap-tap-tap* of Cooper on his laptop keyboard could distract me.

It was my favorite part of my job. Of course all jobs went through the specifically designed CAD program, but for me, this was where each job started.

It was about two hours later that Cooper stood up and stretched. He walked off toward the kitchen and came back with the jar of peanut butter and a spoon. "What?" he asked, when I looked at him. "It was my jar of flattery."

He then proceeded to eat it by the spoonful, and one time I looked up at him, he was concentrating hard at the computer screen with the spoon still in his mouth. It was…cute.

Soon after that, my stomach let me know when it was lunchtime, and sure enough when I checked the time, it'd almost been four hours. I stood up and walked into the kitchen, grabbed two bottled waters and a spoon and went back to the table. I put the two waters down, leaned my ass against the edge of the table near Cooper and picked up the jar of peanut butter.

"How are you going with your wager?" I asked, as I scooped out a spoonful from the jar.

He sighed. "Well, I'm done, but I know it won't be as good as yours."

I stuck the spoon in my mouth and as soon as I tasted the peanut paste, I couldn't help but groan. "This is good."

Cooper looked up at me, seemingly transfixed by the spoon in my mouth. "Told you," he said a little gruffly.

He shook his head, and looked quickly back to his laptop, turning it around to face me. "Not that we really even need to check, because I'm sure yours will put mine to shame."

I looked at the screen. "You've done a really good job," I told him. "The façade looks good, the elevations are clean. It looks good."

"Mmm," he said, not convinced.

"You've got the coding correct," I reassured him. "And considering it's a new program to you, don't dismiss that. You've done a great job."

"Righto," he mumbled. "Let's have a look at yours." He stood up, walked around to my side of the table, and he picked up my grid pad. He was quiet for a long moment, so I walked around and stood beside him. "Jesus," he whispered. "It's…this is amazing."

I smiled at him, and he shook his head.

"The shading, the perspective, the lines…" He seemed lost for words. "Wow. It's um, it's…"

"It's lunchtime and you're paying," I told him, taking the pad and throwing it onto the table. Cooper grinned at me for a beat too long, walked to my front door and held it open for me.

"No jokes about the elderly?" I asked as we got to the elevator. "Yesterday you were full of cheek about my age."

"Can you remember yesterday?" he asked, wide-eyed. "Your Alzheimer's medication must really work."

I pressed the button for the lobby. "You're such a little shit."

I thought I might offend him by calling him that. But by the way he grinned proudly, I doubt I could offend him if I tried.

The streets of New York on a Sunday were still busy, only people had dressed a little more casually than they did during the week. We started to walk and ended up near the park at a vendor. Cooper stared at me. "I might be a lowly intern, but I can afford more than a pretzel for lunch."

I laughed at him. "I happen to like these." So two pretzels later, we found a bench seat and started to eat our lunch.

Cooper was thoughtful as he ate, looking around. "I love this city," he said.

"Me too," I said, and smiled when I looked at him. "It has a hum, an energy, doesn't it?"

He nodded. "Yeah, it does. But" — then he shrugged — "you'll probably think I'm crazy, but you wanna know what I love about New York?" He shook his head like he couldn't believe he was about to admit something. "I love the skyscrapers. I love the glass and steel, I love the purpose this city has. I love how the new buildings integrate with the old ones. I love the history and the modern, I mean some of these buildings are works of art…"

I stared at him, and he stopped talking and blushed, ducking his head. "See? Told you you'd think I was crazy."

I shook my head slowly. "I love that too," I said quietly. "Everything you said, that's what I love about it too." I shook my head, a little perplexed that this man, this man half my age, understood me.

Cooper smiled and looked down at the half-eaten pretzel in his hand. "I've never told anyone that."

I laughed nervously. "I've told people, but they've never really understood me."

He looked at me then and neither one of us spoke. I just stared at him — wondering what on earth it was about him that intrigued me so much—and right there, in a city of millions with the noise of people and cars and buzzing past us, we sat in silence and had ourselves a moment.

He looked back down at his hands, with tinted cheeks, and exhaled as though looking at me had rendered him unable to breathe.

I liked that more than I should. "Come on," I said, standing up. "I want to show you something."

He stood up, threw the rest of his lunch in the bin and looked at me with keen eyes. "What is it?"

"This way," I said, walking in a different direction than the way we'd come. Two blocks over, I pointed up. "See that?" It was a nondescript commercial building, dwarfed by the taller buildings beside it. Usually overlooked by passers-by, it wasn't the biggest or the grandest, but it was a classic building that any decent architect would appreciate for its subtlety.

"The Crawson building?"

I nodded. "I did that."

Cooper's eyes widened. "Really? I mean, I'm not doubting you...it's just...wow."

I laughed. "Yes, really. Complete retrofit. Exterior façade to replicate the existing, even enhance the history of the building, but its interior is something else. You should see it. It's classic art-deco design but completely sustainable." I showed him the cubic forms, the strong sense of lines, the sleek curving forms and illusion of pillars.

When I finally stopped talking, I looked at Cooper to find he wasn't even looking at the building. He was staring at me. "Can you show me?"

"Inside the building?"

He shook his head. "No, show me how you draw. I want to be able to do that."

"Oh."

"Will you show me? I want to learn, I want to see things how you see them."

I looked at him again, and he stared straight back at me. His eyes never faltered, never strayed from mine. All I could do was nod. "Yes."

He smiled magnificently. "No time like the present."

We started to walk back to my apartment. "Are you sure you don't have anywhere else you'd rather be?" I asked. "Working with me on a Sunday is hardly anyone's idea of fun."

"Well, I'm not anyone," he said brightly. "I happen to enjoy it."

"I'm glad you do," I replied.

The rest of the walk back to my place was quiet, but as soon as we were inside, he pulled his chair next to mine at the table. "So where do we start?"

He had the basic, graphic art and technical drawing skills all architecture kids had. He admitted to that — he could draw a building easily enough. But he couldn't draw it to life, he said. Not like me.

So for the next few hours, we sat side by side at my table with my grid pad and pencils. Sometimes our knees bumped, sometimes our thighs were completely touching, sometimes he'd rest his arm on the back of my chair, sometimes our hands would be so close they'd almost be touching.

And we talked, and we laughed, and we told stories and he smelled so good. But he listened, and he studied, and he copied and it was pretty obvious this kid had talent.

It was also pretty obvious there was something between us. I wasn't imagining it. I'd catch him staring at me, or sometimes his breath would catch, and every now and then when our hands touched, it'd make my heart rate take off and my mouth would go dry.

Sometimes I'd catch myself staring at him. I was lost in his brown hair and hazel eyes and kissable, pink lips. When he was concentrating, or lost in thought at the drawing in front him, I'd have to *make* myself look away.

When he turned to ask me about something, our faces were so close, within leaning distance. His question was long forgotten, and his eyes darkened as he stared at me. He licked his lips and leaned in just a fraction.

He was going to kiss me. And I wanted to. I wanted to feel his lips, I wanted to taste him, touch him, and it was that want that made me panic.

I shot out of my seat and went into the kitchen, shaking my head of the Cooper-daze it was apparently in, and tried to calm my hammering heart.

I turned to find Cooper stand up slowly. "I should probably go," he said quietly.

"Okay," I said, out of breath.

His brow furrowed and he collected his laptop and stuffed it into his satchel. He exhaled through puffed-out cheeks and mumbled something about seeing himself out. Unable to do much else, I nodded, compliantly.

He walked out of my apartment and not three seconds later there was a knock on the door. Knowing who it would be, I looked through the peephole anyway and nervously ran my hands through my hair before opening the door.

Cooper looked rattled, confused even, so I asked, "Everything okay?"

He stared at me for a long second then blurted out, "I think we should kiss."

Chapter Six

"You what?"

"I think we should kiss," he repeated, clearly flustered. "We should just do it, and get it out of the way. Then we can forget about it and get over it, move on, clear the air, whatever. But it's just always there," he said, almost pacing in my doorway. "It's right there between us and it's driving me mad. I can't concentrate, all I can think about is what the fuck kissing you would feel like, or taste like."

My heart was hammering and my stomach was in knots. He was standing right in front of me, telling me he wanted to kiss me.

"I'm not concerned about work," he went on to say. "Because I'm sure, I'm *absolutely certain* that if I just kiss you once and get it out of my system, I'll be fine. I'll be back to normal and we can just act like nothing happened. I know you want to kiss me too," he said, still ranting. "I can see it when you look at me. You stare at my mouth and you lick your lips, and it's like you're trying to not want to kiss me and I don't blame you, because it's weird, I get that. But I think if we just did it and got it out of the way, we could work together without all this wondering about what you might taste like…" His eyes went wide and he paled. The look on my face must have scared him. "Or not," he mumbled, taking a step back from me. "I've obviously misread the signs and you're not saying anything and I've just ruined everything." He turned and almost ran for the elevator.

"Cooper, stop," I said, following him and grabbing his arm. "You haven't misread anything."

He exhaled in a rush, pure relief, and ran his hand through his hair.

"But I'm not sure," I said, taking a step closer to him, so we were almost touching.

"We don't have to," he said quickly. "I shouldn't have suggested—"

His words died when I slid my hand along his jaw. I leaned in and could feel his warm breath on my lips. "I'm not sure if once would be enough."

His eyes were wide and he licked his lips. "Probably not."

Our lips met, open and soft. It was a tender and wary kiss; scared of what was happening, of where this was going. Neither of us moved for a long second, but I gently pulled his bottom lip between my lips, and he gasped.

It seemed to kick him into gear because he let his satchel fall to the floor so he could use two hands to hold me. His mouth opened as he deepened the kiss, his hands slid around my waist as his tongue slid into my mouth.

I think I groaned. Or maybe it was him.

I held his face as we kissed, taking in everything about him—the warmth of his body, his soft lips, his taste, his smell. He made my head spin and my knees weak, my heart was thumping and I wanted more.

But then the elevator arrived at our floor and before the door could open, I pulled Cooper's hand, leading him back into my apartment. He grabbed his satchel off the floor and made it inside, just as old Mrs. Giordano walked out of the elevator. I gave her a polite wave and smile as I closed the door and Cooper burst out laughing.

I leaned against the closed door and grinned at him. "Mrs. Giordano doesn't need to see that."

Cooper put his satchel down against the wall near the door, and with smiling lips, he said, "Mrs. what's-her-name might like to see it."

"Mrs. Giordano is ninety-two years old," I told him. I was still leaning against the door and he was right in front of me. He wasn't pressed up against me, but he wasn't letting me move either. His eyes were flickering from my eyes to my mouth, as though he was about to kiss me again. My voice was just a whisper. "I thought you said just one kiss?"

"I thought you said it wouldn't be enough," he whispered back as he pressed his lips to mine again. He held my face this time, as he opened my lips with his own. Our tongues met and he pressed his body against me.

I wrapped my hands around his back and pulled him tighter against me. I couldn't help it. I didn't want to want him. I didn't want to like it. I didn't want to need it.

But I did.

He slowed the kiss, dragging his lips from mine, looking down until his forehead rested on my cheek, then my chin, and eventually he took a small step back. He was breathing hard, but he was smiling. My hands were still on his hips, so he took another small step back, stepping away from me. "I think I should go now," he said.

I worried that he might panic at the realization of what had just happened. We had just kissed. Twice. Me, his friend's father, a man twice his age. His boss.

"There's no need to panic," I said, realizing how stupid it sounded as soon as I'd said it.

"Oh, I'm not panicking," he said gruffly, then he very obviously readjusted the bulge in his jeans.

"Oh."

Cooper laughed, embarrassed. He took a deep breath and exhaled slowly then looked me in the eye. His eyes were bright and playful. "I will see you in the morning at the office."

"Okay," I answered, trying to gauge his mood.

He picked up his satchel, put his hand on the door handle and said, "I'm going to need you to move from the door."

"Oh," I said, stepping around him. "Sure."

Then he stepped right up close and pecked my lips again, kissing me for the third time.

"That's three," I told him.

He opened the door. "I'm not counting," he said as he walked toward the elevator. He looked around and smiled at me before he stepped in.

I closed the door to my apartment, wondering what the fuck I'd just done.

I'd just crossed every professional and personal line I'd ever had. He worked for me, and he was my son's friend. Meaning, he wasn't just someone Ryan knew, he was someone Ryan had gone to school with. As in the same age. As in exactly *half* my age. I tried not to think about that. Or what that meant.

Cooper was an adult. A very willing, consenting adult. A very well-endowed adult by what I'd felt pressed against my hip.

And with that thought, I stripped off and got in the shower, seeking relief. Again. To images of Cooper. *Again.* What he would look like underneath me with his head thrown back, or on his knees with his lips around me.

The lips I'd just tasted.

Fuck.

I came so hard the room spun. I leaned against the tiles in the shower to catch my breath and until I was pretty sure I could stand without falling.

Fuck, this guy was doing my head in.

I thought about him all night, what he'd say in the morning at the office, how he'd react when he saw me. I went to bed thinking about him, I dreamed of him. I needed to jerk off again in the morning.

It was getting ridiculous.

It was with a dreaded anticipation I went to work the next day. An errant thought occurred to me when I was stepping out of the elevator to my office that he could report me for sexual harassment and in that split second, a thousand thoughts ran through my head.

I half expected Jennifer to tell me I had a team of lawyers sitting in my office, but she just smiled and handed me messages. "Coffee is on your desk."

I ran my hand through my hair and huffed out a breath in relief. Jesus, what had I got myself into?

I was at my desk about half an hour later when Jennifer walked in with Cooper behind her. He was dressed in his usual tailor-fitted suit, looking even better today than he ever had, but he said nothing more than a polite and quiet, "Good morning, Mr. Elkin."

I had a lunch meeting, and a consult meeting, and I saw him briefly throughout the day. But not once did he make eye contact. He didn't look at me and smile, or laugh, like I was used to seeing.

He basically didn't acknowledge me. He was professional and stoic, like nothing had happened between us. Maybe he was right. Maybe if he kissed me once, he would get it out of his system and move on like nothing happened at all.

I, on the other hand, was a distracted mess.

I didn't know if he was playing some kind of game. I didn't know if he was just being professional, or if I was truly out of his system and now meant nothing to him.

All day, every time the phone rang, I half expected Jennifer to tell me one of the partners wanted to see me because a complaint had been lodged against me.

That call never came of course, but at six o'clock when Jennifer knocked on my door to say goodnight, Cooper was behind her. I looked up from my desk. "Goodnight, Jennifer," I said. Then I looked back at the papers on my desk. "Mr. Jones. A moment, please."

Jennifer gave a nod and left Cooper to walk in. He sat down and looked around my office, then at me. "Yes?"

I didn't exactly know what to say, or how to say it. So I went with a safer, "You've been busy today?"

He looked at me seriously and said, "It's technically after hours, so can I speak freely?"

I looked at him, unsure of what he meant. "Yes."

But he didn't speak. He threw his head back and laughed. "Jennifer has been on my ass all day," he said with a laugh. "Said you looked stressed this morning and didn't need any interruptions from the likes of me."

"The likes of you?"

"Those were her words."

I smiled, relieved, and exhaled loudly. "I almost had a stress-attack getting out of the elevator this morning," I admitted. "I wondered if my boss and his lawyers would be in my office when I got here."

Cooper's smile died. "What for?"

"A sexual harassment case, from a certain twenty-two-year-old employee," I said, looking pointedly at him.

I could have compiled a list of how I expected him to react, but laughter wouldn't have been on it. He burst out laughing, and when he looked at me again and saw the look on my face, he laughed some more.

"It's hardly funny," I said, rolling my eyes.

"Were you really worried?" he asked, still smiling.

"I didn't know what to think."

"Neither did I," he admitted. "So, is this where you tell me it was just the one kiss and nothing more? Is that what you called me in here for? To say thanks but no thanks?"

"It was actually three kisses."

"I wasn't counting."

I sighed and ran my fingers through my hair. This was it. This was where the line got drawn or where the lines got blurred.

"You seemed pretty into it from where I was standing," he said.

I barked out a laugh. He had no idea how into it I was, how often I thought of him or the positions I thought of him in. *Fuck.*

I had to be losing my mind.

"What do you want?" I asked, trying to take the pressure off making it my decision.

"I want an honest answer."

I exhaled in a huff. He wasn't letting me out of this. "I... I, um..."

"Oh, for fuck's sake," he said impatiently. "If I were to offer to bring dinner to your place tonight, would you say yes or no?"

"Are you always so forthright?" I asked. "Or is it a Gen Y thing?"

He raised one eyebrow at me. "For one of the best, most sought-after draughtsmen in the industry, you're not very good at making decisions."

"Professional decisions are easy," I told him. "Personal ones are not."

"Oh, Tom, just answer the question."

He'd called me Tom. Not sir, not Mr. Elkin, not even Thomas. He'd called me Tom.

"Yes. Yes, I want dinner. Yes, I want more. Once wasn't enough," I blurted out. "Once was never going to be enough."

He grinned at me, and held up three fingers. "It was actually three kisses."

I bit back a sigh. "Are you always so infuriating?"

Cooper laughed. "Yep, it's a Gen Y thing."

I groaned. "Can I take back the offer of dinner?"

"Nope," he said, standing up. "I'm getting Chinese and I'll be at your place in" — he looked at his watch — "half an hour."

I smiled as I watched him walk out. When the door closed behind him, I let out a groan, and ran my hands through my hair. I shut down my laptop, picked up my satchel and turned the lights off when I left.

I think I grinned the whole way home.

Chapter Seven

The air between us was electric as we ate dinner. And the more I tried to ignore it, the worse it seemed to get. It was all suggestive glances, shy blushes and licking lips. I stared as he took food from his chopsticks, as he opened his mouth and chewed. And he seemed transfixed by my hands.

It was…intoxicating.

When the food was all but gone, I stood up to clear the table and offered him another glass of wine. He took the refilled glass then stood beside me, leaning his ass against the table. He was still wearing his suit pants, the first two buttons of his business shirt were undone and his tie was gone. His eyes were bright and his lips were in a smug little smirk. My heart was hammering yet he seemed completely at ease.

"You make me nervous," I admitted.

He looked at me. "You? The great Thomas Elkin, nervous?"

I chuckled. "Well, here I'm just Tom."

"Well, Tom," he said, taking my wine glass and putting it on the table. "I think you should kiss me now."

"Really?" I asked. His confidence was mesmerizing.

He licked his lips and nodded. So I leaned across and brushed his lips with mine. It was soft and sweet, but then he moved to deepen the kiss. I moved from beside him to stand in front of him and pressed my body against his as I opened my mouth for him.

This was a different kind of kiss.

The first time we'd kissed had been just a kiss. But this was going somewhere.

I slid one arm around his back, and kept one hand around his neck as I kissed him, a mass of tongues, lips, mouths and moans. Cooper raked his hands around my back and down, over my ass. He pulled me against him, so I could feel him. All of him.

Fuck.

He was hard and so was I. I knew he could feel it. There was no way he couldn't feel my cock against his through the fabric of our pants.

Then he was pulling my shirt out of my pants and slipping his fingers under the waistband. Before I could pull my mouth from his to ask what he was doing, he'd undone my suit pants and palmed my cock through my briefs.

"Cooper," I started. I wanted to tell him that it wasn't a good idea, but it felt so good. So, so good.

So I undid the button and zipper on his pants and slid my hand over his briefs, wrapping my hand around him the best I could through the fabric.

He moaned so loud, I almost came.

"Fuck," he gasped, and he gripped me harder, pulling, rubbing, squeezing. I did the same to him and he bucked into me, only this time he shuddered and his head fell back as he thrust into my fist.

Watching him come, feeling him in my hand, brought me undone.

His hand gripped me as I erupted between us. I all but fell into him, collapsing with the force of my orgasm, and he seemed to convulse with aftershocks. When the room had stopped spinning, I realized his face was buried in my neck.

He chuckled. "Well, that's dessert."

I laughed and peeled myself off him. We were a sticky mess. "We need to shower," I told him.

He toed off his shoes right there. I hadn't actually meant that we'd shower together, but he took my hand and said, "Where's the bathroom?" He walked toward the hall, and I told him the last door on the right. It was my bedroom, which I think surprised him. He looked at the bed, then at me and he grinned.

"Bathroom," I said, pointing to the door. He still had hold of my hand.

He led the way, smiling as he undid the buttons on my shirt, and as I slid his pants over his hips and as my shirt fell from my shoulders, I knew this was it.

Despite what we'd just done in the dining room, we were about to be naked together. I was forty-four, he was twenty-two. This was where the difference between us would be really evident.

I had a spattering of hair on my chest that was greying, like the hair on my head, and while I worked out, my body was…well, it was forty-four years old. Whereas Cooper's body was taut and trim, his chest was hairless, though he had a light trail of brown hair from his navel to his heavily hung, uncut dick.

He turned to start the water while I took off my socks. He washed the cum from his stomach first, then turned around and put his head under, closing his eyes. "You getting in?"

I followed him into the shower, and taking the soap, I ran it over his body. He smiled, then moved from under the spray of water to let me in. I washed the mess from my stomach and when I turned to put my head under, Cooper put his hands on my chest.

"Mmm," he hummed as he ran his fingers through the hair on my chest. "I like this." Then he snaked his hand down lower and cupped my balls. "I like this, too."

I couldn't help but chuckle, but swatted his hand away. "Are you always so forthright?"

"Yep," he said with a smile. "It's a Gen Y thing, remember?"

I rolled my eyes, so he took his own dick in his hand and gave it a stroke. He was half hard again already.

"Is that a Gen Y thing?" I asked.

He smirked. "That's a twenty-two-year-old-in-the-shower-with-a-hot-guy thing. I can't help it. You're hot and I'm horny."

I laughed out loud, turned the shower off and handed him a towel. "Um, I'll find you some clean clothes," I told him. "I'll send ours to be dry-cleaned."

I wrapped my towel around me and walked from the en suite to the walk-in robe. I pulled on a pair of jeans and took out a pair of cargo-style shorts and a T-shirt for him.

He was standing in my room with only a towel around his waist, looking at my king-sized bed. "Looks comfy," he said with a grin.

Ignoring his comment, I threw the clean clothes at him. "I'll organize the dry-cleaning."

I picked up our soiled suits and shirts from the bathroom floor and when I walked back into my bedroom, Cooper was pulling up the cargos. He was smiling at me, as he shoved his half-hard cock into the pants. "No underwear, Tom? Is it for easy access later?"

I tried not to smile at him, but my belly tightened at the thought. "You're incorrigible."

He laughed, and I left him there. I bagged the clothes and called reception, just as Cooper came out of my room. He looked me up and down. "How come I have a shirt but you don't?" he asked, but it was more of a rhetorical question. "Not that I mind." Then he walked into the kitchen and opened the fridge. "Want a water?"

"Make yourself at home," I said sarcastically, though I kind of liked it that he felt comfortable here.

He handed me a bottle of water anyway and walked out onto the balcony. "Oh my God."

I followed him out to find him staring at the view. New York at its finest — tall gray buildings, narrow roads with yellow cabs sidelined by green trees that led to the enormity that was Central Park.

I smiled at the look on his face. "This apartment is pretty central."

"Pretty central?" he asked. "It's right *on* Central."

I laughed. "Not quite. But close."

He shook his head, then turned back to look up the street at the Empire State Building. New York City lights at night were something special. "How do you not live out here on your balcony with that view? I mean, I've seen it during the day from here, but at night…"

"It's amazing, isn't it?"

He nodded keenly, taking in and pointing out certain landmarks and the buildings he recognized. After a while I started to get cool, so I went inside and came back out with a shirt on. Cooper sighed. "The view was much better without the shirt."

I smiled at his words, but changed the subject. "Dry-cleaning said they'd be a few hours," I told him. "You can wear those clothes home if you like."

Cooper shrugged. "I don't mind. I can wait, but if I happen to fall asleep in that big comfy bed of yours, I won't mind that either."

I wanted to tell him I didn't think that was a good idea, that that would be moving too fast. I looked at him and couldn't seem to find the words.

Chapter Eight

Cooper didn't stay the night. But he did stay till midnight, took his freshly dry-cleaned suit, kissed me in the doorway and left.

At work, he was ever the professional. Never granting me more than a polite, "Good morning, Mr. Elkin," and he diligently did his job.

He was exceptionally good at his job.

As one of the senior partners, I had a slew of architects under me, who were delegated a range of jobs. So while yes, I had chosen him to work on my team, he was one of many. And it wouldn't have been unusual for me not to see him every day.

But I looked for him. I kept an eye on him, and I watched what he did. But I didn't speak to him, not more than a hello or a courteous nod in the hall.

He was really, very good at his job. He was also very good at pretending he didn't know me.

But on the Thursday—four days since I'd seen him outside work—just before closing time, Jennifer's intercom buzzed. "Yes, Jennifer?"

"Did you call for Mr. Jones?" she asked. "He says you asked to see him."

I smiled. "Yes, I did. Please send him in."

The door opened and in he walked, wearing his suit pants, shirt, tie and a waistcoat, no jacket. He looked...hot.

He sat down across from me and smiled. "You wanted to see me?"

"Did I?"

"Yeah, I'm pretty sure you did," he said with a nod. "I'm sure you had work that needed doing tonight. At your place."

I smiled at him. "Oh, yes. Now I remember."

He looked like the cat that got the canary. "And it's your turn to buy dinner," he added. "Not that I'd ever tell you what to order, but I feel like pizza."

I couldn't help but chuckle. "God forbid you tell me what to do."

He stood up. "Half an hour?"

"See you then."

"Pepperoni and peppers."

"I thought you weren't telling me what to do."

"It's a Gen Y thing," he said before he opened the door and walked out.

I was still smiling when Jennifer walked in. "Anything you need me to do before I leave, Mr. Elkin?"

"No, I won't be far behind you," I told her. "I'll be working from home tonight."

"Can I order you something to eat?" she asked.

"No, I've got it covered. Thank you."

"Very well. I'll see you tomorrow," she said. "Don't work too hard."

I smiled at her as she walked out, knowing not much work would be getting done tonight. And thirty minutes later, I was home and pizza was ordered, when the doorman buzzed. "Yes, Lionel?"

"Sir, Mr. Jones is here."

"Send him up."

I unlocked the door, took out two beers from the fridge and smiled when there was a knock. "Come in."

Still wearing the suit and waistcoat he'd worn that day, Cooper walked in to find me in the kitchen. He took the offered beer and didn't hesitate to kiss me. It was a slow, deliberate peck on the lips that made my stomach knot — a kiss that promised more to come.

Then he said, "I don't think Lionel likes me."

"Why?"

"He won't let me come straight up," he said, almost petulantly. "It's like I have to check in with him first."

I took a swig of my beer to hide my smile. "He's doing his job."

"But I've been here like five times, and he's seen us walk in and out together, and he still stops me," he added. "What's it gonna take for him to be cool with it?"

Cool with it? Dear God, he really was twenty-two. "He'll be *cool* with it when I tell him you can come and go as you please."

"What, like I live here or something?"

"Yes, like you live here or something. And you don't live here, and you're not my *something*."

He understood then what I meant. "Oh." He looked down at his beer. "Fair enough."

I lifted his chin and stood in front of him. "Telling Lionel you have access is like my equivalent of giving you a key to my house."

"Yeah, I get it."

I kissed him softly. "I didn't mean you weren't something to me."

His eyes widened and he looked at me squarely. "What am I to you?"

"Mesmerizing. Confounding. Amusing."

He smiled slowly. "They're some pretty good adjectives."

I kissed him softly again. "Yes, that's it. You're some pretty good adjectives to me."

There was a loud knock on the door. "Pizza."

Cooper's eyes narrowed. "He lets the *pizza guy* come up without buzzing?"

I laughed and went to the door, and when I came back Cooper was looking at the intercom. "Which button do I press?" he mumbled to himself. He didn't wait for an answer, he just pressed the first button.

Lionel answered. "Yes, Mr. Elkin?"

"You let the pizza guy up and not me?" Cooper said into the intercom.

"Mr. Elkin, is everything okay?" Lionel sounded alarmed.

I swatted Cooper's hand away and pressed the button. "Yes, Lionel, I'm fine. Mr. Jones here is feeling a little unloved."

"Am I to alert you when Mr. Jones arrives, sir?"

I looked Cooper up and down, finally landing on his face. "Yes, you can still let me know when Mr. Jones arrives," I said, and Cooper's mouth fell open. "For now."

"Very well, Mr. Elkin," Lionel said through the intercom.

I released the intercom button and put the pizzas on the counter. Cooper glared at me.

I smiled at him. "You're cute when you pout."

He huffed. "I think I'll need a lot more adjectives from you yet."

I turned the pizza box to face him and opened it. "Hungry, cute."

"You said that one already."

"Impatient, talented, conceited, smug."

"They're similes. Didn't they teach you similes in school back in the olden days?"

"Smartass, juvenile, petulant, belligerent…"

Cooper picked up a slice of pizza, bit into it and chewed thoughtfully. He swallowed his food and said, "Mmm, well, I like talented and conceited, but smartass and juvenile were a little harsh. I think we might need to go back to cute."

I shook my head and sighed. "Okay, you're a cute, belligerent little shit. How was that?"

He took another bite of his pizza and spoke with his mouth full, "Much better."

I gave up. I doubted I'd ever win. I took a slice of pizza and he clinked his beer bottle to mine and gave me a cheeky grin.

"So do you really think I'm cute?"

"Just shut up and eat your pizza."

Cooper gave me that smug little smile he got, but told me all about his week so far. How he'd been busy with the team getting basics done, and learning what he could. It was easy to see that he loved it, how animated he got, how it seemed he could talk for hours about projects and buildings, and drawings and concepts.

Even long after the pizza was gone and we'd been on the sofa for a while, we were still discussing design theories and building codes and planning laws. It amazed me that he could make me smile with just a pout one minute, then be a professional adult whom I could talk to for hours the next.

Then he changed the subject. "I'm sorry if telling Jennifer you asked to see me was out of line," he said. "But I figured if I didn't, I wouldn't get to see you."

"It's fine," I told him. "I'm glad you did."

He smiled. "Me too." Then he slid himself across the sofa and kissed me. But he didn't stop there. He slowly leaned backwards, pulling me with him, so I was lying over him. He only stopped kissing me so he could maneuver himself into a better position for me to settle between his legs, then his mouth was on mine again.

Cooper opened his legs wider and held on to me tighter, and I rocked a little on top of him while we kissed. But it was languid and soft, there was no hot and heavy desire. His eyes closed gently, sleepily. When I brushed his hair from his forehead, I saw my watch. It was after one, we'd been talking for hours and I'd completely lost track of time.

"Come on, sleepy-head," I said, getting off him, pulling him to his feet. "It's too late for you to go home. You can stay here."

I led him down the hall toward the spare room, Ryan's room, but he turned straight into my bedroom and started to strip off. He threw his suit pants over the chair and climbed into my bed in his underwear.

Into my side of the bed.

I stood there, not sure what to do. I contemplated arguing, but realized arguing with Cooper was futile. So instead, I went back out to the living room, turned off the lights and by the time I'd changed into pajama pants and got into bed, Cooper was already asleep.

* * * *

Waking up to the feeling of being watched isn't particularly pleasant. A sleep-rumpled Cooper looked at me apologetically. "I guess this could be awkward," he said. "I mean, if we let it be awkward. But I'm all for thinking fuck it, let's *not* be awkward. Let's have pancakes for breakfast and then when you're covered in maple syrup, we can shower together, or I can lick you clean. Whichever you prefer."

I smiled. "Good morning, Cooper."

"Morning, Tom," he said with a grin. "So, pancakes?"

I looked at the alarm clock and fell back with a groan. Six a.m. "Pancakes."

He bounced up on the bed, still wearing only his briefs. I could see the heavy outline of his morning wood. He knew I saw, he made no attempt to hide it. In fact, he then walked to the kitchen and proceeded to make pancakes, still only wearing his briefs.

Needless to say, breakfast was a mess, there was a lot of licking and a hot shower where Cooper dropped to his knees and took my hardened cock into his mouth.

I returned the favor on my bed, where he arched his back, gripped the sheets and screamed as he shot hard down my throat. He then chuckled and writhed on my bed until his body recovered while I took a shirt from my wardrobe and laid it on the bed next to him. "You'll have to wear the suit pants you wore yesterday to work, but at least people won't know you didn't go home if you're wearing a new shirt."

Cooper laughed. "It wouldn't have been the first time I've done the walk of shame."

I rolled my eyes at him. "Come on, you need to get up. Don't want to be late."

He stretched lazily and grinned, his spent cock lying heavy across his hip. "I don't know, I think the boss might be in a particularly good mood this morning." Then he added, "Anyway, I think he likes me."

I did up the fly on my pants, not game to look at him in case he saw that exact truth on my face. "Whatever gives you that idea?"

"The way he gripped my hair and moaned my name in the shower."

I blushed. The little shit made me blush. I cleared my throat. "Right, I better go clean up this kitchen."

* * * *

For the next two weeks, we fooled around. Usually at my place, though I went to his apartment on the second weekend. It was small, very small, but clean and small. Did I mention it was small? But it was close enough to the office and he seemed to like it. Compared to my place, it was at the other end of the spectrum of places to live.

So, at his place, or mine, we spent time together. Lost in long conversations, or long make-out sessions, I couldn't seem to get enough of him and as baffling as it was to me, it seemed he couldn't get enough of me either.

But we never had sex. Well, not intercourse-sex. We were close a few times, and it was something we clearly both wanted, but it was something we never discussed. Like it was a step we were too scared to take.

At work, he was always the professional. He kept his cool, though I noticed that smug little smirk every now and then, but to anyone else, from what I could tell, no one suspected a thing.

It was Thursday afternoon and Jennifer's intercom buzzed. "Mr. Jones is here to see you."

"Thank you," I replied.

He walked in with some draughting papers and sat down across from me.

I looked at the plans he was holding. "What are they?"

"Props," he answered. "For Jennifer's sake. I had to come in here with something."

I chuckled at him. "To what do I owe the pleasure?"

"Well," he started, and he seemed nervous. "I know I said I'd come over tonight, but the guys are going out tonight and they asked me to join them. It's been a while…"

I looked at him, a little confused. "Cooper, that's fine. You don't need my permission. You're young, you should go out."

"It's with Ryan."

Oh.

"That's fine," I lied. He was young, he should go out and enjoy his life. Not be stuck at home with some old man like me.

"You can't lie for shit," he said flatly. "And I know what you're thinking. Just because I'm young and we don't go out doesn't mean I don't enjoy spending time with you." He stared straight at me, seeing right through me.

"We should go out more," I admitted.

"No, we shouldn't," he replied. "We can't and you know it." He looked around my office before looking back at me. "And that's okay, Tom. I like what we do. But I'd like to go out with the boys tonight."

"Of course," I said with a smile. "That means I don't have to listen to your shit music tonight."

He smirked as he stood up to leave. "No, you can listen to your Hits of the Eighties crap without me."

I opted for some classical music instead, knowing Cooper would hate it, and spent the night going over some concept budgets. It was quiet and lovely, but something was missing.

Cooper was missing. The noise, the mess, the conversation, the kisses, the cuddling on the sofa.

I'd spent three nights alone that week, so it wasn't like it was *that* different. But it was supposed to be our night, and I'd been looking forward to it.

I got into bed, trying not to think about how different my life had become in a matter of weeks, or what that might have meant. I finally fell asleep, but the intercom buzzer woke me at one in the morning.

I staggered out to the living room and hit the intercom. "Lionel?"

"I'm very sorry to wake you, sir," he said. "But Mr. Jones is here."

"It's one in the morning," I mumbled. "Is everything okay? Is he hurt?"

"No, sir," Lionel replied. "He's drunk."

I sighed. "Can you send him up? Or should I come down and get him?"

"I'll get him into the elevator for you, sir."

"Thank you, Lionel."

Wearing only my sleep pants, I walked out to the elevator just as it arrived. The doors opened and Cooper stood, leaning, half-falling against the back wall. I hit the door button, so they stayed open, put my arm around him and hauled him into my apartment.

"I'm sorry," he slurred. He planted his lips on mine. "You're so sexy."

I laughed. "You're drunk."

"'M sorry. Had to see you."

"It's okay, Cooper," I said, walking him down the hall to my bedroom. "Everything okay? Did you have a good night?" Though it sure looked as though he had.

"'S good," he said. "Ryan knows I'm seein' someone." He fell onto the bed, and I stared at him, unable to speak. Then he mumbled, "Not you, o'course, just someone."

"Oh."

"He wanted to know who I've been spendin' my time with," he said, rolling onto his side. "But I didn't tell him."

My heart was beating double time, but I got into bed beside him. He was quiet for a little while and I assumed he was already asleep. But then he said, "Why won't you have sex with me?"

My heart leaped into my mouth. "What?"

His hand reached blindly for me and now my eyes had adjusted to the lack of light, I could see him watching me. "We've done everything else, why not that?" he asked, his voice slurred. "Don't you want me?"

I squeezed his hand. "Very much."

His voice was sleepy and not too coherent. "Then why?"

"Because it's something we can't come back from. If we do that," I clarified quietly, "what we have, what we're doing, becomes something else."

"Might want something else," he mumbled, and soon after his breathing evened out and he started to snore.

I stared at the ceiling until morning, turning his words over and over in my head, while my heart tried to convince my brain that it might want something more too.

Chapter Nine

The downside of being twenty-two is not knowing when you've had enough to drink. The upside of being twenty-two is how quickly you recover from drinking too much.

Whereas I'd have been hungover for an entire day, he woke up okay. He groaned a bit, didn't speak much, drank his coffee, then he drank mine. He swore he was never drinking again, told me it was my fault for letting him go out, showered, dressed in one of my older suits and went to work.

He left before me, and as I walked through my lobby fifteen minutes later, Lionel winked at me. "He keeps you busy."

There was no point in denying it. "He does." Then I stopped walking. "Did he say anything to you last night?"

Lionel laughed. "Only that he couldn't understand why I didn't like him. I wasn't going to interrupt you, sir, but he wouldn't shut up," he said. "But this morning he was a little less talkative."

I couldn't help but chuckle. "Have a good day, Lionel."

"You too, sir."

I smiled all the way to work, and as I walked to my office. Jennifer being her usual professional self, smiled right back at me. "Good morning, Mr. Elkin. Coffee's on your desk."

It was a completely normal Friday. Busy, productive, but normal. I did see Cooper drink more coffee than normal, but he never missed a beat.

Then just before lunch, Jennifer knocked on my door. "Can I have a moment?"

I blinked in surprise, but closed my laptop, giving her my undivided attention. "What is it?"

She sat down in a chair at my desk, something she'd never done before. "Your meeting with Mr. Takosama," she said quietly, "scheduled for next month in Tokyo, has been brought forward."

"Okay," I said, not fully understanding why she was being so cautious.

"He has two days free this week in Sydney, Australia. I took the liberty of securing the appointment," she said. "I know it's short notice, but it will give you less time to think of a reason not to go."

"Why wouldn't I want to go?"

Jennifer hesitated. "I booked two tickets."

"*Two* tickets?"

She swallowed and whispered, "I thought Mr. Jones could accompany you."

I stared at her. I had to tell myself to close my mouth, while my brain caught up. There was no way Jennifer would say something like this, act so carefully, if she wasn't sure.

Without any doubt in my mind, she knew.

"How did you know?" I asked quietly. "Did someone say something? Has anyone in the office said anything?" Then a cold dread crept up my spine. "Did Cooper say something?"

"Oh, heavens no," she said. "He's not breathed a word of it. Going by him, I'd never have suspected a thing. But you on the other hand..."

"Me?"

She smiled kindly at me. "It's the way you look at him."

"The way I what?"

"The way you look at him," she repeated. "Like the boy hung the moon." I went to correct her on the word 'boy' but she looked at me, daring me to argue. "I'm almost sixty. He's a boy to me. And there's the fact he's wearing the suit you bought last year."

I sighed and could feel myself blush. There was no point in denying it with her. So I confirmed what she already knew. "Yes, he's young, but he's smart, and he's so switched on. He has the tenacity and arrogance that comes with being twenty-something, but he's... I don't know...he's sweet and funny, and when we're together, there's no age difference between us." I didn't know why I was telling her this. But I needed to tell *someone*.

Jennifer smiled. "But?"

"But I don't know what I want. It took a lot for me to finally own up to my wife, and to myself, and admit that I was gay. It's been five years of finally living my real life, knowing exactly what I want, and knowing exactly who I am. But this is the first time that I don't know what I want at all."

Jennifer shook her head. "No, I think it's the first time you know *exactly* what you want." Then she sighed. "Tom." It was the first time she'd ever called me by my first name. "He makes you happy. I've never seen you so happy. It doesn't matter what anyone else thinks or says. It's about you."

There was a knock at the door. I didn't know whether to be sorry or grateful for the interruption. I cleared my throat. "Come in," I called out.

Of all people, it was Cooper. He stuck his head around the door and when he saw Jennifer, without even saying hello, he said, "Oh, I can come back."

"No, it's fine," Jennifer said, standing up. "Mr. Jones, please come in."

Cooper did as he was bid, but looked at the older lady nervously. She pursed her lips. "Have you got a passport?"

He looked at me, then back to Jennifer. "Yes?"

"Good," she said, matter-of-factly. "You'll be going to Sydney with Mr. Elkin for four days. You leave tomorrow."

Cooper blinked. "Um…"

"Mr. Jones," Jennifer said brusquely. "Normally I would accompany Mr. Elkin on such trips, but my granddaughter is the first broccoli singing in a line of vegetables in her first-grade recital. I simply cannot miss it."

Cooper blinked again, and I think he tried not to smile. "Very well. I'm sure your granddaughter will be a great…broccoli…"

Jennifer stared at him. "You'll fly out tomorrow, six a.m. I've booked flights and accommodation, but if you need to make arrangements, please do so now," she said, shooing him, dismissing him.

The door closed behind him, and I looked at Jennifer and laughed. "You scare him, you know."

She smiled. "Oh, I know. Helps keep them in line."

I sighed. "And the trip to Sydney?"

"All legitimate, of course," she said with a sniff. "You *do* have a meeting with Mr. Takosama. He's expecting you. I have updated your schedule, and you'll be busy enough. But Mr. Jones will have a list a mile long of things to do." Then she softened. "But I thought you could use the time away."

I didn't know whether to laugh or cry. "Thank you, Jennifer."

"It's only four days," she said. "Being away from here will put a little perspective on things."

Four days. Four days in a different city, four days to be ourselves.

"His internship is almost over," she said. "Four more weeks. You'll need to keep a lid on things until then."

"I know," I answered. "He knows that too."

She gave a curt nod. "What will you do after that?" she asked, looking me square in the eye. "Will you take him on here at the firm?"

I whispered, "I don't know."

"He's very good," she said from the door. "One of the best."

"Yes, he is."

"But?"

But I can't date a fellow employee. It's against company policy. Fuck, I was already so far in breach of company policy. Jennifer knew this. I presumed this was her point. "But...it's complicated."

"Yes, it is," she said. "For what it's worth, it's good to see you happy." She opened the door then closed it quietly behind her.

I tried to get my head back into the job I was halfway through researching, but gave up and stared out across the blue skies of New York instead. Jennifer came in a few hours later, gave me files and instructions on the Takosama job, handed over the flight confirmation slips and accommodation reservation information and told me to go home.

Figuring I had the next four days with Cooper, I suggested I pick him up from his place at half-past four in the morning. When he got in the car, despite the early hour, he was bright-eyed, but quiet, obviously not wanting to speak in front of a company driver.

He was quiet as we checked in, and he was trying not to smile as we got coffee waiting to board. And by the time we finally got into our seats in first-class, he couldn't stop grinning. "This is awesome!" he whisper-shouted from the seat next to mine. "I can't believe Jennifer passed this up!"

"Jennifer knows about us," I told him as I got settled in. "She made you her replacement because she wanted us to have some time alone."

He was quiet, so I looked over at him. He was gaping. "She...she *knows*?"

I nodded. "Yes."

"How?"

I considered lying but decided to tell him the truth. "The way I look at you, apparently."

He stared at me and blinked, three, maybe four times, seemingly having lost the ability to speak. He fell back into his seat and looked pale.

I turned side on to face him and took his hand. "She won't tell a soul, I promise. She's the utmost professional, Cooper. She won't tell anyone."

"How can you be so sure?" he asked. "If she knows, then maybe someone else does?"

I shook my head. "No, she knows me, she knows me better than most people. She knew I'd separated from my wife by the fact I changed my cologne...well, that and the long hours and sleeplessness. But, believe me, no one else knows."

He sighed and seemed to relax. "By the way you look at me? What does that mean?"

"Apparently I smile when I see you," I told him seriously. "I'm trying to stop doing that."

"Right," he said with a laugh. "Look at me."

I did, I looked right at him. At his smirking lips, the slight dimple in his cheek, his bright and smiling eyes. And I smiled.

"Oh, you're hopeless," he said, shaking his head. Then he sighed dramatically. "Four days, huh? We've got four days before we have to go back to reality?"

I nodded. "We do have work to do on this trip."

"Oh, I know," he said. "The list Jennifer gave me is taller than the Empire State." He shook his head. "She gave it to me, I looked at it and she said if I couldn't manage it, she'd find someone more competent." Then he looked at me. "She doesn't like me, and now you tell me she knows we're…seeing each other?"

"She doesn't not like you," I told him. "She does it to keep you on your toes. In fact, she told me you were one of the best interns she'd ever seen."

"She said that?" he asked brightly. He sat back in his seat and smiled. "I *knew* she liked me."

I laughed at him. "Don't let on, though. She likes everyone to think she's mean."

He grinned like he had her all figured out, but as soon as we were at elevation, he pulled out his laptop and made a start on Jennifer's list.

* * * *

We arrived at the Hilton in Sydney to find Jennifer had booked only one room.

"Is that a problem, sir?" the clerk asked.

Cooper answered quickly, "No, it's fine. We'll take it."

I glared at him, but he just grinned, signed us in and took the key.

The room was extravagant and lovely, overlooking the city and the view was spectacular. But the very large, *only* bed made me nervous. Sure, we'd slept in the same bed before, but this was different.

I knew what we were going to do in this bed.

I put my bags down, and despite how long we'd just spent on a plane, despite the time it was in Sydney, I looked at him nervously. "Wanna go and check out some sights?"

Cooper looked at the clock on the bedside table. "It's almost ten. What *sights* can we see at ten o'clock at night?"

"Let's go find out," I said.

"You know," Cooper said. He was staring at the huge, white bed. "This bed won't bite."

I looked at him quickly then chuckled, embarrassed.

He laughed at me. "I might bite, but the bed won't."

I cleared my throat. "Come on, some air will do us good."

He rolled his eyes, sighed for effect, but then opened his suitcase and pulled out a jacket and woollen beanie. "I can't believe we left summer to go somewhere it's winter. Who the hell does that?" he mumbled to himself.

I grabbed my coat too, and after I'd put it on, Cooper grabbed the key, then he grabbed my hand. "We can hold hands here," he said as we walked toward the elevator. "No one knows us."

I didn't object, and when I looked into the mirrored wall inside the elevator, Cooper smiled at us in the reflection. "Looking mighty fine tonight, Mr. Elkin," he said.

I looked at him in his winter coat and the beanie pulled over his hair. "Not too bad yourself, Mr. Jones."

He kissed my cheek quickly before the elevator doors opened and he pulled me out through the lobby of the hotel and onto the street. He'd never been to Sydney before, and his excitement and enthusiasm was adorable.

It was cold, but we walked a few blocks, looking in shop windows and there were even some souvenir shops and 7-Eleven style shops still open. Cooper dragged me into some. He bought a few things as we went, some I looked at, some I waited outside for, and when he'd obviously seen enough, he declared he wanted to go back to the hotel.

We'd slept on and off on the plane, but figuring he must still be tired, I didn't mind. When we walked in, still holding hands, he led me straight to the bedroom. "Cooper, what are you doing?"

Then he upended one of the bags of things he'd just bought, and the contents spilled onto the bed.

A box of condoms and a bottle of lube.

I looked at Cooper and before I could say anything, he took my face in his hands and kissed me. He held my face to his and kissed me like he'd never kissed me before. I could taste the urgency on his tongue, feel it in his hands.

He finally pulled his mouth from mine, but still held my face to his. "Tom, I need you. Please."

I couldn't argue. I couldn't deny how much I wanted him. So I kissed him in a way that told him I would have him.

Not taking my mouth from his, I reached up and pulled his beanie off, then slipping my hands under his jacket, I pushed it off his shoulders.

He fumbled with my coat and tried too quickly to toe out of his shoes. "Slow down, Cooper," I murmured against his lips. "It's okay, I'll take my time with you."

He nodded, and when he kissed me again, it was slower. He was calmer, but no less certain.

I undressed him, like I'd done plenty of times before, but this was different. I kissed down his neck, I ran my hands over every inch of skin I could reach. And he let me. He let me take charge, he wanted me to.

When he was naked, I told him to lie down on the bed, and slowly undressed myself as I watched him. His long, taut body was stretched out before me, his erection laying heavy across his hip.

I started at his feet, running my hands up his legs, touching every part of him. I wanted his whole body to feel this, to react. When I got to his thighs, he spread them wide and pumped his cock with a groan.

I grabbed the lube and flipped the lid, smearing cool liquid over my fingers then leaned up and kissed the head of his cock, running my tongue over the slit. He fisted my hair and moaned as I took all of him into my mouth, and while he was distracted with my tongue working over his dick, I rubbed his hole.

He cursed.

Then I swallowed around him, and pressed one finger inside him. The sounds he made spurred me on. The more I worked him with my mouth, the more I stretched him, getting him ready for me. It wasn't long before he was begging me, so I turned my fingers, hooking them to the front until I found his gland.

He bucked his hips off the bed, fisted the sheets beside him and threw his head back in a silent scream as he came.

Fuck, it was beautiful.

I pulled my fingers out, and he squirmed and writhed through his orgasm, and I ripped open a foil wrapper and rolled on a condom. I pushed Cooper's legs up and open, and pressed my cock against his ready ass.

I leaned over him and kissed his lips before slowly pushing inside him. His eyes widened and he gasped, making me stop. "Are you okay?" I asked quickly.

"Yes." He nodded and gasped again. "More."

And with every inch I pressed into him, he gasped and pushed his head back into the pillow. I kissed along his strained neck, and he lifted his legs higher and held me tighter. "Fuck, Tom," he whispered. "Oh, fuck."

Only when I was buried inside him did I start to really move, rolling my hips into him. I held his face and kissed him. "I won't last long," I told him. "You feel too good."

Cooper slid his hand between us, taking his cock and pumping himself in time with my thrusts. "I need to come again."

Oh, fuck.

I leaned back to give him room, so I could watch him, so I could see where we were joined. Fuck. It was too much. "Fuck, Cooper, come again for me."

He groaned again and lifted his hips.

So I leaned over him again, thrusting harder, and I whispered into his ear, "I want to feel you come when I'm inside you."

And that did it.

He flexed against me, and he convulsed as his come splashed on my chest. But his ass clenched around me and I thrust hard one last time before I came. I was so lost in the sensation, so lost in the bliss, so lost in him.

When my senses came back to me, Cooper's arms were wrapped around me, his thighs still at my sides and he was kissing my shoulder and my neck. "That was amazing," he whispered.

I chuckled into his neck, still too boneless to move. "You're amazing," I told him.

I could feel him smile into my neck. "While I really don't want to move, we need to shower."

I slowly pulled out of him, rolling us to our sides. But when he shivered from the cold, I took him into the shower.

I poured shampoo into my hand and lathered it into his hair to wash the lube out.

"What time is the meeting tomorrow?" he asked.

"Ten a.m.," I answered. "Lean your head back," I told him and washed the soap from his hair. "There you go."

"Is it all out?"

"Yep, you have lube-free hair."

He laughed, and when we were out of the shower and dried off, he climbed back into bed, naked. He patted the bed beside him so, as naked as him, I joined him and we fell asleep wrapped in each other's arms.

I woke up spooning Cooper. Actually, I woke up to Cooper wiggling his ass against my hardening cock.

When he knew I was awake, he took my hand and rolled onto his stomach, pulling me on top of him, over him.

"Are you sore?" I asked gruffly into the back of his neck.

He shook his head. "Mm-mm, no." Then he spread his legs and raised his ass. "Want you."

"Jesus," I said with a groan. "Are you sure?"

"Please."

Fuck. Reaching over, I grabbed the supplies off the bedside table. I sheathed myself first, then slicked him with lube. He writhed as I prepped him and lifted his ass higher. "Tom, please, baby, please."

I pressed against him, inside him, and sank all the way in one long push. He groaned like I'd never heard him before. He was vocal, not a quiet lover, not a shy lover. If he wanted it, he asked for it, or he just took it.

I kissed the back of his neck as I thrust into his ass and he slid his hand underneath him. I leaned up on my knees and pulled his ass up so I could fill him, and so he could pleasure himself.

It wasn't long before he came with a sharp cry, making me follow soon after.

We collapsed onto the sticky bed, sated and chuckling. "Good morning," he said with a laugh.

I kissed his shoulder. "Good morning."

"Maybe we shouldn't sleep naked," he said.

"Or maybe we should."

He squeezed his dick and groaned. "Jesus, I could almost go again."

I rolled off him. "God, you'll be the death of me."

He laughed, rolled off the bed and slapped my ass. "Up with you, Mr. Elkin. We have a great deal to get done today."

* * * *

The meeting with Tamosaka was long. But considering the sizeable account and the fact we'd just spent twenty-one hours flying to meet with him, it was imperative we were productive.

I'd met with him before. We'd worked on his last build together. He wanted the best for his Fourth

Avenue address, and he'd got the best when he asked for me. This was a different project, his second home, but no less important to him.

He ran businesses in Japan, Australia and America and he had two days spare whilst in Sydney, so that was where I fitted in. We discussed plans and conceptual designs all day, then I'd go back and draft them up that night and show them to him the next day. He'd either approve them or hire someone else.

I spent the day with him in his George Street office, while Cooper sat in the corner quietly taking notes. It was how Takosama did business. He dealt with one man, the man in charge, and only him.

It wasn't strictly how I preferred to do business, but Cooper didn't seem to mind. He said he understood the cultural differences and seemed happy to be in the background writing madly as we talked. He didn't eat with us and when Takosama was called out for an important phone call, I asked Cooper if he was okay.

"Sure," he said with a smile, then went back to writing.

When the meeting was over, Cooper quietly packed away his notepad and pen and stood quietly waiting. When Mr. Takosama addressed him, Cooper bowed his head politely then he did something no one was expecting.

He spoke in Japanese.

I was floored, and Takosama was very pleased. He gave me an honest smile, shook my hand again, and we left. As we climbed into a cab to go back to the hotel, I still couldn't believe it. "What the hell did you say to him?"

"Nothing much," he said with smile. "I simply told him it was an honor to sit in with him."

"Why the hell didn't you tell me you knew Japanese?"

"I don't really," he said. "I studied cultural etiquette at college."

I shook my head. "You're a surprise at every turn."

He grinned at that, then he pulled out his notepad. "I have a lot of notes."

"I have a pretty good idea of what he's after."

Cooper nodded. "I know. You were incredible in there today."

That night, for the next few hours, I drew up some concepts for the job while Cooper worked on the specifications. I had to admit, we worked well as a team. But by the time we were done and jet lag had well and truly kicked in, we fell into bed and slept.

The meeting with Takosama the next day took ten minutes. He looked over the plans, studying each one carefully, read through the spec sheets Cooper had done and he smiled. He shook my hand, then Cooper's and by ten fifteen that morning, we'd won the contract.

Which gave us two full days off.

Cooper was still buzzed about the Takosama job and his excitement was palpable. We got in some sightseeing, though he was more interested in the buildings than in things like the Harbour Bridge or Bondi Beach.

He marveled at the Sydney Opera House. He sat on the steps and just shook his head in wonder. Dragging him from the modern icon, I took him into the oldest part of Sydney, where the buildings were made of sandstone.

Watching him as he took in the history and the designs of each building I showed him was priceless. He commented on the British colonial influences which led to discussion on England and he said he'd never been.

"Oh, London is beautiful," I told him. "I'll take you one day and show you some of the most incredible places. And Paris and Prague. The history in those cities is mind-blowing."

His whole face lit up. "Really? You'd take me and show me?"

I would. I was starting to think I'd take him anywhere, show him anything, to see him smile like that. I nodded. "Yes."

He just beamed, and for the rest of the afternoon, he seemed content to just be with me, enjoying the quiet peacefulness between us. But then as it got later, and as I was thinking of bed, he shook his head.

"Enough old fuddy-duddy stuff for one day," he said. "Now it's my turn."

"Your turn for what?"

He grinned. "Get dressed, old man. We're going out."

Chapter Ten

"A nightclub?" I repeated. "Really?"

"Yes, really," he answered, pulling on a tight-fitting tee. I was going to argue the point, but then he said, "We can't go out together back home. I can't dance with you, I can't be seen with you because of work. But we can here."

I couldn't argue with that.

As we got in the cab and Cooper gave directions, I asked him how he knew where to go. "I asked the doorman," he said, as though it should have been obvious. Then he added, "The one who checked you out every time you walked past."

"Checked me out?"

Cooper laughed at me. "You should get your eyes tested."

"My eyes are just fine," I said indignantly.

He took my hand and gave it a squeeze. "Half the men we walk past look at you, and you have no idea."

We pulled up at wherever Cooper had given directions to, and got out onto the busy sidewalk. It was late and cold, but there were people walking to and from venues up and down the street. Cooper pulled my hand and led me straight into one club, and the first thing I noticed was that they were mostly all men.

We showed our ID, the security guy took a double look at mine, but we walked in and headed toward the bar. Cooper pulled me in close, and I griped in his ear, "The guy at the door had to look twice at my ID."

He leaned in close so I could hear him over the music. "Because you look so good for your age."

I rolled my eyes and looked around the crowded room. I was easily the eldest man there by about ten years. "They probably think you're here with your father."

Cooper grabbed my face and kissed me, right there in a crowded bar, for anyone to see. "Now they don't think I'm here with my father," he said. He leaned over the bar, ordered two drinks and looked at me. "Now drop the age thing. We're here to dance, okay?"

And that was what we did. We danced.

He led the way, of course. I'd expected nothing less. But he wasted no time in putting his hands on me, pulling me in close and making us sway. He kissed my neck and my lips, but it was easy to tell he was lost in the music.

The room was too crowded and the music was too loud, but his eyes were closed, his lips were curled in a small smile as he moved, and I didn't care about anything else. He was beautiful to watch.

I ran my hands over his back, over his ass, and as I ran my hands up his sides, he lifted his arms above his head and swayed. He never opened his eyes, he never stopped smiling. But he danced, and I pulled him tighter against me and his arms came down around me.

I don't know how long we danced for. I didn't fucking care. If he wanted to dance—if that was what twenty-two year olds wanted to do—then I'd gladly do it with him.

We got back to the hotel at some ungodly hour, he pulled me onto the bed and instead of having sex, I sixty-nined him.

We woke up late, spent a lazy day shopping and taking in the foreign city. He was right. It was nice to be able to just be with him. We were free to just walk around, to be ourselves, without fear of being spotted by someone we worked with. And in New York we couldn't do that. Granted it was a much bigger city, but there were eyes watching everywhere there, and someone would be bound to see us together and question why.

By mid-afternoon we were back in bed, both of us sated and breathing heavily. He was threading his fingers through the hair on my chest.

"Maybe we should get some sleep," I suggested. "We need to check out of here at four in the morning."

Cooper shook his head and pulled himself on top of me, sucking my nipple into his mouth. "No, you can sleep on the plane. I'm not done with you yet."

* * * *

Walking back through the airport terminal in New York for me was bittersweet. I loved coming home, but I also didn't want my time in Sydney to end. Cooper sighed. "Wish we had four more days."

"Me too," I replied honestly.

"What happens from here?" he asked quietly. It was rare to see him so unsure.

"What do you mean?"

He shrugged. "Well, my internship is up in four weeks…"

I wasn't sure what he was alluding to. Whether it was that he'd no longer be an employee, or whether he assumed I'd make him a full-time employee, I wasn't sure. "Things will be different, yes."

He nodded slowly. "Good different, or bad different?"

"That depends on a lot of things that aren't necessarily within my control," I answered, knowing he'd understand I was referring to work. "But I'm hoping for the former of the two."

He smiled. "That's good to know."

"Cooper, please understand, I'm not the one who decides if interns stay or go," I told him. "Sometimes none of them do. Sometimes all the interns get is the experience they can take with them."

"I know that," he said. "I wasn't implying that you… I didn't mean for you to…" I'd never seen him struggle for words before. "I know that," he said again. But then he smiled. "Just means we have to make the most of the next four weeks."

We met the driver, he threw our luggage in the trunk of the car and we dropped Cooper home first. It was back to Mr. Elkin and Mr. Jones in the car and at work the next morning.

Jennifer came in with my morning coffee and asked me how the trip went. I told her we'd secured the Tamosaka job, to which she replied she already knew. "Did Mr. Jones get through his to-do list?" she asked.

I smiled at her. "Yes, he was very…good."

She smiled at my choice of words. "Good to hear. Any chance to think on that perspective we discussed before you left?"

"Yes."

"And?"

"I'm happy with what I've got," I answered. "Just not sure on how to keep it."

"I'm sure you'll think of a way."

I sighed. "Well, I hope so." Then I thought of something. "Is Cooper in yet? I haven't seen him."

"Yes," Jennifer answered. "Though I think he's avoiding me. I presume you told him I know about you two?"

I smiled at her. "Yes, I told him. And yes, now he's twice as scared of you." But I stood up and walked with her out of my office. "The Tamosaka job file. Where is it?"

"With Donella."

"And Cooper's at his desk?"

"He was, yes."

I walked down the hall to the cubicle area where the interns and other office staff were. I spotted him talking to the other interns and before I got to him, one of the draughtsmen stopped me to discuss something.

That was when I heard what Cooper was saying. They were discussing Sydney. "Yeah, it's really beautiful, but it was cold. I'd like to go back in summer," he said.

"How was the big meeting?" one girl asked.

"Oh, it was so good," he told them. "Sitting in there with them while they talked business. It was kind of surreal."

"And what was Mr. Elkin like?" someone else asked. "Did you see much of him?"

My heart stopped in my chest, waiting for his answer. I finished talking to the draftsman and walked slowly over toward Cooper.

"Nah, he spent his time doing whatever, and I did my thing," he answered. But then he looked up at me walking toward him, then back to his little audience and smiled when he said, "He's old anyway. What is he? Like fifty-five?"

"Good morning," I said loudly, and every intern there, besides Cooper, looked up at me and scattered in every direction, suddenly very, very busy.

It was almost comical. Cooper certainly tried not to smile. The little shit.

"Mr. Jones? A moment please."

"Certainly, Mr. Elkin," he said, standing up. How he kept a straight face, I'll never know.

I told him with my eyes he was in trouble, to which he replied with his eyes that he'd enjoy every moment of it.

"The Tamosaka file is with Donella, she's one of my head draughters. I thought you might like to follow the job through its stages, considering you were there at inception."

His eyes lit up. "I'd love to."

Then with a stern voice for the benefit of the intern audience, I added, "Though I can probably think of *fifty-five* reasons to have you archive files for the rest of your stay here."

Cooper bit the inside of his lip to stop from smiling, but the poor girl next to him who was staring at her computer screen trying not to listen to us made an odd whining sound. Cooper smiled. "That won't be necessary, sir," he said.

"I'll let Donella know to expect you," I told him. "But you can report to my office before you leave today."

Sure enough, at a quarter to six, Jennifer's line buzzed. "Mr. Jones to see you."

"Thank you."

He walked in and sat in the seat across from me, but he didn't speak.

I raised my eyebrows at him. "Fifty-five?"

Then he burst out laughing. "Oh, my God," he said as he laughed. "That was the funniest thing I've seen."

"The poor girl next to you was almost beside herself."

He laughed again. "She thought you were gonna send me packing."

"I should have," I told him. "I should have kicked your ass out." Maybe he would have taken me seriously if I wasn't smiling when I said it. I shook my head at him and finally laughed. "You're such a little shit."

He cracked up laughing at that, but then Jennifer walked in and Cooper sat up in his seat and straightened out his suit as he tried to stop smiling, which of course made me laugh.

"Not so funny now, is it?"

He shook his head at me, then glanced nervously at Jennifer. She looked at me, obviously not used to seeing me laugh. "I'll be heading home soon, Mr. Elkin. Are you working late or from home tonight?"

"Yes," I told her. "Home tonight. I'll be leaving soon, but I have some work to catch up on."

"You missed lunch today, so I can order something for you to eat before I leave, if you'd like," she said.

The sound of food sounded good. "Actually, that'd be great," I told her. "Thai fish, delivered to home around eight would be lovely, thank you."

Jennifer gave me a smile, then turned to Cooper. "Mr. Jones?"

Cooper's eyes darted to mine, then back to Jennifer. "Pardon?"

I smiled at Jennifer. "He'll have the same as me, and he likes those Thai vegetable rolls."

"Very well," she said and walked out of the door.

Cooper stared at me, wide-eyed and open-mouthed. "What just happened?"

"Jennifer just included you in my dinner order."

His eyes lit up. "Oh, that sounds like fun."

"I didn't mean I was having you for dinner."

"But you can."

I sighed and closed my laptop. "See you at my place in half an hour?"

"Sure," he answered. Then as he walked to the door, he said, "Tell Lionel I'll see him then."

* * * *

For the next three weeks, we worked together, professionally and discreetly, and spent time together in the privacy of our apartments.

I had no qualms in going to his place because, to put it plainly, no one who knew me professionally would ever be anywhere near Cooper's small, not-luxury apartment on East sixty-first street. And if anyone spotted Cooper entering my building, they'd presume he was running errands for me. My interns worked when I did, and I worked all the time.

At the end of the third week, we'd spent an incredible Friday night finishing off some prelims at my dining table, then finishing each other off on the sofa, before moving to the bedroom where we'd spent the night trying to break our record for how many times we could have sex in one night.

He had the libido of a twenty-two-year-old guy, and I told him I'd die trying to keep up with him. He laughed, and told me, "At least you'll die happy," right before he took my cock in his mouth.

Fucking hell.

I knew the countdown to the end of his internship was approaching, but he never brought it up again. Neither did I.

We just spent our time talking and laughing. And fucking. He was insatiable.

By the time we got out of bed on Saturday, it was almost lunchtime. I woke up to hear him in the shower, which was a little odd, but he came out wearing just a towel and a grin. He straddled me, shoving his semi-hard dick near my mouth and told me he'd showered so I could rim him.

No doubt about it. If he wanted something, he just asked. Or, in more cases than not, he *told* me.

I didn't mind. Hell, I didn't mind at all.

So I threw him off me, pinned him face first on my bed and gave him just what he asked for. I left him a quivering, sated lump on the bed and started the shower. He joined me a short while later, but I told him no more sex until we'd both eaten at least.

I left him in the bathroom, pulled on a pair of cargos and went in search of food. I had half the contents of the fridge on the bench, a couple of plates, had the coffee brewing, my stomach was growling, and life was pretty fucking good.

Then there was a knock on the door.

There were only a very few select people who Lionel wouldn't buzz through, and I didn't have to wonder for long when Ryan's voice called out. "Dad?"

Shit.

Shit, shit, shit.

"Um," I answered. "Coming," I said, and when I unlocked the door, Ryan looked at my very rarely worn casual cargos, my shirtless torso and my still-wet hair.

"Did I get you out of the shower?"

"Uh, yeah..." I hesitated, walking back to the kitchen. "I was just making something to eat."

"No worries," he said brightly. "Just haven't seen you much lately, thought I'd call in." Then there was the sound of a door closing. Ryan turned his head toward the hall, then glanced back at me. "Is someone else here?" he asked. Then he grinned. "Do you have *company*?"

"Um, kind of…"

Fuck.

Then Cooper walked out, wearing only his underwear, holding up the new toothbrush I'd bought for him. "Tom, did you get me…"

And his words died away, as did his smile.

There were excuses I could give why Cooper was coming to and from my apartment lobby with his satchel or briefcase, but there was no reason whatsoever I could give to explain why he had walked out of my bedroom in his underwear. Except the truth.

The three of us stared at each other, mouths open and silent, then both of them looked at me.

"Ryan," I started, but he held up his hand. He took a step back from me, then he turned and bolted for the door.

Chapter Eleven

Cooper was quick. I didn't think I'd ever seen him run. Certainly not in his underwear holding a toothbrush, but he beat Ryan to the door.

"What the fuck, man?" Ryan cried.

"You're not leaving until you hear us out," Cooper told him.

Ryan stared at him, but pointed to me. "That's my dad, man!"

"I know that," Cooper said calmly, still holding the toothbrush like it wielded some magical power. "Please. Just sit and listen."

Ryan shook his head, but he turned to me, where I stood half-dressed and helpless near the kitchen counter. The fight in him was gone, or the flight, as the case might be, and Cooper walked him to the sofa and sat him down.

Ryan was now pale and looking a little sick. I took a seat beside my son and sighed. "It's a long story," I said, rather pathetically.

"Oh, Jesus," he breathed. "You're not even denying it!"

Then he started to breathe erratically, like he was going to hyperventilate or throw up. Cooper disappeared into the kitchen and came back with a paper bag. I didn't even know I had paper bags. "Here, breathe into that," he instructed. "Put your head between your knees."

"I'm not on a fucking plane," he said, but snatched the bag and started to breathe into it.

Cooper kneeled down in front of him, still wearing just his briefs and still holding the toothbrush. "Ry, Tom and I have been seeing each other for about six weeks."

Ryan lowered the paper bag. "The guy you've been seeing, the one you were all so secret-squirrel about, *was my dad*?"

Cooper nodded. "Yes."

"Oh, fucking hell," Ryan squeaked. "The one you said sucked dick like a Dyson?"

Cooper shrugged and shot me a not-even-sorry glance. "I was drunk…"

I fell back on the sofa and groaned, and Ryan put the paper bag back to his mouth and started to breathe into it again.

"Look," Cooper said. "Ryan, it's complicated."

Ryan nodded and spoke into the bag. "Tell me about it." Then his eyes fell to what Cooper was holding. "You have a toothbrush here?"

"Tom just bought it for me," he answered with a smile.

Ryan huffed into the paper bag. "You call him Tom?" Then Ryan gaped at me. "He calls you Tom?"

I nodded. "Ryan, we never meant to keep anything from you. I never meant to have secrets, or to go behind your back, but this thing between Cooper and I is… Well, it's complicated."

He lowered the bag. "So you keep saying."

"No one can know," Cooper said. "We work together, I'm an intern at your father's firm, and they have these policies..."

Ryan turned slowly to stare at me. "You'd risk your precious fucking career for him?"

"Ryan," I warned, but it was Cooper who spoke.

"It's mine, Ryan. It's my career he's protecting," he said quietly. "If we were found out, Tom would get no more than a slap on the wrist, but me? I'd be lucky to get a job cleaning floors."

Ryan shook his head. "So why the hell do it?"

"Why do you think?" Cooper asked. "Jesus, Ryan."

"You *like* him?" Ryan asked, staring at Cooper. "You're serious about him?"

Cooper looked at me then at the floor. He nodded and whispered, "Yes."

I smiled, despite the whole unfolding scene. Ryan turned to me, he saw me smile at Cooper, and he rolled his eyes. "And you like him? You want to be with him?"

I was still smiling at Cooper when I answered. "Yes."

"How very fucking Disney," Ryan cried, putting the paper bag back to his mouth. He breathed into it a few times, then lowered it. "He's the same age as me!"

"I know that," I answered quietly. Ryan was angry, and I guessed well within his rights to be so.

Then he stared at Cooper. "My dad?" he asked. "Dude! If older guys are your thing, then find someone else who's not my father!"

Cooper gave him a sad smile. He scratched his head and sighed. "Ry, do you remember back when were in the twelfth grade and you had it so bad for that Rebecca chick? And she was such a bitch, and we all hated her, but you wanted her?" Cooper asked, and Ryan stared at him, confused.

It was weird for me to hear Cooper talk like the twenty-two year old he was, and I wondered what he was talking about too, but then he explained. "Well, this is a bit like that," he said, nodding to himself. "We paid out on you, but when you told me you were serious, I let it go. Regardless of what I thought, I did everything I could to help to help you date her, and you told me it meant a lot, remember that?"

Ryan nodded.

Then he was back to the Cooper I knew. "So, Ryan, you need to let it go," Cooper said simply and seriously. "You need to grow up and realize this isn't about you. I'm sorry to put it like that, but that's just the way it is. What we do, or what goes on between me and your father, ultimately doesn't concern you."

Ryan stared at him. "If you're gonna lecture me, can you at least put on some freakin' clothes?" Then Ryan looked at me. "I fucking hate it when he gets all I'm-tellin'-ya-how-it-is like that. He was like it when we were in high school. He's still fucking like it. He should have been a cop, or a teacher, or a lawyer."

I smiled. "He's fairly straightforward, yes."

Cooper smiled, and the air between the three of us seemed to relax. He stood up and groaned loudly. "You'd think I'd be used to being on my knees by now."

Ryan but the bag back to his face and breathed into it with a groan. "Coop, don't."

Cooper walked toward the hall. "I'm gay. There will always be dick jokes."

Ryan looked at me like it was my fault. I held my hands up. "No dick jokes from me."

"I should think not," Ryan said. Then my son leaned back on the sofa, let his hand holding the paper bag fall to his thigh and sighed. He took a few deep breaths. "Does Mom know?"

"No, of course not," I told him. "No one knows. Well, Jennifer knows, and now you do."

"And you really like him?"

I nodded. "I never expected it, and I never went looking. We started working together and it just kind of evolved." I looked around to make sure Cooper was still out of the room. "We're not even sure if it's going anywhere, we really don't know if it *can* go any further. It just is what it is at the moment. It was never supposed to get serious, with work and all..."

"You weren't kidding when you said it was complicated."

I snorted. "No. And Cooper's right. We need this to stay quiet."

Ryan nodded. "Who the fuck would I tell?" he asked rhetorically. "They'd all think I was bullshitting them anyway."

"How about I finish making that coffee?"

Ryan nodded. "Good idea." Then he added, "How about you put a shirt on while you're at it?"

"Deal," I said, and as I walked to the hall, Cooper walked out. I whispered, "Be nice."

I got to the door of my room when I heard Cooper say, "Hey, douchenozzle, help me get lunch ready."

I took a deep breath and walked into my robe to get a shirt.

* * * *

Ryan left later that afternoon, and I thought he was okay with it. We'd had lunch and Cooper and him had been acting like old times before he'd left, so I presumed he was okay.

He'd said he was okay with it. He'd said he wouldn't tell anyone, but he'd said he'd need some time and asked us to refrain from displays of affection in front of him so he didn't completely freak the fuck out.

His words, not mine. But I agreed wholeheartedly. I had really only gotten my relationship with Ryan back after the split with his mother, so all things considered, he'd taken the news pretty well.

But things between Cooper and I were different after that. Someone outside of us, outside of Jennifer, knew about us. It made it more…real.

We'd admitted, while not to each other, but to Ryan, that we liked each other, and that we were serious about this. And that made it more real.

And of course it was the last week of Cooper's internship, which also made it more real. We were on a deadline, of sorts. One way or another, something would change and now we'd admitted feelings it made something already complicated even more complicated.

It was never supposed to be complicated. It was never supposed to be anything. I certainly was never supposed to be involved with a man I worked with, a man half my age. I was never supposed to have feelings for him, or to enjoy every moment I spent with him.

And as the days drew closer, as the final week wound down, it was the whopping big elephant in the room I was never supposed to deal with.

Cooper seemed to pretend it wasn't an issue, so I did too, despite how much it worried me. The bottom line was, if I told the Board I wanted him to stay at Brackett and Golding, then we couldn't be together. If I told them I didn't want him to work at the firm then he'd never forgive me. Sure, it wasn't my pending decision, but my opinion held water in the firm. If I told them he was as good as I thought he was, they'd want to keep him for sure. It wasn't fair on him, because he was good, and he deserved to work at the best architectural firm in New York.

And like a light bulb popping up over my head, I picked up my phone. "Jennifer, can you get Louisa Arlington's number?"

* * * *

The meeting on Friday afternoon to decide the fate of the interns was awful. I sat there with my head turned, looking out of the window, unable to bear looking at Cooper.

When his name wasn't called as one of the interns offered employment, he stood for a moment, then professionally thanked the other partners for their time and experience before he walked out.

I didn't watch him leave. I couldn't. I felt nauseated, and after I'd sat in my office wondering what the fuck I'd just done, I told Jennifer I wasn't feeling well and I left.

She was concerned about me, probably just as confused by my actions as Cooper. She knew I liked him. She saw how happy he made me, and she'd just seen me throw it away.

I couldn't bear to look at her either.

I went home and threw myself onto the sofa and buried my face in my hands. Not long after, the intercom buzzed and Lionel's voice said, "I tried to stop him, but Mr. Jones is on his way up. Should I call the police?"

I got up and pressed the button. "No, it's fine."

"He's quite upset, sir."

I nodded, though Lionel couldn't see. "I know."

Then there was banging on the door. "Tom, open the door. I know you're in there."

I walked slowly to the door, unlocked it and let it swing open. Cooper walked inside and started yelling. "So is that it? What was I, just some summer fuck? Was that all I ever was?"

"Absolutely not," I said quickly.

"Was any of what you said to Ryan the other day true?" he asked. He was clearly upset, and very angry. "You told him you liked me. Was that a fucking lie too?"

"No," I told him.

"Then why did you tell them not to hire me?"

"I told you it wasn't my final decision, Cooper."

"That's bullshit and you know it. Whatever the almighty Thomas Elkin wants, he gets."

I shook my head. "That's not true."

"Bull. Shit," he said through clenched teeth.

"So was the only reason you were so interested in me was because you thought I could get you a job?"

"What?" he cried. "No, fucking hell, Tom, no! Every single fucking thing I've said to you is the truth. I didn't expect you to get me a job because of *us*. If any interns got offered a job, I would have expected a shot because I'm fucking good at what I do. They hired Anna, and I'm better than her."

"You are!" I said. "You're the best!"

"So put me on the ground floor," he said. "I'll work my way up. I'll be someone's fucking assistant, I don't care."

"You're too good to be an assistant. You've got too much talent to be in anyone's shadow, particularly mine. You need to prove that you can do it on your own and not because of who you're with."

"You're not hiring me because I'm too talented?" He threw his hands up. "Jesus Christ! What kind of fucked-up logic is that?"

"The logic that keeps us together!" I yelled back at him. "If you stay at Brackett and Golding we can't be together. Not permanently, not ever. We could hide it for two or three months when you were working with me as an intern, but on a permanent basis...it just wouldn't work." Then I stared at him. "I don't want to hide anymore. I want more than that."

He shook his head, not believing a word I was saying.

So I told him, "I've lined up an interview at Arlington Initiative for you. They have the same reputation as us. I've specifically called in this favor, telling Louisa Arlington you're the best I've seen. I told her you have ten times the talent I had at your age and I sent over some of your work. She wants to meet you. Tuesday morning, ten o'clock. I've worked with her. She'll give you more than what I could."

"You *what*?"

I nodded. "You should work for the best."

"I want to work for you!"

"You'll go further with someone else!"

Cooper shook his head. "*Why?* Cut the crap and tell me the real reason *why?*"

"Because I want you to move in with me," I told him. "I want you to live with me, to be with me. I want to be with you and we can't do that if we work together."

He stared at me with his mouth open.

"If you work at Brackett and Golding you won't be taken seriously. Your work will be discredited because of me, because if we're together they'll assume you only got the job, got promoted, got whatever, *because of me*. Can't you see that?"

He shook his head. "And who the fuck lets you decide?" he yelled at me. "What makes you think I wouldn't choose the job over you?"

I stared at him. "What?"

"You're so sure we we're going to be together, you're so fucking certain that we'll be together so you decide I can't work there," he spat out. "What if I wanted the job and not you? If we're not together, then I can work there, yes?"

I couldn't speak. My heart was hammering. Breaking. I nodded, and my voice croaked. "I guess."

He walked up to me. His jaw was clenched and he pointed his finger into my chest. "You don't make that decision for me." He backed off, then paced around my apartment, picking up his things and putting them in his satchel. "And you don't ask me to move in with you like that. You don't ask someone to be with you in the middle of an argument, Tom." He shoved a shirt into his bag.

I looked at him packing his things. "What are you doing?"

"I'm going to my apartment," he said. "I need some time without you telling me what to do, without you telling me how to live my fucking life."

"I didn't mean to," I said weakly. "That's not what I meant. I had about two minutes to make a decision. I didn't have time to find you, to speak to you, so I rang Louisa. I thought I was doing the right thing, for you, for us…"

"Without asking me," he said simply. "Without any consideration for what *I* want."

"Cooper, please."

But without another word, he picked up his satchel, turned and walked out of the door.

After the yelling, after all the things he'd said, the silence he left behind was the hardest thing to deal with.

Chapter Twelve

The next four days were hell.

I didn't sleep. I couldn't eat. On Saturday and Sunday, I worked at home, even though everything reminded me of him. He still had clothes and a pair of shoes at my place, and I hoped he'd call me asking if he could come and get them. He never did.

I left a message on the second day, saying I was sorry for being an overbearing ass. He didn't call me back. I went to his apartment. He wasn't home. Or he pretended he wasn't.

I was fucking pathetic.

Ryan came by on Sunday night. He walked in, took one look at me and shook his head. "Jesus. And I thought Cooper looked like shit."

I sat up straighter. "Have you seen him? Is he okay?"

"He's fine," Ryan answered, and his words stung.

"Oh," I said quietly. Then I realized that that was a good thing for Cooper. "Well, good, I guess. I'm glad he's okay." I hardly sounded convincing. "Did he say anything about me?" I asked, and regretted it almost immediately.

"Don't even think about it," Ryan said flatly. He leaned against the kitchen counter and crossed his arms. "Don't think about putting me in the middle of this, because I won't even go there. Don't make me pick sides. You both got yourselves into this mess."

I sighed, and scrubbed my hand over my face. "Fair enough." Then I admitted, "It was my mess. I fucked up."

Ryan didn't even bat an eyelid at my cuss. "I know. He told me."

"Is he still mad at me?"

Ryan snorted. "You've met him, right? He's a stubborn, self-righteous ass. Of course he's still mad."

I nodded. "I shouldn't have done what I did."

"Yes, you should have," Ryan said. His tone was softer. "But maybe you just should have told him about it first."

"I know," I said, sighing again. "He asked for some time."

"Then give him that."

I nodded, but said nothing.

"Jesus, you really do have it bad, don't you?"

I looked at my son. "I wasn't expecting this," I said as a poor way of answering. "I wasn't expecting…him."

Ryan exhaled loudly, walked over to my sofa and threw himself onto it. "So, pizza for dinner?"

I smiled at the welcome distraction. "Sounds good."

Ryan didn't mention Cooper again, but we watched some TV and talked a bit, and it was nice. It was nice of him, knowing I had no one else I could talk about this to, because no one else knew Cooper and I were ever together.

Not that we'd really ever been *together*, either. We'd never discussed anything, we'd never put a label on what we had. We'd just been…us.

That realization, that we'd never officially been anything, made me realize just how foolish I'd been. I'd never told him outright how I felt.

On Monday, after I left another pathetic, barely whispered apology on his voicemail, I spent the entire day staring out across the city, waiting for him to call. He never did.

By Tuesday, I had myself convinced that whatever we'd had was finished and that I was an asshole and I deserved his silence. I knew what I'd done was wrong, how it had ended was wrong, and I needed to pull my shit together. I arrived at work determined to be productive, and it was going well. Burying myself in work to avoid my life had worked for twenty years, so it really shouldn't have been so difficult. I opened files, opened my laptop, and for a few hours, I managed to not stare into space.

Just before lunch, Jennifer knocked on my door, opened it without my saying so and stood aside. Cooper walked in, dressed in his business suit, looking very professional. His chin was raised, his eyes were determined.

I put my pen down and had to close my mouth. I'd missed him so much. Just seeing him made my heart clench. I was filled with equal parts hope that he was here to say he forgave me, and dread that he would say we were over.

I was expecting to hear goodbye. And when Jennifer closed the door and Cooper sat down across from me, after wanting to see him, and speak to him for four fucking days, now I wasn't sure I wanted him to say anything. Hearing him say it was over would make it so final.

"I'm really sorry," I said quickly.

He put his hand up, clearly still angry with me. "Will you let me speak?"

I nodded. "Of course."

"I just came out from my meeting with Louisa Arlington."

"Oh?"

"I suppose I should thank you."

"You're welcome," I told him, though I wasn't sure if he was happy about it. "And I'm very sorry."

He ignored my apology. "She spoke very highly of you."

"Louisa's lovely, and very good at her job," I said quietly. "She's one of the best there is."

"She said the same of you." Then he smiled. "Actually, she said you were the *second* best there was. She was the first."

"Sounds like her," I said softly. He was still angry, and I didn't blame him. "Cooper, I'm really sorry. I fucked up, and I'm sorry."

"You did," he said flatly. But then he sighed. "You were also right."

"Huh?"

"You were right," he said with the start of a smile. "I couldn't work with you, or for you, it would have hindered my career. You were right about that. I can see that now."

I wasn't sure if he was agreeing with me, or insulting me, but either way, I nodded. "I'm still sorry." He had no idea how much. I didn't know what else to say, and he looked like he was done talking. My voice was quiet. "How did it go with Louisa?"

"I start on Monday."

My eyes widened. "That's really good, Cooper. She really is one of the best."

"Hmm," he hummed. Then he looked around my office. "She also said something interesting."

"What was that?"

"She also said you told her why you wanted me to work with her," he said. "She said she was confused at first. Because if I was as good as you said I was, she didn't understand why you didn't want me to work here with you."

I nodded. "I told her the truth."

"Did you?"

I looked at him, fairly certain I knew what he was talking about. I nodded again. "I told her you'd be better off, professionally, with her."

"Well, she agreed with you on that," he said, looking me square in the eye. "Then she told me what you really said. She said she knew I had to be something special for you to call her and ask her for a favor, so she asked you what was so remarkable about me."

I nodded. Yep, he knew.

Cooper shook his head. "She said you told her I *was* special, that I couldn't work here with you no matter how much you wanted me to, because you have feelings for me and you'd rather I *live* with you than *work* with you." Then he spoke slowly, enunciating every syllable. "Because you have feelings for me."

I looked at him, and I knew he saw the truth, the fear, in my eyes. I didn't answer. I didn't have to.

He shook his head. "You inconsiderate bastard," he said, and my eyes shot to his. "Do you know what it's like to hear that from someone else?"

I shook my head. "I shouldn't have said that to her. I'm sorry."

"Damn right you shouldn't have," he said. "You should have said it to me! Jesus, Tom, is it true?"

"Of course it's true! You heard what I said to Ryan…"

"Why didn't you tell *me*?" he cried. "I've just spent the last four days thinking I meant nothing to you. That what you told Ryan was a fucking lie. That everything you said to me was a fucking lie," he said. "And then I have to hear *that* from a complete stranger?" He leaned forward in his chair. "You couldn't even look at me when I walked out of here the other day, you just sat there like I meant nothing to you."

"I didn't tell you because…well, because I didn't know what it would mean to you…"

"It *would have* meant everything to me."

Would have. Past tense. I ran my hands through my hair. I stood up and walked to stand in front of the wall of glass. I turned to face him, so he could see the truth on my face. "I'm sorry. I was scared, because I'm forty-four and you're twenty-two, you have everything in front of you and I didn't want you to feel trapped." I stopped, and my voice was quieter. "I know what it's like to be young and in a relationship you feel you can't get out of. I've been there, when I was your age, Cooper. I know exactly what that's like, and I want more for you. I don't want you to get to forty and have regrets."

"Tom, I might be young. But I know what I want," he told me. "I want a career. I've worked fucking hard for it."

My heart sank, and I nodded.

"I also want you."

My heart leaped in my chest.

Then he said, "But you need to stop going on about our ages. The age difference has never been an issue for me, you know that." Then he added, "And, Tom, there are going to be differences between us. We like different things — different music, different food, different clubs. We have different friends, we have different ideas on a lot of things. There's going to be things that clash, but that doesn't mean it's wrong."

"I know," I agreed quietly. "I like the differences between us. You've opened my eyes to a lot of things I thought I missed."

"I like the differences too," he said with a smile. He leaned back in the chair. "We're like a retrofit project, making the older, classic style integrate with the modern. When everything says we probably shouldn't gel, we just seem to work."

I looked at him. He *understood* me. Like no one else ever had. It was the perfect analogy. "We *are* a retrofit project. *You* are the perfect retrofit for me."

He stared at me for a long moment, then slowly walked around my desk and stood in front of me. He cupped my face in his hands. "You're the perfect retrofit for me, too."

My eyes closed, and I sighed into the palm of his hand. Then his lips were soft against mine, and I threw my arms around him so I could kiss him back. So I could bury my face in his neck and hold him, and he seemed to hold me just as tight. He felt so good against me. No, not good. Right. He felt so *right* against me.

But then he pulled back and put his hand up. "Just so you know, I'm still kind of pissed off at you, but I'm sure I can think of some ways you can make it up to me."

"Anything."

His face was expressionless, but his eyes were serious. "Don't ever make decisions that affect me without asking me first. Ever. That's a deal-breaker, right there. You need to talk to *me*," he said, "Tom, about things like feelings and shit. Not someone else."

"Okay," I conceded. "But to be fair, you never talked to me about how you felt either."

He raised an eyebrow at me. "I didn't go talk to your prospective employer and tell her that you have feelings for me," he said. "And these 'feelings'"—he quoted the air—"that you keep talking about, you still haven't said what they are."

"I really like you, Cooper," I told him honestly. "Maybe it's more than that, I don't know. But I know I *want* more than that with you. I want everything with you."

He smiled. "Thank you, Tom," he said. "Maybe I want more than that with you too."

I couldn't stop smiling. "Really?"

"Don't get too smug, Mr. Elkin. I'm not done with the conditions," he said. "I won't move in with you. It's far too soon for that," he said, and my heart sank. "But I'm open to the whole boyfriend thing."

I grinned at him. "Really?"

"Yes, really," he said, and I leaned in to kiss him, but he put his hand to my chest to stop me. "You said you didn't want to hide anymore, well, neither do I. If we are going to do this, we do it openly. Like we were in Sydney. I want *that* with you. And, now I'm not working here," he said with narrowed eyes, "we have no reason to hide."

I was grinning hugely. "I agree."

His lips twisted as he tried not to smile. "There's one more condition, Tom," he said. "It's the most important."

I was almost too scared to ask. "Yes?"

He looked at me and a slow smile crept across his face.

* * * *

We walked out of my office, and Jennifer took one look at us and smiled. "I'll be finishing up for the day," I told her. "If anything is urgent, delegate it to one of my team. They'll handle it just fine."

Jennifer gave a polite nod. "Of course. Can I do anything for you?" she asked. "Order a lunch? Reservations anywhere?"

"No thank you, I think we'll be okay," I said.

"I'm glad to hear that," she replied. Then she looked at Cooper. "Mr. Jones, it's a pleasure to see you again."

"As always, Jennifer," he replied with a knowing smile.

We walked to the elevator, not holding hands, but when the elevator doors opened, I put my hand on the small of his back as he walked in. He stood a little closer to me than would be considered friendly and he took a deep breath and smiled.

"What was that between you and Jennifer?" I asked.

One corner of Cooper's lips curled into a smile. "When I got here this morning, I asked if I could see you without an appointment."

"And?"

"She's always been so snarly with me…"

"Did she say no at first?"

"Not exactly," he answered. "She told me it depended on what I was there to say. She said if I was there to make you happy, I could see you straight away, and if I was there to upset you any further, I could sit in the hall and damn well wait."

I chuckled. "Wait for how long?"

"I didn't ask," he answered. We stepped out of the elevator and walked through the busy lobby. "But I got the feeling it would have been a while."

We walked out onto the sidewalk, into a rush of people. A warm thrill coursed through me when

Cooper took my hand, and as we weaved our way through the crowd, he said, "Anyway, I told her good news was subjective to what the recipient wanted to hear."

I laughed at him. "She would have loved that."

"I thought she was going to call security," he admitted cheerfully. "But she didn't even glare at me. She smiled sweetly and told me that the recipient, meaning you," Cooper explained with a squeeze to my hand, "was miserable without me."

"Is that what she said?" I asked.

"Yep. Miserable, she said. Were you, Tom?" he asked, looking at me.

I stopped in the middle of the sidewalk, not caring about how the people had to go around us, and looked at him. "I was pathetic. It was disgraceful."

Cooper smiled beautifully. "So, maybe you do like me more than just a little."

I slid my thumb along his jaw, and nodded. "Maybe I do."

Cooper leaned up on his toes and pecked my lips. "Good." Then he looked over his shoulder, to the front door of my apartment. "You ready?"

I rolled my eyes. "It's not me I'm worried about."

* * * *

I led the way, walking into the lobby of my apartment, holding Cooper's hand. We were both smiling, though Cooper's grin was somewhat larger than mine. Lionel stood by the reception desk, watching us curiously as we walked over to him instead of the elevators.

"Lionel," I greeted him seriously. "I'd like to officially inform you that Mr. Cooper Jones has free access to my apartment. He can come and go as he pleases, and doesn't need you to buzz him through."

Lionel barely nodded. "Very well."

"Is that it?" Cooper asked rather disbelievingly. "That's all there is to it?"

I looked at him, trying not to smile. "Yes. It's done."

"Well, that's not as satisfying as I thought it would be."

I chuckled and with a sigh, I looked to Lionel. "You have spare keys to my front door?"

"Yes, sir," Lionel answered. "We keep keys in case of an emergency."

"Would you be so kind as to give one to Cooper?"

Lionel disappeared behind the marble reception desk, and Cooper looked at me. He never said a word, but he rocked up on his toes and grinned. Lionel reappeared and held out a gold key for Cooper.

Before taking it, Cooper looked at him. "This isn't a key to the janitor's closet, is it?"

Lionel smiled. "No, sir. It's not."

Cooper took the key then looked at me and smiled. I thanked Lionel, took Cooper's hand and led him toward the elevator. "We better see if it works," I told him. He was trying not to smile in the elevator, and once he opened my front door with his very own key, I asked him, "Is that better?"

"Much better," he said, grinning, as he slid his arm around me and kissed me soundly.

"Does that mean you'll leave my poor doorman alone now?"

Cooper grinned. "Absolutely not."

I couldn't help but sigh. "You'll send me gray."

"Grey*er*," he corrected. "Now come on, we're going to walk down the street, as a couple, you can hold my hand in public then you can buy me lunch."

I pecked his lips. "You're a bossy little shit."

Cooper kissed me with smiling lips. "I know. It's a Gen Y thing. You'll get used to it."

He pulled the door shut, pocketed the key and we headed back down to the lobby. As we walked out, Cooper grinned at Lionel, who gave me a smile and a nod, and when we walked out onto the New York sidewalk, Cooper held his hand out. I took it immediately and he smiled his smug little smile.

He walked up the street like he owned it. He was so confident, so quietly sure of who he was, what he wanted and where his life was going. He was sexy as hell, had a smile that stole my breath and mischief in his eyes, and for some unfathomable reason, he wanted to be with me.

I'll get used to it, he said.

Would I? Could I?

Cooper squeezed my hand to get my attention. "You okay, Tom?" he asked with a smile. "Because if you're having second thoughts, I'd hate to have to give Lionel back that key." Then he stopped walking and stared at me. "Hey, has anyone else ever been given a key?"

I tried not to smile. "No, only you."

Cooper huffed indignantly. "Just as well. I'd hate to think Lionel gives them out to just anyone."

I laughed at him. "God forbid. I'd hate to think the world revolved around anyone else but you."

Cooper smiled happily. "See? You're catching on with the Gen Y thing already."

He pulled on my hand and led me across the street to some restaurant that had caught his eye. He walked us up to the reception desk and smiled at the maître d'. "Table for two, please."

"Certainly," the man said. "What name?"

Before I could answer 'Elkin', Cooper said, "Jones."

Would I ever get used to him? The attitude, the snarkiness, the sass, the damn Gen Y thing that drove me insane? I doubted I'd ever get used to it, but it was going to be a lot of fun finding out.

* * * *

Cooper

The thing about relationships was that there had to be compromise. And I had to remind myself of that as Tom and I walked into the art gallery. There was some art exhibition opening that Tom insisted he take me to, so I was putting on my grown-up face and doing the grown-up thing.

Well, that wasn't entirely true. I might have griped about it, and I might have possibly pouted. But I went.

I also wore the gray suit pants that hugged my ass and the fitted charcoal-colored waistcoat that I knew Tom fucking loved. He never said he did, but he almost swallowed his tongue every time he saw me in it.

I figured if the art exhibit sucked, at least one of us would have something good to look at.

But Tom was excited about it and that was hard to downplay. It was a joint exhibition opening on expressionism and abstract, and that in itself surprised me. I would have assumed he'd be more into the classics, but no, of course not. I probably shouldn't have been surprised. He was a paradox, that was for damn sure.

He said I kept him on his toes, when really, the opposite was true.

Thomas Elkin was by far the most intriguing, most intelligent, most confident man I'd ever met. Most guys my age mistook confidence for arrogance, but there was something sexy as hell about a guy whose confidence commanded presence. And Tom had it. He was all suave and distinguished without even knowing it. People stared at him—of which he was oblivious—but they knew class when they saw it.

And he was mine.

The great Thomas Fucking Elkin looked at me like I lit up his entire world.

And I'd have been lying if I said that didn't trip my ego. I mean, how lucky was I?

When we walked into the gallery—which kinda looked more like a nightclub than my assumed pretentious art gallery—most of the women and some of the men looked him up and down, undressing him with their eyes. Yet the only one he saw was me.

"People are staring at you," I whispered as we walked in.

Tom looked around, and of course all the people pretended not to be staring at him.

He looked down at his suit jacket, for a stain or whatever. "Why?"

He really was clueless. "Because you're you."

He shook his head, dismissing me. "Don't be absurd."

We stopped at the first painting. "Speaking of absurd…"

Tom chuckled. "Behave."

We stood in front of a wall with a painting that looked like it had been done by a five year old. Monkey. A five-year-old monkey who had been given a box of Crayola, a blank canvas and LSD. "I thought it was illegal to give primates illicit drugs."

Tom cocked his head at the painting, then slowly turned to look at me. "What?"

Now it was my turn to laugh. "Never mind."

But Tom was transfixed by the painting. He stared at it for a long time, tilting his head a little but never taking his eyes from the masterpiece in front of us. I stood diligently beside him, letting him view it in silence.

I'd never been an art lover. Graphic design, yes. Put me in a museum or a gallery of architecture, and I'd love every minute. But the love of paintings and sculptures had always eluded me. Sure, I could appreciate art for what it was, but I was by no means an art connoisseur.

Tom, on the other hand, was taken with it. We moved on to the next painting, then the next, and he stood quietly, just taking them in. Two were bright colors, one with free-formed strokes, the other with layered squares that formed a bigger picture. The third was a black, gray and white piece, with nothing but vertical stripes that somehow made the shape of a man's head. A striking red splatter made it look like the man had blown his brains out.

Nice.

Tom gave it equal admiration as he did the druggo-monkey-painted piece and the I-fell-into-a-tub-of-Lego piece. He breathed in deep, like he inhaled the meaning of life. "What do you make of it," he said, giving a gentle nod to the painting.

"It's...nice," I allowed, "in a Silence of the Lambs kind of way."

Tom snorted, but still didn't take his eyes off the painting. "I will never stop being surprised by what comes out of your mouth."

"Well, it's explicit," I amended. "And confronting."

"Isn't that the beauty of art?" he asked.

I considered this. "True. I mean, there's no real purpose to art, apart from aesthetic value."

Tom turned quickly to stare at me. The look on his face was one of shock. "No purpose?"

"No, don't misunderstand me," I tried to explain. "I can appreciate art as much as the next guy, but art, regardless of medium, is just to be looked at, yes?"

Tom frowned a little and turned back to the painting. "The purpose of art is to make us question, and feel. To evoke emotion and memories, hopes and sorrow."

I looked at the painting of the man with his brains smeared across the canvas. "And what does this one say to you? And you can't say last week's episode of CSI."

He chuckled again. "Why do you assume it's violent?"

"The man has red splatter exploding from his skull. Red is the color of blood," I countered, "and the head wound suggests blunt force trauma."

"Red is also the color for passion and love. Maybe it's his thought process," Tom allowed. "Maybe it's emotion, passion and exuberance, too wild to contain. Maybe the artist's muse comes in pulses."

I looked at the painting. Nope, still didn't see it.

Tom put his arm around my shoulder and leaned into me. "Is it not the beauty of interpretation? What you see is so different to what I see, and that is the beauty of art."

I looked at the paintings we'd already seen. It wasn't easy to explain what I didn't like about it. I shrugged. "There's no structure. There's no confines, and no direct objectives."

That made Tom grin. "And that's what I love about it." He laughed at my expression. "Think about what we do, as architects. Everything is bound by design principles. If not building regulations, then the city's legislation molds what we can and can't do. Hell, even the laws of gravity curb our creativity. Sure, we can pretty up the façade, add some angles and change some basics, but the fundamentals will always be the same."

"Function, practicality and affordability," I added.

"Exactly," Tom said. "Even what you're doing at Arlington, which is a huge leap from what I do at Brackett and Golding, will still have to comply with fundamental building codes." He looked at the paintings and smiled. "But these...these are a creative free-for-all. There are no boundaries. The artist is free to create whatever they want."

Hmm. I could see his point, and maybe, just maybe, I might agree with him. "I still prefer my creations to have a purpose, a functionality. And preferably one that's sustainable and leaves the smallest carbon footprint it can."

Tom threw his head back and laughed. "Ah, you really are a true architect."

"I'm also awesome, dashingly handsome and incredibly good in bed."

He snorted. "You forgot modest."

"Well, I can't be everything. I am but one man."

"Yes, yes you are."

"I am a well-hung man, but one man nonetheless."

Tom smiled a happiness that seemed to come from within. "I'm sure the universe couldn't cope with two of you. Lord knows I couldn't."

With a laugh, I grabbed his hand and led him into the next room. "Come on, show me what you think of the next lot."

There were more paintings in the next room. Each was vastly different, bold colors, no colors, free-formed, straight-lined, oil, watercolor. Tom admired each one, explaining to me what he saw in each piece. I had to admit, I was starting to appreciate art. Or maybe

I was just enamored with how he described it, how his mind interpreted different things.

In the next room were free-standing sculptures. While he admired the artwork, I was stuck staring at the gallery-provided seat. Or maybe it was an art piece. I wasn't sure.

It was black leather, a low ottoman at one end, which rolled like a wave to waist height. It was smooth and somehow resembled black water. And all I could think about—

"Do you like it?" Tom asked beside me.

"Yes," I said, still looking at the furniture piece. "I was just imagining all the positions you could put me into on this thing. I could be on my knees at this end while you stand behind me, or you could bend me over the taller end. God, you could just pin me to it and try to fuck me into it."

Tom cleared his throat, making me look at him. Or, rather, at the now-blushing waiter who was holding a tray of champagne flutes.

"Hi," I said, taking a glass. "I was just discussing the functionality of this piece."

He chuckled a little, blushed some more and went on his way. I shrugged at Tom. "He was totally picturing us fucking on the chair."

Now Tom blushed a little. "Maybe he was picturing you with him, not me." Like it was inconceivable anyone would find him attractive. Jesus, this man was fucking blind.

"I dunno. Have you even seen yourself lately? In case you haven't noticed, you're really fucking hot," I told him, making him duck his head. "And for the record, I don't share my things. And that includes you. You can ask my brother Max. No one touches my things."

"Is this you putting down an exclusivity clause?"

"Hell the fuck yes. I didn't realize I had to. When I said I'd do the boyfriend thing, I assumed it was all-inclusive, terms and conditions apply, that kind of thing."

He was staring at me, the kind of dark and stormy stare that normally ended with fucking. The kind of eyes that made my skin flush warm and made my dick twitch. "I don't want anyone but you."

"Good."

"Thomas Elkin?" someone asked.

Tom and I both turned to the sound. It was a woman, possibly fifty years old, and from her clothes and jewelry, and even her makeup and hairstyle, I could tell she was wealthy. "Alexandra Armitage," Tom said. "What an unexpected pleasure!"

"Oh, Tom, you're looking fabulous," she said, kissing both his cheeks. "Tell me, who is this handsome young man?"

"This"—Tom put his arm around my waist—"is Cooper Jones, my boyfriend."

"Oh," she said, her perfectly manicured eyebrows raised. Whether she had any clue Tom was even gay, or she was just shocked because of our age difference, I didn't know. I also didn't care.

Then Tom explained, "I worked with Alexandra and her husband to get their apartment on East 71st remodeled."

God, how the rich socialites of New York City loved having their prestigious addresses mentioned in conversation. She beamed. "And what a marvelous job you did."

"Thank you," Tom said graciously.

She looked at the black leather chair we were standing in front of. "Interesting piece. Like a modern take on a Victorian chaise."

N.R. Walker

"A retrofit, of sorts," I mused. "A contemporary twist on a classic. I like the sound of that."

Alexandra said her goodbyes, and Tom hid his smile behind his champagne glass. "A retrofit, huh?"

"It always comes back to us, don't you think?" I finished my glass of Moët. "What I really want to get back to is the way you were looking at me before we were so rudely interrupted."

"The way I was looking at you?"

"Yes, all smoldering eyes, like you wanted to see just how many positions this sofa actually has."

His gaze intensified, but it wasn't quite smoldering. "Is that so?"

"Yep. I mean, we could try the sofa at home." I stepped right in close, and whispered, "I'm pretty sure you could bend me over that and fuck me until I pass out."

And there it was. Smoldering eyes and flared nostrils, and the softest, sexiest, bitten-back groan that seemed to pulse in my cock.

He snatched up my hand and stuffed me into a cab, not even caring that the cabbie got a peep show of us making out in the back seat. Fuck, this was so hot.

Thankfully Lionel had gone home for the night, and the other doorman didn't care that Tom and I didn't exchange pleasantries. As soon as the elevator doors were closed, Tom pushed me against the mirrored wall and ground our hips together as he kissed me. My head was spinning so much with lust and pleasure, I almost couldn't stand upright. And when we arrived at our floor, he dragged me inside only to leave me standing just at the front door. He stalked off toward our room, only to come back out a few seconds later with a bottle of lube and a foil packet. And a seriously fucking determined look on his face.

"The couch," he demanded.

I complied, walking around to the back of the sofa, moaning as I pressed my cock against the hard leather. I slowly leaned forward, so my ass stuck out, and rubbed myself against the sofa. The friction felt so good.

The anticipation of what was coming felt even better.

Tom stood behind me. "Like this?"

"Yes."

He put the lube and condom on the back of the couch, where he could grab them easily. But then he put his hands to my front and roughly pulled me back against him, deftly undoing my button and fly. He slid my trousers and briefs down over my ass, pushed me forward against the back of the sofa, and ran his hands down my back to my ass. The cool lube drizzled down my ass crack, then skilled fingers rubbed all around my hole before inching inside me.

But it wasn't what I wanted. I wanted his thick, hot cock inside me. "Tom, please." I snatched up the condom and ripped it from the wrapper. I knew how lube-slicked hands made it impossible to unwrap them, so I did it for him. The sound of his zipper made me moan.

"Want it that bad, huh?"

"Mmm," I answered, rubbing my cock against the back of sofa. "Fucking hurry up, Tom."

He pressed his left hand between my shoulder blades and pushed me down and forward. His right hand gripped my hips and I held onto the seat with both hands. My pants were still around my thighs, and Tom's were only just undone. There was no time for undressing, or perfect, or considerate. I wanted him to fuck me, and fuck me hard, and so God help me, he was going to. The blunt head of his cock nudged against my ass and he pushed inside.

"Oh fuck," I cried out.

He slid all the way, using both hands on my hips to grip me. He took a moment for me to get used to the intrusion before he started to move. He was slow at first, then he thrust a little harder, making my toes leave the floor, but his fingers bit into my hips, pulling me back onto him. I groaned with every thrust, and he grunted as he gave it to me.

This was fucking.

This was pure need and no niceties required.

This was hot.

Then his grunts got louder. "This is what you wanted," he huffed. Every thrust felt like it was deeper, harder.

"Yes," I cried. There was something about being fucked like this. Turning him on so much he couldn't even get undressed, he needed to bury his cock inside me so bad his pants were still around his hips. "Fuck yes."

He groaned long and loud. "I'm gonna come in you." He gasped, and with one long, deep push into me, he stilled. I could feel him swell inside me as he came, pulsing in time with his grunts and cries. Eventually he slowed and fell forward, still inside me. He wrapped his arms around my chest, his breath hot on my back.

"Fuck," he mumbled. "You okay?"

"Mmm," I hummed. "I am, but you need to power up, old man. Your work here isn't done. I'm so fucking hard and you're gonna take me to bed and finish me off, okay?"

He smiled against my back and huffed out a laugh. "You'll be the death of me."

"No I won't," I told him. "But you have to admit, it'd be a helluva way to go."

CLARITY OF LINES

Dedication

For my husband…

Chapter One

The view from my office was spectacular. It was a beautiful clear day, the sky was a brilliant blue and while most people would have cursed having to work, I was still smiling. Line five on my desk phone lit up. My personal line. I picked up the receiver knowing who it would be.

A familiar voice spoke in my ear. "Mr. Elkin."

I chuckled into the phone. "Mr. Jones." It was the third phone call that day. "Don't you have enough to do?"

"Oh, I have plenty," Cooper answered. "But you haven't agreed yet."

"I told you it wasn't really my scene," I replied. "Why don't you take one of your other friends?"

"You mean *younger* friends," he replied. "I don't want any of them to come with me. I want *you* to come with me."

Cooper had two tickets to see some god-awful too-loud band at Madison Square Garden, and right or wrong he wanted me to go with him.

"Is this not something we could discuss over dinner?"

"I like annoying you at work," he said cheerfully. "Usually if I pester you enough, you'll just agree with me to shut me up."

I groaned. "Is that a skill you work on, or is it a natural-born talent?"

"It's a Gen Y thing."

"It's a Cooper Jones thing."

He chuckled into the phone. Then his tone of voice changed to a playful whisper. "Come on, baby. You know you want to. It's Linkin Park. They're my favorite."

"Lincoln who?"

He burst out laughing this time, and I sighed. "I'll talk to you about it tonight," I told him. "Will you come over?"

"That depends."

I could tell he was still smiling.

"On what?"

"On you saying yes to the concert."

"I have a lot to do today…"

"Then agree with me."

"Goodbye, Cooper."

I hung up, still smiling, and not even half a minute later, my private line lit up again. I pressed the flashing button and laughed. "All right, I'll go with you if it will shut you up so I can get some work done."

But Cooper didn't laugh. There was only silence. I quickly checked the line to confirm it was on my personal line and not a business call, just as another familiar voice said, "Excuse me?"

Shit.

Sofia. My ex-wife. I cleared my throat and said, "I thought you were someone else."

"Obviously."

I could have reminded her that *she* had called *me* on my private line at work, but instead I took a breath and started again. "Sofia, what can I do for you? Is everything okay?"

"Everything's fine," she said in a cool tone, like I had no right to ask. "I was just calling to remind you that Ryan's birthday is in three weeks."

"I remembered."

"Yes, well, he's thinking of having a party up at the Casa. I told him he needs to let me know by Friday so I can get it organized."

"Okay."

Then, not being one for small talk, she said, "He tells me you're seeing someone."

"Yes, I am," I said slowly, wondering—dreading—what Ryan had told her. "What else did Ryan say?"

"Nothing really," she said. "Just that you were getting serious."

I exhaled in relief. "Yes, well…" I wasn't sure what to say. I wasn't embarrassed or ashamed of Cooper in any way…it was just that I wasn't about to explain to my ex-wife over the phone that I was dating a man the same age as our son.

"Mmm," she hummed. I could picture the look of disdain on her face. "Well, whatever Ryan decides to do for his birthday, be sure to bring…your friend."

My friend.

Sure, she was ready to admit I was gay, but she wasn't ready to say 'him', or 'he', or 'boyfriend'.

The line clicked in my ear. Sofia also wasn't ready for amicable goodbyes.

Given I'd already just made one faux pas on the phone by assuming it was Cooper and been blindsided by my still-mad ex-wife, I decided text would be safer.

At least I could see who the incoming messages were from.

I pulled out my cell and selected Cooper's cell number and typed out a message.

You're in so much trouble. Just took a call. Thought it was you. It wasn't.

My phone beeped a short time later.

LOL. Did you answer the phone with the offer of a BJ?

I snorted.

Close.

His reply was almost immediate.

LMAO.

'LMAO'? Dear God. I really was dating a twenty-two year old.

I typed, *Keep the first weekend of next month free.*

Okay, he replied.

He didn't even ask why. Then another message, *Keep the fifteenth of next month free. I bought TWO concert tickets.*

Did you ever take my NO seriously?

Nope. Now, about that BJ...

I smiled as I threw my phone into my top drawer. He was so horny. He wanted sex, he thought about sex, all the time. Not that I was complaining. I'd never been more satisfied, and I'd never been fitter.

I needed to be fit just to keep up with him.

* * * *

When Cooper arrived at my apartment, letting himself in with his own key, it was getting late. The sun was setting over the city, casting its final rays across my living room. I was in the kitchen reading through my mail. He walked in and kissed the side of my head. "Good evening, Mr. Elkin."

"Mr. Jones."

"You didn't reply to my text messages?"

When I had checked my phone before leaving, there were three messages from him, all wanting details on this supposed blow job I'd almost offered whoever had called my office.

"No, I didn't reply," I said, taking his hand and leading him to the sofa. I pushed him down so he was seated and I slowly knelt between his legs.

Cooper's eyes widened, as did his smile. "Well, I think I like this better."

Without taking my eyes off his, I undid his belt buckle, then the button on his pants and I gently pulled down his fly. I slid the elastic of his briefs down to reveal my prize and ran my tongue over the head of his cock.

"Oh, fuck," he whispered. He spread his legs wider and lifted his hips, giving me more access.

I licked him again and took him in my mouth, swirling my tongue and sucking him. He was hard in no time, making a whimpering noise.

He always made the sweetest sounds.

His fingers were in my hair and I could tell he was trying not to thrust into my mouth. He wanted more. So I took him deeper, deeper, opening my throat to take him down. Cooper arched his back and moaned, and I knew he was close.

I cupped his balls with one hand and pumped the base of his cock with the other while I sucked the head, making him cry out. His cock swelled in my mouth, he gripped my hair and he spurted hot and thick into my throat.

There wasn't anything like it.

It was empowering to make him come so quick and hard.

He let go of my hair, slumped into his seat and groaned out a laugh. "Tom, Tom, Tom…"

I smiled rather proudly and got up off my knees, only to kneel over his thighs. Cooper's head lolled heavy on the back of the sofa. I put my hands on either side of his face and waited for him to lazily open his eyes. He grinned and put his hands on my hips, so I planted my mouth on his, letting him taste himself in my mouth.

Cooper pulled my thigh down and pushed me sideways, back on the sofa, and lay over me, pressing down on me. He kissed me again, slower this time. "Well, that was better than a text message," he said with a smile.

"Much better," I agreed.

He opened the first two buttons on my shirt and kissed down my neck. "We should text each other more often."

I laughed and ran my hand down his back and over the curve of his ass, pushing his hips into mine. "Having messages from you about blow jobs was too distracting."

I could feel him smile against my neck.

"Mmm, I like making you think about sucking my dick. It makes turning up here a lot more fun."

I chuckled again and playfully bit his neck. "I've been thinking about doing that all afternoon."

Cooper pulled back and pecked my lips, twice. "So what am I doing the first weekend of next month that I would need to make sure I'm free for? Taking me away somewhere for a dirty weekend?"

"Not really. Sorry to disappoint. It's Ryan's birthday."

"Cool," he said, resting his head on his hand, his arm bent at the elbow. "That's not disappointing. It'll be fun. What are we doing?"

"We're heading up to the Hamptons."

His eyes widened, excited. "Really?"

"Don't get too excited," I warned him. "Sofia will be there. She wants to meet you."

His smile faded. "Sofia? Your ex-wife?"

I nodded. "Ryan's mother."

"She knows you're dating me?"

"No," I admitted. "But she's about to find out."

Chapter Two

Cooper took the prospect of meeting my ex-wife quite well. True to Cooper's form, he was inquisitive and asked a lot of questions. "Does she know *anything* about me?"

"She knows I'm seeing someone. She doesn't know who it is."

"How will she take it?"

"I don't know. I'd guess not well."

"Do you care what she thinks?"

"Not about me. Only when it concerns Ryan."

"And she called you?"

"Yes."

"Do you talk to her often?"

"No."

"Do you miss her?"

That question stopped me. "I used to. When we first separated," I told him. "I missed my friend. We were married for almost twenty years. It wasn't easy, particularly for her." I looked at him and smiled sadly. "But I don't miss her anymore."

"Tell me about it," he said softly. "Tell me what happened."

"Why I left her?" I asked.

He nodded. "I know *why* you left. Tell me what made you decide to do it."

I got up from the sofa, walked to the kitchen and grabbed a bottle of merlot and two glasses, then walked back to the sofa. I poured us both a glass and left the bottle on the coffee table. Cooper waited, watching me patiently, and he smiled at me when I handed him the glass of red.

"I met Sofia in college. She was a driven woman, but a lot of fun. I was…curious…with guys. I knew I was attracted to them. I had a few…experiences, but I hung out with Sofia so people wouldn't suspect I was gay. I wasn't gay…well, that's what I told myself."

I sipped my wine, and Cooper curled his legs up underneath him and put his hand on my thigh, giving me his undivided attention.

I took a deep breath then continued, "My father would never have understood. He paid for my college tuition and kept a very close eye on me. He pushed me hard, and I wanted to make him happy."

"You married Sofia to make your father happy?" Cooper asked. There was no judgment in his eyes, just curiosity.

"It was expected of me," I told him. "My parents knew Sofia's parents, and it was just assumed we'd be together. It was a different time then. It's just what you did. You went to college, got married, bought a house, had a family."

Cooper sipped his wine. "Did Sofia ever suspect you liked guys?"

I shook my head. "No. I thought it was an exploring thing. You know, in college you explore, experiment. In

143

my twenties, I thought the attraction to men was just a phase that would pass. But it didn't. I struggled with it. I ignored it. I told myself I was happy with Sofia and that I should be grateful."

Cooper squeezed my thigh.

"But it got harder to ignore."

"Did you ever..." He hesitated. "You know, with a guy while you were married?"

"No," I said adamantly. "Never. I never cheated on Sofia. In my head, yes, a thousand times over I fantasized and dreamt about it..." I sighed. "I don't know, maybe that's just as bad."

"No, it's not," he answered quickly. "It's not, Tom. It's nothing like it. Fantasizing about it and actually doing it are two very different things."

I smiled at how he tried to placate me, and I sipped my wine. "And then I hit my thirties. I knew I had to do something. I knew I couldn't keep living a lie...but Ryan was in high school, and I didn't want to derail him. It wasn't a simple divorce," I said softly. "I didn't just have to tell him I was moving out and that his mom and I were separating. I had to tell him *why*."

Cooper refilled our glasses and patiently waited for me to speak again.

"It was my thirty-ninth birthday and I just knew. I knew I had to come clean. I felt if I got to forty and was still living a lie, then it was all over. I don't know why, it's just how I felt. I'd waited and waited so long then all of a sudden I couldn't wait any more. I felt like I was drowning..."

Cooper moved closer to me and slid his hand into mine. "Oh, Tom."

"I told Sofia the truth, and while it felt like a weight was off my chest, I simply transferred the weight to her. She was devastated."

"I'm sure she'll understand," Cooper said with a nod. "In time."

"It's been five years. She's still very angry with me and I don't blame her," I admitted. "I hurt her very deeply. She was the one who had to face all her friends and associates and tell them her husband was gay."

"But you didn't have a choice," Cooper replied simply. "You couldn't have denied yourself happiness forever."

"My happiness or hers?" I asked rhetorically. "And I *did* have a choice," I told him. "I shouldn't have married her, I should have told her twenty years before, when we were kids in college. But we have Ryan, and he means the world to me. But I still should have told her."

"You couldn't," he countered. "Your father would have disowned you."

"He still would."

Cooper was surprised by this. "Doesn't he know?"

"Well, my parents know I'm divorced of course, much to their disgust," I said. "But not the reason why."

"Sofia never told them?"

I shook my head. "She's mad with me, yes, but she always loved my parents. She'd never hurt them."

"And Ryan?" Cooper asked.

"He was very upset and embarrassed when I told him," I said. "It took a while, but he's okay with it now."

"He looks up to you," Cooper said simply, taking another sip of wine. "It's not hard to see why. You're successful, brilliant, sexy as hell."

"I'm pretty sure that's not how Ryan sees me."

Cooper smiled. "So the Hamptons, huh? You never told me you had a place up there."

"I don't," I told him, finishing my wine. "Sofia does. I used to, but she got the apartment here in the City and the house in the Hamptons in the divorce settlement."

"What did you get?" he asked.

"I got my new gay life," I told him with a smile. "Oh, and I bought this apartment."

Cooper shook his head, downing the rest of his drink. "I don't even want to know how much money you have. This apartment alone must have cost... You know what? Never mind."

I chuckled at him. "It was expensive, yes. But worth it, wouldn't you agree?"

He looked around the large room. "Um, yes I would, very much. And then there's me," he said, putting his glass on the coffee table. "With nothing."

"You don't have nothing."

"No, you're right," he agreed. "I have a small *rented* apartment and a college debt."

I lifted his hand to my lips and kissed his knuckles. "You have more than that."

I didn't have to say any more. I didn't have to tell him he had me. By the way he kissed me, I was pretty sure he knew.

* * * *

"What are you thinking about?" Cooper rolled over and snuggled into my side. It was early morning and I'd been awake for a while, staring at the ceiling, thinking.

I was thinking about what to get Ryan for his birthday, but I was also thinking about what Sofia's reaction would be to meeting Cooper. "I need to know what to get Ryan for his birthday," I told him a half-truth.

"So you keep saying," he said.

"Well, you're his age, what should I get him?"

Cooper laughed into my chest then tweaked my nipple. "It's a gift from you. You need to pick it."

"Ooh, I know!" I said brightly. "You could give him the second ticket to that concert, and you could take him."

"Ha ha, very funny," he said, nipping my ribs. "Suck it up, old man. You're going with me whether you like it or not."

I rolled him onto his back and settled myself on top of him. His morning wood was pressed hard between us and I rocked back and forth. "Oh, that's a shame. I would *suck it* up all right, but I have an early meeting this morning."

Cooper bit his bottom lip and grinned, pushing his hips up against mine. "If you suck my dick, I'll tell you what Ryan told me he wanted for his birthday."

I tried to act like I was offended by his blatant blackmail, but he knew damn well I'd do it. So I took him to the edge of orgasm again and again, making him beg me, literally beg me, to finish him.

When I left for work, he was still a quivering, convulsing mess, barely coherent. But I made the meeting on time, and had Jennifer make some phone calls to find out what the hell an Xbox 3D was.

Chapter Three

Three weeks later on the Friday afternoon after work, I put the suitcases and Ryan's present into the trunk of my Mercedes R171, while Cooper got into the passenger seat. He loved my car. I didn't drive it often — with a company car and driver for all work trips I had no need to — but outside work when we did go somewhere, he loved it.

He was oddly excited about this trip, while I was almost dreading it.

"Did you really get the new Xbox?" he asked excitedly. "From Japan? It hasn't been released here yet!"

"Yes," I told him. "It cost me a fortune."

Cooper clapped his hands and kind of wiggled in his seat. "I cannot wait."

"Did *he* want it, or *you*?" I asked, pulling the car out onto the street. "Because you said *he* wanted it."

"Oh, he does," he said brightly. "I just share his enthusiasm."

I couldn't help but chuckle at him. "Remind me again why my boyfriend is twenty-two?"

"Because I was born twenty-two years after you, my dear forty-four-year-old boyfriend," he said cheerfully. "And because I'm amazing."

I rolled my eyes sarcastically. "Oh, that's right. Now I remember."

"Is your Alzheimer's kicking in?" he asked with a laugh. "Should I drive, old man?"

"You're a little shit," I mumbled. "And don't blame it on Gen Y. It's all you."

He grinned, seemingly pleased with himself. "Oh, my favorite doorman Lionel said to have a good weekend."

"Were you giving him a hard time again?"

"Of course not."

Which meant of course, yes. "What did you say to him this time?"

He chuckled. "I told him your neighbor, old Mrs. Giordano, might like to have your apartment exorcised while you're out. Apparently she hears a man moaning at night time, for hours at a time. I told him I hear it too, but it's really nothing for her to be concerned about."

I stared at him. "You didn't."

He grinned proudly. *Shit. He really did.*

"Leave Lionel alone," I told him. "The poor guy."

"He loves me."

"I thought he hated you."

"It's impossible to resist my charms."

"Yes," I said with a laugh. "I know."

As I maneuvered through New York traffic, Cooper rifled through the backpack at his feet and pulled out an iPod. He grinned at me. The kind of grin that made me worry. "What?"

"How long does it take to drive to the Hamptons?"

"Just over an hour and a half," I answered. "Why?"

"Long enough for you to become intimately acquainted with Linkin Park."

I groaned and he laughed. "You'll need to know some songs before the concert," he told me.

"Resistance is futile, isn't it?" I deadpanned.

He connected his iPod through the car's Bluetooth, looked at me and smiled sweetly. "It really is."

Then he slipped his hand onto my thigh and settled into his seat, and for the whole trip, we listened to Linkin fucking Park.

* * * *

I'd always enjoyed the drive up to the Casa, but it was even better with Cooper. We chatted easily the entire way, and as the city thinned with the traffic, our scenery became more coastal. Though it used to relax me to come up here, the closer we got to our destination, the more anxious I became. I took the familiar road and when we were almost there I turned the music off. "You nervous?" I asked him.

He looked surprised by my question. "No. Should I be?"

I smiled at his confidence. "I just don't think Sofia will be very understanding. No matter what she says, just remember, I'm on your side."

"Ryan's mom always liked me," he said.

"She likes you as Ryan's friend, yes," I told him. "But as my boyfriend…"

He shrugged. "And all the guys who'll be here this weekend?" he asked. "All Ryan's friends, some of my friends, they'll all be here too. We're meeting *them* as a couple too."

Shit. I hadn't given that a thought.

Then Cooper took his hand off my thigh and looked out of the window as he spoke, "If you don't want to…"

I pulled the car off to the side of the road, right near the driveway to the Casa. I think I startled him. He looked at me, wide-eyed.

"Cooper, listen to me," I said seriously. "I don't care what anyone else thinks. I know some people will have a hard time with us being together, because we're gay men, and because of the age difference. But I don't care. I'm proud to call you my boyfriend. For the life of me I can't figure out why you'd want to be with me, but you do, and I'm more than happy to walk in there, holding your hand. But I don't want you to feel pressured."

"I don't feel pressured," he said. "And I can't figure out why you'd want to be with me either, but you do."

I nodded. "Yes, I do."

He smiled, leaned over the console and kissed me. "Thank you."

I sighed and looked out of the windshield. "Well, this is it."

Cooper followed my gaze, to the stone gate posts, to the chiseled sandstone sign on the post that read Casa de Elkin.

"It's named after you?"

I nodded. "I designed this house," I told him. "We named it Casa de Elkin, but have called it the Casa for years."

Cooper gave me a weak smile. "Well then," he said, trying to sound upbeat. "Let's do this."

I slipped the car into first gear and pulled into the drive. I parked the car near the closed garage doors and by the time I'd popped the trunk, Ryan was walking out to meet us. He gave me a bit of a hug, then bumped fists with Cooper. "Hey," he said. "Most of the guys will get here in the morning. Mom said it might be better if they all crash in the pool room, or wherever they pass out," he said with a knowing smile. "But you guys have a guest room in the house."

A guest room.

Ryan looked at me a little apologetically. "Sorry."

"Don't you apologize," I told him. "It's not my house anymore."

We grabbed our bags and the gift box from the trunk and walked toward the front door. Cooper asked me quietly, "Have you been back here in the last five years?"

"I spent two weeks here right after we separated," I told him. "But not since then."

"Come on," Ryan said, opening the door. He turned to us and whispered, "Mom's in the kitchen."

I took a deep breath and followed Ryan through the front living room and into the large open kitchen, where Sofia was dicing fruit.

She looked well. She was wearing a white dress and her trademark gold jewelry, and her brown hair was pulled back in a ponytail. She looked at me, then at Ryan and finally at Cooper. She recognized him immediately. "Oh my, Cooper? Is that you?"

"Mrs. Elkin," he said politely.

She gave me a tight smile, but then leaned in and kissed Cooper's cheek. "It's so good to see you. Ryan never mentioned you were coming." Then she looked at me. "Did you bring Cooper with you? I thought you were bringing your friend."

There was a beat of absolute silence then I said, "I did."

Sofia looked at me then at Ryan and Cooper, then back to me.

"I brought Cooper...my boyfriend."

Sofia laughed, but when I took Cooper's hand, her smile died a slow, painful death. "Is this some kind of joke?"

"No," I said calmly. "Cooper and I have been together for about six weeks, and we...*dated* for six weeks before that."

Sofia took a step back from us, looking at the three of us, but her eyes settled on me. "You're *dating* Cooper?"

"Yes," I answered.

"No," she said flatly. "He's just a boy!"

Before I could answer, Cooper said, "Mrs. Elkin, I'm not a *boy*."

She stared at him. "Did he coerce you into this? Did he mislead you?"

"*What?*" Cooper and Ryan asked in unison.

"Sofia," I said. "That's enough—"

"Excuse me?" Cooper said, interrupting me. He was looking at Sofia, and I could tell by the set of his jaw he was pissed off.

I considered asking both Cooper and Ryan to give Sofia and I a moment to talk alone, but she'd gone too far. She'd insulted Cooper.

"Actually, no," I said. "Cooper you don't need to excuse yourself, or to apologize to anyone for anything." I took a step back, pulling him with me. "Sorry, Ryan, we'll find a hotel."

"No you won't," Ryan said, stopping us. "You're my guest, you can stay here. And, Mom," he said, looking at Sofia, "they're together. You need to deal with it." Then Ryan looked at Cooper and me. "Isn't that what you told me? I just had to deal with it?"

"Uh, pretty much," Cooper answered.

I felt a sudden rush of pride for Ryan. He was defending me, probably more so to keep his parents from fighting and him being caught in the middle, but still...his stepping in was heart-warming.

"Wait!" Sofia cried, turning to Ryan. "You knew about this?"

"Yes," he replied slowly. "I was the one who told you about it, remember?"

"Sofia, it's certainly not Ryan's fault," I said.

She stared at me, long and hard, as though she couldn't understand. "Are there *no* men over forty-five in New York City?" Then she leaned back against the kitchen counter and groaned out a sigh. The fight in her was gone. "Really, Tom?"

I squeezed Cooper's hand. "Yes, really."

Sofia shook her head. She still wasn't happy, but at least she'd stopped yelling. She turned back to her chopping board and took a paring knife to a mango. "I was making a mango salsa to go with grilled chicken for dinner," she said. "I thought it would be nice food for company. I was trying to be supportive and show that I didn't have a problem with you bringing a friend."

"My *boyfriend*," I corrected her. "And I appreciate the sentiment, but we fell a little short on the welcome."

She put the knife down, which was probably a good thing. "How about a little warning, Tom? How about a phone call before you got here, to say you're dating someone who went to school with our son?"

"Okay," I conceded. "Yes, I probably should have given you some warning. I apologize."

Cooper squeezed my hand.

Sofia sighed loudly, put both her hands on the kitchen counter and took a breath. Then she faced us and tried to smile. "Apology accepted. Cooper, I'm very sorry for the way I spoke to you. I was taken off guard, and I'm sorry."

He gave her a curt smile. "It's fine, Mrs. Elkin," he said, but it was clear to see it wasn't fine with him at all.

"We might go freshen up," I told her, giving us all some time to cool down. "Which of the guest rooms is ours?"

She stopped then, and looked down, as though she finally realized I was staying here with someone else. "The blue room," she said quietly. "Second on the left."

All the guest rooms were upstairs so I led Cooper back the way we'd come to the stairs in the foyer. I dropped his hand to pick up our suitcases and he quietly followed me up to the room.

I put the bags at the foot of the bed, Cooper closed the door behind us, and I turned to face him. "I'm really sorry about that," I told him. "I didn't think she'd take it very well, but she seems to have calmed down a bit."

Cooper looked at me. "She might be your ex-wife, and she might be Ryan's mother, and I was taught to show respect," he said, "but she's a bitch."

I cupped his face in my hands, and pecked his lips. "Yes, she was very rude."

"I was just about to tell her to mind her own fucking business," he went on to say. "I don't get angry very often, but she insinuated that you coerced me! Like you were some creeped-out pedophile and I was some innocent kid."

"I know," I agreed, but then he cut me off.

"And thank God you stood up for me," he said quickly, "telling her I didn't need to apologize to anyone for anything, because I was just about to say something I'd probably have regretted."

I held his forehead to mine and took a deep breath. "You would have been well within your rights," I told him. "The fact she'd insulted you is what made me react."

He twisted his lips into a frowning pout. "Yes, she assumed it was you who coerced me!" he sulked. "When it was *me* who coerced *you*!"

"The hide of her," I said with a smile. "Is there anything I can do to make it up to you?"

Still pouting, he pretended to have to think about it. "Well, she did hurt my feelings."

I cupped his balls in my hand. "Does it hurt here?" I asked against his lips. "Want me to kiss it better?"

He smiled. "Would it be considered rude if you were to suck me off with your ex-wife making us dinner downstairs?"

I pulled his bottom lip between my teeth and stroked his cock through his cargos. "Very rude."

He smiled. "Then yes, kiss it better," he said as he rubbed his dick against my hand.

I pushed him onto the bed and undid the fly on his cargos.

"Tom?"

I freed his cock from his briefs and looked up at him. "Yeah?"

"I think she hurt your feelings too," he said, leaning up on his elbows. "I think I might need to kiss yours while you kiss mine." Cooper pulled me onto the bed and within seconds we were sixty-nineing, with our pants around our hips and our dicks down each other's throats.

At least that way Sofia couldn't hear him scream.

Chapter Four

Dinner was much more relaxed. Well, Cooper and I were much more relaxed after 'freshening up' upstairs. Sofia, on the other hand, seemed more resigned.

She was trying to make an effort. Conversation seemed to revolve around Ryan, which was fine, but she eventually asked Cooper about his parents, how they were and what they were doing. She asked him about his job and he answered politely. He could see she was making an effort and he extended the courtesy, though it was fairly obvious she'd done her dash with him.

Not long after dinner, Ryan wanted to know if he could open his birthday present. He'd been eyeing the wrapped gift box since I'd put it on the counter. "If everyone's arriving tomorrow, I won't have much time to enjoy it," he said. "Whatever it is."

Cooper grinned. "You're gonna love it."

"You know what it is?" Ryan asked him, and Cooper nodded. Ryan then looked at me. "Can I open it, pleeeeeease?" he whined like a five year old.

I said, "Yes, but take it into the living room."

Ryan all but raced to the living room with his present, while Cooper quietly thanked Sofia for dinner before joining Ryan in the living room. And no sooner had I picked up the finished plates and taken them to the kitchen than I heard the sound of paper ripping.

Then Ryan yelled from the other room, "Oh my fucking God!" He then appeared at the door holding the box. His grin was huge. "You didn't!"

"I did," I told him. "Direct from Japan. There are only a handful of them in the States until it's released in the fall apparently, so it wasn't exactly easy to get. Though it was Cooper's idea. You can thank him."

Ryan threw one arm around Cooper, hugging him in a man-hug kind of way. "Thanks, man!"

Cooper looked at him seriously, hopefully. "That means I can play too, right?"

They disappeared back into the living room, and I was still smiling when Sofia walked in with more dirty plates.

"Leave them," I told her. "I'll clean up."

She put them on the sink. "Your birthday gift was a hit."

"Yes well, he mentioned he wanted it to Cooper," I told her as I filled the sink with hot water. "I wouldn't have known otherwise."

"Ryan and Cooper are still friends?" she asked.

"Yes, why wouldn't they be?"

She shook her head like I was missing the obvious.

"Look, Sofia, I'm not going to argue with you about him," I told her outright. "You offered for me to bring my partner, so I did. I'm not hiding anything anymore, Sofia. Would you prefer I lie to you? Would you prefer to find out from someone else?"

She exhaled loudly, but didn't answer. Instead, she picked up a dishtowel and started to dry the plates. It was like she wanted to say something, but kept stopping herself, and there was a heavy silence between us.

When we'd finished dish-duty, Sofia seemed to be back to resigned. "I'm turning in for the night. See you in the morning," she said, and without another word, she walked out.

I finished tidying up, checked my emails, watched and laughed at Ryan and Cooper for a while as they played a game I couldn't follow, but then told them I was heading to bed.

I stripped down to my briefs, climbed into bed and closed my eyes. Not fifteen minutes later, warm hands slid around me and a familiar body pressed against me. Cooper whispered in my ear, "No sleep for you yet. I have somewhere else I need you to kiss better."

"Is that so?" I murmured.

"Mm-mm," he hummed. "But it's inside me…about eight inches inside me. I'm sure you can reach it."

I laughed into the pillow before I rolled over to kiss him. "I'm sure I can."

* * * *

Cooper and I woke early, and he decided we should take a walk along the beach, just the two of us, before our day was filled with other people.

He didn't have to say he wanted some time away from Sofia. I just understood. He held my hand as we walked. He was quiet, but he seemed happy. "I think we should have a swim when we get back to the house," he told me. "Then we can have breakfast, have another swim and maybe a bit of a lie down before twenty of Ryan's friends turn up."

I stopped walking on the beach and pulled Cooper against me. I stared at him for a long moment before slowly sliding my hand along his jaw and kissing him. He melted against me, into me, and when I slid my tongue into his mouth he moaned.

I finally pulled away from him, leaving him dazed. And smug. "What was that for?"

"A thank you," I told him. "For being here with me. For putting up with my ex-wife for a weekend. It's a lot to ask of you and I wanted you to know I'm grateful."

He took my hand and we started walking back to the house. "Well, you can show me how grateful you are by making me breakfast, and then how grateful you *really* are when we have a nap."

I was still smiling as we walked back up to the house, still holding hands. Sofia had already put out a spread of croissants and fruit on the back patio table. She and Ryan were there and while Ryan smiled at us, Sofia quickly made the offer of coffee and walked inside.

She came back out a few minutes later with a tray of fresh coffee and some mugs, and to her credit, she did try to get along.

After we'd eaten, Cooper declared it was time for a swim. He and Ryan left me sitting at the table and went to get changed, but then Cooper came back and put his hands on my shoulders. He leaned down and spoke in my ear, "That includes you."

Sofia, who was picking a platter up off the table, cleared her throat. "You boys go and swim while I get things ready," she said, though she was clearly uncomfortable with public displays of affection between us.

I followed Cooper up the stairs and into our room. He was smiling, rather pleased with himself.

"I don't think Sofia appreciated you touching me," I told him as I was getting changed into my swimming shorts.

Cooper smiled. "That's why I did it."

I tried not to smile. "Be nice. She's trying to accept it. She'll be fine with us, you'll see."

He lifted one perfectly arched eyebrow. "Tom, are you blind?" he asked. "She's jealous! She wants you back!"

"No she doesn't," I replied quickly.

"Babe, she looks at you all the time. I'm telling you, she wants you."

"I don't want her," I told him. I tied off my shorts and crossed the room to him. "I don't want her. I don't want to go back. I've never been happier than where I am right now, okay?"

He nodded then his lips curled into a slow smile. "Why do you always know what to say?"

"Years of experience."

Cooper sighed, then changing the subject, he scrubbed his fingers along my unshaven jaw. "You look hot with scruff."

"My scruff, as you call it, is all gray along here," I admitted, rubbing my chin.

Cooper's hazel eyes scanned over my face. "And it's sexy as fuck," he said gruffly.

"Come on," I said, choosing to ignore his comment and dragging him toward the door. "If you keep looking at me like that, we'll need to lock this bedroom door."

He laughed down the stairs. "I'm not opposed to that idea."

No, he never was.

* * * *

We swam in the pool for a while, and I caught Sofia watching us several times. I wondered if Cooper was right—whether Sofia did want me back. I mean, it had been five years. She'd dated other men, though none of them seriously.

Not that it mattered. I mean, it would be unfortunate for her, but I was *gay* and I'd never been happier than I was with Cooper.

He splashed me in the pool then wrapped his arms around me, not caring who saw. "I think we're out of time for that little lie down we were going to have," he said with a smile. "So you'll have to make it up to me tonight. I might be drunk later on, but you have my full consent to have your way with me."

I laughed, but then Sofia called out from inside the house, "Tom? I need you and Ryan to move some tables for me."

Cooper smiled knowingly. "She does know you're not married anymore, yes?"

I kissed him, slow and open-mouthed, knowing Sofia could see. I pulled his bottom lip in between my lips, making him smile. "Yeah, I think she knows," I told him. "Now we need to get out of this pool before we get too carried away."

So Cooper spent the next hour or so playing video games with Ryan while I moved tables and chairs, as per Sofia's instructions.

And it wasn't long after that, that the first cars of Ryan's friends started to arrive. Then the caterers turned up along with the wait-staff, so I told Cooper I was ducking upstairs to shower and change into something a little more appropriate. Of course he joined me, so it was maybe an hour later that we made it back downstairs.

There was quite a crowd gathered, a few faces I recognized, a lot I didn't. Cooper was right by my side when I stopped dead at some unexpected familiar faces.

Fuck.

My parents.

Chapter Five

"Oh, Tom," my mother said warmly. She kissed my cheek. "So good to see you."

My father offered a handshake in greeting. "Son."

"Mom, Dad, I didn't know you'd be here," I said, unable to hide my surprise.

"Oh," my mother said, "Sofia called us and asked us to come over."

Of course she had.

My parents didn't live too far from the Casa so it wasn't too unreasonable that they be there. But still…they were my parents to invite, not hers.

I turned to Cooper and whispered, "My parents. Fuck, I'm so sorry."

But he never missed a beat. He said a polite hello to them as though he was interrupting so he could ask me where Ryan was. There was a loud peal of laughter outside, to which Cooper looked. "Never mind, found him," he said, and he disappeared outside.

I sat with them a while. They told me it was so nice of me to come and spend time with Sofia. My mom told me she'd always hoped we'd reconcile then she smiled and patted my hand.

Sofia was there. She saw it. And she saw how much I fucking hated it. If she thought for one deluded moment that this was some cruel trick to make me see how happy it would make my parents, then the look on my face must have set her fucking straight.

Thankfully my parents were oblivious to me glaring at my ex-wife and equally oblivious to how I looked for Cooper through the glass doors.

Sofia didn't miss that either.

My parents spent a quick ten minutes with Ryan, but wanted to leave before the crowd got drunk and loud. I saw them out, walking them to their car, and told them I'd be in touch. I promised to call them during the week, and I would.

But as soon as they were heading down the drive, I went inside in search of Cooper. I found him through the crowd, drinking and laughing with some of his friends. I wasn't sure if I should walk up to him, or just try to catch his eye. I didn't know what his friends knew, or what they thought.

But he looked around and when he saw me, he smiled and called me over. "Have they gone?" he said in front of his friends.

"Yeah, I'm really sorry," I told him. "I had no idea."

He slipped his arm around my waist, in front of his friends, in front of everyone. "It's okay," he said with a smile. Then he introduced me to his friends—who all *knew* I was Ryan's father—as his boyfriend.

They were all a little wide-eyed, but Cooper didn't seem to care. He squeezed my waist reassuringly and smiled, just as Ryan walked over to my other side and put his arm around my shoulder.

The four pairs of wide eyes in front of us then landed on Ryan, who simply raised his beer bottle at them. "Yep, I know they're dating," he said, then tapped his bottle to the closest guy. "I'm on empty, your turn to get the birthday boy a beer, asswad."

And that was the end of that conversation.

By the quiet whispers and people looking at us, it didn't take long for the word to pass around the party crowd that Cooper and I were together. The fact we stood there with his arm around my waist kind of confirmed it. He was so open, so out and proud, so blasé to what others thought. And even though he was half my age, he was twice as brave as me. I stood by his side with his arm around me as he chatted with his friends, amazed by his confidence and the conviction of who he was.

As the night got later and as the music got louder, the more they drank, the more inclined I was to let him have a night with his friends. He was laughing and talking about college and people they knew, and every time I dropped my arm from around his waist to leave him to it, he'd tighten his hold on me.

So I stayed.

At least I avoided Sofia for the rest of the night. And at two in the morning, I helped carry a very drunk Cooper up the stairs and put him to bed. He was a very giggly, hug-everyone kind of drunk, and when I finally got him undressed and in bed, he was all smiles and slurred words I couldn't make out. It was kind of cute.

His snoring wasn't so likeable.

* * * *

Needless to say, I was up long before any of the bodies strewn across the house, so I decided to make a start on cleaning up. I had a few trash bags full of bottles and cans by the time Sofia ventured out. I avoided her. I was still too mad at her, and she seemed equally pleased to avoid me.

But one by one the party-goers woke up, drank coffee and went on their way. I fed both Cooper and Ryan coffee and greasy bacon rolls until they felt better, and by mid-morning they decided a cool swim would help with their hangovers.

Unfortunately it left me alone with Sofia.

"I think we need some coffee," she said, walking to the coffee machine. "Want a cup?"

"Sure," I told her. "Why not."

She poured two coffees, handed me one then stood leaning against the kitchen counter. She was quiet for a while, so I asked her about her sisters and told her I liked the new pieces of furniture I'd seen around the Casa. She asked how my work was going, how Jennifer was and we talked about mutual friends.

Then she said, "I'm sorry about asking your parents to come last night." She even had the decency to look it.

"You should be, Sofia. I'm sorry to say it like that, but it wasn't your place to invite my parents."

"I thought they'd like to see Ryan for his birthday."

"And you thought you'd like to show Cooper that my parents don't know what he is to me."

"That's not what I meant to do."

"Yes, it is."

Conversation had never been a problem for us, though now it was very strained. There was a very obvious elephant in the room.

Well, the metaphorical elephant who was taking a swim with Ryan.

It was obvious she wanted to say something about him, but she wasn't sure how to bring it up. Then there was a burst of laughter from the pool, Cooper's laughter, and it made me smile.

"You seem genuinely taken with him."

"I am."

"How did you meet?" she asked me quietly. "I mean, this time. How did you meet...again."

"Through Ryan initially," I told her. "But then he had an internship at the office. That's where I got to know him."

"You worked with him?"

"Yes."

"But he doesn't work with you now?"

"No, he works for Arlington. He fits in better there. They're young and innovative."

"And Brackett and Golding are an old prestigious classic," she said. "How ironic."

I ignored the jibe. "He's really very talented," I told her. "He'll go a long way."

Sofia nodded. "He will if he stays with you," she said. "Riding on the coattails of the great Thomas Elkin will get him anywhere."

I put my coffee on the counter with a clunk, probably a little louder than I intended to. I tried to keep my voice down. "It's not like that. That's the very reason I told him to work somewhere else, so he wouldn't be associated with me professionally. He'll go far because he's talented, Sofia, not because of who he's with."

"Tom, forgive me for not understanding the connection between you," she said with hard eyes. "But have you thought of the possibility he could be after your money?"

Anger swelled in my chest, but I tampered it down. She was acting all concerned, but really she wanted to make me angry. She wanted to get a reaction out of me, so I refused to give her one.

"He's not after money, Sofia, and I find it offensive that you imply he is," I said as calmly as I could manage.

"How do you know, Tom?"

"I know he's not after my money because I asked him to move in with me, and he said no."

She stared at me for a long moment. "You asked him to move in with you?"

"Yes," I said with a smile of satisfaction. "And he turned me down."

"Well, at least one of you is thinking clearly."

"Oh, give it up, Sofia," I said, turning to walk out.

"You give it up, Tom," she said, stopping me. "It's embarrassing. You're making a fool of yourself."

"I don't care, Sofia," I told her. "I don't care what you think, or what anyone else thinks. I care what Cooper thinks."

"I don't get it," she said, shaking her head. "I don't understand what you could possibly have in common. He's half your age!"

"You *wouldn't* understand, Sofia," I said, probably too loudly. "He understands me. He *gets* me. The age difference doesn't come into it at all. I'm sorry you don't get it, but you don't have to. What we have, is between Cooper and me, and no one else. It's no one else's fucking business."

Sofia opened her mouth to say something, but I'd heard enough.

"I love him, Sofia," I told her. It was the first time I'd said those words out loud. I'd thought them a hundred times, but never had the courage to say them, to admit them. "You and I won't ever get back together, if that's what you're aiming for here. Beside the fact that *I'm gay*, Sofia, I am in love with Cooper. I *love* him."

Sofia paled as though my words had found their mark, but her eyes darted past me, over my shoulder. I followed her gaze, to see Cooper standing at the back patio doors, looking directly at me.

He was still wet from the pool, shirtless with a beach towel wrapped around his waist. He blinked a few times before he walked inside.

"Cooper," Sofia said, but he put his hand up to stop her talking as he walked over to me.

My heart was hammering, my stomach was in knots. He'd heard everything. He stood in front of me and shook his head. "Oh, Tom, you've done it again."

I could barely speak. "Done what?"

"Gone and spoken to someone else about how you feel about me," he said. His hair was wet and drops of water ran down his body, but he didn't seem to care. He stared right at me. "Don't you think that's something you should have told me first?"

I nodded quickly, petrified of what he might say.

Cooper bit his lip and slowly shook his head. "First you tell Louisa that you want something more with me, and now you tell your ex-wife, of all people, that you love me?"

"I keep getting it wrong. I should have told you."

Cooper looked over at Sofia, who was watching us with a look of dismay on her face, then he turned back to me and he smiled. She'd been blatantly horrible to him, and he wanted me to say this in front of Sofia. He wanted her to see that I was choosing him. "So tell me now."

It was the first time I'd seen him be remotely possessive. It was the first time I'd seen fear in his eyes. There was a bead of water threatening to fall from his hair, so I touched it and pressed my palm to his face. My words were barely a whisper. "I love you, Cooper. I'm *in* love with you," I told him, and he smiled beautifully. Then I told him, "You drive me crazy, you do my head in some days, and you challenge everything I say, but you've breathed life into me. I never expected someone could understand me like you do."

He smiled sweetly, then whispered, "Thank you," before he pressed his lips to mine.

Sofia made some sound that was a half-scoff, half-sigh, and Cooper smiled against my lips. "I think we should go back to New York."

"I think that's a good idea," Sofia said softly.

Ten minutes later we were packed, we'd said goodbyes with Ryan—though he said he'd see us next week sometime—Sofia had bid us a quiet, distant farewell and we were on the road.

Cooper was quiet, but he took my hand and smiled. It wasn't lost on me that he'd not returned any declaration of love—he'd simply thanked me for mine.

But he was just radiating happiness, even hungover. I didn't think he'd stopped smiling yet. Even when he fell asleep in the car, he was smiling.

The quiet drive, with Cooper sleeping in the passenger seat, gave me some time to think.

I didn't regret what I'd told him.

I didn't regret saying it in front of Sofia.

I regretted none of it.

I didn't expect him to tell me he loved me back. I realized when I was driving back to the City that it didn't matter. It only mattered that he knew I loved him.

And when we'd arrived back at my apartment, a still-sleepy Cooper dropped his suitcase inside my front door and went and raided the fridge.

I leaned against my kitchen counter and watched as he mumbled to himself and pulled out two sodas. "Want one?" he asked, but then his smile faltered. He closed the fridge and stood in front of me. "Tom, babe, what's wrong?"

"Nothing," I told him. "Nothing at all."

"You're looking at me funny," he said, but he looked concerned. "Is it because you said you loved me and I didn't say anything back?"

"Sshh," I hushed him, then pressed my lips to his.

"What is it?"

"Take me to bed," I whispered.

He looked at me for a long moment. "Okay," he agreed, but he was worried.

"No, Cooper," I said, holding his face and shaking my head. "I want you to take me to bed," I repeated. He still looked confused, so I spelled it out for him. "Cooper, I want you to top me."

Chapter Six

"Are you sure?" he asked.

I was naked on the bed and he was kneeling between my thighs.

"Yes. I am," I told him, again. He'd asked me in the kitchen, he'd asked me before we undressed, now he was asking again. "I'm very sure. I want to share this with you."

He exhaled with a nervous laugh. "I don't want to hurt you."

He knew I'd never bottomed, he knew this was new territory for me, so he understood how much this meant.

I sat up and swiped the pad of my thumb across his bottom lip. "Take your time and you won't hurt me."

He kissed me then, and we fell back onto the bed. He slicked his fingers and probed my ass while he probed my mouth with his tongue. He was gentle and sweet, he took his time and he took care of me.

He licked and sucked my cock while he slid his fingers inside me over and over, stretching me, preparing me for him. For where I wanted him. He pressed my gland again and again while he worshiped my cock with his mouth.

The intensity of my orgasm was crippling, and amazing. I'd never felt anything like it. I'd never come so hard. It was like he'd rendered my bones to liquid. I heard the rip of foil, then he pushed my legs up to my chest.

I was pliable, like Jell-O. And I still wanted more.

When he pressed against me and pushed inside me, it was a stretch and a burn, but he was slow and careful, and I welcomed it.

He leaned over me while he oh-so slowly filled me, giving me time to adjust. I put my arms around his neck and watched him. I watched his eyes roll back, I watched him tremble, his chest rise and fall in rapid breaths and I watched as he licked his lips and whimpered.

His pleasure was mine.

He kissed me, he gave me his tongue, he pulled on my bottom lip, and he kissed me again. Then his thrusts got a little harder and a little deeper, and he groaned long and low.

"Tom," he whispered gruffly. Then his hands held my face and his lips were touching mine as he breathed, as he thrust into me. He said my name again, and I lifted my legs higher, and he flexed into me as he came.

Completely spent, he collapsed on me, and I traced circles on his back until he'd caught his breath. He pulled out of me, kissed me tenderly then he cleaned me up.

He never said a word.

But when he climbed back onto the bed, he wrapped his arms and legs around me. He'd never held me so tight.

We spent the afternoon in bed alternating between sleep and making out. When I was on top of him, kissing his neck and jaw, I rolled us over so he was on top of me and I asked him to make love to me again.

He made me come again with no less intensity than before, then he laid me face down on the bed. He pressed his weight on me then pressed inside me. He threaded his fingers with mine and whimpered and moaned in my ear.

He kissed the back of my neck and shoulder as he slowly thrust into me. His weight on me, his breath hot in my ear and his teeth scraping my skin set my body on fire. I raised my ass to meet him, to give more of me to him, and his whole body convulsed when he came.

I'd never heard him moan like that.

He collapsed again on top of me, keeping his weight on me. He pulled out of me but continued to rock his hips a little and murmur, "Fuck, baby," over and over.

Eventually we left the bed and showered, and Cooper ordered dinner. We sat on the sofa and ate our takeout, and he was telling me a funny story of something that happened at work. He made me laugh — like he always made me laugh — and I was still chuckling when I speared some of his lemon chicken and shoved it in my mouth.

When I looked up at him, he was quiet and looking at me funny. So with a mouth half-full of food, I said, "What's wrong? I'm allowed to steal some of your dinner. You ate half of mine."

He smiled slowly. "I love you."

I almost forgot to swallow my food, and somehow managed not to choke. "Huh?"

"Do you need hearing aids, old man?" he said with a grin. "I said I love you."

"No, I don't need hearing aids," I told him. Then I giggled. I think I even blushed.

Cooper leaned over the Chinese food and kissed me with smiling lips, then just carried on his conversation about his co-worker like nothing extraordinary had happened.

Except it had.

He loved me. He'd said so. Twice.

He told me he'd had one of the best days of his life, but he said he needed to go home—he had to be at work early and had no work clothes here. I called him a cab and kissed him at the door. "You could always move in," I said again.

He rolled his eyes. "We've been through that," he said and gave me a quick peck on the lips then walked toward the elevator with his suitcase.

"And you turned me down," I called out down the hall.

He pressed the button. "I did," he said, looking back at me with a cheeky grin. "Because you asked me all wrong," he added, then stepped inside the elevator, and the door closed.

I asked him all wrong. What the hell did that mean?

I gave him about twenty minutes to get home and settled, then I sent him a text.

What do you mean I asked you all wrong?

His response took less than a minute. *Aren't you in bed yet, old man?*

I replied, *I'm not old, thank you very much. But I won't sleep if you don't tell me.*

Are you sore? Do you feel okay?

I've never felt better, thank you.

You're very welcome. And thank you for a great weekend and an amazing day.

You didn't answer my question.

You noticed.

Cooper, I need to know. How did I ask you wrong?

Because you didn't ask me right.

You like to challenge me, don't you?

You said it was one of the things you loved about me.

I smiled at my phone, but quickly typed back, *It is.*

Goodnight, Tom. WYWH.

I had to Google what the acronym was, and before I could reply, another message came through.

Did you just Google that?

Little smart ass. *Shut up. Yes, I did. And you wouldn't have to wish I was there if you moved in with me.*

LOL. Oh but Tom, you're asking all wrong again.

I sighed. *Goodnight Cooper.*

Goodnight Tom. ILY.

Just as I smiled at my phone another message came through. *That means I love you.*

I gathered that much, smart ass.

I think we'll need to work on your terms of endearment.

I shook my head and laughed. I doubted I'd ever win with him. *ILY.*

ILY2.

* * * *

Jennifer greeted me with her usual morning message update and the reassurance of hot coffee on my desk. Then she smiled warmly at me. "You look refreshed. I trust you had a good weekend?"

"My weekend was wonderful," I told her.

"How was Sofia?" she asked. Jennifer knew everything there was to know about me, and she knew my ex-wife had met my boyfriend over the weekend.

"Well, she wasn't overly impressed, no." I shrugged, and said, "But we had a lovely time. Ryan loved his gift, so thank you for helping me with that."

She smiled. "My pleasure."

"Well, considering I had the weekend off, I'd better get to it," I told her.

"Yes, looks like a busy week," she said, back to her professional best. "I'll give you twenty minutes to check emails and then we can discuss your weekly schedule."

"Thank you, Jennifer," I said, walking into my office.

I checked emails, responding to anything urgent, then Jennifer and I mapped out the next two weeks' worth of appointments, meetings and deadlines. It was busy, and I knew there'd be work to take home.

Cooper was in the same predicament. His schedule was as busy as mine, though he'd bring work to my place instead of his and we'd work at my dining table. Most nights that week, we spent hours in a peaceful silence as we worked, though we'd stop for 'intermission' as Cooper called it. Which was dinner and sex.

Not always intercourse, but a blow job or mutual hand jobs on the sofa, sometimes too worked up to even get undressed. He was insatiable, completely voracious.

Not that I minded. Hell, I was starting to want it as much as he did.

We were getting cozy on the sofa when I told him of my busy schedule, how I'd be working most of the weekend to get a big contract finalized, and he said he didn't mind.

"I've got some work I can bring over," he said. "I'll be really quiet and won't interrupt you, I promise."

I threw my head back and laughed. "Oh, please," I said. "You can't help yourself. As soon as you get bored, I become a source of entertainment."

He grinned, pushed me back on the sofa and proceeded to unzip my pants and lick and suck me, which proved my case exactly.

But on Saturday, when we'd been working for a few hours, he had his head down going over plans he'd bought with him and hadn't interrupted me once. It was driving me insane. I *wanted* him to interrupt me.

And it was so typically Cooper to *not* interrupt me because I'd made a point of saying he would.

Always challenging.

By lunch time, I couldn't stand it. I'd spent the last hour staring at him, trying to get his attention, and of course he knew. He was trying not to smile. When I got up from the table and pulled out his chair, swinging my leg over and straddling him, he burst out laughing.

"You're such a tease," I told him before pushing his head back and kissing him hard.

When I pulled my mouth from his, he licked his lips. "I wondered how long it would take," he said smugly. "You've got some pretty good self-control." He gripped my hips and rocked me on his lap. "It's been killing me."

I ground down on him. "Your self-control is apparently better than mine," I told him, kissing him again. "Just take me to bed."

I'd never imagined I'd bottom. I'd never imagined I'd want to. But giving myself to him that way was something special. The way he worshiped my body before sinking inside me, the way my body gave him pleasure was empowering.

Since declaring our love, sex was even more intense between us. Everything was more intense — conversations, laughter, touches and even the way we looked at each other.

I told Cooper that I'd spoken to my parents during the week. I'd promised I'd phone them and had arranged to drive up and see them next month. "I'm thinking I should tell them I've met someone," I explained. It was early afternoon. We were in bed, naked, wrapped up in each other.

Cooper leaned up on his elbows to look at me. "You're going to come out to them?"

I sighed. "I think so," I said. "I want to tell them. I want to tell them I found someone who makes me happy, that I've never been happier."

"But you're worried about how they'll react?" he asked.

"Yeah, of course," I admitted.

"I'll go with you," he said with a kind smile.

"Would you?" I asked. "I mean, I'd love to have you by my side. I want them to meet you. But you certainly don't have to."

"I don't have to. I want to."

"Anyway, it's a few weeks away," I told him. "We're both busy here, and we have that bloody concert next weekend," I said, rolling my eyes. But then I rolled us over so we faced each other and ran my hands through his hair. "Is it crazy that I'm considering coming out to my parents?" I asked. "I mean, I'm *forty-four* years old!"

Cooper smiled. "Not at all, Tom. It's not crazy. You still want their approval."

"Well, I'm fairly certain I won't get it," I told him. "But I can hope, right?"

He pecked my lips. "Why are you doing it then?" he asked. "If you know they won't approve and it will cause problems, and you said it yourself, you don't need their approval, then why?"

"I don't want any secrets with them. And I want them to know I'm happy," I told him. "I'm not expecting them to be accepting of it, or even tolerable. They'll more than likely choose to pretend I never told them and keep wishing I'll get back with Sofia."

Cooper snorted. "Maybe you should just tell them you're gay first, before you drop the 'oh, and I'm seeing a twenty-two year old' bomb."

I laughed and pecked his lips again. "I may as well hit them with both bombs. They won't take it well no matter which I tell them."

Cooper sighed and nipped at the skin on my chin. "Tom?"

"Yeah?"

"We'll need to keep one weekend free," he said. Then he bit his lip. "How's your self-defense skills?"

I laughed. "Why?"

"I want you to meet my parents," he said. "And I'm pretty sure your parents are gonna take it a helluva lot better than mine."

Chapter Seven

Well, shit.

"They won't like the idea, huh?"

"Um, your birthday's in November, right?"

"Yeah, why?"

"Well, my dad's birthday is December..."

It took me a second. "I'm older than your dad?"

Cooper laughed and nodded. "Is that weird?"

Weird. That was one word to describe it. "Um, yes." I didn't know why it threw me so much. Our age difference had always been a glaring issue, but I'd come to accept it, ignore it. Yes, I was older than him. So what?

But I was also older than his *father*?

"Hey," Cooper said, putting his hand to my face. "It doesn't change anything."

"Doesn't it?"

"Does it change how you feel about me?" he asked calmly.

"No, of course not," I said quietly.

"Then it doesn't change anything."

There wasn't anything but absolute certainty in his hazel eyes. I smiled and asked him, "How did you get so wise?"

"I'm just smart like that."

I kissed him with smiling lips. "You're just smug like that."

"It's a Gen Y thing?"

"It's a Cooper Jones thing," I said. "Did you still want me to meet your parents?"

"Yes," he said adamantly. "They know I'm seeing someone. They know it's serious, and they know his name is Tom. But that's all I've told them."

"You told them about me?" I couldn't help but smile.

"Of course I did," he said simply. "Just not exactly who *Tom* was. But if we're *that* serious, they should meet you."

"Then I will meet them," I told him. "Again," I clarified, "because I met them years ago, but I was only Ryan's dad back then, not their son's boyfriend."

Cooper chuckled. "They're gonna freak."

"And this is funny because…?"

He sighed and rolled onto his back. "Well, it's not really," he said. "But what else can I do? I've fallen in love with you, and if gender doesn't matter, then neither should age."

I leaned up on my arm and stared at this remarkable man. "You're incredible, you know that?"

He grinned at me. "Actually, yeah. I do know that." Then he added, "But you can keep telling me."

"I might have to write little notes, so I remember," I told him seriously. "You know, my Alzheimer's is getting bad."

Cooper laughed. "Oh my God! Thomas Elkin just made a joke! And it was even funny!"

"Shut up, you little shit."

He leaned up and kissed me. "See? I can go from 'incredible' to 'little shit' in two seconds. It's a talent."

I chuckled at him and pushed him to the side of the bed. "Well then, you incredible little shit, go and look up flights to Chicago, a rental car and a hotel."

"I will," he said, getting off the bed and pulling on his pants. "If you organize dinner. I'm starving."

I watched him walk out of the bedroom and shook my head, still in disbelief that he was mine. Smiling, I pulled on my jeans and followed him out to the living room. He was clicking away at some flight website, so while I scrolled through restaurant phone numbers on my phone, I asked, "Steak, seafood, pasta? Your choice."

"Steak," came his quick reply, so I hit the number on my cell and made reservations for dinner.

Cooper smiled at me and waited for me click off the call. "Are we going out?"

"Yes. You wanted steak."

He smiled warmly at me then looked back at the laptop. "So which dates are better for you?"

Between us, we determined we had something on for the next five weeks. We had that blasted concert, work, a trip to see his parents, then a trip to see mine, more work and Cooper had an energy convention in Philly that Louisa had been priming him for.

I pulled my credit card from my wallet and put it beside him.

"What's that for?"

"To pay for the trip to Chicago," I told him with a kiss to the top of his head.

He started to object to my offer, but I leaned down and gently put my lips to his. "Please, Cooper. Let me do this for you."

185

His lips formed a twisted frown. "Are you sure? I hate that you can pay for things I can't. I feel like a kept boy."

"Of course I'm sure," I told him. "And you're not a *kept* anything. The only thing you *keep* is me on my toes."

He huffed and gave me a small smile. I poured us both a juice while he paid for the trip to Chicago, and when he walked over to me to give me back my card, he slid his arms around me and nestled his face into my neck. "Thank you," he said quietly.

"You're very welcome," I replied with a kiss to the side of his head. "If it would make you feel any better, you can pay for dinner."

I felt him smile against my skin. "I don't feel *that* kept."

I chuckled and dug my fingers into his sides, tickling him. "Too bad, Mr. Jones. You're paying."

"Let me guess, you made reservations at some ridiculously over-priced restaurant."

"No, Perry's bar and grill. Next block over," I said with a smile. "Huge steaks, low prices. All the fries you can eat."

Cooper groaned. "Mr. Elkin, you know me so well."

"Yeah, well," I said, "I'll be having the steak and salad because my forty-four-year-old arteries aren't as forgiving as yours."

He cupped my balls in his hand and gave a gentle squeeze. "Your circulation works just fine."

I turned him around and slapped his ass. "Go, get dressed, or we'll be late."

He walked to the hall, rubbing his ass. "I can't believe you slapped me." Then he stood there and undid his pants, letting them slide down to his thighs, and he rubbed his naked ass. "I think you might need to kiss it better."

"After dinner," I said. "I'll do more than that."

He laughed when I had to adjust the front of my jeans. The little shit.

* * * *

Work was hectic the next week. Hectic, but good. Cooper was just as busy, and I only saw him on Wednesday night when I went to his apartment, and Friday night when he came to mine. We spent the night finalizing some work then crashed in front of the TV.

The next morning, I asked him if he missed going out with the boys, because he didn't do it very often. "I don't mind going out every once and a while," he reassured me. "But I'd prefer to be here. I like quiet nights in, too."

"I just don't want you to miss out on being twenty-two, that's all."

"I'm not missing out on anything," he replied. "I spent four years at college not missing out on much, I can assure you."

"I'd rather not hear the details of that, thanks."

He chuckled and kissed me. "Anyway, we're going out tonight, are we not?"

I rolled my eyes. "We are."

He laughed when I told him one of the other senior partners, Robert Chandler—an esteemed New York architect, who had mentored me ten years ago—had assumed Linkin Park was a period-drama play, because he wanted to know which theater on Broadway it was showing. "He thought it sounded Presidential."

Cooper laughed. "You work with dinosaurs."

I corrected him. "We're very talented, prestigious dinosaurs, thank you very much." Then I teased him, "Aren't you glad you weren't *his* intern?"

Cooper nodded and bit his bottom lip. "Yeah, I wouldn't have fantasized about being pushed against *his* drafting board, letting him have his wicked way with me..."

Forgetting what it was I was reading, I looked up and stared at him. "Fantasized? *My drafting board*?"

Cooper sat on the armrest of the sofa and smirked that smug, salacious smile at me. "You'd make me face the board and I'd hold onto the top of it with my pants around my ankles. You wouldn't even bother to undo the button on your suit pants...just the zip..."

I got up from the dining chair and walked over to stand between his legs, pressing myself against him.

Cooper smiled and his voice was gruff and slow. "And you'd fuck me."

"Jesus, Cooper," I said, pushing my hips against his, and he ran his hands over my ass. He could feel how hard I was. "I just can't get enough of you."

"Good," he whispered. "Because I want you all the time."

I kissed him, filling his mouth with my tongue. He pulled my hips harder into his, but I wedged my hand between us. I undid the button and fly on his cargos first, then on mine until our hardened cocks were pressed together. I gripped us both in one hand, still tongue-fucking his mouth while I jerked us off together. His cock was hot and silky-hard against mine.

He groaned in my mouth, and I needed air. I tugged my mouth from his and sucked back a breath, only to scrape my teeth down his jaw to his ear. "I'd fuck you so hard," I whispered in his ear, his head fell back and his cock surged and swelled in my hand.

Watching him come, feeling his warmth erupt over his stomach and down my hand, down my cock, brought me undone, and I shot white stripes over his skin.

He wrapped his arms around me and we slid over the armrest of the sofa, landing in a sticky mess with me lying on top of him.

The room still hadn't stopped spinning when Cooper chuckled underneath me.

"Fuck, Tom," he murmured. "That was intense."

"You shouldn't talk about fantasies like that," I mumbled into his neck.

He laughed again. "I think I really should talk about them more often." He ran his hands over my back and through my hair. "We should get cleaned up for tonight."

I noticed then that he still had one leg bent over the back of the sofa and his other foot on the ground while I was lying awkwardly over him. "I don't want to move. Too comfortable."

He chuckled. "Is this some old person yoga position? The dual pretzel?"

I laughed as I leaned up off him. "The sticky dual pretzel."

We untangled ourselves, and Cooper suggested we shower together. "To save water," he said. "We should be responsible, ecologically sound citizens," he said.

I rolled my eyes. "You just want to see me wet and naked, don't you?"

He laughed and put his wrist to his mouth, pretending to speak into some covert-operative mouthpiece. "My cover's been blown, I repeat, my cover's been blown."

"You're such a smart ass."

"Yeah, well," he said, pulling me into the bathroom. "You love me and my smart ass."

"Yes, I do."

Once we were out of the shower, dressed and almost ready to go, the intercom buzzed. Lionel's familiar voice said, "Mr. Elkin?"

I walked over and pressed the intercom button. "Yes, Lionel?"

"Sir, sorry to interrupt, but Ryan's on his way up."

That was odd. "Okay, that's fine, Lionel."

"Um, Mr. Elkin?"

"Yes?"

"Your ex-wife is with him."

"Sofia?"

"Yes, sir," he replied. "Just thought you'd like a little…notice."

Cooper walked up beside me and leaned into the intercom. "Lionel?"

"Mr. Jones?"

"You're worth more money."

The doorman laughed. "Just doing my job, sir."

Right then, there was a knock at the door. Cooper looked at me and smiled. "I'll do the honors."

Chapter Eight

"Hey," Cooper greeted Ryan as he opened the door.

"Hey, man," Ryan returned the sentiment.

Cooper stood to the side, gesturing for them to come in. "Mrs. Elkin," he said politely.

"Hello, Cooper," she said. Sofia walked in slowly, looking as uncomfortable as I'd ever seen her. She'd only been to my place once or twice before, and I think she found Cooper being here a little off-putting.

I gave her a light kiss on the cheek. "What do we owe the pleasure?"

Not missing my use of the word 'we', Sofia glanced at Cooper. "I was in town with Ryan and thought I'd call in, if that's okay. Last time we saw each other, we didn't exactly leave on very happy terms," she said, again looking quickly at Cooper.

"No, we didn't," I agreed. But she didn't apologize, and I certainly wasn't about to either. "And it's fine for you to call in, Sofia." I was going to add that a bit of notice would have been ideal, but figured I'd take her olive branch for what it was. The fact Cooper was here, and even felt at home enough to open the door for them should have been enough just desserts, but just in case it wasn't, I added, "Though we were actually just heading out."

"Where you guys going?" Ryan asked, looking up from the inside of the fridge.

"Madison Square Garden," Cooper answered with a grin.

Ryan stood up and gaped at him. "No freakin' way!" he cried. "Linkin Park?"

Then Sofia looked at me. "You're going to see Linkin Park?"

"I am," I told her. "Cooper puts up with my taste in music, so it's only fair that I put up with his."

"Yeah, that's true," Cooper agreed. "But my taste in music is awesome. Tom's is crap."

Ryan laughed, and I rolled my eyes. From the look on her face, it was obvious Sofia wasn't sure what to make of it, or of me and Cooper. He sat on the sofa and pulled on his shoes, then disappeared down the hall and came back with my boots.

"Thanks," I said quietly, taking my boots from him. As I pulled them on, I asked if Ryan and Sofia wanted to walk down with us, basically telling them we were leaving.

The elevator ride was quiet, but when we got to the lobby, Cooper snatched up my hand. It wasn't until we walked past Lionel that Cooper gave him a bit of a wave. "Thanks again, Lionel."

"My pleasure, Mr. Jones," he replied with a smile.

It was then Sofia turned around and saw that we were holding hands. She looked away quickly and pretended not to care, but she pursed her lips in that not-impressed way she always did.

I told Ryan to come over one night, Cooper told him to bring his new Xbox, we bid Sofia a good night then hailed a cab. Standing on the sidewalk with Sofia was awkward, and as soon as the cab pulled up, Cooper and I climbed in.

Cooper laughed. "She hates me."

I gave the taxi driver directions then said, "Don't let her get to you."

"Hmm," he hummed. "Did you see her face when I opened your front door?"

"I don't think she expected you to open the door, that's for sure."

"You know," he said, squeezing my hand, "I normally can't stand it when someone doesn't like me. It annoys me until I find out why, or until I break them down."

"Like Lionel," I added.

"Exactly. Now he loves me," he said simply. "But with Sofia, I just don't care. She can hate me all she likes."

I smiled at him. "I don't think she hates you. You were right—she's jealous."

"Which is irrational," he said. "It's not like I'm a young, blonde woman for her to compare herself to, or someone she could see herself twenty years ago as..."

"No," I conceded, "but I don't want her. I want you."

He smiled. "I know you do." He seemed placated a little. "And that's what she doesn't like."

"Can we not talk about my ex-wife?" I asked. "I'm spending the night with you, going to some god-forsaken concert."

Cooper smiled. "And it's gonna be freakin' awesome!"

* * * *

The concert itself wasn't too bad. Though I didn't want to admit that to Cooper. I was by far the oldest person there from what I could tell, but Cooper didn't seem to notice. I watched him dance and sing almost every word, I watched him get pushed and shoved and he never stopped smiling.

He loved it.

And that was what I went for.

My ears were ringing when we got home, and even when I woke up the next day. Cooper swore the only thing to get rid of the ringing in my ears would be to give him a blow job. He tried to reason that the sucking and swallowing motion would help pop the inner ear. Either that, or make him breakfast. He was pretty sure either would work.

Or both.

The little shit.

He left my apartment on Sunday afternoon, and when I got to work on Monday, I had a text from him saying if I still had ringing in my ears, he could come past the office, I could suck him off then buy him lunch and that might help.

I typed out my reply, *It didn't help for breakfast or lunch yesterday. Why would today be any different?*

Maybe we need to do it two days in a row. Just to be sure. For medicinal research purposes, of course.

Of course.

Is that a yes?

No, I replied. *Aren't you supposed to be working?*

Very productive morning. Apparently two blow jobs yesterday was good for creativity.

I laughed at my phone. *Will I see you this week?*

Maybe Wednesday? he answered. *And I'll stay over on Friday before we leave for Chicago.*

Okay. I'll just sleep in my big bed alone…

Are you pouting?

Yes. And looking at my drafting board, imagining you bent over it…

Jesus, Tom… That's not fair.

See you Wednesday. LY.

There was no immediate reply, but after lunch my phone beeped, and I smiled when I saw his name. *No more sexting at work. I've had a hard-on all day.*

That's a shame, I replied, *because I ordered a drafting board to be delivered to my place this evening.*

His response was almost immediate. *I'll be there after work.*

I chuckled to myself, threw my phone into my drawer and spent the next few hours getting some work done. I had actually ordered a new drafting board and asked for a six o'clock delivery to my apartment, so by five-thirty I was finishing off some financials when Jennifer buzzed me.

"Sorry to interrupt you, Mr. Elkin," she said. "Sofia Elkin is on line one."

I groaned, and Jennifer simply asked, "Would you like me to take a message?"

"No," I said with a sigh. "I'll take it." I pressed the blinking button. "Sofia?"

"Yes, Tom," she answered. "I didn't want to call your personal line. I hope that's okay?"

I repressed another sigh. "That's fine. What are you calling for? Is everything okay?"

This time she sighed. "Yes, everything's okay. I just wanted to speak to you. I'm sorry I called by on Saturday unannounced." Then she said, "How was the concert?"

"It was okay," I told her. Then making a point of calling him by name, I said, "But I wouldn't tell Cooper that. He'd make me go to another one."

"Right," she said.

Sofia was quiet then, so I prompted her, "You said you wanted to speak to me?"

"Well, I just wanted to speak to you...without him being there..."

"Him?" I asked, failing to keep the bite from my tone. "You mean Cooper?"

"Tom, please don't be mad," she said. "I'm trying here."

"Well, you can start by calling him by his name," I told her.

"Can I see you over the weekend sometime?" she asked. "Without Cooper being there? Is that okay?"

She was unbelievable. "I can't this weekend," I said. "We're going to Chicago."

"Oh."

"So Cooper can introduce me to his parents," I told her. "And the weekend after that, I'm taking him to meet my mom and dad, Sofia."

There was a long silence, then she said, "You're really doing this, aren't you?"

I wanted to tell her that I was *with* him, that I loved him, but I didn't. There wasn't any point. Instead, I told her, "Sofia, in the last five years I've spoken to you a handful of times, and now I've finally found someone, you've called me three times in two weeks. Sofia, you can call me about Ryan any time, day or night, but if you're trying to cause problems then I think the calls should stop."

There was complete silence.

So, to soften the blow, I said, "How about I give you a call in a few weeks and we can go out for coffee? I want you to get to know Cooper. I want you to see how wonderful he is, but you never will until you stop seeing him as some kind of threat."

"Okay," she said quietly.

"Sofia, I want you in my life," I told her honestly. "I want us to be friends. I do. I know I hurt you, and I'm sorry for that. I truly really am. But if you fight me on this, on Cooper, I will choose him."

When she didn't reply, I told her I had to go, but I'd be in touch in a few weeks. I put the receiver in the cradle, closed my files, shoved my laptop into my satchel and left.

* * * *

Needless to say, the new drafting board was impressive.

So was Cooper.

He eyed the new addition to the living room somewhat cautiously. He bit his bottom lip and walked over to it, touching it reverently. "It's beautiful."

"It's a nineteen-twenties antique," I explained. "Solid oak, cast iron, adjustable...unbreakable."

He stared at it for a while, running his fingers along the timber. "It's indestructible, right?"

"Sturdy as hell," I answered.

Without another word, Cooper simply disappeared down the hall only to return with a bottle of lube and a condom. He put them on the edge of the dining table near the drafting board and looked over at me with mischief in his eyes, then he stretched up slowly and grabbed the top of the board.

"You're ambitious," I told him. "It's that Gen Y thing that gets you into trouble."

He spread his legs and lifted his ass. "It's a horny thing," he said gruffly. "But I didn't offer myself, in my fantasy," he said quietly. "You...*took* me."

I walked over to him and pressed him against the drafting board. "Like this?"

He moaned his response, so I reached around him and undid his belt and pants, sliding them over his hips. Then I undid mine. I rubbed my naked cock along the crack of his ass, smeared us both with lube, then when he heard the tear of the foil packet, he lifted his leg onto the bottom wooden brace.

"Please."

When I pushed into him, I slid my hands up his arm to the top of the drafting board and gripped my hands over his. And I fucked him. Just like he wanted me to. Just like how he groaned, begging me, pleading with me.

Afterward, when we'd collapsed into a sticky, sated mess on the sofa, I said, "So, you really like the new drafting board?"

He looked at me and waggled his eyebrows. "Yeah, I happen to love antiques."

I narrowed my eyes at him, knowing he meant me, and he burst out laughing.

"You're such a little shit."

"You love me."

I deliberately didn't say anything, so he dug his fingers into my ribs. "Say it! Say it," he said, laughing.

"Yes, I do," I barked out with a laugh. "I *do* love you."

He grinned victoriously, so I added, "You little shit."

* * * *

On Saturday morning, we'd checked our luggage in at the airport and sat down for coffee before our boarding call when Cooper pulled out his cell. He scrolled for a number and pressed call.

"Mom?" he asked. "Yeah, we're just at LaGuardia now." I could hear his mother saying something, then Cooper smiled. "Yes, Tom's here with me," he said. "Actually, Mom, you've met him before."

I put my coffee down.

"Yes, you have," Cooper told her. "Remember my friend from high school, Ryan Elkin?" Then he added ever so calmly, "Well, Tom's his dad."

There was silence for a moment, and Cooper looked at me unapologetically. "No, I'm not joking... Yes, because I want you to meet him..." He was quiet then, while his mother obviously spoke. I could hear her voice through the phone.

"No," he said with less of a smile. "We've organized a car. We'll just see you at your place"—he looked at his watch—"in about three hours."

He clicked off the call and I asked him, "Couldn't wait to tell her?"

He shrugged and sighed. "Now she has three hours to get used to the idea before we walk in the front door."

I sipped my coffee. "True," I conceded. "But over the phone?"

"I know my mother," he said. "Three hours. First hour, she'll be livid with me for dropping that bombshell. Second hour, she'll be mad because, well, you're older than my dad, and by the third hour she'll have had enough time to calm down."

I laughed at his blasé comment. "'She'll be mad because, well, you're older than my dad'," I repeated, shaking my head. "Jeez, Coop. Thanks."

He chuckled. "Don't sweat it, babe. She'll be fine with it…when she gets used to it."

"Don't sweat it, babe?" I echoed. "Is that some Gen Y thing for 'it'll be fine'?"

"Yes," he said seriously. "You should take notes, old man."

Ignoring that, I asked, "And your dad? How will he take it?"

Cooper put down his coffee and said, "I'm thinking not very well." He looked down at the table and for the first time since I'd met him, he looked…uncertain.

"Cooper, I'll be there with you," I told him quietly. "If he… We'll be there together to talk to them."

A voice over the loudspeaker called our flight, and we boarded the plane. Cooper said he wasn't nervous, that he was okay, but the closer we got to Chicago, the tighter he held my hand.

Chapter Nine

Cooper was amazing. Yes, he was nervous but after we'd collected the rental car, I asked him if he'd like to check in at the hotel first. He shook his head. "Nope, wanna get this out of the way."

That was Cooper. Jump in with both feet and tackle it head on. One thing was for certain, when he made his mind up, there was no point trying to persuade him otherwise.

He was remarkable like that. Some might argue that he was more foolish than courageous, but at just twenty-two years of age, sometimes I thought he was light years ahead of me.

And then other times, he was a twenty-two-year-old fucking kid. Like driving, for instance. Claiming I didn't know where his parents lived, he took the car keys then proceeded to drive, according to him, like he stole it.

Twenty minutes and fifteen old-man-with-a-heart-condition jokes later, he pulled the car into the drive of his parent's house. It was a large, double-story house on manicured lawns with well-kept gardens. Cooper's parents had obviously done well for themselves since moving to Chicago.

Cooper exhaled through puffed cheeks and looked at me like 'here goes nothing', opened the car door and got out.

I followed him, and he waited for me to step up beside him at the front door until he rang the doorbell.

Meeting his parents was, for the lack of some profound, life-changing word, weird.

His mother, Paula, opened the door as if she were expecting some other younger Tom, and Cooper's joke of dating Tom Elkin was just that. A joke.

When she saw me, she stared—just stared—before she even remembered to say hello to her son. She kissed his cheek. We walked in and met Cooper's father, Andrew, in the living room. I'd met them both, maybe once or twice, when Cooper and Ryan had been at school, and they hadn't changed one bit.

Cooper and I sat down on the sofa, his parents sat across from us, and still not a word was spoken.

Just awkward stares, coupled with awkward silences.

But then a kid walked in, who I realized must have been Max, Cooper's younger brother. He was seventeen years old and going through what Cooper called an 'emo' phase. He had longish black hair swept over half his face and there was a nose ring on the half I could see.

Max stopped when he saw Cooper, looked at me for a long second, then back to Cooper. "Dude," he said slowly. "He's old."

I looked at Cooper, Cooper looked at me, then both of us burst out laughing. Even his mother tried not to smile. His father on the other hand didn't look so impressed.

Cooper stood up and gave his little brother a bit of a hug, then tried to touch the nose ring, but Max dodged him easily. "Nice silverware," Cooper said.

"Thanks," he replied.

Cooper roughed up his brother's hair. "Do the girls like it?"

Max pushed Cooper and tried to smack him up the side of his head. "Like you'd know."

"Boys," Paula chastised. "Cooper, you've been here for thirty seconds. Leave your brother alone."

Cooper walked over to where I was sitting, and he sat down, a little closer to me this time. Max stood behind his parents, Cooper made a face at him and Max flipped him the bird.

"Cooper," his father said. "Can you be serious for a moment? I think we have some...*issues* that need discussing."

Cooper took my hand. "Mom, Dad, this is Tom. Yes, he's older than me, but we're together, and we're serious."

His parents both stared at him then turned their attention to me and it was my turn to talk. "I know you're thinking this is wrong, or that it can't be real," I said calmly. "And believe me, I don't think we were expecting any of this either, but the fact we're both here must tell you we are serious."

"You're old enough to be his father," Paula whispered.

"Yes, I am," I answered simply.

"Age isn't an issue," Cooper said quickly. "Not for us. It's never been an issue." Then he said, "Well, in the beginning it was a little weird," he admitted, "before we got together and I was attracted to him, and I kept thinking 'Oh my God, he's forty-four' but then I realized it didn't matter."

I looked at him and squeezed his hand.

"It didn't matter?" his father asked.

"No, it wasn't his *age* that I was interested in," Cooper told them. "It was the fact we'd spend hours talking about anything and everything, like I'd met my intellectual match."

I couldn't help but smile, and his admission of exactly how I felt reinforced to me that this was worth it.

His father looked at the both of us, like we didn't understand the obvious. "I'm sorry, Cooper, but it *does* matter."

Cooper's reply was a very serious, "Not to me."

Then his mother asked, "Just exactly how did this all come about?"

I retold the story, *sans* intimate details, of how we'd met, how we'd worked together, how it was then that I saw Cooper to be a person who was strong minded, smart and free-thinking.

Cooper's father glared at me. "You took *advantage* of him while he *worked* for you?"

I didn't have time to speak before Cooper sat forward on the sofa and spoke through gritted teeth, "He didn't take *advantage* of me!" He almost spat the words. "Jesus Christ!"

"Cooper, don't swear in this house," his mother chided him.

Cooper ignored her. "So what you're saying is," he said, "you think I don't have a mind of my own, that I can't make my own decisions and that I'm some easily led kid? Is that what you think?"

"No," his mother said weakly, but his father stared at me.

They didn't think he was a naïve kid, they thought I was some sexual predator. I gave Cooper a small smile and squeezed his hand again. "It's not you they have a problem with."

"You think it's Tom?" he asked, looking at his parent's incredulously.

"I think a forty-four-year-old man should know better," his father replied coldly.

"No," Cooper said flatly, dropping my hand to hold up both his index fingers. "No. Dad, you're not implying Tom should know better, you're implying I don't have the ability to see what's in front of me." He was angry, and his jaw bulged when he spoke. "Like I don't know what's right for me, like I'm some dumbass kid. Yes, Tom's a grown man, but you need to see that I am too."

"You're twenty-two years old," his father said. "And you're our son. We're allowed to be concerned. I don't think you have the perspective to see it for what it is, Cooper."

"I can't believe you have a problem with this," Cooper said, shaking his head.

"I can't believe you thought we wouldn't have a problem with this," his father countered. "Quite frankly, Cooper, I can't see us ever not having a problem with this. I'm sorry, but I don't think it's right."

Cooper scratched his head, like he couldn't understand something. "You told me you'd accept me, all of me. You both said that. When I came out to you, when I finally admitted to you I was gay, you told me you'd love me, no matter who I wanted, or who I fell in love with."

Cooper stood up and walked to the back door, but then turned around. "But what you meant was that you'd only accept me if I fell in love with someone my own age. Or what? Someone that wasn't a guy?" he asked. "Oh God, were you still hoping me being gay was just a phase?" he asked, clearly upset. "Well, guess what? It's not a phase, and neither is this," he said, motioning between him and me. "I am *in love* with him."

His parents sat there, stunned at his outburst, and when they never said a word, Cooper turned on his heel and walked out of the door. I stood up, not excusing myself, not caring, and followed him.

He was walking across the yard to the pool. "Coop, sweetheart," I said, and he stopped and turned around. He had tears in his eyes.

"Can we go?" he asked. "I think I'd like to go now."

I put my hands around his neck and pulled him against me. "Sure," I told him. Not that I thought leaving was the best idea, but he needed me on his side right now.

He nodded against my neck. "I just want to go."

"Okay," I whispered.

"I thought they'd be okay," he mumbled. "I thought they'd be kinda mad, but then they'd see I was happy and they'd be okay."

"Maybe they need some time," I said quietly. "They love you. They just want what's best for you."

"You're what's best for me," he answered, with his face still buried against me.

"Did you want to go?" I asked. "Or did you want to stay and try and sort this out?"

He sighed. "I want to go."

"Okay," I said again. "Whatever you want."

Cooper pulled back from me and took my hand. He led us into the house, but never stopped. "Tell Max I said goodbye," he said to no one in particular and walked right past his parents to the front door.

I stopped him. "Just give me one minute," I said quietly.

He frowned, and said, "I'll see you in the car." And not even looking at his mom or dad, he walked out.

I turned to face his parents. His father looked angry and confused, and his mother looked lost and utterly miserable. "He wants to leave," I told them. "He's very upset. Maybe it's not my place to say, and you can hate me all you like, but please don't lose him over this. Don't cut him off because of me."

"It won't be *our* doing," his father said coldly.

I smiled, despite that he was implying I would be the cause of Cooper losing his family. "I'm sure I don't have to tell you how stubborn Cooper is, or how driven he is. Once he sets his sights on something, he stands his ground until he has it. By the same token, he won't stand for something he doesn't agree with, and he most certainly won't be walked over, and he won't be misled by anyone."

"What exactly are you saying?" Cooper's father asked.

I looked at them both. "That you raised an incredible son."

My words threw them, but eventually Paula asked, "What would you do? If it was your son? If it was Ryan who was dating someone twice his age."

I thought about that for a moment. "If he was happy, if it was what he wanted, then I'd tell him I loved him, knowing I'd be there for him if it fell apart."

Cooper's father scoffed. "Of course you would."

"All we can do is love them, and hope they make the right choices," I said, with my hand on the door handle. "Unconditional love is exactly that. We don't get to choose."

I opened the door wider but before I left, I said, "We're staying at The Peninsula, on the eighteenth floor. Don't let him go back to New York thinking you don't love him."

I walked out to find Cooper in the passenger seat of the car, instead of the driver's seat. I got in and pulled the car out onto the street and headed toward the city. Cooper was quiet and stared out of the window for the trip to the hotel, and even after we'd checked in and went up to our suite, he was still silent.

He sat on the bed, and it was then he asked me what had been said between me and his parents while he'd waited in the car, and I told him every word. His face fell and he frowned. "It wasn't supposed to go like that," he said.

It was heartbreaking to see him so upset. I pulled him against me and we lay back and while he snuggled into me, I stared out over Chicago for I don't know how long.

When it started to get dark, I asked him if he wanted something to eat. "Or we can go out?" I suggested. "We can find whatever food takes your fancy, or if you want to get drunk, we can do that too."

"Can we just stay in?" he asked. "I'm sorry, I'm not really in the mood to do anything."

"Don't apologize," I said, kissing his forehead. "Of course we can stay in. We can get room service."

"Sounds good."

"I can run you a bath. The spa is huge."

He finally smiled. "Maybe later."

I ordered us dinner, which he only picked at, and he declined the bath, opting for a hot shower, then he climbed into bed. I joined him, he slid into the crook of my arm, nestled into me and fell asleep.

I lay there, staring at the ceiling, with an awful lot to think about.

I wondered if I should back off from Cooper, if I should urge him to choose his family over me. I certainly would never *make* him choose. But I had the perspective of both sides—as the boyfriend, and as a father. It angered me that his parents wouldn't even consider the idea of Cooper and I being together. Maybe they were hoping I'd be the one to call it off with him, knowing as a parent, I wouldn't want to be the cause of such a conflict.

And, well, that just pissed me off.

I wondered if this would change things between us. I wondered, if his parents did give him an ultimatum, who he'd choose. As a parent, I wondered who I'd *want* him to choose.

I couldn't imagine leaving Cooper. I knew we'd only been together for a few months, but I loved him. I *adored* him—this incredible man who, for some reason, seemed to love me just as much as I loved him.

I wondered if he could leave me. I wondered if he should. And as that thought unsettled me, I tried to get out of bed, but Cooper's hold tightened on me. "Don't go," he mumbled.

I rolled so I faced him instead and wrapped him up in my arms. Even in his sleep he needed me. How could I ever leave him? I hoped to God it wouldn't come to that. Instead, we could prove to them that we were serious. It wouldn't be easy, it would take patience and understanding, and it could very well take years.

But he was worth it. *We* were worth it.

I kissed the side of his head. "I'm not going anywhere."

* * * *

In the morning, I woke up to find Cooper sitting on the bed with his phone in his hand. "Hey," I said, my voice still sleepy. "Everything okay?"

"Just got a message from Mom and Dad," he said, giving me a guarded smile. "They're coming to see us before we go back to New York."

Chapter Ten

It was a very different meeting this time. Andrew and Paula Jones walked into the café at the hotel, looking more nervous than anything. Cooper's mother looked like she'd barely slept.

I knew how she felt.

Cooper was stoic, his jaw was set and his chin was raised defiantly. I'd told him earlier, if he wanted to, he could listen to what they had to say and if it didn't go well, the power was his to end the meeting.

If they didn't meet him halfway, at least.

He'd told me he'd hear them out, but he wouldn't put up with any bullshit about me coercing him into bed. He wouldn't cop being told he was just a kid, or that I had no right to take advantage of him. He was hurt and angry, and I didn't blame him.

As tough as he tried to make himself out to be, he wanted their approval. He wanted his parents in his life, without any disagreements, without any tension. He wanted them to be happy for him.

Thankfully the waiter followed them in and took orders for coffee, which was an ice breaker for all of us.

His mother started first. "Cooper, honey, I'm sorry yesterday ended up the way it did," she said. "I don't want to fight with you."

"I don't want to fight with you either," he said softly.

Then Paula stared at her husband, prompting him to speak.

"Look, son, we might not agree with everything you do," he said cautiously. He sighed and started again, "But it's not our choice. We know that."

I half expected him to say 'it's not our mistake to make' but thankfully, he didn't.

"No, it's not your choice," Cooper said. He wasn't letting them off easily. "It's my choice, and I've made it."

"We can see that," his mother said, trying to smile.

Just then, the waiter returned with our coffees and asked if we were ready to order breakfast.

Cooper looked at his parents. "Will you be eating with us?" he asked. It wasn't really a question of food, it was a question of tolerance. If they stayed and ate with us, it meant they wanted to try to accept us.

"Yes," his mother said. "If that's okay with you?"

Cooper looked at his very-quiet father. "Dad?"

"Yes," he said, clearing his throat. He looked to the waiter. "We're ready to order."

Cooper smiled and finally exhaled. He looked at me. "I'm starving. What are you having?"

It was hard not to smile back at him, even with his death-grip on my hand under the table. "Eggs Benedict, I think."

Cooper looked up at the waiter. "One pancakes with maple syrup *and* bacon, and one eggs Benedict, with ham not salmon, sauce on the side, thanks."

The fact he ordered for me, knowing exactly how I liked my eggs done made me smile. It wasn't lost on his parents either.

It was pretty clear it was Paula, Cooper's mother, who had insisted on this visit. His father was still standoffish, obviously not pleased with the idea of his son dating an older guy. But they were making an effort.

"Where's Max?" Cooper asked.

"Still in bed," Paula replied.

"He won't surface until lunch time," his father mumbled.

Cooper looked up thoughtfully and sighed. "Ah, the good old days."

His mother smiled at him. "You should invite him to New York for a weekend," she said. "He'd love that."

"That'd be great," Cooper said. "I'm pretty busy with work, but we could line it up with a concert or something he wants to see." He looked at me, and smiled. "Max loves thrash death-metal."

"Oh, excellent," I said sarcastically. "Another concert."

Cooper laughed. "You went to *one*, and you liked it."

"You went to one of his concerts?" Paula asked, surprised.

Cooper answered for me, "Of course he did. He takes me to those boring art exhibition openings, so it's only fair."

"You went to *one*," I countered, trying not to smile. "And you liked it."

Paula and Andrew looked on, not very sure what to make of our banter. Cooper smiled as he sipped his coffee. "You guys should come to New York," he said to his parents. "We could spend the weekend, I could show you where I work, we could go to Broadway or something equally as boring."

They agreed, but didn't commit to anything, and conversation turned to Cooper's work, a subject he could talk about for hours. I just loved his enthusiasm for what he did, for what *we* did. He asked me a question or two, trying to drag me into the discussion, but I was happy for him to have this time with his parents. It didn't have to involve me at every turn.

I wanted them to see he was still the same person.

I answered him, of course, but let him take center stage. Not that I minded. I could listen to him talk about architecture all day long.

Cooper's parents might have caught me smiling at him a few times, but I didn't care. Let them see how much I admired him. I wasn't about to deny it.

Breakfast arrived and as we ate, Paula directed her questions at me. She asked about my work, how I found New York and she even made small talk about the Yankees.

But Andrew barely said a word.

When it was time to go, I told Cooper I'd give him a few minutes with his parents while I checked us out of the hotel and organized the car. When I couldn't put it off any longer, I met them in the lobby.

Cooper gave me a tight smile and quickly took my hand. After we'd said goodbye and were in the car on our way to the airport, I asked him what was said in my absence.

"Well, they're still not exactly happy about us," he said quietly.

"I'm sorry," I told him.

"Don't you apologize," he said quickly. "For anything."

"Still, I'm sorry it didn't go how you'd hoped."

"Well," he said with a shrug, "they're prepared to put up with it, so I guess that's all I could hope for." He looked at me as I drove, and gave me a sad smile. "Last night, I really thought they weren't going to accept it all, so I guess *tolerance* is good."

"Coop, sweetheart, they're still a part of your life," I said. "They're talking of coming to New York to visit you. They might not 'accept' us being together, but they're trying. Give them time."

"I just wish they could see us, ya know?" he said, slowly shaking his head. "If they could see us, the way we are together, the way we talk and laugh…"

"I think they saw how happy you were, how serious we were," I told him, "and I think that's what scared them."

"Why would it scare them?" he asked. "Shouldn't they be happy for me?"

"Give them time," I said again. "I know it's a Gen Y thing to want everything yesterday, but some things take time."

He sighed and was quiet for a little while. Then he looked at me curiously. "What generation are you anyway?" he asked.

"Generation X," I answered.

"You had to Google that, didn't you?"

"Yes," I admitted with a laugh.

"So if I'm Gen Y and you're X, then together we are the chromosome code for male," he mused.

"Yes, I am X marks the spot, and you are the dear God, why, why, why."

"Fucking hell, Tom," he deadpanned. "We need to work on your jokes."

* * * *

Cooper and I got back to New York and slipped easily into our routine. He was busy with work, and it was something I understood well. I actually condoned it. If he wanted to be the best—and he could be with his talent—he needed to put in the hours.

It was what I'd done. It was what had got me where I was today.

So if he had to work late, I didn't mind. If he brought work over to my place, I did my work alongside him.

It was what we did.

We worked, we talked, we laughed, we made out then we worked some more. He didn't stay over every night that week, but almost. "It really would be easier if you moved in here," I told him.

Cooper was standing near the dining table, packing some papers into his satchel. He dropped his hand. "Really, Tom?" he asked, not too happily. "*Easier*? It'd be *easier*?"

"Well, it's a pain you always having to come here, or me going to your place," I said, but my words lost steam with the look on his face. "Easier was the wrong word, wasn't it?"

He nodded. "Yeah, it really was."

"I'm sorry," I started to apologize.

Cooper finished stuffing his belongings into his satchel and walked over to me, kissing me with smiling lips. "You keep getting the whole move-in-with-me speech wrong."

"Can I try again?"

"Not tonight."

Damn, he was a demanding little punk. "Let me call you a cab."

"I can call my own cab," he said with a smile. "Well, Lionel will call one for me."

"Lionel hails you a cab?"

"Yep," he answered with a grin. "I told you he loves me."

"Did you bring him a jar of peanut butter?" I asked with a smirk. "Did you *flatter* him, the way you *flattered* me?"

"No, I bought him struffoli from the Italian bakery on East fifty-third," he said simply. "Well, technically I bought them for his wife who's from Naples, so he was in her good books, and I'm in his."

"I can't believe you did that," I said, shaking my head. "Wait. Wait, you gave him fine Italian pastries and all I got was peanut butter?"

Cooper laughed. "I bought you peanut butter because I wanted a sandwich. The coffee was to win you over."

"You're unbelievable."

"I know," he answered simply. "Coffee and sass. I bought you coffee and sass."

I chuckled as he got to the door. "Cooper?"

"Yeah?"

"I'm glad you bought me coffee."

He grinned and walked out. I heard him yell from the hall. "And sass."

I nodded and grinned to myself. "And sass."

* * * *

I spoke to Cooper every day, on the phone or via text, but didn't see him for the rest of the week.

I missed him.

So on Friday night when I was supposed to be meeting some business friends of mine, I called and asked Cooper if he'd like to come.

"They're your friends," he said. "They've known you for twenty years. Is that a good idea?"

"Of course it is," I told him. "I want them to meet you."

I heard him switch his phone to his other ear. "But it's Chaney, Hilderbrandt and Myer."

"So?"

"Jesus, Tom," he whispered into the phone. "They're like the holy trinity of architecture."

I laughed. "Really, Cooper? They're just friends of mine."

"They're just friends of mine," he repeated sarcastically. "God, I keep forgetting you're in the same league as them."

"Thanks," I scoffed.

"You know what I mean," he tried to explain. "I studied their work in college. They're like legends."

"Did you study *my* work in college?"

"Enough of the ego, Elkin."

I laughed into the phone. "You *did* study my work!" I cried, but all he did was mumble some noncommittal response. I took a deep breath and tried not to smile. "Will you please come to dinner with me?" I asked. Then I whispered, "I've missed you."

"Okay," he relented petulantly. "I'll be nervous, and probably say something to embarrass you and they'll laugh at me and I'll never work in the industry again, but I'll go because you asked."

"You'll be fine," I told him. "Just be yourself. They'll love you."

* * * *

Well, he was a little late, but that gave me enough time to tell the three men I met there I was expecting my date.

My boyfriend.

They'd known I'd split from Sofia, although I hadn't really found the courage to tell them the real reason

218

until almost a year after. The three of them were what Cooper would call *old school*, but they were also my friends. They'd said they didn't care that I was gay, and I'd met with them many times since and things between us were the same as they'd always been. Granted, I'd also never brought a date.

The restaurant was on Madison and Fifth, fine dining and strict dress code. I wondered briefly if I should have elaborated that fact to Cooper earlier, but when he walked in, he was still wearing his suit.

I stood when the maître d' escorted him over, and gave him a reassuring smile. He was nervous. "Sorry I'm late," he said quietly. "Louisa has me working on the Philly project."

Cooper took off his jacket, revealing his charcoal waistcoat and gray shirt and tie, and looked expectantly, nervously, around the table. I made introductions, and Cooper smiled and said polite hellos. I'd never seen him so anxious. I didn't want anyone to be uncomfortable with public displays of affection, Cooper included, but I wanted to reassure him. So under the table, I slid my foot alongside Cooper's, silently telling him I was there. He gave me a small, appreciative smile.

Hal Meyers spoke first, "Tom says you're working with Louisa Arlington?"

"Yes," Cooper said. "She's great. I'm working on a project at the moment that we're taking to the Green Exhibition in Philly next week. It's amazing."

And so conversation turned to architecture, but with five architects at the table, it was inevitable. I kind of hoped it would, knowing it was a safe topic of conversation for Cooper. And I also wanted them to see how switched on he was.

He was quiet at first, but as conversation opened up, he spoke animatedly, reining himself in every now and then. I think the others asked him questions to test him, but he spoke about new design concepts, and how air flow principals and insulation should co-exist to reduce energy output, and how sustainability was the responsibility of his generation of designers.

I was sure Cooper would start on a tangent, then remind himself just who he was sitting at the table with. Whether it was his nerves or his blatant love for what he did, I wasn't sure.

After we'd eaten and when he'd excused himself to go to the bathroom, the three men watched him leave. Lloyd Chaney raised his eyebrows. "He's certainly on his way in the world, isn't he?"

"Yes," I agreed. "He's very passionate about what he does."

"He's very young," Ro Hilderbrandt said. He wasn't talking about Cooper's age for his profession. He was talking about his relationship with me.

"He is," I conceded. "But I assure you, he has twice the talent than what any of us did when we were his age."

"Are you hoping he'll tutor you?" Hal joked.

"I shouldn't laugh," I said with a smile. "Because I promise you, new design principles will leave us old fogeys for dead. He probably could teach me a thing or two about where our industry's going."

"Old fogeys?" Ro scoffed. "We're not that old. You might feel it because you've scored yourself someone half your age."

I ignored his jibe about us. "He's really nervous about being here tonight."

Lloyd turned his wine glass in his fingertips. "You must be serious about him, if you've brought him to meet us."

I sighed. "Yes."

"How did you meet?" Hal asked.

"He's a friend of Ryan's," I said, deliberately not telling them about Cooper's internship. It was a discussion I didn't want to have knowing Cooper would be back any second. So I changed the subject. "When I told him who we'd be having dinner with tonight, he called you three the holy trinity of architecture."

Cooper came back to his seat, as the three of them were still chuckling, and looked at me nervously. "I just told them how they'd be known as the holy trinity of architecture from now on."

Cooper groaned. "Yeah, thanks. I was going to make the Godfather analogy but figured I didn't want to give you ideas about young architects offending his mentors," he said, looking at me pointedly. "Besides, I hear horse heads are hard to come by this time of year."

Ro, Hal and Lloyd all laughed at his joke, and I slipped my hand on Cooper's leg under the table.

Hal said, "Well, if we're the holy trinity, what's the great Thomas Elkin?"

Cooper looked at me and shrugged. "He's just Tom."

They all laughed again, but Ro laughed the loudest. "That's the first time I've ever heard Thomas Elkin be called 'just Tom'," he said.

Lloyd nodded. "I like you, son," he said to Cooper. "It's about time Tom here had some ego checks."

Cooper looked to the table, a little embarrassed, so I gave his leg a squeeze. "Gentlemen, on that note, before I'm the punchline to any more of your jokes, we'll bid you goodnight," I said with a smile. I knew they meant no harm. It was just how they were.

"Yes, I must be getting home too," Hal said. "Sue's had one of her book-club meetings on, so I think it'll be safe to go home by now."

We paid our bill and walked out, shook hands and agreed we'd do it again in another month or so, like we always did.

Cooper was quiet on the way back to my apartment. I asked him if he wanted to go home, but he held my hand tighter and said no. When we finally got inside, he was frowning. "Did I say something wrong?"

I walked around to where he was leaning his ass on the dining table. I put my hands on his face and made him look at me. "Cooper Jones, you were perfect tonight," I told him. "Their jibes at me were nothing to do with you. It's how we are when we all get together. They're old country-club style, men's-club boys. They're always like that. Actually," I said, "I think they took us pretty well, all things considered."

Cooper nodded, but didn't seem convinced. "I just felt stupid."

"You're *not* stupid. You're far from stupid," I said seriously. "They said to me when you'd gone to the bathroom how switched on you were."

He looked at me with imploring eyes. "Really?"

"Ready to take on the world."

"I called you 'just Tom'."

I nodded and pecked his lips. "So? I like being just Tom."

He gave me a half-smile. "You're *my* just Tom."

"Yes, I am," I whispered, before I kissed him again.

222

Chapter Eleven

Cooper worked most of the weekend. He spent the day with his head in books, looking at the laptop screen or scribbling down notes.

I didn't mind.

I lounged on the sofa for a while, read the papers, made him coffee, nuzzled his neck, made him lunch, made him laugh, then annoyed him some more.

Eventually, realizing I wasn't going to deter him, I pulled out my own work, cleared some room on the dining table and joined him. We had a lazy dinner, I gave him some stress relief in bed by lavishing his entire body with my mouth, and we fell asleep wrapped around each other.

Sunday was much the same. It was a perfect way to spend the weekend. Well, it was for me, but Cooper was looking a little stressed. He was sitting at the dining table and had just run his hand through his hair for about the twentieth time.

"I just want this to be perfect," he said when I asked him what was wrong. "It's my first big project, and Louisa trusts me with it. I know it's not my project alone, but I need to make sure what I contribute is perfect."

I kissed the top of his head. "Don't underestimate yourself," I told him. "Everything you do is perfect."

He looked up at me and grinned. "Everything?"

"Mm-mm," I hummed. "Some things a little more perfect than others, but yes."

"Excuse me, Mr. Elkin, do I hear a sexual innuendo in your tone?"

"There's quite the possibility you do, Mr. Jones," I said with a smirk.

Cooper stood up from the dining chair, and kissed me. "No innuendos for you, Mr. Elkin. I need to get going home."

I raised my eyebrows. It was the first time he'd ever not been interested in sex. "You know, I think that's a first."

He smiled. "I have laundry to do, and I need to get organized for tomorrow…"

"You're passing me over to do laundry?"

He laughed, but then he groaned. "Aw, that's not fair."

I smiled and kissed him. "Seriously, Cooper, I don't mind. I'm just joking."

"I'll make it up to you during the week," he said.

I sighed dramatically. "You know, if you lived here…"

He narrowed his eyes at me. "You want sex that bad?"

I barked out a laugh. "No!"

"Then what?"

"Well, I have a laundry service—" I stopped mid-sentence from the look on his face.

"So, I should move in for sex and free laundry?"

"No!"

"That is the worst move-in-with-me speech ever," he said. "In the history of the world."

I was gaping, but smiling and shaking my head. "No, that's not what I was saying at all."

Cooper shook his head then clicked his tongue. "Tsk, tsk." Then he sighed dramatically. He was trying not to smile. "That was your worst one yet."

My head fell back and I groaned. "Cooper Jones, you're infuriating and unreasonable, and *you* made it all about sex and laundry."

He laughed. "Infuriating and unreasonable? Jeez, this just gets better. Remember when I used to be cute?"

I grabbed his chin between my thumb and forefinger and kissed him. "Have fun doing your laundry."

"I will," he said cheerfully. "And I will see you on Wednesday after work." He packed up his papers, his laptop and threw it all in his satchel and we walked to the front door.

I leaned against the jamb and stopped him from leaving. "You're still cute. You're still infuriating and unreasonable. But you're addictive and you're wonderful."

He stepped up close and kissed me softly. "I love you too, Tom."

I smiled and rested my forehead on his. "One day you'll agree to move in, and you won't have to keep leaving," I said quietly. "And my place wouldn't feel so empty."

A slow smile spread across his face and he sighed. "Mmm, almost. Not quite, but that's the best by far."

"I wasn't trying to ask you to move in."

He kissed me sweetly again. "Maybe that's why." With that, he walked out and down the hall, smiling as he looked back at me.

"Did I mention infuriating?" I asked.

He pressed the elevator button. "Good night, Tom."

"Maddening?"

The elevator doors opened, and he smiled. "I'll call you later."

"Exasperating?"

"Love you," he called out as the doors were closing.

"Love you, too," I called back. "You little shit."

"Heard that," he said quickly, but the elevator closed, then he was gone.

I shut the door, and when I looked around my apartment to see his mess strewn all over it, I smiled.

* * * *

I'd spoken to Cooper on the phone several times over the next few days, and he'd said he would be over at my place on Wednesday after work. He'd thought it'd be about seven by the time he finished up for the day, so I was surprised to hear his keys in the front door barely after six.

I walked around from the kitchen just as he was coming through the door. "Hey you," I said. "You're early. Everything okay?"

Cooper nodded as he dumped his satchel on the floor. He walked directly up to me and smiled. "I missed you," he said, then he kissed me. Hard. And he pushed me backward toward the hall, toward my bedroom. He broke the kiss to say, "I shouldn't have said no to sex on Sunday."

I laughed as I pulled his shirt up and loosened his tie. "Tell me what you want."

"I want it all," he murmured, trying to kiss my neck while undoing his pants. "I want you to do everything to me."

"Everything?"

Cooper undid my pants and wrapped his hand around me. "Everything."

By the time we were naked on the bed, by the time I had made him come the first time, he was begging me. I kissed him, licked him and sucked him. I rimmed him, fingered him then I fucked him.

He wanted everything. So that was what I did to him.

Afterwards, when he'd come the second time, I discarded the condom and lay back beside him. He looked at me with glazed-over eyes and he chuckled. "Jesus," he said, still catching his breath.

"You said everything."

He laughed again, just as his cell phone rang. With a groan, he rolled to the end of the bed and almost fell off trying to get his phone from his pants pocket. He was still laughing when he answered. "Yes, Louisa?"

He was quiet while his boss spoke to him, but he was still naked in my bed so I commando-crawled over to him, licking his spent cock, seeing if there was a third time in him.

He squirmed and pushed me back, somehow rolling on top of me, still with his phone to his ear. "Louisa, I don't think I can," he said seriously. His eyes flickered between mine. "I have plans...well, they're important plans."

Then he climbed off me, sat cross-legged on my bed, still naked. "Louisa, Tom and I are going to see his parents," he said. "It's kind of important..." He ran his hand through his hair. "Well, actually, he's right here... Okay," he said slowly. "I'll put him on." Cooper frowned and held out his phone. "Louisa needs me to work this weekend."

I took the phone. "Hello, Louisa, it's Tom."

"Oh, Tom," she said into the phone. "How are you? Cooper talks about you all the time."

"I'm really well," I answered. I looked at the man in my bed. "Never better, actually. How are you? It's been a while."

"I'm great," she said. "I've been meaning to call you and thank you for recommending Cooper. He's really taken strides since he started."

"Yes, he has."

"Cooper says you have a family commitment this weekend," she said.

"We had plans, yes," I explained. "We were heading up to see my parents."

"You know we have the Philadelphia exhibition coming up," she said.

"Louisa, I can't tell him what to do, or make decisions on his behalf," I said. "I did that once and he tore shreds off me. But I can *suggest* to him, in my professional opinion, that it'd be in *his* professional interest to work. We can see my parents another time."

Cooper shook his head. "We said we'd go," he whispered.

Louisa said, "Tore shreds off you, did he?" I could hear the smile in her voice.

"Yes, it wasn't pretty."

She laughed. "He's a strong-minded one, isn't he?"

"You have no idea," I said with a smile.

Cooper snatched the phone off me and rolled his eyes.

"Louisa, can I call you back?" he asked into the phone. "Five minutes."

He threw his phone beside us on the bed and took my hand. "Tom, we agreed we'd go and see your parents."

"And your Philly exhibition is extremely important."

"So are you," he said quickly. "So is telling your parents."

I squeezed his hand and smiled. "Coop, sweetheart, we can go another weekend to see my parents, the date of your first exhibition can't change."

He sighed. "I don't want you to think — "

"I understand. I truly do." I lifted his hand to my lips and kissed his knuckles. "You've worked so hard on this job, you need to go."

He frowned and sighed again. "What will you do?"

I smiled at his concern that I couldn't possibly survive a weekend without him. "There's no reason why I can't go see my parents anyway," I told him. "I haven't spent much time with them lately, aside from the occasional phone call. It'll be nice."

He was quiet for a long few seconds. "Will you tell them?"

"I don't know," I answered honestly. "I'll test the waters first. I want to tell them. I need to tell them. I'd kind of psyched myself up for it to be this weekend, but I know I said we'd do it together."

"I want to be there for you," he said quietly. "In case…well, in case it doesn't go well."

"I'm a big boy," I said with a smile. "I love that you want to be there. But if I get there and the timing is right, I'll tell them. I want to tell them about you, that I finally met someone who understands me. It's not the oh-by-the-way-I'm-gay speech I want to tell them, it's that I met you. *That's* what I want to tell them."

He smiled shyly for me. "Maybe giving them some warning might be a good idea," he said. "Before we go up together."

"And you need to kick ass in Philly."

"I don't exactly have that much to do there," he said with a shrug.

"Louisa wants you to see the whole process," I presumed. "It'll be good experience for you."

He turned my hand over in his and pouted. "Will you miss me?"

I lay back on the bed and laughed. "Every minute."

"Just every minute?"

I reached over, picked up his phone and tossed it to him. "Call Louisa, I'll organize dinner."

I pulled on a pair of jeans and left him to make the call. After I'd ordered some takeout, I grabbed two beers from the fridge just as Cooper walked out. He was wearing a pair of my sleep pants.

I looked him up and down. "Not wearing those home, I hope."

"Not going home tonight."

I handed him a beer and kissed him lightly on the lips. "When do you leave for Philly?"

"First thing Saturday morning," he said. "So I might have to stay here Friday night as well."

I grinned. "I think you might."

* * * *

I offered to drive Cooper to the airport to save him the cab fare, so as a trade-off, he went for two takeaway coffees while I finished getting ready.

I told him I'd bring our overnight bags down to the car and when I got to the lobby, Cooper was walking back in with three coffees in a cardboard tray. He handed one to Lionel, who at first refused the offer, but then took it at Cooper's insistence.

I put the overnight bag and Cooper's satchel down, and Lionel jumped with a start. "Oh, let me get those for you, Mr. Elkin," he said quickly. He looked at the coffee he was holding, not sure where to put it.

"It's fine, Lionel," I said with a smile. "We're heading down to the parking lot."

"Are you heading out of town?" Lionel asked. "How long can I expect you gone?"

"Just overnight," Cooper answered. "I'm leaving first, then Tom will go before lunch, in different directions this time. Not sure how Tom will cope without me."

I rolled my eyes and took my coffee from him. "You can carry your own bags."

Cooper feigned offense. "Hey, I thought the elderly revered chivalry."

I looked at Lionel. "See what I have to put up with?"

Cooper nudged poor Lionel with his elbow. "And he absolutely wouldn't have it any other way."

Lionel hid his smile behind his coffee cup. "Well, I hope you both have an enjoyable weekend, even if it's in different directions."

Cooper walked over toward his bags and said, "Lionel, tell Mrs. Lionel I said hello. If she needs any more of that struffoli any time soon, you just let me know."

"Will do, Mr. Jones," Lionel said with a nod. "Thank you very much."

I shook my head at him and his ability to charm anyone. "You ready?"

He nodded and smiled handsomely. Then he picked up his overnight bag and held it out for me to carry. He batted his eyelids and with a sigh and dramatic eye roll, I took it with my free hand. He picked up his satchel, looked back at Lionel and grinned.

"You're such a little shit," I mumbled.

"It's a Gen Y thing," he said cheerfully.

"It's a Cooper Jones thing." Then I added, "It's a pain in the ass thing."

"You love the pain in your ass thing."

Knowing I would never win, I chose to give up on that line of conversation and pressed the elevator button to go to the parking lot instead. And as we got into the car and headed out into New York traffic, Cooper said, "You know, Mr. and Mrs. Lionel don't have kids."

"Mr. and Mrs. Lionel?" I asked. "You do know that's his first name?"

Cooper nodded. "Yeah, but I don't know his last name, or his wife's first name so I call them Mr. and Mrs. Lionel."

"Yet you know she likes struffoli?"

He smiled proudly. "Of course. It's all in the questions."

"Apparently you ask the wrong ones."

"Or the right ones," he said with a smirk. "Anyway, as I was saying, they don't have kids." Then he added thoughtfully, "I think they might want to adopt me."

I laughed at him. "You're incorrigible."

He smiled as though I'd complimented him. "It's a talent."

"It's one of your finest."

Cooper grinned at me. "So, are you going to see me off at the airport? Stand in the terminal lounge, staring out the window, waiting for my plane to take off?"

I snorted. "Um, no. I was going to drop you off at the departure terminal so I didn't have to get a parking spot."

He gaped and narrowed his eyes. "When you get home, do me a favor and Google the word chivalry," he said flatly. "It's spelled c-h-i-v —"

"Shut up," I said with a laugh.

"Or even look up the definition of 'nice boyfriend'. I'm pretty sure it says 'does not drop off loved one at terminal gate' or 'does not tell boyfriend to shut up'."

I laughed at him, but he smiled smugly when I turned into the ludicrously expensive parking lot instead of pulling up at the terminal doors. I even carried his bag *and* his satchel to the check-in counter.

"See, I know what chivalry means," I told him.

Cooper hooked his arm through mine. "And you do it well."

"Do I really have to wait until your plane leaves?"

"Maybe just until I board."

"Even that long?"

"Your chivalry is starting to wane."

"It comes and goes."

He rolled his eyes dramatically. "Oh, just like you. You came this morning, and now you want to go."

I barked out a laugh. "Okay, you win. I'll buy you another coffee."

"And a croissant."

I led him to a coffee shop in the terminal and it wasn't until he was about to board his plane that he was serious. "If you want to tell your parents today, then tell them. Do what feels right," he said. "If you think it won't go well, you can wait and we'll tell them together."

I pulled him in for a hug and kissed the side of his neck. "Thank you, Cooper. You have a good time down in Philly, show them what you can do."

He sighed against me. "Call me if you need to talk," he said. "About anything."

"You'll be so busy," I told him, pulling back so I could see his face. "How about you call me when you get to your hotel tonight? It doesn't matter what time."

"Okay," he agreed.

I knew exactly what he was about to say. "Don't apologize. Last time you saw my parents, at Ryan's birthday, you had to pretend we weren't together. The next time you see them, I want them to know exactly who you are."

"Oh, they'll love me," he said casually. "Everybody does. I'm more worried how they'll be with you."

I rolled my eyes and sighed loudly. "Go get on your plane. Before you take off, do me a favor and Google the word 'cranter'."

I could tell by the look on his face he didn't know what the word meant. I smiled and kissed him lightly. "Bye."

I hadn't even got the car out of the parking lot before my phone beeped with a message.

Your use of the Urban Dictionary is outstanding, smartass.

When I pulled up at traffic lights, I typed out my response. *Your proper nouns could use some work.*

From chivalry to insolent in twenty minutes.

I replied with his earlier comment to me. *It's a talent.*

I'm putting in my earphones and ignoring your insolent, gorgeous smartass.

I smiled as I typed out my response. *I love you too.*

* * * *

I smiled all the way home, packed my bag, and by the time I'd driven up the coast to my mom and dad's house, I was even more determined to tell them.

I wanted them to know about the person who challenged me, who drove me crazy, who made me laugh. Who loved me.

I wanted them to know. I knew they wouldn't take the news very well, but Cooper was worth it.

The closer I got to my parents' house, the more determined I was. But as I pulled into their street, everything changed. Because there were blue and red flashing lights, and an ambulance in their drive.

Chapter Twelve

I pulled up and raced out of the car to the back of the ambulance. My father was lying on the gurney, with an oxygen mask on his face marred by pale puffs of breath. He looked asleep as they loaded him in the back of the vehicle.

Despite my father obviously being unwell, I knew things really weren't good from the look on my mother's face. Her soft, ever-smiling face was etched with worry and stained with tears. There was a female paramedic standing beside her.

"Mom, what's wrong?" I asked, almost running to her. "What happened to Dad?"

Her eyes darted to her husband, then the paramedic gave me a sad smile. "You're Tom?" the woman asked. "Your mother said you'd be here soon."

"Yes," I answered. "Can you tell me what's going on? What's wrong with my father?"

"Your father has suffered what we suspect is a massive stroke," she answered. "We're taking him to hospital."

"Okay," I said rather stupidly, trying to process everything. "Which one?"

"South Hampton," the paramedic said, and she moved to the back of the ambulance.

Another paramedic gotten out from the back of the ambulance and gotten into the driver's side. She looked pointedly at Mom. "We need to go."

"Mom, you go with Dad in the ambulance," I said, ushering her toward the van.

She seemed unable to move.

"I'll lock the house up and meet you there. You go."

Mom blinked a few times. The paramedic kindly helped her into the back of the ambulance, the lights started to flash and they left.

And I stood there, staring at where they'd just been.

That wasn't how it was supposed to go at all.

I stood, lost, stuck, until my mind finally told my body to move. I ran inside, closed and locked windows and doors, grabbed my mother's handbag and keys and locked the front door behind me.

I don't remember the drive to the hospital.

When I gotten to the emergency room, after telling them who I was there to see, I was ushered through the double white doors, and found my mother, sitting, waiting, alone.

"They're working on him now," she said quietly. "He had another turn in the ambulance."

Fuck.

I took her hand and held it as tight as I dared.

"He said he was feeling funny this morning," she whispered. "Said he thought he should have a lie down. I took a cup of tea in to him not long after," she said, starting to cry. "But he couldn't move. He just stared at me."

I pulled my mom against me and held her while she sobbed quietly in my arms. And then a man in scrubs walked out to stand in front of us. "Mrs. Elkin," he said. "We're taking your husband in for surgery. He's had scans. There's considerable swelling on his brain and a blockage. We'll do everything we can..." His words trailed off.

"But?" I asked.

"But it doesn't look good," he replied gently.

My blood ran cold and my stomach knotted. I squeezed my mom's hand.

"If there's any other family you need to call..." he suggested, then turned and walked down the hall.

I let his words sink in for a long moment before I took my phone from my pocket. I scrolled through my contacts and hit call.

He picked up on the third ring. "Dad?"

"Yeah, Ryan, it's me," I said softly.

* * * *

It was a long, anxious wait sitting beside Mom in the waiting room, waiting for word, waiting for anything.

I was hoping Ryan would get there before the doctors came out to speak to us, but it didn't work out that way.

The same doctor as before walked out and I knew from the look on his face that the news wasn't good. He looked at me first, then to Mom, and he frowned. "I'm sorry," he started. "Your husband suffered a heart attack and with the blockage in the brain... We did everything we could."

Mom's hand went to her mouth and she started to cry, saying, "No, no, no," over and over. The doctor offered quiet condolences and as he left, Mom surprised me and stood up. "I want to see him."

The doctor looked at me, then back to the heartbroken woman in front of him. "Come with me," he said gently.

They disappeared through the doors he'd just came through, and again, I was left not knowing what to do.

My father was gone.

Forever.

He was only sixty-seven.

I heard a familiar voice and turned to see Ryan come down the hall. He was almost running, and his mother was behind him. Sofia must have driven him here. "Dad?" Ryan asked. "How is he?"

I stood up and I was pretty sure I didn't have to say. The look on my face must have said enough. I shook my head and said the hardest words I'd ever said to him, "He's gone."

Ryan's whole body sagged. "He what?"

"Your grandfather's gone," I said again. "It was a massive stroke."

Ryan shook his head, and looked disbelievingly from me to Sofia. His eyes welled with tears. "No."

I put my arms around him and held him while he cried. I looked at Sofia, who had fresh tears running down her cheeks. "Thank you for bringing him," I said softly. "Thank you."

She put her hand on my shoulder. "Are you okay, Tom?"

"I'll be fine," I answered, nodding weakly. I *had* to be fine. I needed to be strong. My mother and my son needed me and I had to be the strong one. I pulled back from Ryan and let him wipe his eyes with the back of his hands.

"Mom's just gone with the doctor," I told them, as we sat down in the waiting room chairs. "She wanted to see him before... She wanted to see him."

239

Ryan nodded. "Where's Cooper?"

"He's in Philadelphia," I told him in a whisper. "He left this morning for the green energy convention he's been working on."

Ryan wiped at his nose and nodded. "That's right. I forgot." Then he said, "What do we do now? With Grandpa? And Grandma? What happens?"

"I don't know," I answered honestly. "I'll see what Mom wants to do. I might suggest she comes home with me, but knowing her she'll want to go home."

"If you need me to do anything," Sofia said softly. "Please, just ask."

I gave her a nod. Sofia always loved my parents, and they loved her, so it really wasn't surprising that she'd offered to help. It wasn't surprising that she was here. She would take the loss of my father similar to the loss of her own.

My mom walked through the door, strangely composed though she looked like she'd aged a decade.

Ryan, Sofia and I all stood to meet her, and it was Ryan who was the first to hug her, then Sofia then me. I knew my mom would probably just like to go home, but I didn't want her to be alone. "Mom," I said gently. "How about you stay with me tonight? You can have Ryan's room. I don't think you should be alone tonight."

Her bottom lip trembled, and all she did was nod. She didn't want to leave Dad, she didn't want to go home without him. I understood that, and I was helpless to do anything about it.

I put my arm around her and led her out to my car. The drive to the city, to my place was quiet, the both of us lost in our own thoughts. Through all of this, with my grieving mother in the seat next to me, all I could think about was Cooper.

I needed him.

I felt selfish for wanting him. I wanted to call him, I wanted to talk to him, I wanted to hear his voice. I just needed him.

But I couldn't.

He couldn't do anything by being here. He just had one day away for work, and he'd be back tomorrow.

I could hold out until then.

I gotten Mom inside my apartment, and Ryan and Sofia followed us in. Mom didn't want anyone to fuss, she didn't want to eat, she didn't want anything.

Just my dad.

I'd never felt more helpless.

Everyone was hurting and I couldn't do anything. I ordered food that no one ate, I only seemed to say the wrong thing, or not enough, or too much.

Mom said the doctor had given her a few pills to help her sleep tonight. I couldn't protest, I couldn't tell her she hadn't eaten all day, I couldn't say anything. I just gave her a hug, tucked her into bed and told her we'd deal with tomorrow together.

When I walked back into the kitchen, Sofia and Ryan both stood up and looked at me. "How is she?" Ryan asked.

"I think she's in shock," I told them. "Dad was fine at breakfast, and now he's gone. That has to be hard for anyone."

Ryan walked over to me. "You okay, Dad?"

No. No, I wasn't. "Yeah, I'm okay." I looked at both Ryan and Sofia. "You don't have to stay…" I was fighting to keep it together, swallowing back tears.

Then Sofia, who had been relatively quiet the entire day, came over to me and put her arms around me. It was kind and familiar, and it should have comforted me.

But it felt wrong.

She was soft and gentle, smelled floral and womanly, when all I wanted was firm and hard and the smell of cologne.

I pulled out of her embrace and took a step away. I swallowed hard, and took a shaky breath.

"Tom, do you want us to stay?" she asked, looking a little concerned.

"No," I answered, trying not to cry. "I mean, you can if you want, but I'll be fine."

I didn't want to be rude. Sofia had been very gracious today, very kind and supportive.

But she wasn't who I needed.

I walked around my ex-wife toward the sofa when there was a familiar sound of jingling keys in the lock of the front door.

I looked at Ryan.

"I called him," he said. "For you."

I turned back to the door as Cooper walked in. He looked worried, urgent, like he'd run all the way from Philly. He didn't look at anyone else, he put his bag on the floor and never took his eyes off me.

I'd never needed someone so fucking much.

There was a burning in my eyes and a heavy relief in my chest. I couldn't fight the tears, and a quiet sob escaped me.

Cooper crossed the floor and pulled me against him. He wrapped his arms around me, and I buried my face in his neck. He had one hand around my back and the other holding my head. I'd never held anyone so tight. My hands fisted the back of his suit jacket and he held me while I cried.

He fit against me perfectly. He felt right—his arms, his smell. Everything. He was…everything.

I didn't want to let go, but eventually pulled back and wiped at my face. "I'm sorry you had to leave work. I'm sorry you had to come back," I said quietly. "But I'm so glad you're here."

Cooper nodded and wiped my face with his hands. "Tom, I'm so sorry."

"Thank you for being here," I whispered.

He held my face and kissed my cheek then my forehead. He replied softly in my ear, "I couldn't be anywhere else."

I looked around then, at Ryan and Sofia, who were looking at Cooper and me. Cooper looked at Ryan, and didn't hesitate. He took a few quick strides to him and hugged him too. "Thank you for calling me," he told him. "I'm really sorry, Ry."

Ryan hugged him back, and Cooper looked at Sofia. He walked slowly over to her. "Mrs. Elkin," he said gently. "I'm very sorry for your loss."

Sofia gave him a small, kind, but genuine smile. "Thank you, Cooper."

Then Cooper came back to me. He slid one hand around my jaw and gave me a quick kiss on the cheek. He wiped my face dry with his thumbs. "Have you eaten? Can I get you a drink of wine? A coffee?"

I smiled, despite my tears, and put my hand on his chest. "I'm so glad you're here."

Cooper took my hand and led me to the sofa. "You guys sit down. I'm sure you have a lot of things to discuss," he said to us. "I'll make some hot tea."

He just took charge. He tidied up, put the leftover, uneaten dinner in the fridge and came back with a tray of herbal tea and cups.

"When my grandma died," he explained softly, "my mom served a lot of chamomile and peppermint tea. It's supposed to be calming and good for the soul." He sat down next to me and started to pour some of the hot brew into one of the four cups, then he stopped and looked up. "I think that's the gayest thing I've ever said."

Ryan snorted out a laugh, which made me chuckle. Even Sofia smiled. It was a much-needed release from the tears and the grief.

Cooper finished pouring the tea and I told him my mom was asleep in the spare room. We weren't sure what tomorrow would bring, but we'd deal with it the best we could.

He sat particularly close to me, with one leg tucked up underneath him, a part of him always touching me. Just having him there was a relief, like I could somehow bear the loss of my father if Cooper was with me.

The weight of the day, the irreparable loss, finally settled over me. I was suddenly exhausted and could barely keep my eyes open. When I stifled a yawn, Cooper suggested I go to bed.

He gave my leg a squeeze, gotten up from the sofa, then cleared away the tray and the tea. Cooper disappeared down the hall, came back with linen and kicked us off the sofa so Ryan and Sofia would have somewhere to sleep. I think his insistence might have surprised Sofia, but Ryan and I weren't surprised at all.

I offered to help, but he shooed me away. "You go in and have a hot shower," he said gently. "It will make you feel better. I'll get this all sorted."

I loved his ability to just take charge, to know I needed someone to take care of things, to take care of me. And he just did it. He just knew.

I stood under the stream of the hot water and the realization that I'd lost my father hit me again. My own mortality hit me. How quickly life could change, how it could be changed forever in a heartbeat. I worried about my mother, how she would cope, how she would get through this.

Selfishly, I wondered how my life would change after today. Would my mom need to live with me? What would that mean for me and Cooper?

I shut off the water, and as I gotten dressed into sleep pants and a T-shirt, I could hear someone was in the other shower in the main bathroom. Then I could hear two voices coming from the living room.

Soft voices, and at first I assumed it was Cooper and Ryan. But as I gotten to the hallway, I realized it was Cooper and Sofia.

I knew I shouldn't have been listening. It was a private conversation. But it sounded amicable, so I stood there, where they couldn't see me, and listened.

"Did he really ask you to move in with him?" Sofia asked.

"Yes," Cooper answered honestly. "Several times."

"Why did you say no?"

Cooper laughed. "I like to keep him on his toes."

"But you want to move in with him?" Sofia asked.

I thought about moving, walking out so they'd hear me. I wasn't sure I wanted to hear his answer. I didn't think I could cope with hearing why. But then he spoke.

"Of course I do," he said quietly. "I love him."

My heart swelled in my chest at his words, my eyes filled with tears as I smiled.

"You know," Sofia started, "I've known Tom for a long time. Since we were kids ourselves. We've been through a lot," she said. "I've been with him through everything— the highs and lows of his career, parenthood..."

I wondered where she was going with this, and I almost interrupted them.

But then she let out a nervous breath. "But tonight, when you walked into this apartment, when he saw you…the way he looked at you…" She paused for a moment and her voice was quiet. "In all the years we were together, not once did he ever look at me like that."

"Sofia…" Cooper started to speak.

"It's okay, Cooper," she said. "Really, it is. In a way, I'm glad."

"Glad?"

Sofia sighed again. "When I first learnt that he and you were… Well, I thought it was just some fling. I thought it was something he'd get over," she admitted. "But I can see now that it's not."

"No, it's not," he replied. His tone was soft and agreeable.

"So I'm glad," she repeated. "I'm glad he has you."

The water from Ryan's shower cut off, and so I wasn't caught eavesdropping in the hallway, I had to move. I walked out into the living room. Cooper and Sofia were sitting at the dining table, and he stood up when I walked in. "Feel a bit better?"

I smiled at him. "Yeah, but I should go to bed. No doubt Mom will be up with the sun in the morning." Sliding my hand along Cooper's arm, I gave him a soft kiss.

"I won't be long," he whispered.

I mouthed the words "I love you" so only he could see, then I kissed Sofia on the forehead. "Thank you for being here," I told her. And I meant it.

I said a quiet goodnight to Ryan as he walked out, gave him a hug, and I climbed into bed. As exhausted as I was, as emotionally drained as I was, I closed my eyes but sleep wouldn't come.

Soon after, familiar, strong arms wrapped around me and I turned to face him. It was only when Cooper tucked me into his side, and kissed my forehead, that I fell into sleep.

Chapter Thirteen

I woke up and smiled at Cooper's sleeping form beside me. Then I remembered the events of yesterday — that my father had died.

My stomach knotted and my heart sank.

Then I remembered my mother was asleep in the room across the hall.

It was still early, so I threw on some jeans and a shirt and set about making breakfast.

Cooper, sleep-rumpled and gorgeous, woke up at the scent of coffee. Ryan woke up at the smell of toast. Sofia smiled at the both of them playfully bickering over who would eat first as she packed up the bed linen from the sofas in the living room.

I worried Cooper might find it weird that he was having breakfast with my son and my ex-wife, but he seemed to take it all in stride. He took over the kitchen like he owned it, finishing up cooking and cleaning.

But then my mother walked out to where we were. She looked like hell. Her eyes were red and puffy, she was pale and...heartbroken.

I walked over to her and gave her a hug. "Coffee?" I asked, and she nodded.

She sat down on the sofa, and when I glanced over at Cooper, he seemed nervous. He grabbed a coffee cup and before he could pour it, Sofia was beside him. "Go," she murmured.

It was then that my mother looked to who else was there. Her eyes landed on Cooper.

I cleared my throat. "Ah, Mom?" I said, and she looked at me. "I want you to meet someone."

Cooper's eyes darted to mine, but he walked around the kitchen island bench, nervously wiping the palms of his hands on his thighs.

I took Cooper's hand and we sat down across from my mother. "Mom, this is Cooper Jones," I said. I figured there was no easy way to say this, and there was no point in beating around the bush. "Cooper and I are together, Mom. We're dating."

My mother blinked. And then blinked again.

"I'm gay, Mom," I told her. "I know the timing is horrible. I know you're dealing with a lot right now, but in light of yesterday…with Dad… I don't want to wait another day. I don't want to keep any secrets from you."

Mom was quiet, unmoving.

"I'm in love with Cooper," I told her gently. "And life's too damn short, Mom."

Cooper squeezed my hand, just as Sofia brought over a cup of coffee and handed it to Mom. Then Sofia sat down next to my mother and squeezed her hand.

Mom looked at her. "You know about this?"

"I do," Sofia said with a gentle smile. "It's okay. I didn't take it well at first, I'll admit to that. But yesterday, well, yesterday I saw them in a different light."

Mom looked at Cooper then, studied him for a long moment then looked at me. "A boy?"

"Not a boy," I corrected softly. "A man. And yes."

Mom put her coffee down on the side table untouched. "You're telling me this today?"

"Today especially," I said softly. My eyes burned with unshed tears. I didn't want this to go to badly. I knew the timing was awful, but I had to tell her. She had to know. "Today especially, Mom. After yesterday…losing Dad… Mom, if there was ever a day to tell you how much I loved someone, then today is it."

Mom's lip trembled, and she blinked back tears. Deciding to ignore my point of conversation altogether, she picked up her coffee again with shaking hands and said, "I need to call the hospital, I guess. I need to make a lot of calls and tell people…"

"Mom, I can phone them," I offered. "Just tell me who you want me to call."

Then Mom started to talk about letting the Country Club know, and an aunt who lived on the West Coast, and how Julia, her next-door neighbor, must be worried sick.

"I'll take you home if you want," I said softly.

"Would you, dear?" she said. "I have a lot to do." Then her eyes welled with tears. "I'm not sure how I'll do it without him…"

Ryan walked around then, and hugged his grandma. "We're here to help you," he said. "All of us." I couldn't help but smile at Ryan's inclusion of Cooper, and I squeezed Cooper's hand.

"I'll just go freshen up first," Mom said before she stood, leaving us all in the living room and walked down the hall.

Cooper ran his hand up my back and into my hair, and he pulled me against him. "I'm sorry," I whispered to him.

He kissed the side of my head and whispered, "Don't apologize."

Sofia stood up. "I can take her home, if you'd like, Tom."

For a moment, I considered it. "I'll take her," I said. "But thank you for the offer." I looked at Cooper. "I just wish I didn't have to leave you."

"You need to go," he said with serious eyes. "You need to be with your mom."

As much as I needed to be with Cooper, I needed to be with my Mom more. "What will you do?"

"He'll come home with me," Ryan interrupted. "I have a new Xbox 3D that needs playing," he went on to say. Then he shrugged. "And I could use the company."

Cooper smiled, and looked at Ryan, Sofia then me. "Don't worry about me, silly. You go, take care of your mom."

I think everyone knew I was worried about how I'd be without him, not the other way around, but no one acknowledged it out loud.

Five minutes later, I kissed Cooper soundly, told them I'd call each of them, and took my mother home.

We spent the day making phone calls, and making arrangements. It was emotionally draining, and by the time Mom put herself to bed, I didn't want to leave her in the house alone.

I called Ryan then Sofia, like I said I would, then I called Cooper. I spoke in a whisper, not wanting to wake my mother, but desperately needing to hear his voice.

I told him I wouldn't be back for another night at least, that I'd call the office in the morning and request a week's leave. "They're hoping to have the funeral on Thursday," I told him. "Do you think you could come with me?"

"Oh, Tom," he whispered into the phone. "Of course I'll be there."

I sighed, almost with relief, knowing he'd be with me. "I miss you," I said rather pathetically.

"Babe, I'm just a phone call away," he replied. "But if you need me to come there, I'll leave right now."

I smiled sadly into the phone. "Just hearing your voice is enough. But thank you."

"You sound tired," he said softly. "Don't hang up. Go to bed, and we can talk again when you're ready for sleep."

I walked into the guest bedroom and leaving my jeans on the floor, I climbed into bed, and we talked.

Quietly, tenderly, without any physical contact, we spoke for hours. Cooper knew I needed him on some level, like he always just knew.

I loved him, this man who was half my age and twice as strong as me.

I'd never loved him more.

* * * *

The next morning, I called work and spoke to Robert Chandler and explained I needed some time off. He sent warm, honest condolences and told me to take as much time as I needed. Then I spent the rest of the day at the hospital and it was that night it really hit my mom that my dad was gone.

She cried and cried and spent the entire evening wandering around the house, trying to keep busy. She had phone call after phone call of people with good intentions, but in the end I started answering the phone for her.

It was a restless night, but Tuesday was marginally better. I spent the entire time with her, rarely leaving her side, yet she never once mentioned my little coming out speech, and she never mentioned Cooper.

It wasn't surprising. It was typical of my mother to ignore subjects she didn't want to discuss. I did mention Cooper in conversation a few times, but she never asked me anything. It was hardly the time to bring it up. She knew I was gay, she knew I was in love with someone special, and that was all I wanted.

By Tuesday evening, I couldn't put it off any longer. I needed to go home, back to New York. I needed to get clothes for the funeral, so Mom's neighbor Julia kindly offered to stay with her. I drove straight back to the city, and didn't even bother going home.

I drove straight to Cooper's.

He opened the door to his shoebox apartment and the second he saw me, he pulled me straight into his arms.

He was like fucking oxygen to drowning lungs.

He took me straight to bed, holding me so damn tight as he made love to me. He kissed me so reverently, he wiped my tears and his eyes never left mine as he rocked his hips into mine. He filled me so completely — physically, emotionally.

He just knew. He knew exactly what I needed, and he gave it to me without question.

I woke with my face to his chest, and his long fingers tracing circles on my back. He had to go to work, and I had to go back to Mom's. But with a soft kiss and a whispered 'I love you' we went our separate ways.

I was kept busy with final funeral arrangements, and organizing the wake. I spoke to Cooper briefly on the phone Wednesday night, and by the time we were ready for the funeral on Thursday, I was just about ready to unravel.

Mom wanted to get to the church early. She wanted to be there to greet the good people as they came in. All things considered, she was coping quite well. It was the first time in two days that I'd had time to stop, and standing alone beside a flower-covered casket didn't help.

I said somber hellos and thanks to the people who came in, lots of faces I recognized, lots I didn't. Most surprising was two very familiar faces from work—Jennifer and Robert had wanted to show their support in being there for me. I'd worked with them for a decade, and I was touched very deeply with their presence.

Then Sofia walked in, looking lovely and impeccably dressed, and she gave me a sad smile. Behind her was Ryan, all suited up, then behind him was Cooper.

Wearing a black suit, his hair styled and clean shaven, he walked into the fast-filling church and he visibly sighed when he saw me.

I can't begin to describe the relief I felt when I saw him. It rocked me. I took a steadying breath and blinked back tears.

Sofia gave me a soft pat on the arm and took a seat at the end of the front row. Ryan gave me a hug and took his seat next to his mother, then Cooper was standing in front of me.

I didn't care that people were watching. I didn't care what they thought. I hugged him, and I hugged him hard. It wasn't a family-friend hug, it wasn't a thanks-for-coming hug. It was an embrace.

Cooper pulled back and whispered, "You'll be okay."

"I will now," I told him.

Cooper took a seat next to Ryan, and when my mom came in, I put my arm around her and led her to the front row. I sat next to Cooper and took his hand immediately, and slid my other arm around my mom as the funeral started.

The priest talked of a well-loved man, whose life was cut far too short. He spoke of family, loss and of acceptance and love, and when he said I'd be getting up to talk to the congregation, I didn't hear him call my name.

"Tom?" Cooper said quietly beside me. "Did you want to get up and talk?"

"Oh," I said, apparently a million miles away.

"You don't have to," he said, concerned. "Everyone will understand."

"No, I'm okay," I told him then I stood up and walked up to the parapet. I ran the prepared notes through my head, and when I looked at the faces staring back at me, all the words in my head were gone.

I glanced over at the priest, and exhaled through puffed cheeks. "I, um," I started. "When I was asked if I'd like to say something in honor of my father, I said I would. Of course I would." I swallowed hard. "But what I was going to say doesn't seem fitting.

"My father was a good man. A good father, a good husband and a good friend," I told them. "My father was one of the biggest influences in my life. He hated architecture," I said, and a few people smiled. "He told me I should get into banking, or teaching, but I followed my heart. And it was his initial disapproval that pushed me to be the best. I didn't want to disappoint him."

My gaze fell on Cooper then, and I swallowed back my tears. If only my father knew how much I would have disappointed him...

I shook my head and took a deep breath, so I could keep talking. "But funnily enough, my dad and architecture were a lot alike. And whether he knew it or not, he taught me more about architecture than college ever could."

I looked at my mother, then at Ryan and Sofia. "He taught me that solid foundations gave me strength and stability. He taught me that the only principles of design should be honesty and integrity, and above all, that there was a truth in the lines that we drew."

Finally I looked back at Cooper and had to blink back tears. "It's unfortunate that some of life's greatest lessons come from death. Because without knowing it, my father taught me that *every* design has a clarity of lines. Lines that bind it, that define it, that make it— lines that sometimes other people can't see." I scanned the faces around the church then, not ashamed of my tears. "And that's what I'll take with me—what my father taught me. That sometimes the lines seemed undefined, but they aren't blurred at all. Sometimes they are crystal clear."

I thanked everyone for coming, to help celebrate the life of a good man, then I walked back to my seat and slid my arm around my crying mother. Cooper took my hand and held it tight, and for the rest of the service, he never let it go.

Throughout the wake, Cooper was never far away. I didn't care if distant relatives, work colleagues or complete strangers saw me with my arm around his waist, or if they saw the way I looked at him.

Life was too damn short.

We'd done the rounds of talking and thanking the guests, and after many stories of my father's life, the crowd eventually waned. Mom had tired quickly, and when I had suggested I take her home and stay with her, Sofia put her hand on my arm. "I'll take her. I'll spend the night with her. You should go," she said with a kind smile.

"Are you sure?"

"Of course I'm sure," she said. "You look tired, Tom. Let Cooper take you home."

I hugged her, taking her off guard, and I thanked her. Her final acceptance of Cooper in my life meant the world to me.

Then Cooper hugged her as well. "Thank you, Sofia," he said softly.

We said goodbye to Ryan, and Cooper took my keys and told me he was driving. I didn't even argue. Instead, I half turned in my seat so I faced him, and watched him while he drove. He held my hand over the console and after a little while, he told me he'd had a few talks with Sofia these last few days.

He told me of the conversation I'd half over-heard, about how she could see now that we were the real deal. She admitted to him the age difference between us had worried her, but she knew now it didn't matter.

"Plus, she thinks I'm charming and handsome and awesome," Cooper said.

"She did not say that," I said tiredly.

"I'm paraphrasing," he said.

Leaning my head against the headrest, not taking my eyes off him, I smiled. "God, I've missed you."

Cooper smiled and squeezed my hand. "We're almost home. Do you want dinner? A bath? Alcohol?"

I shook my head. "Nothing. I just want to be with you."

He pulled the car into the parking lot then took the elevator straight to our floor. He threw the keys to my car onto the kitchen counter and led me down the hall to my bedroom.

He took of his jacket then helped me out of mine. "Does it feel good to be home?"

"It does," I agreed. "It's weird though," I told him.

Cooper undid his shirt. "What's weird?"

"I'm the next in line now. Genealogically speaking, father-to-son, I should be the next one to go."

Cooper shook his head. "No. Don't say that."

"Not now," I amended. "Just...next. Now that my dad's gone, like his father before him, and his before that."

Cooper frowned and he started to undo the buttons on my shirt. "I called my dad," he said. "After... When you took your mom back to her house and after Ry and Sofia left and I was alone here, I called him."

"Really?"

He nodded. "I didn't want to leave things bad between us. I mean, the last time we spoke wasn't exactly on the best of terms." His brow pinched. "I told him about your dad... I told him I didn't want that to be us. I'm sorry if that sounds bad..."

"I understand, Cooper," I told him honestly. "And he was okay?"

Cooper nodded and gave me a small smile. "Better. He was better."

I slid my hand around his neck and pulled him in for a kiss. "That's great."

He smiled and went to put my pants and jacket on a hanger, but felt the folded paper in my breast pocket. "What's this?" he said, as he passed the handwritten notes to me.

"It's the speech I was going to say at the funeral," I said with a shrug. "Instead, I just...spoke from the heart. What I said at the funeral probably didn't make much sense."

Cooper stopped undressing and put his hand to my face. "What you said in the church made a lot of sense," he murmured. "It was beautiful."

I nodded then undressed down to my briefs, pulled back the bedcovers and gotten into bed. Cooper quickly joined me, lying on his side, facing me.

I took his hand and played with his fingers. "These last few months, people have judged us, told us that us being together is wrong, just because I'm twice your age, or if they think it's just some fling," I told him. "I wanted to tell people that the lines aren't blurred for me. I know exactly what I want. And having my father taken away so suddenly was like a wake-up call for me."

"Your speech was lovely," he said simply, threading his fingers through mine. Then after a quiet moment, he asked, "What were you going to say? What was written on the piece of paper?"

"It was just some childhood memories of my father," I told him. "It was nice to relive those memories, but no one really wants to hear those kinds of stories at funerals. They mean a lot to me, but not to anyone else."

"Tell me," Cooper said softly. "Tell me your childhood memories, like what was your favorite memory of your dad when you were little."

I leaned in and kissed him lightly. "You're amazing, you know that?"

"Yes, I do," he said with a smile. "It's a Cooper Jones thing, remember?"

"How could I forget," I said, and for the next little while, until I couldn't fight sleep any longer, I relived childhood memories of a boy and his father.

* * * *

Two weeks later, it was a Saturday and I was drawing at the drafting board in the living room. Cooper said he had some errands to run in the morning, but had arrived not long after lunch and threw himself onto the sofa.

He was agitated, which was very un-Cooper-like. "You know, you haven't asked me to live with you for a while."

I smiled at the board. "I got sick of hearing no."

He tapped his fingers on the arm of the chair. "I kept saying no because you kept asking me wrong. Did you want to try it again?"

"Is your lease finishing?" I asked with a smile, putting my graphite pencil down. "Is that why you want to move in with me? Is this some Gen Y, the-world-revolves-around-me thing?"

He sighed dramatically. "Oh, Tom. You're getting the move-in-with-me speech wrong *again*."

I laughed at him, but realizing he was finally asking me to do this, I quickly walked over and knelt between his legs. I looked up at him. "Move in with me, Cooper. I want to go to sleep with you, I want to wake up next to you. Every day. I want to live with you, I want to know everything about you. I want you to show me how you see the world." Then I added, "I want to show you things like the different architecture all around the world, all the amazing places. I want to share *that* with you. You are perfect for me, Cooper." I sat back on my haunches and shrugged. "You've changed me, and I don't want to live without you."

He smiled slowly.

"Did I get it right that time?"

He nodded. "And just so you know, I have a month left on the lease on my apartment, but I've given notice. I'm completely packed and ready to move in."

Grinning, I leaned up and pecked his lips. "A little confident that I'd still want you to live with me, yes?"

He closed his eyes and smiled. "It's a Gen Y thing."

"It's a Cooper Jones thing."

"No, it's an I-love-you thing."

"It's an I-love-you-too thing."

"So are we doing the whole-live-in-boyfriend thing?"

"Yes."

He grinned. "Lionel will be so stoked."

"Are you moving in here because you have a crush on the doorman?"

"No, no," he said, like I'd missed the point. "He has a crush on me."

"You're incorrigible."

Cooper leaned forward and kissed me with smiling lips. "You really shouldn't talk about your live-in-boyfriend like that."

I sighed. "There really is no point in arguing, is there?"

He shook his head. "No. But Tom?"

"Yeah?"

"Don't ever stop arguing with me."

"I won't."

"Promise?"

"Promise."

Epilogue

Cooper

My cell phone rang. It was my dad's number. My heart leaped and sank at the same time. I'd called him after Tom's father had died, telling him perspective put a new light on things, and he'd seemed to agree. I refused to apologize for falling in love — not that he asked me to apologize — but it was really only time that would tell if he was truly okay with me and Tom. And that's why I was nervous.

"Hey," I answered.

"Hiya." He sounded upbeat. "How's things?"

"Good, good."

"Settling in to domestic life okay?"

I snorted. "Just fine. How's things with you?"

He launched into telling me about some dinner Mom was making him go to, and he wanted some tips on any serious illness he could fake to get out of going. So in between suggestions of chest pains, spider bites and actually growing a set of cojones we were back to good.

Just like old times. I sat my ass on the sofa, put my bare feet on the coffee table and laughed with my dad.

It was such a relief, such a weight off my chest, that even after we'd said our goodbyes and disconnected the call, I sat there and smiled at the wall for a while. I couldn't wait to tell Tom.

Eventually I got up and padded around the apartment. Well, it was Tom's apartment, where I now called home. I'd officially lived there a week. Just seven days. My things—the few things that I owned—were here, looking all sorts of cheap and tacky compared to Tom's expensive and classical taste. The differences stood out ridiculously.

But Tom refused to hide them. "They remind me that you live here," he'd said. Then he'd looked around our bedroom at all my clothes and shit on the floor. "Not that I could ever forget."

But he was serious. He wanted my things here on display as much as his own, and the truth was Tom didn't see my belongings as inferior in any way. They belonged to me and that was enough for him to want to show them off proudly.

And people wondered why I loved him?

I picked up my dirty socks and threw them in the clothes hamper. I really had to make more of an effort now. Be more grown up, I supposed. Tom might think my clothes strewn across the bedroom was cute now, but there would no doubt be a time when it would piss him off, and I just didn't want that day to come.

So I tidied up everything then collected my suits and shirts ready for dry cleaning, then seeing Tom's, I added his to mine and called for a service collection. I didn't go as far as cleaning the bathrooms or anything. I didn't have to. Tom had cleaners for that.

Such luxury would never get old.

Nothing in this apartment would ever cease to blow my mind. Tom included.

He was with Ryan and Sofia, having lunch downtown. He'd asked me to join them of course, but I wanted him to have some alone time with them. Especially with the death of his father just over two weeks ago, they needed to decompress and take some time to be together, just the three of them.

Tom had kissed me and whispered, "Thank you." Whether he was thanking me for understanding, or thanking me for just being fucking awesome, I wasn't sure. It could have very well been both.

I'd just pulled his chin between my thumb and forefinger and kissed his lips. "Be home at two, and be alone," I'd told him. My voice had been gruff and dripping with sexual promise.

I couldn't help it. I was a twenty-two-year-old gay guy living with the sexiest man on the fucking planet. I was horny all the damn time. It was Tom's fault completely. He stimulated my mind and my body equally.

My boss, Louisa, benefited from the former, Tom from the latter. Not that he minded. Hell, he didn't mind at all.

My plan was for him to come home and find me, stark naked and ass up on the bed, ready and waiting. I wanted him to fuck me for hours, and when he was done fucking me, he could damn well fuck me some more.

But I lost track of time. It was the first time I'd really been in the apartment by myself for any great length of time and somewhere between spending an hour on the balcony overlooking my kingdom—which some folk liked to call New York City—and going through Tom's wardrobe seeing which of his suits might fit me, time just got away from me.

I'd barely got myself douched in the bathroom before I heard his key in the front door.

Shit, shit, shit.

I quickly pulled on my jeans and went out to see him. He stopped when he saw me, his eyes were dark and focused, and he looked a little peeved.

"Hey. What's up?" I asked.

He put his keys on the table as he walked in. "Be home by two." He repeated my earlier demand, striding over to me. "Be alone." He walked around me and sniffed me.

Was he smelling the douche? Jesus. My dick stirred.

He huffed his disapproval, his voice was deep and low when he whispered, "Your promise had me distracted all lunch and I come home to find you not naked."

Oh, wow. That demanding tone in his voice buzzed straight to my cock. "I ran out of time," I offered meekly, playing along. I went to undo my jeans fly, but he stopped me.

"Leave them on."

I did as I'd been told, trying not to smile.

He stood in front of me, put a finger under my chin so I looked up at him. His eyes were on fire, making me swallow hard, then he almost—almost—pressed his lips to mine. But he didn't. He teased, taunted instead of touched, and withholding the kiss I craved, he said, "Go stand at the drafting table."

Oh, holy fuck.

Now, I'd never let anyone boss me around but this…this was different. *This* was about to be a whole lotta fun.

I walked slowly over to the drafting board and stood facing it, hands by my sides. I could feel his eyes on me, every hair on the back of my neck was on end, my dick was hard and my skin flushed warm with a promise of what was to come.

He waited a long moment, and I wondered if he was about to laugh and this game would be over, but he didn't. I turned to find him walking from the hall with a silver foil packet and lube in his hand.

"Turn around," he demanded.

I quickly did as he'd said. My skin prickled with gooseflesh and my nipples hardened. I widened my stance and rolled my hips so my ass stuck out more. Fuck. This was too good.

He stood behind me, close enough that I could feel the warmth of his body, but he didn't touch me.

"Grip the top of the board," he said, all gruff like sex and honey.

Every cell in my body caught fire at his words. He knew this was a fantasy of mine—I'd told him it was. We'd had sex against the drafting board before, but my fantasy wasn't just having sex. It was him taking me, dominating me, fucking me so damn hard… And holy Jesus, he was making it happen. Aching in all the right places, I bit back a moan. I reached up over my head and gripped the top of the drafting board.

He pressed himself against me then. "Keep your hands up there." He reached around to my front and undid my jeans, deliberately brushing against my hard-on, then he roughly pulled the denim down over my ass.

"Fuck," I whispered, and I could feel my blood pump hot through my whole body. I was so turned on.

Tom put his legs between mine and shoved my feet out wider still. My jeans were tight across my thighs, my ass exposed, and I let my head fall forward with a moan.

Like every sense was on keen alert, I heard the pop of the lube bottle and the sound made my skin tingle. Then his slick fingers were rubbing over my hole and pushing inside me. I cried out, not because he was rough or hurt me, but because it wasn't enough. It was torture. The very best kind of torture.

"I know what you want," he murmured in my ear, sliding in a second finger. I lifted my ass to give him more access. It felt so good, so very fucking good, but it still wasn't enough — and he knew it.

Then his fingers were gone and I heard him undo his fly, and I almost came right then. He never took his boots off, so I knew his jeans were still on, only opened at the fly. I heard the foil packet rip open and my body instinctively pushed my ass out. God I wanted him inside me, like I never had before.

He pressed the head of his blunt cock against my ass and his breath was hot in my ear. "This what you want?"

All I could do was nod.

And he thrust inside me. Hard and deep, he grunted and groaned, and his hands gripped my hips as he buried every inch of his cock in me. Then his hands, his oh-so talented hands, raked roughly up my sides, up my outstretched arms and held my hands over the drafting board.

"Fuck," he cried out, gruff and hot, as he started to thrust.

He wasn't gentle. He fucked me. He fucked me like I wanted him to, needed him to. I was so stretched and full, my arms reaching out above my head and my toes barely on the floor as he drove up and into me, over and over.

I tried to pull my hand down so I could grip my aching dick, but he forcefully grabbed both my hands and held them in one of his at the edge of the drafting board. He took hold of my cock in his now-free hand, and jerked me hard and fast as he filled my ass.

I wanted to tell him to never stop, to keep doing exactly fucking that, but I couldn't even speak. All I could do was groan as I came. My orgasm obliterated my insides, pleasure so intense and hot barreled through me, and he never stopped fucking. I let my head fall back against his shoulder, my body completely at his will — he owned me. I was his. I never had any doubt.

He grunted in my ear, words I couldn't understand, and he roared as he climaxed. His cock surged and swelled inside me, and I could feel his knees and thighs shake before he leaned against me, spent. Exhausted.

I felt him grin against my back before groaning as he pulled out of me. I turned around as he threw the condom in the wastepaper bin, and ignoring the wonderful ache in my ass, I cupped his face and kissed him. When I wrapped my arms around him, he kind of fell into me, pressing my back against the drafting board.

He was all slow and languid, his eyes barely open. He had a blissed-out look on his face. "You okay?" he asked, his voice husky and low.

I snorted and held him tighter. "I'm so fucking better than okay right now."

I pushed him back a little so I could grab his hand. I led him down the hall to our room, my jeans still around my thighs, his softening dick still heavy and glistening, hanging free, and I pulled him onto the bed and snuggled into him.

"I'm still dressed," he mumbled. "Should probably shower."

"Mh mm," I protested, holding him right where was. "Nap first, you can fuck me again later."

He snorted, his eyes still closed, and relaxed. "Haven't you had enough?"

"Never."

"You're insatiable."

"Can't help it," I said, drowsily. "My live-in boyfriend is really fucking hot."

He smiled against my forehead. "Is he just?"

"Yeah, and I want to spend the rest of the day with his dick in my ass."

Tom opened his eyes at that. They took a second to focus. "Is that right?"

"Yep."

"Do you always get what you want?"

I grinned, closed my eyes and snuggled in warm against him. "You've met me, right?"

He laughed, a deep rumbling sound in my ear. "It's that damn Gen Y thing."

I snuggled in some more and sighed, more content than I'd ever been. "It's a Cooper Jones thing."

Tom took a deep breath, and tightened his arms around me. He pressed his lips to my forehead. "It's an I-love-you thing."

"Just as well," I mumbled sleepily. "I'd hate to think I moved in with just anyone."

He sighed and gave me a gentle squeeze, but never said anything more.

"Tom?"

"Yes?"

"I love you, too."

SENSE OF PLACE

Dedication

For my husband…

Chapter One

Definition: Sense of place — a quality of design where the building and/or space achieves a sensory, emotional and spiritual connection to the site in which it is placed.
Source: Architecturewiki

I did up the last of the buttons on my shirt, and my doctor sat down in his chair behind his desk. "Well, Tom," he said. "Your blood pressure is fine, and," he said, looking down at the piece of paper in the file, "all test results came back clear. Cholesterol is good, blood glucose is fine, STDs all clear, PSA is good."

I nodded and sat down across from him. "And everything else looks okay?"

He double-checked the papers in front of him. "I have to say, you're the healthiest I've ever seen you. What's your secret?"

"Um…"

The doctor smiled. "Who is he?"

I let out an embarrassed laugh. "He's, um…he's a lot younger than me."

My doctor smiled and nodded, knowingly. "Well, whatever he's doing is working. I know you're concerned about your health, with the passing of your father, and that's completely understandable. But, Tom," he said, "I'd say you're a picture of health. Diet and exercise looks good on you."

"I need to work out, just to keep up with him," I admitted.

The doctor laughed at that. Then his smile faded. "Do you practice safe sex with your partner?"

"Yes, of course."

"How long have you been together?"

"About six months."

"Are you exclusive?"

"Yes. We live together." Then I added, "Well, that's kind of new. He moved in with me two weeks ago."

My doctor tilted his head. "Will you be looking to have unprotected sex with him?"

I hadn't even considered the idea. "Um, no..." I started. "Well, maybe... I'm not sure. We've not discussed that."

"When was he last tested?"

"Um—" Shit, I had to think about that. "He was tested just before he moved here. He's only been with me since."

"Anyway," he said casually, "if you do decide it's something you want to explore, then I'll be more than happy to run the necessary tests for him too."

I shook my head, a little daunted by the concept. "Okay."

"Don't feel you *have* to have unprotected sex, Tom," he went on to say. "A lot of gay couples don't, a lot do. It's something you need to discuss with your partner."

I left the doctor's appointment probably more conflicted than when I'd arrived. It had been a late appointment and when I got home, Cooper was cooking dinner. Well, he was making a mess — dinner, not so much.

"Oh, hey," he said with a smile, looking up from the stove. "Working late?"

"No," I said, putting my satchel on the table. "Doctor's appointment."

Cooper looked up at me, alarmed. "Everything okay?"

"Yeah," I said, giving him a kiss on the cheek. "Everything's fine. Just got the test results from my full checkup."

Cooper still looked concerned. "You sure you're okay?"

I gave him a bit of a nod and a shrug. "It's just with the way Dad died," I said. "I think I need to keep an eye on my health."

Cooper frowned and his eyebrows furrowed. He stopped stirring a pan of sauce, and put the spoon down. "Tom, please don't talk like that."

I cupped his face in my hands and kissed him. "Cooper, sweetheart, no one expected my dad to have a stroke. I'd be foolish not to take that on board."

"I just can't think about you like that," he said quietly. "I can't even begin…"

"Hey," I said, kissing him again. "My doctor actually said I'm the fittest he's seen me. I told him I can credit you for that."

He smiled then. "He said you were okay?"

"A picture of health."

His eyes widened. "What tests did you have?"

"The usual," I answered. "Cholesterol, blood sugar, HIV, PSA…"

"What's PSA?"

"Prostate test."

"Prostate?" Cooper asked, looking a little miffed. "I hope he bought you dinner first."

I snorted out a laugh. "It's a standard lab test these days."

"Oh," he said, seemingly disappointed. "That's a shame."

Smiling, I looked around at the kitchen counter. "What are we eating?"

"It's supposed to be poached chicken," he said, turning back to the stove. "Well, it will be if I can get it cooked. And there's a mango dressing to go on it, but I haven't got to that yet."

"Where did you learn to cook this?"

"I called my mom for the recipe," he said with a grin.

"Can I do anything to help?"

"Yeah, you could cut up the mango, and add all the dressing stuff," he said. "There's a recipe here somewhere."

I smiled as I scoured through the mess on the counter until I found the piece of paper with a handwritten recipe. I cleared a space, cleaning up what I could, and set about doing my task.

"Oh," I said as nonchalantly as I could. "My doctor said he'll add you to his list of patients if you wanted to go to him to have any tests done."

He looked thoughtful as he turned the chicken. "Mmm, I'm about due to be tested again."

I slid the diced mango into a mixing dish. "I know it's not exactly pleasant dinner conversation, and the fact we have to have tests done at all is an awful reality, but it's something we should talk about."

Cooper shrugged indifferently. "No, it's not that," he said. "I was just hoping to find a doctor who did prostate exams the old-fashioned way."

I laughed at him, and he smirked as he put the cooked chicken on a plate. I squeezed some lemon over the mango, and told him, "I can check your prostate for you later, if you'd like."

He slid in beside me and playfully bit my shoulder. "Do you want me to call you doctor?"

I kissed his cheek. "No, Tom is fine." I took a clean board and chopped red peppers. He threw in some type of canned bean, stirred it all together and spooned it over the chicken.

It was pretty freakin' good.

"This was beautiful," I told him. "How come you don't cook more often?" I asked.

"Did you like it?" he asked excitedly. "My mom makes it all the time."

"We eat a lot of takeout," I mused out loud.

"You can cook tomorrow night," he told me. "I think we should have grilled Thai fish with a bean shoot salad."

I chuckled at him. "I think you overestimate my cooking ability."

Cooper stood up, took my plate and walked into the kitchen. "Just as well you're good in bed."

Smiling, I cleared the table and followed him into the kitchen where I kissed the back of his neck. "I'll clean up. You start the work you brought home."

When I had the kitchen back to spotless, I pulled out my laptop and a job file and set up my own work space across from Cooper.

He was engrossed in his work. His head was down, looking from his laptop to the file in front of him and back again, and there was that concentration line between his eyebrows which meant he was trying to get his thoughts around something.

I opened my job file and flipped open my laptop, but I just couldn't get started. My mind was elsewhere.

"You okay?" Cooper asked.

I looked at him then, not even aware I'd zoned out. "Um, sure. Just not really in the mood for work tonight."

"Oh…" he said, then he looked at his own work. "I can pack this up if you'd prefer."

I laughed. "No, keep at it. You look engrossed in whatever it is you're doing."

Cooper sighed. "Actually, I'm stuck on something. Can I pick your brain?"

"Sure," I said, brightening. "Of course you can."

"Well," he started. "We've just signed with a developer who I met with at the Philly energy convention. He wants to incorporate the design concepts in a commercial refit. He has a list of requirements and I'm not sure they'll work."

"How so?"

Cooper launched into how the existing building structure was confined by New York building restrictions, and how the desired energy compliance wasn't feasible without some external façade changes, and how he had to find a middle ground. "He really liked the glazing concept that I used on the Philly design, but I can't use that if I keep with the façade guidelines for the Riverdale district."

"Can I have a look at it?" I asked.

"Please do," he said, and pushed his laptop out a little.

I pulled my seat around to his and for the next hour and a half, we went over the plans, job specifications and New York City building codes. It was fascinating how his ideas differed from mine. His were new and exciting whereas mine were traditional and tested.

"I can bring home some old job sheets from work," I said. "I've done work in this district, so I can see what council certificates we needed. You might be able to find a loophole."

"Would you?" he asked. "That'd be great! I mean, I don't want you to get into trouble."

"It's not privy information," I told him. "Anyone could check city records, but this will just save time. Is the original structure pre- or post-1940?"

"Pre."

"I'll check our records with the Preservation Commission," I offered. Then I smiled. "I'm sure you can figure out a way to make the new and old coexist."

"Yes, between us we have the whole retrofit thing covered, don't we?" he said with a nod. "You know, me being modern, you being antique."

I rolled my eyes at him. "At least I'm post-1940."

"Just as well," he said with a laugh. "Because I didn't get a permit from the Preservation Committee to date you."

"You're such a little shit," I said, grabbing his chin between my thumb and forefinger and planting a kiss on his lips. "I offer to help and you insult me."

Cooper grinned and stood up, only to straddle me in the seat. "You're so sexy when you try to act all hurt."

"Sexy, huh?" I asked with a smile. "Now you're just trying to sweet-talk me."

He leaned down and kissed me, pulling my bottom lip between his. Then he whispered gruffly, "You have no idea how sexy you are."

I looked into his darkening eyes. "I could say the same about you."

He kissed me again, rocking his hips on mine. "You promised me a physical examination."

"Then I best make it thorough."

He grinned, and I kissed him, then I stood us up and walked him backward to the bedroom, never taking my mouth from his.

He wanted me to check his prostate. So I did.

Twice.

* * * *

I walked into my office on Monday morning and smiled at my personal assistant. "Morning, Jennifer."

"Good morning, Mr. Elkin," she replied professionally. "I trust you and Mr. Jones had a good weekend."

"Yes, we did," I answered, flipping through my messages. We'd gone out on Friday night for a few drinks. Cooper had spent the weekend going over the old files I'd brought home for him while I did some work, but mostly I'd annoyed him. We'd worked out, we'd cooked lunch and dinner both days. "It was lovely, thank you. And how was yours?"

"Very well, thank you," she replied. "You're early today. If you'd like, I can bring in fresh coffee."

"That'd be great," I told her.

Barely two minutes later, Jennifer carried in my coffee. But she frowned. "Were you expecting a meeting with Robert?"

Robert Chandler was one of the other senior partners here. He'd mentored me, and even though I was on an equal footing as a senior partner, I'd always thought of him as a boss. He'd even gone with Jennifer to my father's funeral just four weeks ago.

"No, I wasn't expecting a meeting, why?"

"He's asked to see you," she said.

"Oh, okay."

"Did something happen between you?" she asked, rather cryptically.

"No. Why do you ask?"

Jennifer wasn't displaying her usual cool demeanor. She even seemed concerned. "Well, he asked to see you *now*. Told me to hold all calls, and asked that you see him first. He didn't exactly seem happy about it."

Chapter Two

Grace, Robert's personal assistant, opened the double doors for me and announced my expected arrival.

"Robert, you wanted to see me?" I asked, walking into his office. He was about sixty-five years old, with gray hair and jowls that reminded me of that cartoon dog.

"Yes, Tom," he said somewhat pleasantly. "How's your mother?"

"She's okay," I answered, unsure of where he was going. "She's determined to stay at the house, though. I call her every night, just to check on her," I said, though I got the feeling he didn't really care. He was simply making polite conversation until he got to the subject he was after.

"I saw that young intern of yours at the funeral..."

And there it was.

"His name is Cooper."

"Yes, that's it," he said, like he didn't know. "Cooper Jones." He stared at me for a long moment. "You seemed very...familiar."

I couldn't believe it. I could not fucking believe it. "He's my boyfriend, if that's the information you're fishing for," I said, not caring if he didn't like my tone. "Actually, we now live together."

Robert tilted his head. "Were you seeing him while he was your intern?"

Fuck.

"No," I lied. "Strictly professional while he was here."

"I'm glad to hear that," Robert said with a smug smile. "Because you know it's a breach of company policy to date staff. Particularly impressionable interns."

I almost laughed at that. Cooper was anything but impressionable, but that was not Robert's point. I'd broken company protocol, and we both knew it.

"Am I being officially reprimanded?" I asked him outright.

He smiled a little more genuinely this time. "Heavens, no," he said, though I didn't believe him. "Though I am curious about one thing."

"What's that?"

"Why didn't you recommend we hire him?"

There were two ways I could answer that question. I could tell him I hadn't wanted him to work here because then we couldn't date, and basically admit that I'd been seeing him while he'd worked here. Or I could lie and tell him I didn't think Cooper was good enough.

Instead, I answered his question with a question. A conversational trait I *knew* Robert detested. Maybe that was why I did it. Sure, Robert had mentored me when I started at Brackett and Golding, and I admired him professionally. But as employees in this company, we were on an equal footing, so the words *fuck you* echoed in my mind.

Cooper was starting to wear off on me.

"Why are you bringing this up now?" I asked. "One month after my father's funeral, where you saw Cooper and me together. Why now? Why not the day I came back to work?" Then it dawned on me. It had taken a month for him to find out information. "Did it honestly take you that long to find out anything on him? Because really, Robert, you just could have asked me."

"A little defensive, don't you think, Tom?" he asked dismissively.

"Not at all," I said. "But tell me this, Robert. You've known I am gay for five years. Why act all homophobic and discriminatory now?"

That stopped him. Two very carefully chosen words, with a lawsuit ring to them. Not that I would go down that route, but he didn't know that.

"Tom, that's not what this is about," he replied. "That's not why I wanted to speak to you at all."

He had made me so damn angry I wanted to let him have a piece of my mind. I'd probably already said too much, but I needed to play his game. "I'm glad to hear that, Robert," I said. "Because we wouldn't want to have a conversation one might deem inappropriate."

"No, we wouldn't," he replied with a knowing smile.

"Robert, if you're alluding to an official reprimand, please, by all means, have it on my desk by lunchtime and I'll have my lawyer look it over. But just so you know, I first met Cooper through my son, Ryan. Not Brackett and Golding. I chose him to be my intern because he was the most talented one there." Then I added, "But you're right about one thing. I didn't want him to work here. I called Louisa Arlington and lined up an interview for him, but he got the job on his own merit. And she has since thanked me for suggesting he work with her."

I stood up and went to the door. "And if you want to know the reason why I didn't want him to work here, it wasn't because I wanted to be with him and couldn't because of *company policy*." I took a breath to make sure my voice was steady when I spoke. "I didn't want him to work here because the staunch traditionalism and lack of free thinking would have suffocated him."

And with that, I walked out.

I stormed back to my office, past Jennifer, who had the grace to leave me alone long enough to calm down.

I waited for an official letter to come from the Chairman of the Board, upon recommendation from Robert. But it never came.

By the time I got home, I was calmer and had let most of the residual anger go. I knew Cooper had wanted me to cook, but I really wasn't in the mood. I had dinner ordered by the time he got home. "I ordered you the Thai fish you wanted," I told him.

He finished putting his work satchel on the table and pulled his tie off, then he gave me a proper kiss. "If I hadn't come home right now, would you have pretended you cooked it thinking I'd be all impressed and love-struck?" he asked, batting his eyelashes.

I snorted. "There's no way I could fake that kind of cooking skill."

"You cook just fine," he said, opening the fridge and pulling out two bottled waters and handing me one. "I went to see your doctor today," he said casually. "I called to make an appointment, he had a vacancy, so I went. Had all the usual screening tests done." Then he sighed dramatically. "No prostate exam, though."

I laughed. "Did you ask for one?"

He pretended to be offended. "Not on the first date! I'm not that kind of guy."

Still smiling, I took a sip of water. "What else did he say?"

"That you were handsome and dreamy."

"He did not," I said flatly. "He's a straight man."

"Oh," Cooper said with a grin. "Maybe that was me who said that."

"You're such a dork."

"Dork?" he replied. "Really, Tom? No one's used the word 'dork' since the nineties."

"Oh my God," I cried sarcastically. "They should archive it with Olde English. The nineties were sooooo long ago."

Cooper rolled his eyes at me. "So how was your day, anyway?"

"Well," I said slowly, "I had a very interesting conversation with Robert Chandler this morning."

"The old fogey with the gray-helmet hair?"

I snorted again. "Yes, that's him."

"What did you talk about?"

"You."

"Me?"

I nodded then relayed the entire conversation to him.

"An official reprimand, Tom!" he cried. "Jesus Christ!"

"I never got one," I said, trying to calm him down. "I think he was just trying to gauge my reaction, that's all. So in hindsight, I probably shouldn't have lost my temper."

"That wasn't losing your temper," Cooper said, shaking his head. "Telling him to mind his own fucking business would be losing your temper."

I smiled. "Actually, I thought of you and almost told him to fuck off."

"I would have," Cooper replied. "What we do is none of his fucking business."

"Well, technically it was when you were my intern," I amended. "I knew I was breaking company policy by seeing you." Then I shrugged. "And I did it anyway."

"Ugh," he groaned. "That's so not fair."

Then dinner arrived, and he spent the entire meal stabbing his fish with his fork, or pointing it at me while he ranted about the fucking politics of fascist corporate leaders who should have retired in the Middle Ages.

All I could do was smile at him.

"Why doesn't it bother you?" he asked.

"It did when it first happened this morning," I said. "I was livid. But at the end of the day, it's just one reprimand. We don't work together anymore. I'm not bringing any disrepute onto the Brackett and Golding reputation with a sexual harassment case or anything. He's got nothing else on me."

"Yeah," Cooper agreed. "But what's he really after?"

"What do you mean?"

"You've been friends with this guy for years," he answered. "He went to your father's funeral, and now this? It doesn't seem right."

"Maybe he's not as tolerant of same-sex couples as he thought he was," I answered.

Cooper growled. "Well, maybe someone should suggest the old fart retires and lets the rest of the twenty-first century get on with their work."

I picked up his plate and gave him a kiss. "I love the way you think."

"What if you get to work tomorrow and there's a letter on your desk?"

"Then I'll deal with that tomorrow," I said, walking into the kitchen. He followed me, so I said, "But let's not worry about it anymore tonight. What's done is done." He didn't seem exactly happy with the idea, but with a pout and a sigh, he let it go.

Later that night when I was getting ready for bed, a naked Cooper snuggled down on my side of the mattress. "The doctor said something else," he said quietly.

I threw our dirty underwear into the hamper. "What's that?"

"He said he'd spoken to you about the possibility of unprotected sex."

Oh.

Cooper smiled. "It's okay, Tom. He never told me what you said or anything. Just that it's something we should talk about, if it's something we might want to do."

"I, um…" I said, then climbed onto the bed and took his hand. "I didn't mention it to you yesterday, because I don't know how I feel about it."

Cooper nodded thoughtfully. "It's weird, huh? Condoms are just something I assumed I'd always need." He shrugged one shoulder. "It's not just a safety thing, but it's a security thing. I'm not sure if I'm explaining that correctly…"

I snuggled in beside him and kissed him softly. "I understand exactly what you mean. And when he first mentioned it to me, I was like no way, it's condoms or nothing." Then I exhaled slowly. "But the more I thought about it…"

Cooper leaned up on his arm so he could look at me. "The more you thought about it, what?"

"Well, I'm not opposed to sharing that experience with you," I hedged. "As long as we're both given the all-clear and we both want it."

He bit his lip. "I'm not sure."

"Truthfully, neither am I," I said honestly. "But we have a few weeks before you get your test results, and even then we don't have to agree to it. We can wait a year, or ten years before we need to decide."

Cooper smiled and settled down into the crook of my arm. "Thank you for understanding."

I kissed the top of his head. "Thank you for understanding, too."

He sighed contentedly, and after a long moment, he said, "What do you think Robert will say to you at work tomorrow?"

I tightened my hold on him. "I don't know. It doesn't matter. If he wants to reprimand me for dating you, then let him. I don't care." I rolled over so I faced him, so our noses were almost touching. "Because given the chance to go back and do it again, I wouldn't change a thing. I should be sorry for breaking company policy, but I'm not. I'm not sorry at all, and if he has a problem with that, he can get fucked."

Cooper laughed and put his hand to my face. "I think I'm starting to rub off on you."

I kissed him with smiling lips. "I know you are," I agreed. "But if I'm going to get reprimanded over anything, it will be because I told him the reason I didn't want you to work with me was because people like him would suffocate someone like you with their institutionalized way of thinking."

Cooper's eyes drilled into mine. "But you don't think like that."

"Not anymore," I whispered.

He smiled, slow and shy. "I think that's the best compliment you've ever given me." I opened my mouth to speak, but he put his thumb over my lips. "Shh, don't ruin it."

I took his thumb between my lips, sucking it into my mouth. His eyes darkened and he groaned low in his throat.

I pulled off his thumb. "Want to put something else in my mouth?"

He nodded. "God, yes."

"Get up on your knees," I urged him. So while I lay on the bed, he knelt near my face, offering me his dick.

I slid one arm around his thigh and ran my fingers over his ass to cup his balls from behind while I took his cock into my mouth. He gripped the headboard and moaned, threading his fingers through my hair.

"Oh fuck, Tom," he gasped, then moaned long and slow.

I worked him over, while his thighs trembled and his cock grew impossibly harder. He was trying not to thrust into my mouth, trying to restrain himself, so I sucked him harder, deeper. He stuttered out a warning, "Tom, gonna—gonna—fuck, Tom, I'm gonna come."

So with a final thrust, I took him into my throat and his whole body shook as he cried out some strangled cry and he came.

When he could form coherent words, he said, "Your turn."

I stopped him. "No, just for you tonight."

He was too spent to argue. He burrowed himself into my side and fell asleep with a smile.

* * * *

"Good morning, Lionel," Cooper said cheerfully as we walked through the lobby.

"Good morning, Mr. Jones, Mr. Elkin," Lionel said, addressing us both with a smile.

"How's the weather out there today?" Cooper asked, looking out at the rather gray-looking New York day.

"Getting colder," Lionel said with a nod. "It'll be snowing before you know it."

"I trust Mrs. Lionel is well?" Cooper asked with a smile.

"She's still wonderful," the old man said proudly. "Don't know what I ever did to get so lucky."

"Aw," Cooper said. "Tom says the same thing about me!"

I rolled my eyes, and Lionel tried not to smile. Instead, he said, "You gentlemen have a great day."

"Thank you, Lionel," I said. "Same to you."

Cooper and I stepped out onto the sidewalk, ready to go our separate ways. "Don't let that Robert dickhead say anything to you today," Cooper said. "I'd hate to have to come over and kick some old guy's ass."

I couldn't help but laugh. "Do you have some tough-guy persona I haven't seen yet?"

"Absolutely," he said brightly. "I have a black belt in sarcasm, and my wit is like lightning."

I laughed. "Goodbye, Cooper."

I walked to work with a smile. Although I was dreading another *meeting* with Robert, he never spoke to me, came near me or even looked at me. That was more than fine by me.

Jennifer was her cool, professional self, but she looked troubled by my conversation with Robert, or at least by the residual tension that seemed to settle over the office because of it.

Never one to look like anything affected her, she seemed a little on edge all week. When she brought in some files on Friday, I asked her if she was okay. "Yes, I'm fine," she said plainly. "Why wouldn't I be?"

"Just with my meeting with Robert earlier this week, I don't want you to worry about it, that's all," I told her.

"Nonsense," she said, dismissing the notion completely.

Of course she said she was fine. On the outside, nothing seemed to faze her. I remembered when I'd told her I'd separated from Sofia because I was gay, she hadn't even blinked. She'd just asked if I was okay then proceeded to hand me my coffee and tell me of my day's appointments.

But this seemed to have put a chink in her well-polished armor. Knowing Jennifer, if she didn't want to discuss it, it wasn't up for conversation. She obviously didn't want to discuss it, so I let it go.

I went about my work, and was having a rather productive afternoon, when my phone buzzed. Cooper's name flashed across the screen, and I smiled as I answered. Without so much as a hello, and not giving me time to speak, he said, "Oh my God, Tom. I got it." His voice was fast and excited.

I couldn't help but smile. "Got what?"

"The job!" he cried. "I got the Xavier Baurhenn contract."

"Oh, Cooper, that's excellent," I said. I was grinning, knowing what this meant to him.

"He saw my proposal and loved it."

"Of course he did," I said. "Because it was amazing."

I could tell he was grinning when he spoke. "He said it was a standout."

"I thought you weren't showing him until Monday?"

"We weren't supposed to," he explained. "But Xavier called and asked Louisa how we were coming along with the prelims, and she told him I'd done more than just the prelims. She told him I was almost done, so he came over to look at it."

"And?"

"And he freakin' loved it," he cried, and I laughed. "We're going out for celebratory drinks," Cooper said.

"You have to come, Tom. It's my first contract and you need to be there."

"Of course I'll be there."

An hour later, still dressed in my work suit, I walked into the young and trendy bar, through the young and trendy crowd, to find some young, trendy, good-looking guy with his arm around Cooper.

Chapter Three

Cooper's face lit up when he saw me, as though he couldn't get away from the other guy quick enough. He left him standing there, and the others he was talking to, and quickly walked over to me. He kissed me, right on the mouth.

"Thank God you're here," he said.

"Everything okay?" I asked.

"Yep," he said brightly. Then he took my hand and led me back toward the group of people he was with. "I want you to meet everyone."

I was introduced to a Skye, Tyson, Ben—all of whom gave me wide-eyed nods—then Cooper turned and proudly, nervously, introduced me to Xavier, the guy who had had his arm around him.

"Hello," I said, shaking his hand. He was about twenty years younger than I'd expected him to be. "It's a pleasure to meet you."

Xavier shook my hand firmly then looked at Cooper. "You said his name was Tom!"

Cooper smiled. "It is."

Xavier shook his head. "Not Thomas fucking Elkin."

Cooper burst out laughing. "He's just Tom to me."

I smiled at Xavier. "It's true. I am just Tom to him."

Cooper slid his arm around my waist and leaned into me. "Can I get you a drink?" he asked me.

"Shouldn't I be buying?" I asked. "I believe congratulations are in order."

Cooper rolled his eyes and ignored me. "Scotch and soda?"

I gave him a nod, and was left with Cooper's colleagues and Xavier staring at me.

One of the young guys, Ben, stuck his hand out. "Mr. Elkin, it's a real pleasure. I've admired your work for years."

Skye was next. She shook my hand nervously. "I had no idea when Cooper talked of Tom that he meant you," she said.

Before I could be any more embarrassed, Louisa Arlington, Cooper's boss, saw me and made her way over. She kissed my cheek. "Tom, it's so good to see you!"

"Louisa, you look great," I told her honestly. She did. She'd lost weight, or gotten taller or done something to her hair.

She smiled genuinely. "Cooper's been doing some excellent work," she went on to say. "He has an eye for fine detail."

"He puts the hours in," I told her.

"Cooper told me about your father," she said with a kind smile. "I'm very sorry."

"Thanks. And I'm sorry Cooper had to leave Philly early," I said. "He worked hard on that project."

"And it showed," she said with a nod. "It was his work on that project that got him seen by Xavier, here," she said, including him in our conversation.

Cooper came back with two drinks and handed me one. He smiled and again slid his arm around my waist.

He wasn't being possessive. He was just showing Xavier, who quite possibly fancied him, that he was with me. Well, maybe just a little possessive.

And while we talked and mingled with his co-workers and with Xavier, it wasn't lost on me that he'd not told any of them about me. Well, he'd told them about a 'Tom' but not who I was exactly. I was a little put out at first, thinking maybe he didn't want them to know he was dating a man twice his age. But then it occurred to me that it was me who had insisted he work for Arlington so people wouldn't mistake his talent for my reputation.

So as much as I didn't really like it, I had no right to complain.

For most of the night, Cooper was with me. He either had his arm around my waist, or his hand on my back, my ass or my arm. But when Cooper got chatting with Ben, Skye and Tyson, it left me alone with Xavier.

"He's very talented," Xavier said. He was looking over at Cooper, smiling as he sipped his drink. "I've worked with him a lot over these last few weeks, and he has a gift."

"He does."

"I just think it's funny that in all that time, talking about architecture the way he does, he never mentioned you."

"He's professional," I agreed lightly.

Xavier nodded thoughtfully. "I wouldn't have pictured him to like older men," he said casually. "Just with how vibrant he is, he has so much energy. Thought he'd be with someone his own age, that's all."

The little fucking punk was giving me attitude! Implying he knew Cooper better than me, and that

Cooper would be better off with someone his own age. So I smiled at him. "Maybe he should be, maybe not. I'm sure there's a lot you don't know about him. One thing I will say, though, with all due respect" — which was minimal, I thought to myself — "is that what Cooper does outside of your project isn't really your concern."

With that, I said, "Excuse me. It was nice meeting you," and I left him there, and walked over to where Cooper was. I very deliberately slid my hand over his ass, so Xavier could see it, and offered to buy the next round of drinks.

By the time I got back from the bar, Xavier was in my place. There was no doubt — he wanted Cooper. He was also a pompous little brat. When the group had decided they were headed to a nightclub, Louisa put up her hands and gracefully declined their offer.

"You'll come out with us, won't you, Cooper?" Xavier asked loudly, so everyone could hear. "You're not ready to call it a night yet, are you?"

Cooper's eyes darted to mine, and I shrugged. "You can go," I said.

His eyes narrowed briefly at me, then he turned to Xavier. "No, I won't. Thanks for the offer, but I have an early start tomorrow. I have your project details to finalize."

"But it's the weekend!" Xavier said as though it was a foreign concept, and I wondered whether he'd ever worked a weekend in his life.

"No rest for the wicked," Cooper said with a smile, though it was hardly genuine. He glanced at me again, and it took me a second to recognize the look on his face. I'd never seen it before. Well, I'd seen it, but it was never directed at me.

Cooper was pissed off at me.

He announced that he should be going, did the rounds of smiling goodbyes, shook hands with Xavier and told him he'd see him Monday, and without our usual conversation, we went home.

By the time we walked through the door and I'd pulled off my tie and shoes, Cooper was quiet, his anger was just bubbling under the surface. I had no idea what he was angry about, what I'd done wrong, but I knew with Cooper it would only be a matter of time before he told me.

I asked him if he wanted a coffee as I set the machine and got two cups from the cupboard. His silence was unnerving. Cooper was never silent. So I figured I'd throw it out there. "Xavier is impressed by you. Though I didn't realize he was gay."

"Does that matter?" Cooper asked.

"Well, no," I replied. "Of course not." Then I shrugged.

"Then why bring it up?"

"Just that you never mentioned it."

"Because it's not important," he said curtly. "You should know that, Tom."

"I do know that, Cooper," I said calmly. "But he basically told me he thought you should be with someone like him, not me."

"He said that?"

"Not exactly," I conceded. "But he alluded to it."

"What did you say?"

"Nothing. Just smiled at him, told him maybe you should. But that it was none of his business, and that's when I walked over to you."

"You said *maybe I was better off with someone like him*?" he asked like he couldn't believe it.

"I did tell him, very diplomatically, that who you're with doesn't affect how you do your job. But apart from that, what was I *supposed* to say?" I asked. "I'm just not sure how I feel about people like that."

"Feel about what?" Cooper asked incredulously. "What is there to *feel* about it?"

"I don't know…jealousy. Insecurity. Self-doubt."

Cooper's mouth fell open. "Who? *You?*"

"Yes, me!" I replied. "He'd be perfect for you! He's brilliant, successful…younger."

Cooper groaned. "I don't want him! I've never even thought of him like that! He's an immature little brat whose daddy has handed him everything. And stop with the 'I'm too old for you' bullshit, okay? Because I'm sick of fucking hearing about it."

His outburst surprised me. "Okay," I said.

"Jesus, Tom," he went on to say, "your whole 'I'll set you free if it's what you want' mindset drives me insane! It's so *noble* of you," he added sarcastically.

I'd obviously touched a nerve. "Well, it's true. I love you enough to not stand in your way."

Cooper rolled his eyes and groaned loudly again. "That right there! Some people might find that sweet, Tom, but you know what? It pisses me off!"

"Jesus Christ, Cooper," I said back to him. "I will never win with you! What the hell am I supposed to do?"

"I want you to get all pissy," he shot back at me. "I want you to show some asshole who might hit on me that I fucking belong to you, that's what. When the likes of *Xavier* tell you they think I should be with them instead, I want you to tell them to back the fuck off. I want you to tell them I am yours. Tell them you're the one I go home with, you're the one I want." He ran his hand through his hair. "I want you to show some emotion. I don't want you to act like if I *did* leave with

299

someone else that you wouldn't give a shit. It's not that hard, Tom."

"Wouldn't give a shit?" I asked. "It would kill me, Cooper. Do you think by my wanting the best for you, if that means you moving on, that it wouldn't fucking kill me? Jesus, Cooper, you're *it* for me. I want everything with you. I want to spend the rest of my life with you—I'd fucking marry you, Cooper, in a fucking heartbeat. I want you to have it all, so how could I ever stand in your way?"

Cooper's mouth fell open and he slowly raised his hands so he could rub his forehead. "For the love of fucking God, Tom, please don't tell me that was a proposal. Because fuck, that was the most woeful excuse for a marriage proposal ever."

I exhaled in a rush. The argument in me was gone. "No, it wasn't. But I would marry you. And I do know you love me, that's not what I'm insecure about," I said. "I just want you to have everything. I don't want you to choose anyone else, and it scares the shit out of me that one day you will." I ran my hands through my hair. "To be honest, Cooper, I'm not even sure I know what we're arguing about."

Cooper sighed and walked over to me. He fisted my shirt at my stomach. "We're not arguing. It's just when someone basically tells you they want me, it'd be nice if you acted like you cared."

I cupped his face. "I care, so fucking much," I said before I kissed him. "Don't ever think I don't care. It's just the likes of Xavier don't deserve the reaction. He's your first contract client, and as much as I'd have liked to tell him to fuck off, I couldn't. I wouldn't do anything to jeopardize your work."

"Ugh," Cooper groaned and leaned his forehead on my collarbone.

This whole outburst was just so not Cooper. I rubbed his back. "Now would you like to tell me what's really bothering you?"

He lifted his face and his eyes flickered with doubt. It wasn't something I saw very often. He frowned. "I know he likes me, I'm not stupid."

"So?"

"So what if he only picked my proposal because he thought he could have me with it?"

"Oh, Cooper, sweetheart," I said softly, running my hand down his face. "He picked yours because it was the best."

Cooper huffed. "The guy doesn't even know his left from his right."

I smiled. "He's a Baurhenn. His family has been in the real estate development field for decades. So his parents or grandparents might hold the purse strings, and he might not know the technical terms, but he knows good architecture when he sees it."

"I just thought, when he was trying to get me to go out with him, that that's all he wanted me for," Cooper said quietly. "That it wasn't my work. I put hours into that project."

I shook my head. "Have you got a copy of your project blueprints here?"

"On my laptop," he said with a nod. "Why?"

"Can you open it for me?" I asked. "I want to show you something. Just give me a sec."

I walked back out to the living room with a rolled set of blueprints that had yellowed with age.

Cooper was waiting for the CAD program to load on his laptop, and when his familiar plans came up on screen, he pushed his laptop out for me to look. That was when he noticed the old plans in my hand. "What are those?"

"These are the blueprints to my first ever contract job," I said, then I pointed to the laptop screen, "just like yours."

His eyes widened. "Really?"

"Yes."

"Can I look at them?"

"Please do," I said, unrolling the delicate paper. "I want you to look at them. Actually, I want you to tell me what you see."

Cooper almost frowned, and as I laid the plans flat on the table, I used the corner of his laptop as a paperweight and held the other side with my hand. Cooper stood right up close to me and put his hand on my hip as his eyes scanned over the old plans.

"These are incredible."

"Well, no," I added. "Not compared to what I've done since, but these were my first project plans. Simple, residential, but mine."

Cooper traced his finger over the lines on the paper down to the bottom right-hand corner. He read the words out loud, almost reverently. "Drawn by Thomas Elkin. July 13th, 1991." He looked at me and sighed. "That was the year I was born."

"Yeah, thanks," I said, rolling my eyes. "Don't rub it in."

"No," he said quickly. "I mean, I think that's significant, don't you?"

Oh.

"Oh, um…" I paused. "I hadn't thought of it like that." I smiled at the sentiment. "I actually wanted you to look at both of these plans, my very first, and yours, and tell me what you see."

There were huge differences between the two. Not that one was computer-generated on a laptop screen, and the other was a twenty-two-year-old, hand-drawn lithograph plan. The difference was in the complexity, in the inventiveness. Cooper's plans were intricate, almost genius. And mine…were not.

Cooper saw it—he knew exactly what I meant. "Of course they're different. Technology from then to now is like night to day, Tom. Legal requirements, regulations, energy, it's all so *different*. So while the plans look a world apart, they're not really. Yours was a residential, mine's a commercial-residential."

He was trying to justify why his looked so new and grand, and mine looked pale in comparison. I chuckled at him and ran my hand up over his back. "Cooper, sweetheart, you want to know why yours is so much better than mine?"

He looked at me, but said nothing, waiting for me to continue.

So I told him. "Because it *is* better than mine."

Cooper shook his head. "That's like comparing a computer from 1991 to a computer released today. You just can't."

"Look at them," I said to him again. "The fundamentals are the same, yes. But see this?" I asked, pointing to the laptop screen. "See how you've used this space? See how you've used the positive flow you've created through the commercial floor area, and then the functionality of the apartments above it? How you've used the energy created by venting the window cavities to source the internal air flow…" I shook my head. "Cooper, I don't think you understand just how talented you are."

He stared at me and bit the inside of his lip. Then he shook his head.

"Cooper," I whispered. "You have more natural talent for this than I could have dreamed of at your age."

Still biting his lip, he still had disbelief in his eyes. "Really?"

I gave him a smile and a kiss on the cheek. "Yes, really. So don't let clients like Xavier bother you too much. There will always be clients who grate on you."

"I have to work with him pretty closely on this for the next few months."

"So you be your professional self, and if he's still inappropriate toward you, go over his head. Ask Laura to speak to his supervisor, or his father, or whoever." Then I smiled. "And failing all of that, tell him young and successful isn't your thing. Tell him you like graying hair and a sagging ass."

Cooper smiled and even managed a bit of a laugh, and he ran his hand over the curve of my ass and gave it a squeeze. "Graying hair, yes. Sagging ass, no."

Then he looked back over my paper blueprints and sighed. "I love these plans. I can't believe you don't have them framed or something."

I shrugged. "They've been up the top of the robe in Ryan's room. Who knows?" I said. "Maybe one day I will."

Cooper looked into my eyes, and shook his head as though he couldn't believe something. "How do you do it?"

"Do what?"

"Know exactly what to say," he said. "Like showing me these." He waved his hand at the plans on the table. "Knowing it was exactly what I needed to hear." He smiled and sighed contentedly. He even leaned against me as he kept his gaze on the plans. But then he said, "And then you can completely balls something up as important as a move-in-with-me speech, or a marry-me speech."

I could have argued the whole point, that it technically wasn't a proposal, but with Cooper there was no point in arguing. In fact, I was just happy he hadn't freaked out when I'd even mentioned getting married. So instead of arguing, I playfully growled and pretended to bite his neck.

"Come on," he said, taking my hand and pulling me down the hallway.

"What about the plans?"

"Leave them," he said. "You might not be able to show that dickhead Xavier that I belong to you, but you can damn well show me."

* * * *

Monday morning at work was interesting, to say the least. We had our usual senior staff meeting, and all the usual things were discussed — portfolios, budgets, projections and schedules.

Robert never looked at me or even spoke to me, until we were walking out of the conference room.

"Nice photo in yesterday's paper," he said coolly.

I, of course, had no clue what he was talking about, but I replied with a cheery, "Thanks." And as soon as I was in my office, I Googled *New York Times* and there on page six of the social pages were me, Cooper, and of all people, Xavier Baurhenn leaving the bar we were at on Friday night. I hadn't even known Xavier had left the same time as us.

But it was the story with the photo that made me both smile and cringe.

Esteemed architect Thomas Elkin and his boyfriend, Cooper Jones, and development heir Xavier Baurhenn, was written underneath the photograph. But the story itself read, *Thomas Elkin looks like the responsible dad driving the kids home after a night out, but he is in fact the live-in boyfriend of the much younger up-and-coming architect Cooper Jones.*

The article about us stopped at that, and went on to talk about who else was seen out and about.

I picked up my phone and dialed Cooper's number. He answered the call with, "Look, I've already told you, I like my men with gray hair and a saggy ass."

I snorted into the phone. "Just as well."

"I only left you a mere two hours ago," he said brightly. "I know I'm amazing, but surely you don't miss me that much."

I sighed into the phone. He really was incorrigible. "Have you seen page eighty-seven of yesterday's *New York Times*? Well, page six of the social pages."

"No," he replied. "We didn't leave the apartment yesterday. Actually, we barely left the bedroom, remember?"

"Did you want to look it up online?" I asked a little impatiently.

"I already am," he answered, just as impatiently. "Holy shit!" He'd just seen the picture, obviously.

"That's what I thought."

"I didn't even see anyone with a camera when we left," he said.

"Neither did I." Then I said, "What the freakin' hell are we doing in the social pages?"

"Well, I'm awesome, and you're hot," he replied casually. "What's not to love? Well at any rate, I think it's fantastic!" he cried. "The old and the new in New York."

"I'm being serious!" I cried. "It's ludicrous."

Then Cooper burst out laughing. "*You look like the responsible dad driving the kids home...* Oh my fucking God, it actually says that!"

"Yeah," I grumbled, "but you don't need to laugh about it."

And yet he was still laughing. The little shit.

"It's not that funny."

"I'm gonna send this to Mom and Dad," he said, still chuckling. "They might put it on the fridge."

"I don't think they're ready for that," I said.

"It's not like we're snogging in the gutter or anything," he replied. "You're not even holding my hand... Hey, you're not even holding my hand!"

I rolled my eyes, even though he couldn't see it. "You were pissed at me, remember? Because I didn't beat my chest and drag you back to my cave by your hair."

Cooper laughed into the phone, then he spoke like a caveman, "Cooper laugh. Tom. Make funny."

I couldn't help but laugh at that. "I'll see you at home tonight."

"Yes, and thanks for offering to cook Thai fish for dinner. Sounds great."

"I didn't," I started to say, but was only talking to a dial tone.

I hung up the phone and rubbed my temples.

I really should take a vitamin pill, a shot of Scotch and one shot of adrenaline before having phone conversations with him.

Chapter Four

I was in the kitchen, trying to separate fillets of fish with one hand while I held my cell to my ear with the other. "Well, I'm trying to cook dinner," I mumbled into the phone. The line was quiet for a long moment. "Sofia?" I asked. "You still there?"

"Yes," she said. "What exactly are you cooking?"

"It's supposed to be some Thai fish thing."

She snorted out a laugh. "Seriously?"

"Cooper's mentioned it a few times," I told her. "I thought I'd try. We order it, so I know what it's *supposed* to taste like…"

She chuckled, somewhat amused at the idea. "Anyway, what I was calling for," she said lightly, "was that there are a few things up at the Casa that belonged to your dad… I thought you might want them."

"Oh."

"Yes, I know they came with the house, and technically they're mine," she said. "But they're not, Tom. They're yours. It's the old telescope in the study, and there's a chessboard in the den."

This was the Sofia I knew — this was the Sofia I'd been married to for twenty years. "Um, thank you, Sofia," I said. "That means a lot to me."

"It's no problem," she said. "Not this weekend, but the weekend after, you're more than welcome to go up to get them. You and Cooper can stay…if you want."

I could hardly believe it. I smiled into the phone. "Thank you, Sofia." I wasn't thanking her for the offer of the Casa for a weekend. I was thanking her for her acceptance. "That means…that means a lot."

"It's okay, Tom," she said.

"So, what are your plans this weekend?" I asked. "You mentioned plans?"

Sofia cleared her throat. "Well, there might be someone…"

"Really?" I asked with a smile.

"Yes, Tom." Then she mumbled something about how the girls had set her up through a friend of a friend, how she'd seen him a few times since and his name was Phil. She seemed nervous, but happy. It sounded like she was finally starting to move on.

"That's good, Sof," I said softly. "I'm so glad to hear it."

There was the familiar jingle of keys at the front door, and when the door opened, Cooper walked in. Well, it was more *New York Times* than Cooper. It was his legs and hips, but he was holding up the social page, page eighty-seven, with the picture of us on it.

I laughed at him, and he shook the paper and hollered, "We're in the *New York Times*, baby!"

"Is that Cooper?" Sofia asked, obviously hearing him through the phone.

"Yes, that's Cooper," I answered into the phone, making Cooper lower the newspaper to see who I was talking to. "He's being…Cooper."

I grinned at him, walking around the island bench to kiss him. He swatted me with the newspaper and gave me a pouty smile. "That's for calling me names."

I chuckled, still holding the phone to my ear. "Thanks again, Sofia. I'll check with him and let you know, if that's okay?"

Realizing I was talking to my ex-wife, Cooper raised an eyebrow and walked into the kitchen. He inspected the fish and the tube of Thai spices, and looked at me, rather alarmed. Then he called out, "Sofia, dear God help me, he's going to try to cook!"

"Ignore him," I told her, knowing she'd heard him. I followed him into the kitchen. "I cook sometimes."

Cooper held out his hand, and reluctantly, I handed the phone over. While I separated the fish and dabbed it with paper towel, Cooper spoke to Sofia. He gave her a commentary of my culinary skills and I heard her laugh through the phone. The entire conversation lasted all of thirty seconds. And when he slid my phone onto the counter, he sighed. "She loves me."

I rolled my eyes. "Well, she can take a number."

"She told me to tell you that you should cook more often."

"Of course she did."

"Even though you're cooking fish, when I specifically asked for chicken."

"You did not!"

"Well, I meant to," he said. "And she said you should stop looking so damn sexy in jeans with no socks and shoes," he said, looking at my feet.

I smiled at him. "Right. She said that."

Cooper nodded shamelessly. "She also said you were lucky to have someone as awesome as me."

"Oh, yes, we all know that," I said flatly.

"Then she said you should stop what you're doing, drop to your knees in the kitchen and give me a blow job."

I laughed at him. "Are you sure she said that?" I asked. "It wasn't a very long conversation, and that's hardly an icebreaker for short conversations with ex-wives."

"Yes, that's what she said," Cooper said seriously. "Or something like that, I was having trouble concentrating. I was distracted by your naked feet."

I washed my hands in the sink, dried my hands on the dishtowel then walked over to stand in front of him. I pulled his chin between my thumb and forefinger and pulled his lips to mine. Sliding my hand down his neck, his chest, further down his stomach and even lower, I expertly popped the button on his suit pants with one hand.

He smiled against my lips then he nodded. "Do it."

I slowly lowered to my knees and, right there in the kitchen, undid his suit pants and freed his semi-hard dick from his briefs. I took him into my mouth, and sucked his cock to life.

I listened to him moan, and just before my eyes closed, lost to the feeling of him in my mouth, I saw his fingers grip the marble countertop. I loved how his cock hardened, how it felt like silk on steel in my mouth — hot, hard and pulsing.

I wrapped my arms around his thighs and opened my throat to take all of him. I skimmed my fingers between the cheeks of his ass, over his hole to his balls, and with a strangled cry, he came. His cock swelled and lurched in my mouth as he tried not to thrust into me, and his cum shot thickly down my throat.

I licked him clean and when I let go of his hips, he slumped against the countertop and slid down so he sat on the floor in front of me. He had a blissful, lazy smile and his eyes were heavy-lidded. He chuckled. "Jesus, Tom."

"You're gonna have to get up," I told him.

His eyes took a second to focus on me, and grinned. "Why?"

"Because I'm old and my knees are locked up from kneeling on the floor."

He laughed, really loudly. I pushed his shoulder. "It's not that funny, asshole. Now help me get up."

He was still laughing, but got to his feet and pulled me up. He slowly tucked his spent cock back into his briefs, making sure I watched, then took my face in his hands and kissed me. He was still smiling.

"I suppose I should cook dinner now," he said. "Considering you just ate."

"You're such a little shit," I said. Then I squeezed his ass and gently pushed him out of the kitchen. "You go get changed, I'm cooking."

"Only if I get dessert later on," he said as he walked toward the hall. "But I'll make sure your knees don't lock up."

I was frying fish, and still pouting by the time he came back out. He'd changed into cargos and an old college shirt, looking like he was about to play football in the park. I huffed at him. "If you don't mind not looking so fucking cute when I'm mad at you, thanks."

He slid his arms around me from behind and nuzzled my neck. I could tell he was smiling. "Don't be mad," he mumbled into the skin behind my ear. "You're perfect and gorgeous, so incredibly sexy, even if your old knees find tiles unforgiving."

I sighed. "You know, maybe I wouldn't have such a complex about my age around you if you'd stop making fun of it."

Cooper stood back and with a hand on my shoulder, he turned me around. There was no joking in his eyes, only concern and a seriousness I rarely saw in him. He opened his mouth, unsure of how to say something. Then he shook his head and whispered, "I don't mean it. I don't care about the age difference, I promise. I just joke about it...well, because that's what I do. I'm sorry. I'm sorry, I didn't—"

I put my hand to his lips and smiled at him. "I know you don't mean anything by it."

He shook his head, and he looked genuinely worried. "I don't. I don't mean anything by it. Don't be mad. I'm fucking cute, remember?"

I pretended to have to think about it.

So then he kissed me.

All-consuming, hands, lips, mouth and tongue. Soft, slow, deep and sure, he held my face to his and kissed me like I'd never been kissed.

I forgot about the sizzling fish. Hell, I forgot my own name.

He pulled away, licked his lips and took the spatula out of my hand, while I stood there, dazed and out of breath.

Cooper turned the fish in the pan and nodded smugly.

I exhaled in a rush and wiped my thumb across my bottom lip, feeling where he'd just been. "Jesus, Cooper. You can kiss."

"You're not the first person to tell me that."

"I better be the last."

Cooper turned the fish again. "Is that some Thomas Elkin way of telling me you want to be with me forever?"

I leaned against the countertop and sighed. "I'm pleading the Fifth on that, because no matter what I say, it will be wrong."

Cooper laughed at that. "Yes, it probably will."

Seeing the fish was nearly done, I grabbed two plates. "It seems whenever I ask something, it's wrong."

"Only the big stuff."

I snorted. "Good to know."

Cooper plated the fish, threw on some sliced lemon and I carried the salad and cutlery to the table. He sat at the table, still smiling. "What did Sofia call for?" he asked as he dished up the salad.

"There are a few things that belonged to my dad at the Casa," I said. "She offered for us to have the place to ourselves next weekend."

"The Casa?"

I nodded, spearing the first mouthful of fish. "Do you think you might want to spend the weekend in the Hamptons with a sexy, older man?"

"Do you know any?" he asked.

I tasted the fish. "Mmm, this is really good," I said. "And yes, I think I know someone who might be available."

Cooper slipped a forkful of fish into his mouth, and smiled as he ate. "This is good," he said, finally swallowing his food. "So is this guy hung?"

"Like a horse," I answered. "Or so he's been told."

Cooper laughed, but we ate in silence until our plates were almost empty. "My next two weeks are busy as hell, so I'll probably look forward to a weekend away," he said, leaning back in his chair. "I have the next two weeks working with Xavier, so God knows I'll be needing some serious, sexy-older-man-who's-hung-like-a-horse time."

I pushed my plate away, leaned back in my chair and smiled. "Then you shall have it."

Cooper rubbed his stomach. "Dinner was good. I should cook more often."

"Cook?" I scoffed. "You turned the fish in the pan."

"Like a chef," he said proudly. "Oh," he said as though he'd just remembered, "I spoke to my mom today. I told her about the photo in the paper. I emailed it to her."

"What did she say?"

"That I'm awesome!" he said simply. "Well, she's my mom. Of course she thinks I'm awesome."

"I happen to think you're awesome too."

"You're my boyfriend. You have to say that."

"I call you a lot of things."

"I know. Some of them not very flattering, I might add."

"Such as?"

"You call me a little shit all the time."

"Because you are...some of the time."

"I think I prefer the term sassy."

I laughed at that. "So, if I call you sassy, it will be like a secret code instead of little shit?"

"Exactly!" he said. "Like if I stop saying 'because you're old', I could say you were being 'funny'."

"Funny?"

Cooper nodded brightly, apparently thinking this was a great idea. "Mm-hm. Funny is much nicer than old."

"What if you wanted to actually call me funny?"

Cooper cocked his head and looked off into space. "Well, it hasn't happened yet."

"You're such a —"

Cooper raised one eyebrow. "I'm what?"

"Sassy. You're a sassy little shit."

Cooper sighed, trying not to smile. "Well, it's true. You can't teach an old dog new tricks."

* * * *

Cooper was right. For the next week, work kicked his ass. Early mornings, late nights, but he never lost that buzz for what he was doing. He'd get home late and show me the latest developments, excitedly demonstrating what he'd done that day.

On the Friday night, Cooper got in around eleven and as he sat on the edge of the bed, he took his shoes and socks off and sighed tiredly. He said Xavier was still all over him like a rash, but he had told Xavier again and again he wasn't interested. "If he stands too close, I talk about you," Cooper said. "If he even looks at me like he's about to say something not work related, I talk about you."

I put my book on the bedside table and smiled. "Don't let him bother you."

"Does it bother you?" he asked, stripping down to his briefs.

"No," I said quietly. "If it upset you, then that would upset me, but he can *want* you all he likes. Doesn't mean he'll *get* you." I pulled back the bed cover and Cooper climbed onto the bed.

He rested his head on my chest and snuggled into my side. "No, it doesn't."

We'd had a similar conversation to this that had ended in a fight, so I was wary as to how this would go. I kissed the top of his head. "I trust you, sweetheart."

This time he didn't argue. Instead, he whispered, "Thank you," then he just kissed my chest, held me tighter and fell asleep in my arms.

* * * *

He worked most of the weekend at his office, which was fine. I got work done from home, but it was eerily quiet. No music, nothing to trip over on the floor, no smell of food cooking in the apartment, no one swearing at the coffee machine.

It wasn't lost on me just how much he brought to my life.

Or how much I missed him when he wasn't there.

When he got home late on Sunday, I asked him if he wanted me to heat his dinner for him. He shook his head tiredly, and without a word, he took my hand and led me to bed.

He was tired, his movements were unhurried, his kisses slow and languid. "I really need you," he said gruffly. "Please, Tom." It didn't take much for me to be turned on by him.

I laid him on his stomach on the bed, and I lifted his ass. Slowly, tenderly, I readied him for me, and when I finally pushed my sheathed cock inside him, he arched his back and moaned.

I lay down over him, filling him completely. His eyes were closed and I slowly rocked my hips into him, savoring every moment. "Fuck," he moaned, long and low.

I kissed his neck, his shoulder, everywhere I could reach, while I thrust slowly into his ass. Cooper put his hands over mine, threading my fingers with his, and spread his thighs even wider.

I was buried so far inside him, every inch of me, and he lifted his ass for more. I rocked harder, I thrust deeper and when his ass squeezed my cock, I couldn't hold off anymore. "Gonna come," I rasped in his ear.

He threw his head back and groaned, while I filled the condom, deep inside him.

When I pulled out of him, I rolled him over. His eyes were closed, and he was smiling, his cock still hard. "You didn't come," I stated softly.

"Didn't need to," he replied sleepily, still with his eyes shut. "Just needed you."

I discarded the condom and licked the length of him, from his balls to the glistening tip of his cock. When I took him into my mouth, I slipped my finger into his still-slicked ass in search of his gland.

He bucked his hips, gripped the sheets and his eyes shot open. "Fuck!" he croaked out.

I sucked and licked, and rubbed and swiped his prostate until he came with a hoarse cry. His body convulsed, wracked with waves of pleasure. Completely spent, boneless and smiling, he fell asleep.

* * * *

The next week was much the same. He worked hard, as did I, and I missed him terribly. I still got a text message when he had a spare moment, a phone call at work every now and then, though he sounded tired.

He'd come home late every night, crawling into bed and falling asleep, only to wake up and go into work early. I knew he had to do it. Long hours came with a successful career. So as much as I missed him, I understood.

On Thursday night after work when I walked into the lobby of our apartment, Lionel beamed. "Special delivery for you, Mr. Elkin," he said, the crinkles at his eyes telling me it was a genuine smile.

I walked over to the reception desk, where there was a wrapped box and a bouquet of a dozen red roses. "Are these for me?"

Lionel nodded. "I think someone misses you."

My eyes darted to the doorman's. "Is there a card?"

"Of course," Lionel answered, handing me a small white envelope. "But Mr. Jones phoned ahead. He wanted to make sure it arrived. He said to say he'll be late again, and thank you for understanding."

I grinned so hard it was ridiculous, thanked Lionel then took my gifts and went upstairs.

I opened the card first.

Saw this. It reminded me of you, of where it all began.

I ripped open the wrapping on the box, confused at first at what I saw. Then I burst out laughing and my heart warmed in my chest.

Of all the things it could have been, it was a box of fucking Lego.

Of where it all began...

The Architecture Lego of the Sydney Opera House.

Where we'd gone together, where we'd first made love, where I'd first realized the lines had blurred, where I'd been falling in love with him.

Where it all began.

Chapter Five

When Cooper got home, it was almost midnight. I was sitting on the sofa with the coffee table in front of me, music playing softly. I'd drunk a bottle of wine and had almost finished the Sydney Opera House.

He set his satchel down at the door, looked at the empty bottle of wine, then at the Lego masterpiece and finally he looked at me.

"Having fun?"

I chuckled at the look of disbelief on his face. "Actually, I am." Then I added, "But if you tell anyone, I'll deny it."

He fell onto the sofa beside me with a sigh and kissed me soundly.

"You're up late."

"Someone gave me Lego."

Cooper laughed. "And flowers, I hope." He looked around the apartment and found the vase full of roses on the middle of the dining table.

When he turned back to me, just about to speak, I slid my hand along his jaw, leaned in and kissed him.

"Thank you. No one has ever bought me flowers before."

His eyes widened. "No one?"

"No one, ever."

Cooper smiled proudly, but then his brow furrowed. "What about Lego? Has anyone ever bought you Lego?"

I couldn't help but chuckle at him. "I had wooden blocks as a kid. No Lego."

Cooper leaned back into the sofa and pulled his tie off. He was exhausted. "I saw it, and thought of you," he said, smiling tiredly. "Going to Sydney was like the beginning of us, wasn't it?"

"It was," I agreed. I looked back at the almost-completed Lego Opera House. "What other Lego buildings did they have?"

Cooper had to think. "Um, Seattle space needle, Empire State, Eiffel Tower…"

"We should get them all," I suggested. "Then we can go see the real thing."

He raised one eyebrow at me. "The Eiffel Tower?"

"Absolutely," I said, squeezing his knee. "There is so much I'd love to show you in Paris…actually, there's a lot of Europe I'd love to show you."

Cooper leaned his head on the back of the sofa and smiled warmly at me. "I would love that."

"You're so tired," I stated the obvious. "Come on, let's get you into bed." I pulled him to his feet, and while I turned off lights, he walked down the hall, stripping off his shirt and vest as he went. He dropped them where he was. I picked them up as I followed him, then his crumpled suit pants off the bedroom floor.

He was crawling into bed, wearing only his briefs. "Are we leaving after work tomorrow to head up to the Hamptons?"

"Yeah, if you want."

He nodded. "Looking forward to it," he said with a yawn.

"How was Xavier?"

Cooper groaned. "I don't want to talk about him. He's a sleaze."

I got into bed and pulled up the covers. "Has he hit on you again?"

"All the time," Cooper mumbled, almost asleep. "But I'm not privileged. He's like it with everyone."

I leaned over and kissed his closed eyelid. "Go to sleep, sweetheart. Thank you again for my gifts."

"Welcome," he mumbled, and his lip curled up in a tired smile.

"I love you," I whispered.

"'Cause I'm awesome," came his mumbled response. His hand reached for mine, he threaded our fingers and brought our hands to his chest. His breathing evened out, and he fell into sleep.

* * * *

Cooper brought so much work with us when we went up to the Casa, I wondered if it was even worth the break away.

It also reminded me of what Sofia had put up with for years. I'd worked so much when I was Cooper's age, and for the twenty years after. I'd taken work with me when we vacationed, on weekends and nights out.

I didn't begrudge Cooper for the workload. I didn't envy him either. But it was something I understood.

I carried in the overnight bag of clothes and dropped it at the foot of the stairs, while Cooper unloaded his satchel, laptop and briefcase onto the dining table.

It was ten in the morning, but Cooper hadn't eaten before we'd left. He'd barely woken up. "Are you hungry?" I asked him. "If you want, I'll make you something to eat while you have a swim to wake yourself up?"

Cooper smiled. "You just like to see me wet."

"True."

"Will you join me?"

"Maybe later," I said. "I want you to relax first. You've been working so hard. Relax first, work later."

"You relax me," he said, smirking at me. "You, wet, in the pool, with me. *That* would relax me."

I rolled my eyes. "I'm sure it would."

But then his eyebrows pinched, and he said, "We didn't bring any food. We can't eat Sofia's food, that'd be rude."

"I organized a grocery delivery yesterday. Sofia was here when it arrived."

Cooper walked over and pecked my lips with his. "You think of everything."

I smiled, but then I admitted, "Well, Jennifer asked if I wanted to have food delivered. She knew we were coming up here for the weekend, and thought it was a good idea. She organized it."

"Remind me to thank Jennifer," Cooper said with a smile.

"She likes you," I told him.

"Of course she does," he said. Then he took a fistful of my shirt and led me to the back doors, toward the pool. "Come on, old man, you're coming with me to get wet."

I tried to protest. "I'm not wearing swimming trunks."

Cooper laughed, opened the door and pulled me outside. "You won't need them."

* * * *

After we were both wet, and *relaxed*, we got dried and dressed and Cooper suggested a walk on the beach before an early lunch.

He seemed to be a little quiet, which I presumed was from being tired, so I never questioned it. I just held his hand as we walked, and was more resolved to make sure he had a relaxing weekend away.

The afternoon got cool, and Cooper started to organize his workspace on the large dining table. Sofia had left the two items from my father on the dining table, so I told Cooper I'd put them in the car so he had more room.

Cooper ran his hand over the telescope. "It's beautiful, Tom."

"It is," I agreed. "It was nice of Sofia to give it back to me. I didn't think of taking it when we split. She got the house and everything in it, and by the time it all went through, I just wanted to move on, you know?"

Cooper nodded thoughtfully. "Where will you put it?"

"I don't know," I answered honestly. "Somewhere in the apartment, or I'll store it, or give it to Ryan."

"Do you play chess?" he asked, eyeing the wooden board.

"Not for a long time."

"You'll have to teach me how to play one day."

"I'd love that," I said, a warm smile spread across my face. "Not this weekend, though. You have enough work to keep you busy."

I took the telescope and the chessboard and loaded them into the trunk of the car, and when I came back inside, Cooper was leaning against the door frame looking at me.

"You okay?" I asked.

He smiled warmly. "I am. Are you?"

"Of course," I answered. I leaned in and kissed him. We turned and as we walked through the foyer into the living room, I noticed Cooper was looking around. He didn't look his usual comfortable, confident self.

I stopped and faced him. "What's bothering you?" I asked outright. "I mean, about this place? Since we got here, you've been quiet. I thought you were just tired, but now I'm not sure."

Cooper shrugged and spoke to the floor. "I don't know...it's a bit silly, actually."

"What is it?"

"Just that you designed this house. This is yours. For Sofia."

I knew something had been bothering him. "And Ryan," I corrected. "And for me. This holiday house was for me too."

"But it's not anymore."

"No, and you know what?" I asked rhetorically. "I don't regret it. Sure, I loved this house. I loved the fact that I could design something for my family. But I'm happy Sofia has it. I'm happy she wanted to keep it and not sell it to some stranger. I know you don't really like that I have a history with Sofia, but I do. And I can't change it. But, Cooper, please understand, I'd give up this house a hundred times over if it means I get to keep my life as it is now. It's kind of perfect."

He smiled at me. "That's because I'm in it."

I rolled my eyes at his way of making everything about him. Even if it was.

"It's funny," he said thoughtfully. "I mean, I can see how, fifteen years ago, this was the perfect holiday home for a family. I can see that. But it's big, and I don't know…" He trailed off. "But what bothers me is that this house," he said with a sigh, "this house isn't the Tom I know."

"The house isn't me?"

He shook his head, looking around the room. "No, I don't know *this* Tom."

"You mean you didn't know me fifteen years ago when I designed it?"

"Yeah, I'm probably not explaining it right," he said. "It's just not what I would see you in now, if you designed something to suit your life as it is now. The Tom that I know."

"What do you think I would design?"

"Something smaller. Earthier. With more wood and stone. Something more rustic, not the vast open spaces this place has. More cabin-like, with a fire and a small marble kitchen. I just see you in something more honest and genuine, no pretenses."

I smiled and shook my head slowly. "You read me so well."

"I know you," he said simply. "And there would be a room like a study or an attic, with a wall of glass or dormer windows for the telescope, and a drawing board where you would get lost for hours."

"Well that's where you're wrong," I said softly.

He tilted his head and raised one eyebrow in question.

"There would be *two* drawing boards."

Cooper smiled and ducked his head, almost shyly. "Yes, there would."

I walked over to him and kissed him. "It still amazes me how much you see the real me."

He exhaled contentedly. "I am kind of awesome like that."

"Yes, you are," I said, before kissing him again. "Why don't you get some work done while I work my culinary magic in the kitchen."

Cooper raised a sarcastic eyebrow at me. "Culinary magic?"

"Oh, shut up," I grumbled. "I suck at cooking and you know it."

He had a glazed, dreamy look on his face and after a while, he said, "I'm sorry, you mentioned sucking and I got distracted. I didn't hear a word after that." I rolled my eyes and walked into the kitchen, but he called out, "Your cooking is fine, Tom. But your sucking skills are your true talent."

I ignored his comment, and set about getting a dinner ready while Cooper got lost in his paperwork and laptop. As I chopped and diced, I thought about what Cooper had said.

It made total sense. Then again, most of what he said did.

This house, the Casa, was big, purpose-built for a family. Large open spaces, and maybe there was a detached feeling to that, which Cooper had picked up on. Maybe there was a detached feeling to the man who had designed it, all those years ago.

I loved how he said this house wasn't the Tom he knew.

I loved how he could identify the architect with a building, but then differentiate them as well.

He knew me so damn well. We'd not even been together a year, and yet he knew things about me I didn't even know.

"You'd better be thinking of me when you smile like that," Cooper said, now standing beside me.

I hadn't heard him come into the kitchen. I bumped his hip with mine. "Of course I'm thinking about you."

"Then why aren't you hard?" he asked, looking pointedly at my crotch. Before I could say anything, he said, "They have pills now, for old guys who can't get hard."

I pointed a carrot at him. "I can get hard just fine," I said. "You know that damn well...unless you need reminding?"

Cooper leaned forward and bit the end off the carrot. He grinned and waggled his eyebrows, as if he was daring me. "I think I might need reminding." He chewed the mouthful of carrot and swallowed. "But dinner first. I'm starving."

After dinner, Cooper went back to work while I cleaned up. And by the time I fell onto the sofa, Cooper shut down his laptop and shuffled in beside me. We watched some TV and even though I finally got him to relax and have some downtime, I could tell he wasn't too comfortable in the Casa.

Not that he was *un*comfortable, just not his usual vibrant self. I think it was because it reminded him that I'd had a life before him. I'd shared this house, the bedroom upstairs, with Sofia...

"Oh, Jesus," I groaned. "I shouldn't have brought you here."

Cooper sat up and stared at me, confusion clear on his face. "What? Why not?" His voice was quiet and worried. Oh, God. He thought I didn't want him here.

"No, I didn't mean it like that," I said quickly, taking his hand. "I just meant that I don't want to be in this house. You were right. I don't like what it represents, my life with Sofia, and I shouldn't have expected you to stay here."

"Tom..."

I shook my head. "I didn't even think of it like that, until just now. I didn't mean to bring you to a place that reminds you of me with someone else."

"Tom?"

"Come on," I said, standing up. "We'll find a hotel, or just drive back to the city."

"Tom!" Cooper said, louder this time. He pulled on my hand, pulling me back onto the sofa beside him. "It's fine. We don't have to leave." Then he leaned up and swung one leg over me, so he was straddling me. He pushed me back into the backrest of the sofa, and looked down at me. He softly planted his lips on mine. "But maybe you needed to come here one more time, so when we leave tomorrow it will be like a final goodbye...to this part of your life."

"It will be, yes," I whispered. I leaned up and kissed him. "It's kind of fitting that you're here with me, actually."

He smiled and nodded. "So we don't have to leave?"

I shook my head slowly. "If you want to stay, we'll stay."

"Good. I want you to take me to bed. Last time we were here, we fooled around, but we didn't really get to christen the bed properly. I was too drunk at Ryan's party, if I remember correctly," he said. His eyes sparked with mischief. "So I think we better do it twice tonight to make up for it."

"Is that so?"

Cooper nodded. Then he was serious. "Thank you for thinking of me," he said. He pecked my lips with his own. "I'm lucky to have you."

"I was just thinking the same thing."

"Take me upstairs, Tom," he said. "I don't think Sofia would appreciate stains on her sofa."

I did as he asked, of course. Then he did the same to me.

* * * *

The next morning, we took a long walk on the beach. It was getting cool, and Cooper tucked himself into my side as we walked. He talked of the project he was working on with Xavier and how the job was moving along nicely. He seemed content to just talk, and I could listen to him forever.

He was even okay when I called in quickly to see my mom. He walked in, smiled as he said hello and politely accepted the offer of coffee. Mom was doing okay—she missed Dad terribly and said she always would, but I wanted to check in on her, considering we weren't too far away.

My mom was pleasant enough, she wouldn't ever be rude to Cooper, but she also didn't acknowledge our relationship. I doubted she probably ever would. But she knew I was gay, she knew I was with him, she simply chose to not talk about it. And that was okay.

When we'd said goodbye and were on our way back to the city, Cooper sighed contentedly. "You know, I think your mom is starting to warm to me."

"How so?"

"She offered me coffee," he said with a smile. "She doesn't have to start any new PFLAG chapters or anything, but she smiled when she saw you, and she offered me coffee. That's pretty lucky."

I took his hand over the center console. "I was just thinking the same thing. She'll probably never say the word 'gay' or 'boyfriend', but as long as she smiles and offers us coffee, then we're good."

Then right on cue, Cooper's cell phone rang. He checked the screen before answering. "Mom?"

I watched the road, but I could hear his mother's voice through the phone.

"Um, two weeks?" Cooper said. "Hang on, I'll check." He put the phone against his chest so his mom couldn't hear. "Mom wants to come to New York in two weeks, just for the weekend. Is that okay?"

"Of course it is, you don't need to ask me," I said.

Cooper smiled and lifted the phone back to his ear. "Sure, Mom. Weekend after next would be great."

After a short conversation, he disconnected the call and smiled. It was obvious the offer for a visit was one of acceptance. "There's some show Mom wants to see," he said, still smiling. "Thought it would be a great excuse to come for a visit."

"That's great, Cooper," I said, taking his hand again, giving it a squeeze. "You know my apartment's yours now too, you live there. You don't have to ask permission for anyone to stay. Your entire family is welcome."

"Good," he said with a grin. "Because my entire family is coming."

Chapter Six

Work that week was hectic, as per usual. Cooper's was even busier than mine. He was hoping to wrap up the job with Xavier soon and was putting in the hours to get it done.

I couldn't say I blamed him. Xavier Baurhenn was a jerk, and Cooper was fed up with him.

Cooper was really looking forward to his family visiting, and truth be told, as much as it made me nervous, it was a positive step forward. Cooper needed them in his life. He wanted their approval, whether he admitted it or not, and I wanted him to be happy. So we were planning a dinner at home on the Saturday night, hoping they'd see Cooper was still the same.

The weekend before his parents were due to visit, he'd taken a break from work and decided he was going to cook for the dinner party. He had the menu planned and everything. The only thing he wanted my help with was to choose the wine, but then he proceeded to tell me which types of wine his parents preferred, so he ended up taking that task off me as well.

Sitting at the dining table, he was writing lists and recipes, while I watched on in wonder. He was a control freak, through and through. "Cooper, sweetheart," I said with a kiss to his temple. "They're coming here to see you, which shows they're making an effort."

"Which is why it has to be perfect!" he cried.

"It will be. Just be yourself."

He exhaled through puffed-out cheeks. "Tom, I just want them to see *us*, you know?"

"They will," I reassured him.

"How come you're so confident?"

"Because they love you," I answered. "And because you're cooking, not me."

He finally smiled. "That's true."

I snatched the shopping list. "At least let me get the grocery items."

Cooper smiled at me. "You mean, let Jennifer order them for you."

I resisted sticking my tongue out at him. "Jennifer doesn't do *everything* for me."

His lips twisted as he tried not to smile. "Oh, okay, if you say so," he said, rolling his eyes. "Tell her it doesn't matter what kind of flowers she orders, just as long as they're bright."

I didn't even try to deny that I'd be giving the list to Jennifer. I lifted my chin with dignity. "Jennifer knows where to buy the best stuff."

Cooper laughed. "So, if the day ever arrives when I get flowers delivered, or cool Lego sets, or new Prada boots from the new winter collection, I'll just presume Jennifer buys them for me?"

This time it was me who laughed. "New Prada boots?"

"Well, they *are* nice," he lamented. "They're black, and pull-on, and they have this stitching patterned across the toe...you know, just in case you were wondering which ones..."

I shook my head at him. "Your ability to drop a subtle hint is sorely lacking."

Cooper got up from his seat, sat himself on my lap and kissed me. "You know what else is sorely lacking?"

I smiled. "No idea."

"You."

I quirked an eyebrow at him. "Me?"

"I've been so busy, and I feel so bad, and this week will be even busier, and then next week my family will be here," he said. "I don't want you to feel like you're second place for me, because you're not." He held my face in his hands. "You're first place, all the time. Even if I'm at work, or in a meeting, or whatever, you're always first."

His words and the sincerity in his eyes made me smile. "I know that."

"I know you say you understand how busy I am, but, Tom, I can't see it slowing down any time soon, and if anything, the more my name gets out there, the busier I'll be."

"Cooper, it's fine, really."

"You say that now," he said. "But what about later, in a year or five years' time, when you're sick of being alone?"

"I won't be alone," I told him. "I have my work, too. And Ryan, and my mom—and, Cooper, I have you. We'll just have to plan around our schedules and work in some time for us."

He smiled. "I'd like that. Maybe one weekend a month, we could take off. Get out of the city, or book a mystery flight away for a few days every now and then, or even if we stay here, we can tell Lionel we've gone, turn our phones off and block out the world."

"That sounds perfect."

"I just don't want to lose us. Life's gonna get busy, and I want to keep us in check, you know?"

I kissed him sweetly. "God, I love you. You're just…"

"Awesome?"

"Sassy."

"Did you just call me a little shit?"

I shook my head slowly. "Maybe."

"And to think I was going to ask you to take me to bed." He sighed dramatically. "Now I might just insist on you cooking me dinner."

"How about both?"

"In what order?"

"Does it matter?"

"Yes."

"How hungry are you?"

"Starving."

"How about I order dinner to be delivered, which should give us about forty minutes to fill in."

He smiled when he kissed me. "I do believe I like the way you think."

* * * *

First chance I got at work on Monday, I Googled Prada stores, then the boots he had mentioned. One thing was certain. Cooper had expensive taste. Whether he was joking about wanting the boots or not, I bought them.

But then knowing ordering them online wouldn't be good enough, I went to the store in my lunch hour. I had the store wrap them and courier them to his office, with a handwritten note attached that read, 'Anything for you…'

I got sidetracked with new clientele, and it wasn't until I was walking home that I realized I'd not heard from Cooper. I was a little disappointed, but looked forward to seeing his reaction first-hand when he got home.

It was late, well after I'd gotten home, and he walked through the door looking tired. He slumped his satchel on the floor next to the sofa then sat across from me on the other sofa. I put the job file I was reading through down and watched him.

Without a word, he lifted his newly-Prada-booted feet and slid them onto the coffee table, and a slow smile spread across his face.

"Anything for you," he repeated what I'd written on the card.

I stared straight at him. "Yes."

"You didn't have to actually buy them, you know. I was only joking."

"Your wish, my command. Or something like that," I said, smiling back at him.

"My wish?"

"I believe I said 'anything', yes."

"My wish is you, in me."

My eyes widened at his blatant request. "Is that so?"

"Yes."

"You're very tired."

"Then fuck me slowly."

I shook my head at him, but stood up and held out my hand. He took it, and I pulled him to his feet but as I stepped toward the hall, he pulled me back to him. Cooper slid his arms around me and held me, nuzzling into my neck.

"I was having such a shitty day today," he mumbled into my collarbone. "And then I got some boots delivered and you have no idea how much I wanted to leave right then and come see you."

I tightened my hold on him and ran one hand over the back of his head.

"It wasn't even the boots, really." Then he amended, "Don't get me wrong. They're great, but the card…"

"Anything for you," I whispered against the side of his head.

He nodded. "It was just what I needed to hear. Thank you."

"You're very welcome."

"Take me to bed, Tom."

"You're so tired, sweetheart."

He pulled back to look at me. "Are you going to make me beg?"

I shook my head and kissed his lips. "Never."

I made love to him, softly, slowly. I savored every movement, every thrust. Cooper was on his back, with his legs bent to his chest. He never took his mouth from mine. He kissed me deeply, keeping rhythm with every roll of my hips. His orgasm surged through him, his eyes fluttered closed and his fingers dug into my skin.

By the time I had us both cleaned up, he was half asleep. When I crawled in next to him, he burrowed himself into my side. I kissed the side of his head and whispered that I loved him, but he was already asleep.

* * * *

Tuesday at work was productive. I got in early, left late and got a lot of work done. Jennifer came in just before she left for the day, and sat down across from me. She looked worried.

"Tom," she said. "Robert's up to something."

N.R. Walker

I put my pen down and sighed. "What do you mean?"

"He's been asking questions around the office, apparently. Not just on this floor either. I don't know what his problem is."

"His problem is that I'm gay," I told her outright.

"He never had a problem with it before."

"He never saw me with anyone before," I said. "I'm presuming when he saw me with Cooper at my father's funeral, he didn't like it much."

"He never said anything to me," she told me. "He sat with me the entire time."

I shrugged. "It's the only thing I can think of."

"Well, I don't like it, Tom. It makes me feel uneasy." She shook her head. "You've given so much of your life to this place. I just don't know what he's trying to achieve."

"Maybe he wants me gone."

Jennifer blinked. "I work for you. I don't want to work for anyone else."

I gave her a smile. "I'm sure it won't come to that. He simply can't just say he wants me fired because I'm gay. He'd be in court faster than he could blink, and he knows it. I gave him the perfect opportunity to issue me with a written notice, citing violation of policy, and he didn't do it."

"Because he couldn't prove anything."

"That was just him letting me know he knew damn well I'd breached policy," I told her. I exhaled loudly. "Jennifer, I don't know, to be honest. But as long as I keep doing my job, he can't say anything. He might not like my choice of partner, but it doesn't concern him."

Jennifer frowned. "Well, I don't like it."

I gave her a smile. "I know, but try not to worry. It'll be fine, you'll see."

She gave me a nod, though she hardly looked convinced. "Give Cooper my best."

"I will," I told her. "I'll just wrap up this file and be heading home myself."

"See you in the morning," she said, and the door closed quietly behind her.

Needless to say, my mind was hardly on the job folder in front of me.

Whatever Robert's issues were, they were with me, and I hated that Jennifer was worried over whatever nonsense he was hell-bent on proving.

I'd given ten years of my life to Brackett and Golding. I'd worked seven days a week, putting in countless, endless hours. I'd won contract after contract, award after award — they were on shelves and walls, peppering my success in this company over the last decade.

Admittedly, the success was for me as much as it was for Brackett and Golding. But the feeling of being shunned, ousted, was not pleasant.

Actually, it was pretty fucking awful.

I packed up my satchel, needing to talk to Cooper. I knew it would piss him off and that I had to tell him, but it was late when he got home. He was stressed enough with the Xavier job, and his parents visiting this weekend, so I tried to let it go.

But when we were lying in bed, with Cooper's head on my chest, me tracing circles on his back, I had to tell him. I didn't want to keep anything from him. I took a deep breath, and said, "I think Robert's trying to get rid of me."

He leaned up on his elbow. "Seriously?"

I nodded. "Yeah."

He opened his mouth, no doubt to rant, but I rolled onto my side and faced him. "Cooper, don't worry. I haven't been issued with any kind of warning or anything like that. He's just been snooping, trying to find something that will stick. Nothing may come of it. I just wanted you to know."

Even in the darkened room, I could see him frown. "What's his problem? Is it me? Is it because I was your intern? Is it something you did? Is it something I did?"

I traced my fingers across his cheekbone. "I think it's because I'm gay."

Cooper's mouth snapped shut, and I knew he was mad. So I leaned in and kissed him, soft and sweet. "Cooper, sweetheart, I've told you before. I wouldn't change a thing I've done. I wouldn't. I don't care what he thinks, or anyone else for that matter. He can fire me for all I care, because I somehow got you. And I'd choose you every day for the rest of my life over Robert Chandler."

Cooper fell onto his back. "Jesus, Tom. Don't ask me to marry you when I'm mad. Fuck."

I laughed and pulled him against me. "Was there a proposal in there somewhere, on some Cooper frequency that I didn't hear?"

He sighed. "You keep talking forever."

I nodded. "And marriage and forever are the same?"

"Yep."

I kissed the top of his head, unable to stop smiling. "Go to sleep."

He mumbled, "Don't tell me what to do," but tightened his hold on me, and soon was sound asleep.

* * * *

I went about my work on Wednesday, like any other day. I kept an eye out for Robert, but didn't see him. Cooper called me after lunch to see how things were, and I told him it was all just normal. "Maybe I'm imagining it," I said.

"And Jennifer?" he asked. "She doesn't miss a thing in that office."

I sighed. "She's the one who told me she thought something was wrong."

"Fuck, Tom," he said with a groan.

"We'll talk about it tonight," I said.

"I'll be late," he said. "I'm so close to finishing this, and then Xavier Baurhenn will be out of my life."

"I'll wait up."

"You better."

I smiled as I hung up the phone. But we didn't talk about it when he got home.

The doctor called him at work with his blood test results, and we talked about that instead. Everything was clear and physically he was in perfect health. But he was unsure about something. He was leaning against the kitchen counter, frowning.

"Cooper, what is it?"

He shrugged. "Well, just about the unprotected sex conversation we had before…"

"We don't have to not use condoms," I said. "Like we said before, no pressure. When we're ready."

"I want to," he said quietly. "Not yet, I don't think. But one day, soon maybe, if you want…"

I lifted his chin, and kissed his lips. "I want to, but when we're ready."

He bit his lip and nodded. "Okay."

"No pressure," I added. "We'll know when it's the right time."

His stomach grumbled, interrupting the conversation. I insisted he eat something, which he did, then I ran us a steaming hot shower and we fell into bed where he made love to me.

It was slow and deep, and when I imagined what it would be like to one day have him inside me, condomless, skin on skin, how he'd come inside me, I came.

* * * *

On Thursday morning, we walked through the lobby saying a quick hello to Lionel and chatting about New York winters. Cooper had reminded me of the grocery order I had to make today for his parents' dinner party. "Oh, and the little Italian patisserie on Eighth has these little fig tarts. I'm sure Mrs. Lionel would love them heated up."

Lionel was quick to object, "No, Mr. Jones, you don't have to do that."

"I don't," Cooper replied simply. "Tom does."

Lionel looked at me, somewhat alarmed, and I just smiled and rolled my eyes. "Really, Lionel, there is no point in arguing."

Lionel gave me a smile and a shrug, and Cooper nodded like his work here was done. With a quick kiss, Cooper and I went on our separate ways to work.

My morning was uneventful, but just before my ten o'clock meeting, Jennifer buzzed through my intercom. "Mr. Elkin?"

She sounded worried. "What is it, Jennifer?"

"You have a phone call on line one. He said his name was Lionel."

I frowned at the blinking button on my phone. "Thanks, Jennifer. I'll take it." I picked up the receiver. "Thomas Elkin speaking."

"Mr. Elkin," Lionel's familiar voice said.

"Lionel, is everything okay?"

"Well, yes," he said unsure. "I've tried calling Mr. Jones, but he's in meetings all day, apparently. I hope you don't mind me calling you at work. I have your office number in case of emergencies."

"Lionel, it's fine," I said, knowing he'd never call me if it wasn't warranted. "What is it?"

"There's a young gentleman here who says he's here to see Mr. Jones. He says his name is Maxwell Jones. He says he's Mr. Jones' brother?"

"Max?"

"Yes, sir." Then Lionel said, "I don't want to send him out onto the streets, Mr. Elkin, if he is indeed Mr. Jones' brother."

"Does he have long black hair, a nose ring?"

"Yes, sir."

Shit. "Tell him to wait. I'll be there in ten minutes."

Chapter Seven

When I walked into the lobby of my apartment, Lionel was laughing with our surprise visitor, who was indeed Max.

Cooper's brother's eyes brightened when he saw me. Whether he was just happy to see a familiar face or me in particular, I wasn't sure. Considering I'd only met him once, and he'd called me old, I assumed it was the former.

"Hey," Max said, by way of greeting. His longish black hair hung over half his face.

"Hey," I said, as casually as I could. "We were expecting you tomorrow. Cooper never said you were coming a day early."

"Oh, he doesn't know I'm here," Max said, as though it was no big deal.

"Max," I said, using my talking-to-teenagers voice. "Do your parents know you're here?"

"Yeah," he said. "I told them Coop knew I was coming, but I just forgot to call him. I was gonna call him from the airport, but then I forgot." He looked me up and down, seeing I was wearing a suit. "Oh, man. Did you leave work?"

I smiled at him, considering it was just after ten in the morning on a workday. "Ah, yes."

I glanced at Lionel then, and it prompted him to speak. "Max here was just telling me about his flight here." The crinkles around his eyes deepened when he smiled. "They don't look much alike, but they're definitely brothers."

I smiled a little more genuinely then. He wasn't just some seventeen-year-old kid. He was Cooper's brother. Then I noticed a backpack near his feet. "Come on, we'll take your things upstairs."

Max picked up his bag, and as we headed toward the elevator, I turned back and gave a nod of thanks to Lionel. He gave a knowing smile in return. As we took the elevator to my apartment, I wondered what the fucking hell I was supposed to do with a seventeen-year-old kid.

"Hey, sorry to be a pain in the ass," Max said.

I wasn't even sure if I should be correcting his language. I decided no, it wasn't my place. "It's okay," I said, as I let us into the apartment. "You can put your bag in the spare room. First door on your left down the hall, bathroom is the second door. I'll just try calling Cooper."

Max disappeared and I pulled out my cell. Of course he didn't answer. Twice. So I called his office, something I really didn't like doing. A bright and cheerful female voice answered, only to tell me Cooper was out on the job site and would be back in another hour or two.

Shit. Shit, shit, shit.

Since I couldn't very well leave him in the apartment by himself, the next number I dialed was my office.

Jennifer answered promptly. I told her I wouldn't be back in today. I had two appointments this afternoon, and told Jennifer one of my team could sit in on my behalf and fill me in later.

Then it occurred to me that Cooper would be even busier tomorrow, trying to get everything finalized on the Baurhenn job, so I told Jennifer to clear my schedule for tomorrow as well, just in case.

As I clicked off the call to Jennifer, Max walked back out and was looking around the living room. He inspected the photos, the antique drafting board then the Lego Sydney Opera House, but before he could touch it, I said, "Max, Cooper won't be back for a few hours."

He stared at me from behind his half-wall of hair. "Oh."

"So you're stuck with me."

"You don't need to babysit me."

I rolled my eyes at the very Cooper remark. "I'm hardly babysitting. Been to New York before?"

"Not since I was a kid."

"Well then," I said. "Where did you want to go first?"

Max smiled. "Really?"

"Just let me get changed," I said, but then stopped halfway to my room. "As long as it's not some death-metal concert crap. It's bad enough I have to listen to Cooper's taste in music, and I won't be responsible for tattoos. You do that with Cooper, not me."

Max grinned at me. "Deal *and* deal."

I quickly dressed in jeans and a light jacket, and suggested we go get some lunch. As we sat and ate, we made small talk and I learned a few things about him — he had a girlfriend called Ashley, she had pink hair and liked a list of bands I'd never heard of. At first appearances, Max didn't look like Cooper, at all. But underneath the dyed black hair and silver ring through his face, they were a lot alike.

They both had curious, keen eyes, a sense of self and strong opinions. I smiled when Max said he wanted to go to the University of Illinois and study computer science.

"There's a science of computers?" I asked.

He looked at me like I'd sprouted a second head. "It's programming and software design."

"So, you're exceptionally smart?"

He smiled at that. "I'm a four-point-oh."

He looked like a goth-wannabe kid with attitude, but he wasn't that way at all. "So the clothes, the hair, the nose ring?"

"Just part of my awesomeness."

I burst out laughing. "Oh, my God. You are so much like your brother."

Max chuckled quietly but shrugged one shoulder. "Never really thought about it."

"You and Cooper both have to know how things work, yes?"

Max half shrugged. "I guess." Then he added, "When we were younger, he'd build stuff and I'd watch. I wasn't allowed to play with his Lego," he said with a roll of his eyes. "But he was older than me, so he'd build houses and buildings and castles…"

"And what did you do?"

"I watched him. Sometimes I'd play with his stuff when he wasn't there, so he wouldn't know," Max said with a grin. "When he got older, all he wanted to do was draw. He did graphic arts and shit like that. Went from building houses, to drawing 'em."

"And you like computers?"

He nodded and sipped his Coke. "Yep. It's just what I know. Natural progression from playing games to designing them," he said simply.

"You design computer games?" I couldn't hide my surprise.

One corner of his lip curled up into the same smug smile Cooper had. "Only basic ones, but yep. Working on more complicated programming, but it takes time."

I smiled knowingly. They were so alike. Not in looks, but personality-wise they were. And more obviously, they were both very smart, and both designers, creators. It was kind of remarkable. "Maybe one day you can create a design program for architects to make our jobs a bit easier."

"Nah, not really my scene." Max pushed the rest of his uneaten lunch away. "I'm thinking more along the lines of the next Google or Windows."

I laughed. "Nothing like aiming high."

"Go hard or go home, right?"

"You're so much like Cooper," I said, shaking my head. "Come on, let's go see if he's back in his office."

We started walking the three blocks to Cooper's office and I pointed out a few buildings of interest. Max wasn't particularly interested, but nodded just to be polite, I'm sure.

He and Cooper definitely didn't share a love of architecture.

I'd only been to Cooper's office a couple of times, and only ever on a weekend when it was all but empty, but I knew which floor he was on. Getting out of the elevator and facing Arlington reception, we were greeted by a woman I'd not seen before.

"Can I help you?"

"I'd like to see Cooper Jones, please," I said giving her my most pleasant smile.

She tapped on her keyboard. "Is he expecting you?"

"Well, no actually, he's not," I explained. "But if you tell him Tom is here"—I looked at Max—"and a surprise."

Max spoke then, "He's Tom, I'm the surprise," he said with a disarming grin. God, he was so like Cooper.

"I'm afraid you'll need to make an appointment..." she started to tell me.

I put my hand up. "Never mind, thank you." I pulled my cell phone out and pressed redial.

Cooper answered on the second ring. "Hey."

"Hey," I replied. "I'm in reception."

"Where?"

"At your office," I explained. "In reception. I have...something for you." I looked at Max and smiled.

"Is it a matching Prada leather jacket?" he asked, but I could hear he was walking as he talked. "Because they have these black jackets with these tags and buckles. They're incredible."

"No, it's not a matching Prada jacket," I said, rolling my eyes.

Max smiled.

"Is it two tickets to Muse?"

"No, it's certainly not," I answered, wondering how long it would take, and how long the list was of possible gifts he was giving me hints for.

"Tickets to Paris?"

"Are you even in the building? Because this list is getting more expensive the longer I wait."

He laughed, but I heard him down the hallway, rather than through the phone. Cooper appeared at the door, and his smile died, his eyes widened.

"Max?"

"Surprise," Max said flatly, almost sarcastically.

Cooper crossed the floor and hugged his brother. "What are you doing here? Are Mom and Dad here?" he asked. Then he looked at me, then back to Max. "Why are you with Tom?"

"I came a day early. Mom and Dad aren't here. I flew in this morning."

Cooper blinked. "You came to New York City? By yourself? Are you insane? You're seventeen! What the hell were Mom and Dad thinking?"

"Well...well, they thought you organized it..."

That was news to me as well. Cooper's face paled. "Max, do they even know you're here?"

Max looked at me then back to Cooper. "Yeah...they... Well..."

Cooper grabbed Max's arm and led him down the hallway he'd just walked out of. I smiled at the receptionist, who was watching in wide-eyed wonder. I gave her a smile. "Brothers."

I followed Cooper and Max down the hall to Cooper's working station. The Arlington offices were an open-floor area, with communal tables and spaces which apparently encouraged teamwork and brainstorming. They were all about pushing boundaries on modernization and contemporary planning and design. It was...exciting.

It was so different from Brackett and Golding.

In all honesty, I preferred my private office. I did like working alone. But the concept, the enterprise of Arlington, was definitely modern and would see it lead the direction of where architecture was going. It reminded me that I'd made the right decision in calling Louisa Arlington to get Cooper an interview here.

Cooper led Max into a conference room, and I followed them in.

"Sit your ass in a chair," Cooper barked at his brother. At the same time he had his cell phone out and to his ear, waiting for whoever he was calling to answer. "I can't believe you just turned up here. I can't believe you came here on your own!" Then he spoke into the phone. "Hi, Mom, yeah, it's Cooper. Give me a call."

Cooper clicked off the call and exhaled loudly, and finally looked at me. Seeing I was dressed casually, he said, "I'm not even sure how you're with him, but I'm grateful. And I'm sorry. Jesus, Max. A little warning next time."

"I was going to call," Max said. "But then I got busy, then I forgot, and then I was going to call from the airport but I forgot."

"It's okay, Cooper," I said. "Lionel said he tried calling you a few times this morning, but you didn't answer, so he called me instead. I don't mind, really."

Cooper shook his head. "But you're so busy, and I was out all morning. I'm trying to get this Baurhenn job finished by tomorrow… Oh my God, tomorrow…" He looked at his brother. "Crap. I can't take tomorrow off, I'm totally swamped."

"I can look after myself," Max said. "I don't need a babysitter."

Cooper raised one eyebrow and pursed his lips. "You are not walking around New York City by yourself."

"Jeez, Coop," Max said, rolling his eyes. "Gettin' your Dad voice on."

I chuckled at that. His biting, sarcastic comments were so much like his brother's. "Cooper, it's fine. I've already told Jennifer I won't be in tomorrow."

"You can't have two days off!"

I scoffed. "I've had a total four weeks off in about ten years. I'm sure I'm entitled to two days' family time. Anyway," I added, "I'm kind of glad not to be there right now."

Cooper frowned. "Oh, Tom. I'm sorry. I know you're having a shitty time at work right now, and I wish I wasn't so damn busy. I'm not being much help right now, am I?"

"Max and I are fine," I reassured him. "I'm sure we'll find something he wants to do."

Max spun himself around in the swivel chair. "As long as it doesn't involve thrash metal or getting tattoos. Those are Tom's rules."

Cooper looked at me. "Rules?"

I shrugged one shoulder. "Thought they were fair."

Cooper stared at me for a long moment, as though trying to think of the right thing to say, then he sighed. "Thank you."

I smiled back at him. "You're very welcome."

"Ugh," Max groaned. "You two finished with the heart-eyes? Because no one should see their brother getting it on."

"Hey," Cooper said, pointing his finger at his brother. But before he could start ranting, his cell phone rang. He growled as he answered the call. "Hello…oh, hi, Mom." Cooper pulled a face at his brother. "Yeah, he's here, safe and sound."

Max pulled a face back at Cooper. Cooper tried to swipe Max's face. Max ducked and softly jabbed at Cooper's ribs. "Yeah, of course he asked me. We had it all lined up… Okay, we'll call you later."

Cooper disconnected the call and stared at Max. "I just lied to our mother to cover your ass." He shook his head and exhaled through puffed-out cheeks. Then he and Max stared at each other until they started to smile. "Come on, I'll show you my desk."

Cooper held the door open for us. Max walked out first and when I got to the door, Cooper quickly ran his hand over my back and pecked my cheek. "Love you."

I smiled and told him what he always tells me. "I know you do. It's because I'm awesome."

Cooper laughed, and for the next ten minutes or so, Cooper showed Max his work station. Max was more interested in the computer system of course, and spoke in some foreign binary language I couldn't follow. I just stood back, leaning against the wall to let them have some time, albeit brief time, together.

I didn't even notice a group of people approaching until they walked past. Then they stopped. And stared at me.

There were three of them — two men and one woman, all about the same age as Cooper or a bit older.

"Oh my God. You're Thomas Elkin?" one of the men said. The other guy was wide-eyed, and the woman slack-jawed.

I leaned off the wall and extended my hand. "Yes, I am. How are you?"

By the time I'd introduced myself to the three of them, Cooper and Max, and some others at the other end of the large office space, were watching us.

"What are you doing here?" the first guy asked. "Are you overseeing something?" Then his eyes brightened. "A collaboration with Arlington?"

The three of them waited eagerly, and a silence fell across the room waiting for my reply. Luckily it was lunchtime and half the room was empty. "Uh, no. I'm just here with Cooper," I said, giving a pointed nod to him.

All eyes went to Cooper, who opened his mouth to say something, but it was Max who laughed. "Is Tom like some kind of celebrity or something?"

I laughed at that, and Cooper blushed and mumbled, "No, he's just Tom."

One of the three people, I think it was the woman, whispered, "Just Tom?"

I nodded, and told them, "It's true. I am just Tom." By this time, Cooper had pulled Max away from his desk, leading him toward the door. But then he stopped and faced his co-workers who were all now watching us.

"Everyone, this is my brother, Max," he said, waving his hand in introduction. "And my partner, Tom Elkin."

I waved my hand. "Hi."

I got a collective shocked, mumbled response, and Cooper turned on his heel and Max and I followed him out. I felt bad, because I knew only a select few of Cooper's co-workers had known about me. "I'm sorry," I said. "I did try to call."

Cooper shook his head. "No, don't apologize. They were all bound to find out sooner or later." He looked back to the way we'd come. "I'm about to get a gazillion questions." Then he looked at Max. "You behave yourself. And here, take my credit card," he said, pulling out his wallet. "Don't let Tom buy you anything."

Then Cooper looked at me. "I'm so sorry. I promise I'll make it up to you."

We said goodbye, and when we walked back out onto the New York City sidewalk, Max burst out laughing. "Oh my God, that was funny," he said. "You're like someone famous or something?"

"Only to those who know architecture."

Max grinned. "Okay then, Mr. Ce-leb-rity, what are we doing now?"

"Something awesome."

"If you say 'because that's how you roll' I'm boarding the next plane back to Chicago."

I barked out a laugh. "You're so much like your freakin' brother."

Chapter Eight

When Cooper got home, I was in the kitchen cleaning up after dinner. He dropped his satchel at the door and without a word to his brother, he walked up to me and slid his arms around my waist. I threw the dishcloth into the sink and hugged him back. His face was buried in my neck and he mumbled, "Thank you, Tom. For everything."

"You're very welcome," I whispered back to him. "Have you eaten?"

Without pulling away, he shook his head. "No."

"We ordered pizza. Max said Chicago pizzas were the best, so I thought we'd have proper New York pizza just to prove him wrong," I said. "I got your favorite."

Cooper gave me a squeeze. "You're so good to me."

"Coop?" Max said. He was now standing in the kitchen beside us, not seeming to care that Cooper was still wrapped around me. Max was still excited. He'd been waiting for his brother to get home. "You'll never believe where Tom took me this afternoon."

Cooper pulled away then, to look at me, then to Max. "Where?"

I took out a plate and put some pizza in the microwave for Cooper, as Max said, "First stop was Academy Records. Best vinyl album shop, they have all this vintage stuff. It was really cool. Then we went to Café Wha?."

"Café where?"

"No, Café Wha?," he repeated. "Where Jimi Hendrix played! We couldn't go in, because I'm seventeen, but Cooper, we went to where Jimi Hendrix played!"

Cooper was smiling at Max's enthusiasm. "That's so cool!"

"But then," Max said. "The best place ever... Tom took me to Generation Records."

Cooper blinked, then his eyes darted to mine, and back to Max's. "And that's cool because...?"

"Because it's the best metal and punk record store, ever. Like, ever. If it's metal or punk, they have it," Max said. "Coop, it was so freakin' cool."

I handed Cooper his reheated pizza. "I am officially the coolest guy on the planet."

Cooper took the plate and stared at me. "You really took him there?"

"I did."

Cooper took a step closer and planted his lips on mine. "Thank you." Then he looked at Max. "Did my credit card survive?"

Max laughed. "Yeah, yeah. But I bought you something, so that makes it okay."

"With my own money. How thoughtful of you." Cooper took a bite of pizza and spoke with his mouth full, "So where is it?"

"Well, Tom picked it," Max admitted. "I said I wanted to get you something cool, so Tom found you this..." Max walked over to the sofa and picked up the bag and held it out proudly.

Cooper followed him over to the sofa, put his plate on the coffee table and threw himself onto the sofa. Max handed him the shopping bag and we watched as he pulled out a Ramones CD and a Sex Pistols shirt.

"Oh, man," Cooper said quietly. "Did you pick these?" he asked me.

"Yep. I figured the Ramones were easier to listen to than the Sex Pistols, plus I liked the shirt. Well, for you. Not for me."

Cooper held up the white, sleeveless shirt with a washed-out Union Jack Flag on it, and the anarchy A. "I love it." Cooper took another mouthful of pizza and started to unbutton his shirt.

Max looked at Cooper. "Dude. What are you doing?"

"I'm gonna wear my new shirt," he answered.

"Thank God I didn't buy you the briefs."

"Did they have Sex Pistols undies? Because I would totally wear those," Cooper said seriously. He grabbed his slice of pizza and sat back down on the sofa.

I laughed, leaned over the back of the sofa and kissed the side of his head. "I'll leave you two to chat. I'm going to our bedroom to check emails and catch up on the critical stuff I missed today."

Cooper stood up. "Are you sure? Tom, you can stay out here."

I walked back over to him and kissed him. "I'm sure. You two can catch up, I can get some work done," I said. "Plus, I walked the entire length of the city today. I could put my feet up for a while. I'm old, remember?"

Cooper rolled his eyes, but put his hand on my chest. "Okay. I won't be too long. I'm tired, myself."

I looked at Max. "Thanks for a good day. I had fun."

"Thank *you*," Max said. "Can't wait to see what we're doing tomorrow."

I groaned at the thought, and left them to it. As I walked down the hall, I heard Max say, "He's not, you know."

"He's not what?" Cooper asked warily.

"Old," Max answered. "He said he wanted to put his feet up because he's old. But he's not."

"I know that," Cooper said. It sounded like he was smiling.

"He's pretty cool actually," Max said.

Cooper laughed. "Yeah, I know that."

Smiling, I shut the door quietly and left them to it. They could use some brother time, and quite frankly, I really needed to put my feet up. I'd literally walked all over the city and was feeling every one of my forty-four years.

I got through a swarm of emails and replied to the urgent ones. Then I emailed Donella, my lead draftsperson, and roped her into taking on the critical jobs for tomorrow. She was more than capable of stepping up for a day, because I was spending the day with Max.

And the truth was, I wasn't loving my job.

It was the first time ever that I'd not loved my job. I still loved architecture — that would never change — but I wasn't loving my *job*. This bullshit with Robert had put a cloud over everything to do with Brackett and Golding.

I didn't know what he was playing at, or what he was after. But I had bigger things to worry about.

I had to spend another day trying to up the ante in the cool stakes tomorrow with a seventeen-year-old punk kid, then spend the weekend with Cooper's parents.

My apartment, which had been just mine for four years and now was Cooper's home as well, was going to be very crowded for the weekend. With people who didn't particularly like me.

And the weird thing was? I was looking forward to it.

It meant a lot to Cooper, and I wanted it to work out for him. I wanted his parents to like me, to like *us*. Not for my sake, but for Cooper's.

I just hoped once they saw us, together, in our home, that they'd see the real us. That we were just a normal couple. Age differences aside, we *were* just a normal couple.

I had a quick shower to wash the grime of the city off me and crawled into bed. Not too long after, Cooper slid in behind me, and wrapped his arm around my waist. He kissed the back of my head. "You impressed Max today."

"He had fun."

Cooper wriggled closer and nuzzled my neck. "What you did today... It means a lot to me."

I rolled over to face him and he hitched his leg over mine. His hand cupped my cheek and he kissed me. "I really do love you, Tom."

"I know," I whispered. "And I really love you."

He smiled and closed his eyes as if he were basking in sunshine. "I wish I could spend tomorrow with you and Max."

"I wish you could too," I said. "But I don't think I'll be earning any cool points with Max tomorrow. We have a very important dinner party we need to get produce for."

"You're taking him grocery shopping?"

"Yep."

"Yeah, you can hand your cool-card in," Cooper said with a smile.

"I have in-laws to impress, remember?"

"In-laws?"

"Well, your parents."

"In-laws?"

"Wrong word choice, again, huh?"

"Hmm," Cooper hummed. "On a scale of one to ten on the romantic marriage proposals, that was about a minus eighty."

"I didn't ask you!"

"You called my parents in-laws."

I chuckled and pecked his lips. "One of these days I might ask you for real, and you'll shoot me down and break my heart."

"You have been asking me for real," he said, shaking his head. "I'll only say yes when you get it right."

"You're impossible."

"Ah, Tom, that's not getting it right. Were you *even* trying?"

"I wasn't even asking."

Cooper sighed. "You're impossible."

"I learned from the best."

Even in the dark, I could make out his grin. He kissed me with smiling lips, but then he stifled a yawn. "I know this is a first," he said, "but I'm too tired to do anything tonight."

"Oh, thank God," I said with a laugh. "I wasn't kidding about having to walk five hundred miles today."

"Aw, my poor baby," Cooper said in a baby's voice. "Did dat bad teenager wear you out today?"

I dug my fingers into his ribs, tickling him and making him squirm. "Yes, he did. He's almost as bad as you."

Cooper laughed. "I don't make you walk from one end of the city to the other."

"No, you wear me out in other ways."

"Better ways?"

"Much better ways."

Cooper pecked my lips with his. "Good." Then he rolled over and wiggled back against me. "I need big-spoon cuddles."

I laughed into the back of his head, but I nuzzled my nose into his hair, and put my arm around him. "I'll always be your big spoon."

He snorted. "Unless I'm being the big spoon. Then you'll be my little spoon."

"Always."

"Mmm, cute. But no marriage proposal should ever involve spoons."

I sighed. "Goodnight, Cooper."

* * * *

I'd forgotten how teenagers could sleep. Max stumbled out of bed around ten, and according to him, even that was getting up early. The good part was, it gave me plenty of time to read emails, make phone calls and basically work from home for a few hours.

Max griped about having to go grocery shopping, but once I explained it meant a lot to Cooper, he was okay with it. "He wants everything to be perfect for the dinner party tomorrow night," I said. "It's kind of a test by your parents of sorts, whether intentional or not, that Cooper and I are serious."

Max nodded, and only after a long stretch of silence did he reply. "They're trying to make an effort, you know."

"Your parents?"

"Yeah," he said. "They didn't like it at first, as you know. But what you said to them about pushing Cooper away kinda hit home. Well, for Mom anyway."

"What do you mean?"

Max looked around the fresh produce store and shrugged. "Mom told Dad she'd intentionally lose her husband before she'd ever intentionally lose a child, and she warned him not to make her choose." Max picked up a durian and studied it like it was from outer space. "I don't think Dad would ever let it get to that. He loves Cooper, and what Coop said was right. If they didn't care if he liked boys or girls, then they shouldn't care how old they are." He held up the spiky fruit. "What the hell is this?"

"It's a durian," I said. "And I think your parents just want him to be happy."

"He is."

"I know."

"What do you do with it?"

"Pardon?"

"A durian. What do you do with it?"

"It's a fruit. And I have no clue. Apparently they're banned in some places of Asia because of the putrid smell. Why anyone would actually taste something that smelled like skunk, I'll never know."

Max dropped the fruit and wiped his hands on his pants. "Eww. That's just nasty."

I smiled. "I think your parents just need time."

"They miss Cooper."

"He moved to New York before we were together. He'd still be living away from home if he was with me or not."

"I know that. They know that," Max said. "But they still miss him."

"They've still got you at home," I said, as though it lessened the loss.

"Until next year, then I'll be going too." Max shrugged, and spoke as though he couldn't have cared less. "I think Mom always hoped he'd come back to

Chicago... But then he met you, and I think she knows he's not going anywhere in a hurry. I think that's what scared her the most, you know."

"I'm not holding him ransom here or anything," I said.

Max rolled his eyes. "I heard them talking one night, not long after you and Cooper visited. It's not really about you. It's about Cooper moving away and settling down. They weren't expecting him to bring anyone home, let alone you."

"Let alone me?"

"Yeah, you're like twice his age."

"Thanks for reminding me," I said. I was going to ask him if it bothered him, but I suddenly didn't want to know. Instead, I said, "Thanks for being honest with me."

Max shrugged again. "No worries. You know, growing up we were never that close. There's five years between us, so we were always at different schools, at different stages, know what I mean?" he asked. "It's only now that he moved away that we're kind of getting on better. We make the effort to talk more, I guess."

"Cooper was so excited that you were coming."

"I came a day early to spend some time with him," he said quietly. "I didn't let him know I was coming in case he said no."

"He'd never say no, Max," I said softly. "He wishes he could have taken today off work to spend with you."

"Yeah, he said that. It was good to catch up with him last night," Max said with a bit of a smile. "He's real busy with work, isn't he?"

"He is," I agreed. "But you're more than welcome to come and stay any time."

Max gave me a half-smile. "Don't tell him I didn't call him on purpose. He'll be mad."

I grinned at him. "Deal."

My cell phone rang, and when I pulled it from my pocket, Cooper's name flashed on the screen. I handed the phone to Max. "Here. You talk to him." I turned and looked over the rows of fruit to find what I was after.

"Hey," he said into the phone. "No, we're in the grocer's. Tom's picking mangoes..." There was a moment's silence, then he said, "No, that's not a euphemism for anything. He's honestly looking at mangoes."

I laughed, but let him talk to Cooper while I picked all the fresh produce on Cooper's list. As I got the register, Max handed me back my phone. "He needs to tell you something."

I took the phone. "Hey."

"I'm so fucking jealous of you two right now."

"Oh, sweetheart. I'm sorry."

"No, don't be," he said. "I just wish I was there, that's all. Max said he's had a pretty good day."

"Not as cool as yesterday."

"Well, no. But that would take some beating. What I was calling for, it looks like we're going to wrap up the Baurhenn job today. It's all but done. Louisa just needs to go over the job file and sign off on it."

"Oh, that's excellent!" I said into the phone. I handed my credit card to the cashier and paid for the groceries.

"I think they're having celebratory drinks somewhere," he said. "I should be there for that, but my parents and Max..."

"Tell them to have a little party at the office," I suggested. "That way your parents get to see where you work, and Max can go. If it's at a bar, then he can't, and, Cooper," I said, "he wants to spend time with you."

"I know," he said with a groan. "I'll see what I can organize, and let you know. Are you still right to collect my parents from the airport?"

I looked at my watch. I had three hours. "Of course I am."

"Tom, thank you."

"You can pay me back later."

"Dude!" Max said beside me, obviously hearing what I'd said to his brother. "Ew."

I laughed into the phone. "Cooper, I'll speak to you later."

We got home, I put everything away and checked emails, while Max spent the next two hours glued to his phone. His interest in doing anything was kind of wavering, but then I said we were heading to the airport, and he saw my car.

"Holy shit, dude!" he cried. "You serious?"

I laughed. "Cooper loves this car."

"I can see freakin' why!" he crowed. "Can I drive it?"

"No freakin' way," I copied his tone.

Max grinned all the way to the airport. Whether or not he knew I was nervous and needed some reinforcements, just like Cooper, he took charge. He chatted and kept me busy the whole time. His parents came through the terminal gates, searching the crowd. I think they were looking for Cooper, but they spotted Max and both of them smiled.

Then they saw me.

Andrew, Cooper's father, tried to smile but failed. However, Paula, Cooper's mother, managed just fine. It was a brief but polite hello, and the attention revolved around Max, which was fine with me.

Max told them all about the shirts he'd bought yesterday, for himself and Cooper, and the music he'd got. But then we got back to my car, and he started talking about it.

He assumed he'd be sitting in the front again, but I threw my thumb toward the back seat. Max grumbled at me but he did climb through to the back. I'd never had anyone in the back seat of my car, so Max and Paula were the first. Which left Andrew in the front with me.

And funnily enough, he spoke to me. It was about the car, but it was unprompted conversation. Admittedly, I didn't know a great deal about cars in general, but I knew enough about this car to have a conversation with Cooper's father.

"Where is Cooper?" Paula asked from the back.

"At work," I said. "He's wrapping up his first project. It should be signed off this afternoon. Well, he's hoping it will be. The developer is driving him insane." Then I said, "Actually, he won't be home till late, so he's hoping we can all go to his office. They might be having a little party to celebrate the completion of his first solo job. It's, um…it's kind of a big deal."

"Oh, okay," Paula said, unsure.

"But he's going to call to let us know," I told them. "It's just unfortunate timing that this particular job is being signed off on on the same weekend of your visit. But that means he's free for the rest of the weekend. I think that's what he was aiming for. He's looking forward to having you all here."

In the rear-vision mirror, I watched as Paula smiled then frowned as she must have remembered something. "Oh. Cooper presumed he'd have some work to catch up on tomorrow, and he told me not to get extra tickets to the show."

Max snorted. "He told you that because musicals suck."

"Max," Andrew chastised his son. "I'm sure Cooper would go and suffer along with the rest of us for the sake of his mother."

Max nodded in agreement, and Paula rolled her eyes. I couldn't help but laugh. Not that what Andrew had said wasn't funny, just that I'd never expected Cooper's sense of humor to come from his dad.

"Well, Cooper has a dinner planned for you tomorrow night," I told them. "So while you're out at the show, it will give us time to get it all ready."

We got to the apartment, and I showed them to the spare room. "I had housecleaning change the linen today," I told them. "Max, you're on the sofa."

"Oh, nice," he said. "Kick me out." Then after a second, he cocked his head. "You have housekeeping? So I didn't need to make my bed this morning?"

I didn't get a chance to reply. Paula beat me to it. She hissed at him. "Max. Don't be rude."

Max rolled his eyes. "Don't stress. Tom's cool."

I don't know why it embarrassed me, but his acknowledgment made me blush. "Ah, bathroom through that door," I said, pointing the way. "That's mine and Cooper's room," I added, then regretted literally pointing to the bedroom I shared with their son. I cleared my throat, and led them back out to the living room. "Balcony out there."

It was obvious they were a little impressed by the apartment—the place Cooper now called home. But it was still a bit awkward.

Thankfully Cooper called soon after, and after chatting for a short while, invited us all to his office for some celebratory drinks. Paula and Andrew suggested they take a walk for a look at the city before we were due to leave, so the three of them left for an hour or so. And quite frankly, it was a much-needed reprieve.

The first meeting with his parents — on my own, no less — had gone quite well, I thought.

I called the office and spoke to Jennifer for a while. She said nothing was that urgent that couldn't wait until Monday, that Robert was curious as to my absence, but apart from that, all was well.

I spent the rest of my time alone choosing something to wear that wasn't too old or too young, wishing Cooper was there to just pick it for me. So I phoned him, and he roared with laughter. "Just pick something," he said. "Be yourself. They will love you."

"Cooper," I whined, rather childishly.

"Your black jeans, white button-down shirt and my charcoal vest," he rattled off quickly.

"Okay."

"God, Tom, are you that easy?"

I sighed. "You know I am," I said, and clicked off the call before he could answer.

But an hour later, dressed in the outfit he had suggested and with his family in tow, I walked through the lobby of Arlington for the second time in as many days. The receptionist nodded me through this time, and we walked down the hall to the large communal office room where the party was being held.

I was quite looking forward to it.

Until I saw Xavier Baurhenn with his arm around Cooper.

Fuck.

Chapter Nine

Cooper saw us as we walked in, and peeled himself away from under Xavier's grasp as we approached. He hugged his parents first, bumped fists with his brother then slid his arm around my waist. "Thank you," he whispered, leaning into me.

"Is he annoying you?" I didn't have to say Xavier's name.

"Hasn't stopped yet," he said, then turned to his parents who were watching us. "Let me show you around."

Cooper took his parents and showed them around his office, the place where he spent so much time, and in particular the boards and scaled model of the project he'd just completed.

Which left me alone with Xavier. Thankfully before we could say more than a brief hello, Louisa saved me. "Tom!" she said, kissing me on the cheek. "So good to see you again."

"Louisa," I said. "Exciting times for Cooper."

"Oh my God," she said. "He deserves this. He's really worked hard for this." Then she included Xavier.

"Xavier can attest to that. He's gone above and beyond."

The slimy bastard smiled at me. "Oh, he sure has," he said, with innuendo dripping off every word. "Mr. Elkin," he said, sipping his champagne, "it's good to see you again. But if you'll excuse me, I'll be with the man of the hour." He looked over toward Cooper, then back at me as if daring me.

Xavier turned on his heel and walked over toward Cooper and his family, and Louisa handed me a glass of champagne. She put her glass to her mouth and mumbled, "He's an arrogant prick."

I hid my smile behind my drink. "Cooper can't stand him."

"Oh, I know," Louisa said, still smiling behind her glass of champagne.

We watched as Xavier introduced himself to Cooper's parents and brother.

"I think the reason Cooper pushed so hard to finish the job was to be rid of him. It's a blessing and a curse that Cooper had a Baurhenn job as his first," Louisa said. "Great on the portfolio, but putting up with Xavier is…" She seemed stuck for the right word.

"Trying?"

"I was going to say 'skin-crawling'."

I laughed. "Well, there's that."

We were interrupted by two people whom I'd met before. Skye and Tyson were happy for Cooper, and as much as they assured me it was his job and his alone, Cooper would assure me it was a team effort.

It was pretty obvious word had spread around the office that the 'Tom' Cooper had talked about was in fact Thomas Elkin. There wasn't a huge number of people there, but they all eyed me and took turns at introducing themselves.

I kept a bit of an eye on Cooper as he mingled, and over the course of the evening, I saw first-hand just how much Xavier touched him. No wonder Cooper hated to be around him. And it seemed the more glasses of champagne Xavier had, the sleazier he got. Admittedly, it wasn't just with Cooper, it was with anyone, but it still irked me.

I finally had a quiet moment, so I grabbed a champagne for me, and a soda for Max and saved him from dying of absolute boredom. "What's with the douche-king?" Max asked, giving a pointed nod to Xavier.

I laughed again. God, he was so like his brother. "He's the grandson of a property developer millionaire who's been given permission from his father to try his hand at real estate development."

Max sipped his soda. "He's a wanker."

I snorted into my drink just as Cooper snuck up beside me and slipped his arm around my waist. "Oh my God," he said. "This is a bit insane. I've just been lined up to do an interview for *Architect* magazine next month. Can you believe that?"

"I can," I said.

"We were just talking about the douchebag," Max said with another pointed glance at Xavier, who was talking rather loudly to a group of Cooper's co-workers.

Cooper gritted his teeth. "Thank God today's the last day. After tonight, I'm done with him." Then Cooper looked at me. "You don't seem to mind letting him put his grubby hands on me."

"Mind?" I asked. "It's disgusting."

"Well, tell him to stop it," Cooper said with a smile, like it was the most obvious thing to do.

I spoke to him through smiling lips and gritted teeth. "I didn't want to make a scene in front of your colleagues."

Cooper rolled his eyes, which silently said, *That's the lamest excuse ever.*

"After tonight, you don't have to see him again," I said, trying to placate him, just as Paula and Andrew came up to us.

"It's getting kind of late," Paula said, obviously wanting to go home. "It's been a long day."

But then, like the slimeball he was, Xavier came over to us and put his arm around Cooper's shoulders. "How about," he said just to him, "we go out? This party is all but over, but the night is still young."

Cooper's eyes darted to mine, so I stepped in closer to Xavier, looked pointedly at his offending arm around Cooper and said, "The funny thing about architecture, Xavier, is that there's a distinct rule on space. You don't encroach on what's not yours," I said, still smiling but with fair warning in my tone. "There are boundaries. You should learn them."

Xavier shrugged like he didn't care, like the arrogant little fuck he was. "My school days are over. No one owns me," he said, which I'm sure was a jab at Cooper. "I'm free to do what I want."

"I'll be sure to tell your father all about that," I told him cheerfully. "I'm meeting with him on Wednesday. We're discussing tenders for the Eccleston Apartment complex. I'm sure he'll be very interested to hear it."

A few shades paler, Xavier smiled, though it was more of a sneer. "Well, then," he said. "I should be going. Pleasure to meet you all," he said to Cooper's parents. Then he turned to Cooper, but glanced at me first. He extended his hand, which Cooper shook. "It's been a pleasure. Hope we can continue this professional relationship in the future with new projects."

It was a practiced spiel, translucent as he was.

When Xavier had gone, Cooper shuddered. "Are you really meeting the Baurhenn group on Wednesday?"

"No," I said with a smile. "But he doesn't know that."

Max laughed. "He was whistling a different tune after that, though."

Cooper chuckled but looked at his parents. "Come on, let's go home."

We said goodbye to Louisa and the others, and when we stepped into the elevator, Paula sighed and said, "It just goes to show that all the money in the world can't buy you class. That guy was a…"

Max finished for her, "A douche!"

Cooper smiled and leaned into me. "Yeah, the last few weeks have been…character-building."

Cooper's father looked at his son, and said, "Don't know how you haven't punched him."

Then Paula looked at me and said, "I don't know how *you* haven't punched him!"

I laughed quietly. "If it wouldn't have ended Cooper's career, I probably would have."

Cooper snorted and shook his head at me, disbelievingly. "No, you wouldn't have. You'd find some other way to shame him, professionally, publicly, by proving what a dick he is. But not punching him."

I conceded a nod. "Maybe."

"The likes of Xavier Baurhenn will never amount to anything," Cooper said confidently. "Not long term. I don't care who his parents are, he has no integrity."

I smiled at him and kissed the side of the head, not caring if his parents were right there, just as the elevator doors opened. As we walked through the lobby,

Cooper took my hand and asked, "Have you guys had enough to eat? We could pick up a pizza if you want?"

And so began the friendly debate over New York pizza versus Chicago pizza, which lasted until the last slice was eaten and I bade Cooper and his family goodnight. I thought they could use some time to catch up. Cooper had missed them, and even though it was late, they sat around the living room talking long after I went to bed.

* * * *

I woke up to the sound of banging on my door. I sat bolt upright, making Cooper, who had been half wrapped around me, startle awake. "Wuh?"

"Cooper, get your ass out of bed and make me pancakes!"

I sagged.

Max.

Cooper laughed sleepily and fell back on the bed with a groan. If Max was awake, it meant his parents were, and figuring I'd rather not venture out in front of them half naked in my sleepwear, I headed straight for the shower.

When I came out, appropriately dressed in jeans and a T-shirt, there was a wonderful smell of bacon and pancakes cooking, and Max and Cooper were arguing.

"Dude," Max said, "you need to add the bacon to the batter."

"No, you don't," Cooper argued. "You fry the bacon first then add the batter."

"Mom!" Max called out. "Please tell him he's doing it wrong."

I walked in behind the kitchen counter and headed straight for the coffee machine. Cooper smiled at me, and said, "Tom, tell him how it's done."

"Well, I would say fry the bacon first," I said.

Cooper grinned hugely at me, and Max groaned. "You *have* to say that. Mom!" Max called again. "They're picking on me!"

Cooper launched himself at his brother, collecting him in a headlock and dragging him out through the living room to the verandah, where I presumed their parents were sitting enjoying the morning sun. But just as they got to the door, Paula walked through it. She looked at her two sons and sighed. "Cooper, leave your brother alone." It sounded like it was something she'd said a thousand times.

Max spoke from the headlock he was still in. "Mom, do you cook bacon first, or in the pancake batter?"

Cooper looked at his mom and smiled, as though having his brother in a headlock was nothing out of the ordinary. "Tell him I'm right."

"I always cook the bacon first," she said.

Cooper raised his free arm and crowed in victory. But then Andrew called out, "I pour the batter over the bacon."

Cooper dropped his arm, deflated, and Max sprang up and out of his headlock. "Ha! Told ya!"

Before Max barely had the words out, Cooper tackled him onto the sofa. Paula looked at me. I smiled, shrugged and turned the bacon. "Can I get you another coffee?" I asked her.

She smiled and walked over to the kitchen island bench. "I can get it," she said. After she'd poured herself another cup, she leaned against the kitchen counter, holding the cup with her two hands. "Boys!" she chided. "Stop wrestling."

Cooper got off his brother, ruffled his hair for good measure, then walked into the kitchen. He took the tongs out of my hands, snapped them at me then ordered Max to set the table.

"I was quite capable of turning bacon," I said.

He grinned at me and bumped his hip into mine. "I have it all under control," he said. "You just need to stand there, drinking coffee and looking handsome."

I rolled my eyes at him, and Paula smiled behind her coffee cup. And the rest of breakfast went pretty much the same. We all sat around the dining table and listened as Cooper told stories of his time here in New York.

He was so excited and happy to have his family here, and I couldn't help but smile at him as he chatted animatedly. And as they all got dressed and ready for their lunch and theater show, Cooper and I cleaned up the mess in the kitchen. Yes, it was cute to watch them wrestle and jibe at each other, but tidy cooks they weren't. And as his parents and brother were getting ready, walking in and out of the open living area, every chance he got, Cooper would grope my ass or kiss me.

We finally got the mess cleaned up, and they all looked very well-dressed and ready to go. Paula offered one last chance for us to go with them. "Can't, Mom," Cooper told her. "I have the best dinner to cook. It's gonna take a while. By the time you get back, it'll all be done and we can sit down and you'll tell us all about the show."

Paula looked at me. "Are you really sure?"

"It's fine, truly," I told her.

"How come they have a choice?" Andrew asked. "I don't mind staying and cooking, if it means I get out of going to this musical."

Max gasped at his father. "You'd leave me to go alone? Nice. Real nice."

"You're both going," Paula said, putting an end to that conversation.

Cooper laughed and offered to walk them down to the lobby. "I want you to meet Lionel," he said. "Then I need to come back up here and cook up a storm."

When he was done harassing poor Lionel, he walked back into the apartment. I was in the kitchen with most of the ingredients on the bench. "Okay, what do we need to do first?" I asked. "I thought we might start—"

Cooper spun me around and pressed me against the kitchen counter. "We need to fuck."

My mouth fell open. "Such a romantic way to put it."

He took my hand and led me to our bedroom. "There won't be anything romantic about it," he mumbled. "I can't wait any longer. I thought they'd never leave."

I laughed, but then he turned and kissed me, hard. He was so damn eager. And hard.

I kissed him back, running my fingers through his hair while he slipped his tongue into my mouth. He walked us backwards to the bed, but before I could push him onto it, he turned in my arms and leaned over the mattress. Quickly undoing the button on his cargos, he slid them over his hips, exposing his bare ass to me.

"Cooper," I whispered gruffly.

"Just do it, Tom," he said. "I really need you."

I reached over to the bedside table and pulled out one foil packet and the small bottle of lubricant. I undid my jeans and pulled my dick from my briefs, tore open the condom wrapper and rolled the latex barrier down my cock.

Only then did I notice Cooper, rubbing his slicked fingers over his ass, inside his hole.

"Fuck."

Cooper moaned. "Please. Tom, I'm ready. I just need you."

I rubbed some lube over my cock, and with my jeans still around my ass, and Cooper's cargos down to his thighs, I pressed against him. As the head of my cock breached his hole, Cooper gripped the bedcover and moaned. And the further I slid into him, the louder he became.

I leaned over him. "You okay?"

"Don't stop," he bit out. Then he groaned again. "Fuck, Tom."

Putting my hands on the bed above his shoulders, I leaned over him and kissed the back of his neck, and I rolled my hips into him, over and over. Cooper gripped my hands and my wrists and he lifted his ass for me. It didn't take long for that familiar draw in my belly, in my balls, and I knew I was close to coming.

Then Cooper bucked his hips, like he was working my cock, and my body seized and my senses obliterated as I filled the condom. Cooper moaned deep and low as I came, and when I pulled out of him, I spun him around and leaned him back onto the bed.

I lifted his legs so his feet were on the edge of the bed and took his still-hard dick into my mouth. I slid two fingers into his ass, twisting them up, searching, feeling for his gland.

His reaction told me I'd found it.

He gripped the bedcovers in his fists and he threw his head back. "Fuck!" he growled out. "There!"

I sucked him and fucked him with my fingers, and when his cock pulsed in my mouth, he shot cum down my throat. I pulled my fingers out of him, my mouth off him, licking as I went and he squirmed under my touch. I leaned over him and put my head on his chest.

His heart was hammering and he clumsily put his hand on my hair. "Fuck," he murmured. "That was exactly what I needed."

I looked up at him and smiled. "What we need now is a shower."

Cooper squirmed again. "No round two?"

I grinned at him. "We have dinner to make."

"We can order takeout."

I barked out a laugh, and taking his hand, pulled him off the bed. "No, we can't. You've been planning this for a week."

He followed me into the bathroom and as I threw the used condom in the trash, he slapped my ass. "I hate it when you're responsible."

"I love it when you're horny," I said. I turned the taps on in the shower, and pointed to the water. "Now get in. I'll make sure you're all clean."

He stepped up close to me. "You'd better be thorough."

I pecked his lips. "Just do as you're told, Jones."

He raised an eyebrow at me. "Bossy in the bedroom, I'll take any day. Bossy out of the bedroom, not so much."

I laughed. "You're the bossiest person I know."

"And you love it," he replied, stepping in under the streams of water.

"Is there any point in me arguing that?" I asked, stepping in behind him.

His answer was short and sweet. "Not if you're smart."

I pressed him up against the tiles and scraped my teeth against the back of his neck. "Oh, I'm smart," I murmured.

He moaned and his skin covered with gooseflesh, even under the hot water. "If you do that again, Tom, we'll be ordering in dinner."

I smiled into the skin on his shoulder, but picked up the cake of soap and started lathering his body. I soaped him over, feeling every inch of his skin under my hands, and he soon turned around so he could kiss me.

We made out like college kids in the shower, and still even had everything done for dinner by the time his family came back.

And yes, Paula told us about the musical they'd just seen, while Andrew and Max rolled their eyes. I poured some wine, and as we served dinner, talk turned to the food, and I promised them that I was just the apprentice—Cooper was the one who did everything, I just did as I was told.

"Tom very rarely does what he's told," Cooper said, taking a bite of his chicken.

"Which is rather surprising, considering how bossy he is," I replied to everyone at the table.

Paula laughed at that. But then Cooper said, "Tom asked me to marry him."

I dropped my fork. "I what?"

Despite the stunned silence at the table, Cooper rolled his eyes. "You know you have."

I looked at his parents. "I haven't, not really."

"Well, okay," Cooper added, "so they weren't traditional proposals by any means."

His mother's eyes were wide. "They? As in a few?"

"Well, I keep saying no," Cooper told her, as if he were talking about the wine.

"I haven't asked him," I told everyone again. "He keeps telling me I have, but I've said no such thing." I didn't dare look at Andrew. He'd only just started to warm to me. I pushed my plate away, and decided that drinking wine was a much better idea.

Max burst out laughing. "And that, boys and girls, is what we call a conversation-stopper."

Cooper laughed, and, more surprisingly, Andrew did too. "Good one, Grandpa," Andrew said, which confused me even more. I was, however, one hundred percent certain I would never understand the Joneses' sense of humor.

Then Cooper said, "Okay, so he hasn't technically. I just thought I'd do a Grandpa. You know, keep the tradition alive."

According to legend, Cooper's grandfather, at a family gathering once, had stood up and announced he'd won a few million dollars, which he hadn't. He'd just wanted to spark up conversation, see people's reactions purely for entertainment purposes. And now, apparently, at most Jones family functions someone made some outlandish comment, just for laughs.

"I'm guessing the sense of humor is hereditary," I said, still preferring my wine.

"Well, my father was a very funny man," Andrew said. And so the conversation resumed around the table. I did notice Paula looking at Cooper a little weirdly, though he seemed oblivious, as they talked about some cousin I'd never heard of.

Later that night, when Cooper was sound asleep beside me, and unable to sleep myself, I got up for a drink of water. Knowing Max was asleep on the sofa, I didn't turn on any lights, and after I'd poured myself a glass of water, I noticed the door to the balcony was open.

Thinking someone might have left it open, I stuck my head out to make sure I wasn't locking anyone out, when I found Paula looking out over the city. I must have startled her, because she put her hand to her heart. "Jesus."

"Sorry," I said softly, grateful I'd worn sleep pants *and* a shirt to bed. "I was just checking I didn't lock anyone out here, or if the door was just left open." Then I added, "I was just getting a drink."

"I was just enjoying the view," she said with a smile. "It's so quiet up here."

Not sure if I should, but not wanting her to think I was ignoring her, I walked out and leaned against the balcony railing, overlooking the city. "It's really beautiful."

She smiled, and sighed, and for a long moment we both just stood there and admired the city lights. Paula had been a little quiet since Cooper's marriage statement at dinner. "I'm sorry about what Cooper said about us getting married," I offered quietly. "I haven't asked him. Not officially. But he keeps alluding to the fact as though I have." Paula didn't answer me, so I added, "I just didn't want you to think I was being misleading or that we were hiding anything, because we're not." She still didn't say anything, so I thought I'd aim for funny. "He keeps telling me I'm proposing, but then turns me down, so I can't win anyway."

Paula looked at me then, and smiled. But she still never said anything, and I realized I'd probably said too much.

"Well, I'll leave you to it," I said, taking a step toward the door. "Goodnight."

Before I walked back inside, she said, "He used to do that, as a kid."

I stopped, and looked at her, waiting for her to continue.

Paula looked back out to the city, but said, "When he was younger, he used to do the same thing. He'd twist the story all round, as though buying him a new bike was my idea, then tell me I didn't have to. Or the time for his birthday, he wanted a new phone or a new laptop, he'd bring it up in conversation, I'd say something about it and he'd tell me I was bad at keeping secrets about what I was getting him."

I chuckled quietly. "That sounds like him."

Then her smiled died. "It's hard for me to watch him grow up. No matter how accomplished he is, or how successful he is, he's still my little boy."

"He'll always be your son," I told her honestly. "He loves you very much."

"He loves you too," she said, looking back out to the city before looking at me.

"Yes, he does," I told her simply.

She gave me a sad smile. "He wants you to ask him to marry you."

I ran her words through my head a few times, and still wasn't sure how she had come to that conclusion. "Pardon?"

"He wants you to ask him to marry you," she repeated. "That's why he keeps bringing it up. That's what he does. Whether it's a new bike, a new phone, a computer…that's what he does. He keeps talking about it like it's your idea."

I looked back out across the neon-lit sky, so Paula wouldn't see the surprise on my face. But then she startled me by laughing. "He told me you bought him some Prada boots. Was it your idea, or did he suggest them *as though* it was your idea."

I smiled. "It was his idea."

Paula smiled. "See? That's what he does." Then she looked back out over the New York skyline. "You don't seem too deterred by the idea."

"I'm not," I told her honestly. "But for what it's worth, he might think he's ready, but he's not."

Paula laughed again. "Oh, Tom. You know he always gets what he wants, right? Whether he works hard for it, or simply demands it."

I couldn't help but chuckle. "I guess."

She nodded knowingly and sighed again, looking out over the city. "For what it's worth, Tom, I'm not opposed to it either. I thought I would be, but I'm really not. I just want him happy, and I can see that he's happy with you."

I gave her a smile. "Thank you." I bade her goodnight then slid into bed with Cooper. Even though he was sound asleep, I kissed the back of his head and smiled as I fell asleep.

Chapter Ten

We said goodbye to Cooper's family at the airport, and he grinned the entire trip home and for most of the afternoon. He was still buzzed about having his family here and the acceptance they seemed to show in regards to our relationship.

I didn't tell Cooper about the conversation I'd had with his mother. Though I had to admit, I liked knowing. I liked knowing that this man wanted to marry me, even if he didn't know that I knew.

I pulled out my laptop and sat at the dining table, when Cooper walked over and kissed the side of my head. "Whatcha doing?"

"I need to catch up on work," I explained. "I haven't been in the office for four days."

"Surely they can't be pissed at you for that," he said.

"I don't care if they are," I said honestly. "I've enjoyed this weekend, and I wouldn't change it."

"You were amazing this weekend."

I smiled up at him. "I missed a lot of family stuff working so much. It's about time I spent time on what's really important."

"Well, work, then dinner, then you can do what's *really* important." Then he added, "You know I'm what's important, don't you? I meant that you can do me."

I laughed. "I got the reference, yes."

He leaned down and nuzzled my neck. "You know, if you haven't worked all weekend, another few hours won't hurt." He then rubbed my shoulders, massaging me with his fingers. "Leave it until tomorrow. We can lie on the sofa and watch some hockey or something. We've had the perfect weekend, don't ruin it now with work. Let the likes of Robert Chandler ruin your day tomorrow. Spend today with me."

* * * *

When I walked into my office on Monday morning, I wondered what would greet me. But Jennifer smiled, asked me all about my extended weekend, and how I had coped with Cooper's parents. We chatted for a brief moment, she told me my coffee was on my desk, then it was business as usual.

But then at three o'clock, Jennifer knocked quietly and let herself into my office. "Robert wants to see us both," she said in a hushed tone.

"When?"

She looked at the clock on the wall. "Now."

Well, shit. I closed the file on my desk then Jennifer and I walked the short distance to Robert's office. His receptionist buzzed us through, but before we got to the door, I stopped us. "Jennifer, whatever he says, it doesn't matter. It will all be okay."

And with that, we walked inside.

Robert sat smugly at his desk, and Peter Sleiman and Donald Croft sat at the side of the desk. As surprised as

I was to see them, I gave them a smile and said, "Good afternoon," as Jennifer and I both sat down across from Robert.

They both nodded, but it was Robert who spoke.

"I have asked Peter and Donald to sit in on this meeting, because I believe some interesting developments have come to light."

He then licked his fingers, like the uncouth slob he was, and turned the first page of the file in front of him. I recognized it immediately. It was Cooper's approval for the Baurhenn job.

I looked at Robert curiously. "How are those plans relevant to anything here?"

Robert smiled at me, but then looked at Jennifer. "Jennifer, I need to remind you that you're here in an official capacity, and what you say will be taken seriously." He looked back down to the file in front of him. "Did you request the job files from archives for the 1994 Graham's Corporation job Mr. Elkin did here in Riverdale District?"

"I retrieve a lot of files for Mr. Elkin," Jennifer told him.

"These Brackett and Golding plans were used by Mr. Elkin for personal reasons. He shared these plans and specifications with a Mr. Cooper Jones, who then went on to win the contract to build for the Baurhenn Group. I wouldn't have known this, only the plans that Mr. Jones submitted for approval have a distinctively similar façade—elements that have Tom Elkin written all over them."

"I wouldn't remember specific files," Jennifer said. "Though if you have archives records of the request, then you already know."

He smiled again. "Yes, you're quite right."

I sighed. "Those plans are available at the City Library. Hell, they're probably online. You'd only have to drive down the damn street to see the façade, Robert. Any architect knows the city has design clauses and restrictions because it's pre-1940 with the Preservation Committee, and anyone with half a brain would know that what was approved by city planners less than ten years ago would be approved again." I shook my head at him. "You're really clutching at straws this time, Robert."

Robert ignored me completely and again turned to Jennifer. "Jennifer, were you aware that Brackett and Golding also filed submissions for the Baurhenn job? And that in fact helping another firm win a contract is a breach of policy?"

"Oh, enough, Robert," I said flatly. "For fuck's sake, that's enough. If you have something against me, if you're that damn homophobic, you speak to me, not Jennifer."

"Tom, it's fine," Jennifer started to say.

"No it's not," I answered. "It's far from fine. He wants to get rid of me, and is using you as bait, and that's *far from fine*."

Robert was still smiling, as though it was just the reaction he was after. "Tom, it's also been brought to our attention that you may have used the Brackett and Golding contracts you've completed to purchase real estate in districts you knew were undergoing development."

I think my mouth fell open. "You can't be serious. You taught me how to do that, Robert, remember? When I worked with you when I first started here, you told me it was a smart financial decision to follow developmental trends."

"No, I never," he lied outright. Then he changed the subject again, swiftly putting the emphasis back on me. "And then there's the little problem of you...and your intern."

"Oh, that's enough, Robert. Enough." I shook my head. "I'm not even going to justify that with an answer. The problem here is that I'm gay, but of course you can't say that trying to fire me, can you?"

"The problem is with your work ethic and bringing this company into disrepute."

I laughed at that. "I'm done." I stood up. "I'm so fucking done here."

Jennifer stood up beside me. "You're what?"

"I'm done. I quit. Hereby tender my resignation, citing Robert as a homophobic asshole and I'm better off somewhere else that doesn't confine creativity and expressionism."

Jennifer shook her head. She didn't say anything, but she looked worried, scared even.

I put my hand on her arm. "I know you don't want to work for anyone else. But this way you don't have to. You can come work for me."

Then I turned back to the other two men seated at the table. "I've done nothing wrong, but I won't stand for this. You can have my termination papers drawn up and forwarded to my lawyer."

Jennifer stood beside me and looked to the other men sitting with Robert. "Gentlemen, Robert's already familiar with his legal firm, he can give you those details. In case he's forgotten, it's the same lawyers who took care of a little problem for Robert about fifteen years ago when he got his intern pregnant. You remember that, don't you, Robert?"

Robert's face went red, his eyes bugged out and he sputtered something unintelligible. I couldn't stop the bubble of laughter that escaped me. This was news to me.

Jennifer folded her arms. "Did you forget I've been here as long as you, Robert? I've seen every single thing that's gone on in this office for the past sixteen years, including your indiscretions with numerous young female staff. More recently, how you've snooped for information on Tom, trying to ruin his career for your own satisfaction, how you've intimidated staff to try to leach details. I've seen it all, and you'll do well to remember that." Jennifer sniffed, then raised her chin and spoke to Peter and Donald. "I'll be happy to testify to anything I've just said. But you can finalize my papers and entitlements and forward them with Tom's papers to his lawyer."

I looked back at Robert, who was now looking a little pale. I would have smiled at him if he wasn't so pitiful. Instead, I said, "You, Robert, are a disgrace to this firm." And with that, Jennifer and I walked out of his office. We packed up our belongings, to a hushed disbelief across the entire office floor.

And with a strangely enlightened feeling, we walked out of Brackett and Golding for the last time.

* * * *

I heard the familiar sound of keys at the front door, and I laughed. "Cooper's home," I said, and Jennifer started to giggle.

Cooper walked in, and stopped when he saw Jennifer was in our living room, sitting with me on the sofa. We were both grinning like idiots so he smiled cautiously at us. Then he saw the two empty bottles of wine, and the half-empty third, and looked at me. "Celebrating something?"

"Kind of," I said, and Jennifer giggled again.

"We're unemployed," she added cheerfully.

Cooper dropped his satchel along with his jaw. "You're what?"

"I prefer the term 'newly self-employed'," I amended.

Jennifer laughed again, and Cooper sat down next to me, ignoring our drunken merriment. "Tom, what the hell happened?" he asked. "Did something happen with Robert?"

"Well, yes," I said. "He called Jennifer and me in for a meeting with Peter and Donald and threw accusations at me. First, that I'd helped you secure the Baurhenn contract because it 'looked like my work'. Which I told him was bullshit. Then he accused me of profiting personally by using Brackett and Golding information to purchase real estate in areas about to be developed. Which is kind of true, but it's not illegal and anyone with half a brain and the financial backing can do it. But then," I continued, "*then* he tried to blame Jennifer, and I drew the line."

"You quit?"

"Kind of. I was pushed," I said, taking another sip of wine. "I told them to forward my termination papers to my lawyers. Peter Sleiman didn't look too pleased with Robert. I'm guessing we haven't heard the last of it."

"Tom," Cooper whispered. He shook his head, unsure of what else to say. "I can't believe it."

"You know what?" I asked rhetorically. "This isn't what I had planned. At all. But I think this could be the best thing to happen to me…" Then I corrected, "Well, the second best thing to happen to me." I took his hand. "You're the best thing to ever happen to me."

Cooper ignored what I'd said. "Tom…" He shook his head. "Oh, my God. I can't believe it."

Giving him a moment to get his head around it, I asked him if he wanted some wine. He shook his head. Instead he asked, "Why didn't you call me?"

"It only happened late this afternoon," I said. "Jennifer and I left and thought we could do with a drink. Here we are! I knew you wouldn't be far away, and I didn't want you to worry."

He rubbed his temples and forehead. "Was it because of me? Really? Because I…"

"No," I interrupted him. "No. It had nothing to do with you, Cooper, and everything to do with me. Not you, so don't even think that."

He shook his head again and exhaled through puffed cheeks. "And you two are celebrating? Or commiserating?"

"Celebrating," Jennifer and I answered at the same time, which made Jennifer start to laugh again.

"I told Tom last week I didn't want to work for anyone else at that firm," Jennifer explained. "I'm near retiring age anyway, but Tom said he'd need me if he's going to go out on his own."

Cooper's eyes shot to mine. "On your own?"

"Yes," I said, nodding. "I'm going to do my own thing. Someone taught me to say 'fuck it' every now and then, and do what's in my heart."

Cooper's eyes then darted to Jennifer. "I apologize for the language, Jennifer." Then he swatted my arm. "Don't swear in front of a lady."

Jennifer roared laughing. "Oh, Cooper, you're a sweetheart. Thank you, but I must be going home. I've had far too much to drink to keep up appearances" — she smoothed down her hair — "and will bid both you lovely gentlemen goodnight."

"I'll walk you down and see you into a cab," Cooper said, not taking no for answer.

I kissed Jennifer on the cheek, told her goodnight, and Cooper returned a few minutes later, and we played a game of three hundred and seventy-four questions. He was shocked, but after he got over that initial reaction, he could see my point of view.

Yes, it was scary and daunting and exciting and new.

"I needed the challenge," I said. "I've seen what you do, all the new concepts and principles and I want to be able to have the freedom to do that too."

And just like that, he understood.

"Have you eaten?" he asked.

"Have you?"

"No," he answered. "What do you feel like?"

I was going to answer something sex-related, but feeling the wine buzz in my system, I said, "Pizza," instead.

* * * *

The next day, just as Cooper was about to leave, the intercom buzzed. "Sorry to bother you, Mr. Elkin. Jennifer Huddleston is here to see you."

I slowly walked over to the intercom and pressed the button. "Does she have coffee?"

"Yes, sir, she does."

"Then please, let her up."

Cooper laughed. "Bit hungover, are you?"

"How much wine did I drink last night?"

"About a bottle too much."

"Do you have to talk so loud?" I asked. "Because honestly, I don't think that's necessary."

Cooper laughed again, just as there was a knock on the door. He let Jennifer in, who bought with her a tray of coffees. She handed one to Cooper, which he took gratefully. "I wasn't sure if you'd still be here," she said.

"Just about to leave," he said. "How are you feeling this morning?"

"Oh, I'm fine," she answered.

She looked fine. I, on the other hand, felt like crap. "Could you two keep it down a bit, thanks," I mumbled from the kitchen.

I was trying to fill the coffee machine when Jennifer handed me a coffee. "I'm feeling every ounce of the wine we drank last night."

"I made him get up and shower, at least," Cooper gloated. Then he kissed my cheek. "You two seriously aren't going in to Brackett and Golding today?"

I shook my head and sipped my life-saving coffee. "No."

"But we have much to do," Jennifer said. As she rattled off a list of things to do to a very amused Cooper, I sank back onto the sofa with my coffee and picked up my notepad.

"Can you two do all that important talking a little quieter?" I mumbled. "My head hurts."

Cooper laughed and walked over to kiss the top of my head. He wished Jennifer the best of luck, and with a grin, left for work.

"Tom," Jennifer called me by my first name, and it was nice to have her so relaxed with me. Gone was the stiff-backed personal assistant. She sat down across from me. "Hungover or not, I think we need –"

Yet, she was still my ever-efficient Jennifer. I interrupted her by handing her my notepad. "Business plan – financials, projections, goals and mission statement," I said, taking a sip of my coffee. "Hungover, yes, but I'm still me."

Jennifer grinned. "Okay, so where do we start?"

Chapter Eleven

As I drove out of the city, I thought about the last month. It had been interesting, that was for sure. It had been four weeks since I'd left Brackett and Golding. Four weeks of getting my own business started. It was only early days, but things were going well.

Peter Sleiman had called to tell me Robert had been fired. Jennifer's claims of numerous affairs with staff had proved true, and Peter said they really didn't like the way he'd tried to defame me. Robert had admitted to 'not appreciating working with a homosexual' and finding my relationship with Cooper a 'bad reflection of what Brackett and Golding stood for'.

They'd asked me to come back to work for them, and I, of course, had said no.

I loved working for myself. Along with the stress of starting over and fear of failure, there was also a freedom. A freedom of time, yes, but a freedom of expression. I'd been studying up on ecologically sustainable development, and had a fantastic teacher in Cooper.

Cooper had been amazing. He'd work all day at Arlington, then come home and want to know everything I'd done. I only had two contracts in the first four weeks — though they were pretty big jobs. But he was fascinated with the inception of my business, getting more excited with each step I took.

He was almost as excited as me.

I was still working from home. I'd told Jennifer we'd look for an office soon, but while I started out, working from the apartment was logical, practical and economical.

I insisted Jennifer start with six-hour days, for the same pay of course. The truth was, I couldn't have done it without her. She was more than a personal assistant. She was like some organizational guru who held it all together for me.

She argued about the hours, of course, but I explained that this was about reducing stress and getting back to basics. Not like starting over, but more like regrouping and doing what felt right, not what was expected. So if she wanted to take some hours to see her grandkids at school, then she absolutely should.

When I put it like that, she didn't argue. She was amazing, and had helped me more than she could possibly know.

But it was Cooper…

In less than twelve months, he'd changed my life. He'd changed the way I thought, the way I saw the world.

He'd changed *me*.

I got out of my car, took a single key from my pocket and opened the door. It was a small, cottage-style bungalow not too far from the Casa in the Hamptons. It wasn't on the beach, though, it was on a nature reserve.

It was a disaster.

Half-shelled, walls missing, drywall sheeting strewn across the floor, covered in dust, and damp. The last owner had run out of money, and it was in dire need of a very good architect with a very keen eye.

That was where I came in.

It was a project. Just not one *I* alone was contracted for.

"Hello?" I heard a familiar voice call out. "Tom, is that you?"

Grinning, I made my way to the front door. Cooper was standing there, looking handsome as ever, but extremely confused.

"What's going on?" he asked. "Louisa told me I had an appointment booked for a new contract. Said I was to meet the guy on site, but when I got here, your car was out front..." His words trailed off. I thought the penny had just dropped. "Tom, what are you doing?"

"I wanted you to see this place," I said. "I spoke to Louisa, and told her I wanted the very best architect she had."

Cooper looked around the construction site I was standing in. He was still in the doorway. "Um..."

"Come in, I want to show you around."

He stepped inside. "Tom, what is this place?"

"A dump at the moment," I said honestly. "But I was thinking a collab between Arlington, meaning you, and Thomas Elkin Architecture, meaning me."

"A collaboration?" he said, still looking around, taking in the ceiling and windows. "Between you and me?"

I nodded. "Yes. I thought it was something I would do on my own, but the more I thought about it, the more I wanted your input."

"Tom...who owns this?"

I smiled. "A woman who ran out of money."

"Then what are you doing here?" he asked. "If she's not remodeling it..."

"I want to buy it," I said. "But I wanted your opinion."

Cooper's mouth fell open. "Buy it?"

I nodded. "Do you remember when we were at the Casa, and you said that house wasn't the Tom you knew? It was too big, too cold and distant?"

He nodded warily. "Yeah?"

"I want this to be the Tom you know."

He blinked, twice. "You want me to design it? What for? Are you selling the apartment? Are you moving? What are you doing?"

"Come through here," I said, and he followed me into one of the rooms. There was a mantel amongst the mess, and on top of it, a rolled-up blueprint. "I want this to be ours. *We'll* still have the apartment, because that's where *we* live. And no, *we're* not moving. But this place…well, this place will just be ours. Where we come to get away, to spend time alone, for weekends."

I took a nervous breath and handed him the tightly rolled blueprint plan.

And waited.

Cooper slid the metal band from the plans, and unrolled them. He looked over the plans, which were basically blank. I saw the confusion on his face, then he realized he was still holding the metal band in his hand.

He looked at it.

Then at me, then back to the silver ring in the palm of his hand.

I saw the rapid rise and fall of his chest. I swear I could hear his mind racing, and when he looked up at me, I saw it in his eyes.

He knew what it was. He swallowed thickly. "Tom?"

I smiled. "You know what a sense of place is?"

Cooper nodded. "It's when the place you're in feels like home. Where you're at peace."

I nodded. "That's exactly right."

Cooper looked around. "This place?"

I shook my head. "No."

His voice kind of squeaked. "Me?"

I nodded and grinned. "You're my sense of place, Cooper."

He looked back at the ring he was still holding.

"Marry me," I said. "Build me a house that's made of us, that reminds you of who we are."

Cooper bit his lip, and his eyes welled with tears. Then he nodded.

"Yes?"

He nodded again. "Yes."

"Did I ask right this time?"

He nodded then the first of his tears fell. "Yes."

I wrapped my arms around him and he held onto me so tight and buried his face into my neck. "Did you want to see the rest of the house?"

He nodded, but didn't move to let me go. Eventually he pulled back, and handed me the ring. Before I could ask, he said, "You have to put it on my finger. You need to do it properly."

I took the silver ring, then his left hand and slid the ring over his finger. He took my face in his hands and kissed me tenderly. "I'm so in love with you," he whispered. Then he wiped his face and laughed before he took my hand. "Come on, show me the rest of the house."

He led me through each room—granted, there weren't many of them—and I could see his excitement grow with each new discovery. I could also tell he was mapping out and planning, seeing visions in his head.

"How am I supposed to go back to work now?" he asked, as I locked the front door behind us. "I'm too excited!"

"You have a lot to plan," I said, kissing him at the Arlington company car. "You need to tell Louisa you'll be doing your first joint account."

"What are you doing?" he asked.

"I need to drop off the key back to the real estate agent, and sign some papers. I'll need to call my lawyer, and my accountant," I said. I was playing with his left hand, turning the ring around his finger. "I'll have some papers for you to sign as well."

"Pre-nup?" he asked. "I have no problem with that."

I laughed. "No, silly. Papers to sign for the purchase of this place. It will be in both our names."

"Tom, I… I can't afford it—"

I kissed him quiet. "I don't care. This place is ours." Then I told him, "And you'll need to think of a name. It doesn't have one currently. The old owners never called it anything."

Cooper exhaled through puffed cheeks and took another deep breath. He looked at the ring on his finger and touched it, then he looked back to me. There was a humbled softness in his eyes. "How did I ever get so lucky?"

I kissed him again. "I often ask myself the same question." He held onto me and kissed me deeply, and when he pulled his mouth from mine, he left his forehead pressed to mine. "Drive safely," I said. "I'll see you at home tonight."

* * * *

I'd only been home for a short while, sitting on the sofa, looking through some legal papers when I heard the familiar sound of Cooper's keys in the door.

He came through the door like there was a demon behind him, and never took his eyes off me.

"You're home early," I said.

"I couldn't wait," he said. "I couldn't concentrate and I was bouncing in my seat apparently. Louisa told me to go home."

Without another word, he took the papers from my hand and put them on the coffee table, took my hand and led me to our bedroom.

"Uh, Cooper," I said with a laugh.

He didn't answer me until we were next to the bed, when he turned to face me. There was a look of love, a little fear and a lot of determination on his face. "I said I couldn't wait," he whispered.

"Cooper, what is it?"

"I want you," he said softly. "I want you to have me...bare."

My eyes widened. "Cooper..."

"You don't have to if you're not ready," he said quickly. "I probably should have asked first. But I have this feeling, this need, that if you don't do it, I think I'll die."

I would have laughed if he wasn't so serious. I put my hands to his face. "Are you okay?"

"I've never been better," he replied. "Just today has been so much emotion, and I can't seem to contain it. I can't... I'm not making much sense."

I kissed him then, softly, deeply, and started to undress him. I knew exactly what he meant. "You're making perfect sense."

There was a desperation in his touch, in his kiss, and when we were both naked on the bed, I took the lube, but left the foil wrappers in the bedside table. "Are you sure?" I asked one final time.

He nodded. "Yes."

I knelt between his spread thighs, prepping him while I kissed over his chest, his jaw, his neck. He was so desperate, panting and pleading, with frantic fingers and grinding hips. When he was ready for me, I leaned over him as I pressed the head of my cock against his hole. He held my face as I pushed inside him.

"Oh my God," I mumbled. It felt so good, so real. I slowly slid all the way inside him, giving us both time to adjust. When he lifted his hips and thrust against me, I cried out, "Slow. Please, baby, slow."

His eyes were wide and he brought my face to his, kissing me passionately. I tried to rein in my body's desire to fuck hard, but it was getting too much.

I leaned back, resting my weight on one hand, and took his cock in my other hand. He batted my hand away and started to pull himself, while I thrust slowly into him. "I need you to come first," I said with a groan. "Please, come for me."

A few more strokes of his hand and his body went rigid beneath me, his head pushed back and he groaned as stripes of cum lined his stomach. I couldn't wait any longer. I thrust into him, deep and hard, making his eyes pop open, and he cried out in pleasure as my cock swelled and emptied inside him. Like my body splintered into a thousand pieces, and he held me together while I surged inside him.

"Oh, Tom," he murmured, over and over. I buried my face into his neck, and he held me so tight. When I finally moved to pull out of him, he stopped me. "Stay inside me," he whispered and kissed my neck, my shoulder. "I never want you to leave."

I could barely form a coherent thought, but I managed to tell him I never would.

Chapter Twelve

Two years later

I turned into the drive, and like every time I saw it, I smiled when I saw the name on the gate. 'Winston' was the name Cooper had given this place. He'd wanted to name it after me, but I'd told him it should reflect him, too. So then he'd wanted the name of the cottage to somehow reflect some translation of 'sense of place' and I'd told him maybe he was over-thinking it.

Then he'd thrown his arms up and yelled at me. "At this fucking rate, I may as well call it Gary or Ian, or fucking Winston!"

Well, we had dropped the 'fucking' prefix, but kept the Winston.

No matter what we called it, it was home.

During the course of construction, Cooper would bring something home, be it a small floor rug, or a frame for the wall, and when I'd ask him who it was for, he'd smile and answer, "Winston."

It was like the small cottage became a living entity, another person, and in many ways, I guess it did. Winston was a huge part of our lives.

Even if we only spent every other weekend there, or any vacations we could, it was home. Sometimes, when work allowed, we'd base ourselves there. It was serene, peaceful—it was a part of us. I'd asked Cooper to design it, to decorate it, so it was indicative of both of us, and he'd done it well.

It was a place that as soon as you walked through the front door, you felt at ease. It was like pulling on an old favorite pair of jeans or a favorite sweater. It was comfort, it was familiar and it was…home.

Just as he'd said it should be, it was now warm timbers, slate floors, rugs and rustic stonework. Books, plans and maps adorned the walls. It was perfect.

I pulled my car in behind Cooper's. He'd driven up earlier today, saying he could work from home while I had some meetings in the City, and I told him I'd meet him here.

I walked in, taking in the familiar smell and the warmth of the fire, and headed straight for Cooper's favorite room, knowing that was where I'd find him.

He turned from his drawing board and smiled at me as I walked in. "Hey, you."

"Hey, handsome," I replied, kissing him softly. He had on a long-sleeved knitted top and jeans, and was looking particularly comfortable.

He sighed contentedly and looked up at me. "You ready for tomorrow?"

"I am so ready," I said, taking off my glasses. A testament to my age and too much time looking at computer screens, my failing eyesight now required glasses. I was almost afraid to show him, but Cooper loved them on me.

Cooper took the pair of glasses from me, folded them and rested them on the lip of his drawing board. "Sofia called," he said. "Mom, Dad and Max are on their way."

I smiled and kissed the top of his head. "Ryan and Bianca are driving up after work," I said. "And Jennifer will be here in the morning."

Cooper smiled again. "Isn't it against tradition for us to see each other in the morning?"

I kissed him softly. "I don't care much for tradition."

We were having a small ceremony here at the cabin. Our guests, who consisted mostly of family, were staying at the Casa, thanks to Sofia's generous offer. Everyone had pretty much organized the entire thing for us, including the catering and decorations. All Cooper and I basically had to do was be here.

"I can't wait to marry you," he said reverently. "I wish it was happening today."

"You're so impatient," I said with a smile.

"It's a Gen Y thing, remember?"

"How could I ever forget?"

"Did you remember the rings?" he asked.

I resisted rolling my eyes. I pulled a small box out of my pocket. "Want to see them?"

Cooper's eyes lit up and he nodded. So I opened the box for him, and he took out both metal bands. He'd picked them out, but we'd needed them resized, so I'd added a surprise engraving. I waited for him to notice it then he looked at me.

Written inside both bands were three words.

"*Et cor domum,*" I murmured. "It's what you are to me."

His eyes darted to mine. "What does that mean?"

"It's Latin," I murmured. "It means 'heart and home'."

Cooper's eyes softened and he smiled, almost tearful. "Oh, Tom. It's perfect. That's what you are, that's exactly what you are."

I leaned down and kissed him softly. "Heart and home."

"Always."

Epilogue

Four years later
Cooper

I sat in my office, staring out of the window. I'd been at Arlington Initiative for six years, and I was as happy there now as I had been the day I'd started. I had my own office, got my own jobs, secured my own contracts, and had complete control from the first meeting until construction completion. Tom kept asking me to quit so we could work together, but I was happy where I was. I saw how much he loved being his own boss, but I told him until such a time when Arlington impeded on my creativity and stopped encouraging me to flourish, then I'd forgo branching out on my own with the added stress of being self-employed.

My email pinged on my laptop, and I saw it was from my boss, Louisa.

I smiled as I opened it and when I read the words 'vacation time approved' I turned to the glass wall that fronted the main office area and found her grinning back at me.

Without wasting a second, I opened my Internet browser and began my search at the same time that I called the only person on the planet who could help me. "Hi, Jennifer. It's Cooper. Listen, I need your help."

* * * *

Tom had been avoiding any discussions about his birthday. He wanted no part of it — he wanted no party, no celebration, and certainly no reminders.

Turning fifty was hitting him hard.

It was so unlike him to be bothered by a number. I knew he'd had his freak-out before he'd turned forty, but that was for a different reason. He'd needed to stop living a lie, he'd needed to come out before he'd turned forty — or so he'd convinced himself. But maybe the problem was that I was still in my twenties. I was twenty-eight. The twenty-two-year age gap between us would never change, but something in his head told him being fifty while his husband was in his twenties made him...old.

The fact that some waiter at a restaurant last week had assumed I was his son didn't help matters either. I'd laughed it off, but it had really bothered Tom. And his impending birthday, his dreaded fiftieth, loomed over him like a dark cloud.

That's why I needed to make his gift special.

I needed to remind him that I loved him when he was twenty-two years older than me when we got married, and I loved him still, when he was twenty-two years older than me today.

I needed to find the perfect gift. One that would show him exactly how I felt, exactly what he meant to me. I needed to show him that the age difference between us was what made us work. So, with that in mind, I let my mind wander…

Tom.

Love.

Timeless.

Architecture.

The perfect retrofit.

An absolute sense of place.

I smiled and searched up the most perfect gift.

* * * *

Two weeks later, against Tom's wishes, I held a small party for him at our apartment. He'd tried to argue with me — seriously, he should have known better by now — but to relent a little, I invited strictly family and closest friends only.

There were about twenty people in all, including Ryan and Bianca, Sofia and her new husband Phil, and Jennifer and her husband of thirty years.

I'd hired wait staff to serve food and drinks, so all I had to do was entertain and be awesome. Truly, I didn't even have to try. Tom, on the other hand, was struggling.

"Can you try to smile?" I asked him gently. We finally had a moment alone near the kitchen. I put my arm around his waist and gave him a squeeze. "The birthday boy is supposed to be happy."

"I am," he said. "It's just… I didn't want a fuss."

"This isn't a fuss," I said, looking around at our guests, all of whom were chatting and laughing. "Me paying the City to stop traffic in Times Square so we could waltz in the middle of the street in front of the world's media would be me making a fuss."

He groaned painfully and downed his champagne. "You wouldn't."

"No," I admittedly cheerfully. "But just so you know, my thirtieth is in a year and a half and if you can't think of any ideas…"

At least that made him smile. For a moment. Then he frowned.

Shit. I had to mention my age, didn't I.

Just then Sofia came up to us. "Is something the matter?" she asked quietly.

I shouldn't have been surprised that she could tell. They'd been married for twenty-something years, and were now back to being close friends.

I sighed and spoke for him. "He says he's fine, but this whole turning fifty thing is stressing him out. He hasn't said as much, but he doesn't like the idea of being in his fifties while I'm…" I cringed. "Not quite thirty."

Tom stared at me.

I eyeballed him. "Tell me I'm wrong."

Tom made a face and looked away.

"See? I'm never wrong," I said to Sofia. "Can you tell him he's being ridiculous, please?"

Sofia pursed her lips. "No, I won't."

Wait, what? No?

Tom looked at her, his whole face indignant.

Sofia pointed a well-manicured finger at his chest. "You're not being ridiculous, Tom. You're being selfish, rude and disrespectful to Cooper."

Oh.

She wasn't finished. "Tom, I love you dearly. But pull your head in. He loved you then, he loves you now. You'd think after fifty years you'd have learned not to waste a minute, yes?"

I could have hugged her. Then I thought fuck it, so I did hug her. Then I hugged Tom. "I can see why you married her," I said, thinking that would finally make him laugh.

It didn't. "I'm starting to think I must like being bossed around," he replied with a smile that didn't quite work.

"Tom, what's really wrong?" I asked. Maybe it was the look on my face, maybe he could tell how scared I suddenly was. Maybe it was how my voice was quiet or the look in my eyes. This was not the place I would have chosen to have this conversation, not at his birthday party, but something wasn't right. "Please?"

Tom swallowed hard and stared at me. "Do you remember Robert Chandler?"

I nodded. "He was the prick who tried to get you fired from Brackett and Golding."

"He had a stroke two weeks ago," Tom said quietly. "He's bed-ridden, needs around the clock care…"

I shook my head. *No, no, no. Just no.* "Tom, you listen to me. You're fit, healthy. You're not like him."

"My father had a stroke," he whispered.

Oh, fuck. How did I miss the connection?

"Oh, Tom," Sofia whispered.

He was still staring at me. "What if I…? I can't expect you to… You're only twenty-eight."

My heart literally fell through the floor. Yes, we were standing away from the crowd, but we were still at a party. In our living room. Surrounded by our nearest and dearest. I wanted to cry. I wanted to scream and punch something. Instead, I took a deep breath and spoke as quietly as I could. "Tom, do you remember when we got married, and I said in sickness and in health?"

He balked.

"You remember that, right? Because I do. I said it, because I meant it. Do you know what it does to me when you tell me it didn't mean anything to you? That you'd think so little of me as to assume I wouldn't care for you?"

"Oh, no," he said, shaking his head. His eyes were wide and filled with remorse and fear. "That's not what I meant at all."

"Because you have to believe me when I say this, Tom, it fucking hurts that you would think that."

He threw his arms around me and pulled me in tight. My face was buried in his neck. "No, Cooper, my love. That's not what I meant. I'm sorry."

"You should be," I told him. I pulled back so he could see my face. "There was no fine print, Tom. There was no sub-clause to revoke vows because one of us might get sick. Do you under-fucking-stand me?"

He nodded.

"Do you need me to write down a definition of forever, you know, with your Alzheimer's and all."

Sofia snorted a teary laugh beside us. I'd forgotten she was there, and this time when Tom smiled, it was genuine. "I love you," he said to me. "Sometimes I forget just how much you love me in return."

I looked at Sofia. "See? Alzheimer's. He forgets all the important stuff." Then I gave him a quick kiss. "I love you too. Next time, please talk to me. Or Sofia. Or Jennifer, or Ryan. Okay?"

He nodded again, but looked like the weight of the world was off his shoulders. When I finally let go of him, Sofia kissed his cheek. "Happy birthday, Tom," she said, walking back to Phil with a smile.

Tom put his hand on my waist and pulled me against him. This time we danced. Like we'd done countless times in our living room when it was just us, slow and sensual. Normally this kind of dancing ended in bed or with an epic make-out session on the sofa that normally ended in bed. And it wasn't long before the other guests noticed us in the corner, slow dancing and soft kissing.

So I grabbed his hand and led him to the table where the gifts were and asked for everyone's attention. "First of all, I'd like to thank you all for coming. It means a great deal to both of us," I said. "Tom, very adamantly, didn't want any speeches. He also told you all not to bring any gifts, and the fact that you all still did just shows what impeccable taste in friends he has.

"Now, I'm allowed to break the no-speech rule because, well, because I never do anything he tells me to do anyway."

"It's true," Tom said. He was blushing and looking all sorts of handsome.

In fact, his shy smile and nervous lip-bite made me lose my train of thought completely. "Um... What was I saying?"

Everyone laughed, and of course that only embarrassed Tom some more.

"Right," I said with a chuckle. I put one arm around his waist, and continued, "I was telling you all about this wonderful man I married who, despite not wanting to turn fifty, is the smartest, most brilliant, sexiest damn fifty-year-old I know." I raised my champagne glass and made a toast. "To Tom."

Everyone raised their glass and repeated my toast and, rather reluctantly, Tom decided to respond. He'd gone from looking shy to resigned, and even a bit sad. "It's true," he started. "I didn't want to turn fifty. I guess saying you're in your forties is still kinda young, but..." He shrugged. "Saying you're in your fifties isn't. But then tonight I was reminded by someone younger and wiser than me"—he looked squarely at me—"of what love really is. Of what life really is. And I'm truly grateful. For everyone here. For everything."

After everyone had toasted once more, I couldn't wait anymore. I handed him his gift. It was a rectangular box and the noise it made kind of gave it away, but he grinned anyway. Whereas I would have just torn at the paper, Tom slid his finger under the tape and unwrapped it delicately to reveal the box of Lego.

Those who knew us knew the significance. Our little cottage in the Hamptons had a cabinet of a few Lego built buildings from their Architectural range, from all the places we'd been together. It had started with the Sydney Opera House, and now included the Flatiron Building, the Lincoln Memorial and the Seattle Space Needle.

This particular one was the Eiffel Tower.

Tom tilted his head. "We haven't been there," he said, clearly confused.

"Look in the box," I told him.

He hadn't even noticed that the Lego box had been opened. But his eyes went wide when he pulled out the envelope with a flight itinerary on it. "Paris?"

I nodded. "Two tickets, a tour of the Eiffel Tower and a private showing of the Rudy Ricciotti exhibition at the Cité de l'Architecture et du Patrimoine," I said, no doubt butchering the French language.

Everyone awwwed at the gift, but it was only Tom who really got the significance. I knew he would. I had no doubt.

He got a bit teary. "Are you trying to tell me something?"

I nodded. "I knew you'd get it. I thought you might need reminding."

"Get what?" Ryan asked. "Reminding of what?"

Tom read over the itinerary and his grin grew wider and his eyes got even more teary. "The Louvre, the Eiffel Tower and Rudy Ricciotti's work are just three of the world's best examples of retrofit. Where the new and old meet, complement and enhance. Both generations of design contribute equally to make each structure what it is."

I nodded. He got it.

"How did you get all that from *that*?" Ryan asked, clearly oblivious to the elements of architecture, and how they related to his father and me.

"Because I did need reminding. And because Cooper knows me better than I know myself."

I nodded. "It's true. I do."

Tom pulled me in for a warm embrace. "And I'll never forget it again. I promise," he whispered in my ear.

"Good," I told him. "But don't worry. I'll always remind you."

He laughed. "Thank you."

"And when we're in Paris," I added, "we might want to get some inspiration for our first public Elkin-Jones design."

He pulled back, his eyes wide. "Serious?"

"Don't get too excited. I'm not leaving Arlington, but I think it's time we let the world see what we can do together."

Tom smiled like I'd never seen him smile before. "You really are kind of awesome."

I rolled my eyes. "For the love of God, Tom. I've been telling you that for six years."

Our friends, all still gathered around us, laughed. Tom raised his champagne glass. "A toast to the last fifty years"—he smiled right at me—"and may the next fifty be just as blessed."

I clinked my glass to his. "I'll drink to that."

About the Author

N.R. Walker is an Australian author, who loves her genre of gay romance. She loves writing and spends far too much time doing it, but wouldn't have it any other way.

She is many things; a mother, a wife, a sister, a writer. She has pretty, pretty boys who live in her head, who don't let her sleep at night unless she gives them life with words.
She likes it when they do dirty, dirty things…but likes it even more when they fall in love.

She used to think having people in her head talking to her was weird, until one day she happened across other writers who told her it was normal.
She's been writing ever since…

N.R. loves to hear from readers. You can find her contact information, website details and author profile page at http://www.pride-publishing.com.